# A LONG WAY HOME

# A LONG WAY HOME

MARGIE WILLIS CLARY

Palmetto Publishing Group
Charleston, SC

*A Long Way Home*
Copyright © 2019 by Margie Willis Clary
All rights reserved

First Edition

Printed in the United States

Paperback: 978-1-64111-422-6
Hardcover: 978-1-64111-577-3
eBook: 978-1-64111-578-0

# DEDICATION

This book is dedicated to the memory of James Irvin Willis, great-grandfather of the author. He served in the South Carolina Confederate Light Artillery 1862 to 1864, and was stationed at Minott's Bluff on the James Island side of the Stono River. He actually saw the Isaac P. Smith gunboat that was captured by the Confederate army on the Stono River in January 1863, and wrote home about it. The family has copies of the letter.

And to the memory of James Irvin Willis' three brothers who lost their lives in the American Civil War: Marcus McKibben Willis, Erastus Rowley Willis, and John Javin Willis, all of Spartanburg County, South Carolina, sons of Daniel S. Willis and Elizabeth Clement of Boiling Springs, South Carolina, Spartanburg County, great-great-uncles of the author.

# TABLE OF CONTENTS

# ACKNOWLEDGEMENTS

In the writing field, it has been said that every writer desires to write a novel. That may be true for the majority of writers, but I never dreamed that I could write, let alone publish, a novel.

Having attempted for years to have one of my children's stories published, I was overjoyed in 1995 when my book, *A Sweet, Sweet Basket*, was published by Sandlapper Publishing in Orangeburg, South Carolina. Not only was the book published, but it received the honor of being named a notable book for children by *Smithsonian Magazine*, November, 1995.

I continued to write for children and published five more books: *Searching the Lights*, *The Beacons of South Carolina*, *A Gullah Alphabet*, *Make It Three*, and *Spirits and Legends of the South Carolina Sea Islands*.

In 2015, out of the blue, a story for a novel came to mind. I imaged it would take place in the old South. Characters began to come to life. It was unbelievable. So, I began to write *A Long Way Home*. My writer friend, Dr. Linda Cantey Slonim, thought it had great possibilities and encouraged me to continue writing. Thank you, Linda for your professional input and help to get this book published.

My granddaughter, Jill Clary Coggins of Hanahan, being proud of Grandma's efforts, became a great proofreader and an advisor for the timeline of the story. I love you, Jill. My niece, Jane Woodberry Fordham has been a cheerleader for me getting the novel completed for publication. Thanks for being my friend as well as my kin.

I finally completed *A Long Way Home*, a 120,500-word manuscript, in March of 2019.

Many thanks to Kathy Judd for her hours typing the first draft.

I definitely want to thank the many members of the Writing Circle of the Low Country Senior Center for their wonderful support and suggestions as they walked me through the pages of my manuscript, always encouraging and helpful, even when critiquing. They were there for me at the beginning of the novel, supporting me all the way to finally getting the manuscript put together and sent off to the publisher. I appreciate you guys and gals: Bernie Ditter, Al Stiles, Bob Kelly, Frank Johnson, Jo Ann Flynn, John Kotila, Karolea Lucas, and Lane Reed, as well as others who came and went.

I give my nephew, Joseph Strafford Woodberry, praise and thanks for his excellent rendition of the poker game. Without his help, it would have been a real game loss for the story.

Last but not least, I wish to thank to Karen Stokes, a local author who gave me advice in what a publisher needs from a writer. Karen willingly gave of her time to help me follow through to the completion of my work. Thank you, Karen.

# PREFACE

From 1861 to 1865, the American Civil War's intent was to control the destiny of the United States of America, from the first bombing of Fort Sumter to the signing of surrender at Appomattox, Virginia, April 1865.

The Northern side of the war was known as the Union, or the Federals, and the Southern army was known as the Confederacy, or the Rebels. The general color of the rebel uniforms was gray while the Federals was blue.

In early 1861, thousands of men from the South volunteered to defend the rights of their beloved South. These men knew little about fighting a war, but the words "duty" and "honor-bound" enticed them to become fighting men for The Cause.

On the Southern plantations, many masters and sons left home to join the ranks, leaving the women to run the plantations and supervise the enslaved.

In *A Long Way Home*, we meet Charlotte Grimball, who finds herself managing the family's island plantation while her husband and son are away fighting in the Confederate army. Being in charge of some eighty-two enslaved Africans was Charlotte's greatest challenge, until she realized that the enslaved Africans were willing and able to help her in situations other than harvesting the rice.

With Civil War ending, transportation was somewhat asunder. James Grimball and his son, Jimmy, found that the road home was a long one, and getting there was an experience in itself.

Once home, Master James is faced with running a plantation without enslaved help, and realizes that a rice plantation is no longer possible. By late 1865, the Grimball family hired an employee who later invested money to enable them to turn the plantation into a much-needed business, supplying employees with jobs and housing for the future.

Margie Willis Clary

# CHAPTER 1

# MISS CHARLOTTE

*May 25, 1865*

As the wagon rolled onto dry land and headed to the Battery of the city of Charleston, Charlotte Legare Grimball was anxious to see her home at 10 South Bay Street. She had been away from Charleston since 1863, before the city was taken over by the Northern troops. She worried about the damage she might find. Truthfully, she expected the worst. Her brother-in-law, George Grimball, stopped the wagon at the front door of the house.

Charlotte jumped out to survey the damage. Giving the house a quick once-over, she noticed two chimneys with missing bricks. The only other real damage was some water damage to the windows of the drawing room. In the side yard, two large oak trees were partially destroyed from cannon fire. Tree limbs covered most of the yard. Otherwise, the house looked surprisingly unblemished, too good to be true.

Charlotte was so thankful she raised her hands in praise and shouted, "Thank you, Lord, thank you!"

George hitched the wagon to a post and went ahead to unlock the front door. Charlotte walked into the foyer, then to the parlor, the dining room, and into the kitchen. She was amazed by how clean she found the house. It looked as though things had recently been dusted, though to her knowledge, no one had slept in the house since November 1863.

George had checked on the house often, but he did not clean. For a moment fear engulfed Charlotte's mind. Had the Yankees been in her house? She laughed to herself, answering her own question. If they were Yankees, they would not clean a Rebel's home.

After checking all the rooms, George began bringing Charlotte's belongings into the house. Pug and Ham carried the empty trunk up the stairs to Charlotte's chamber, making several trips to put things in place. It was nighttime when they finally got everything unloaded from the wagon, too late to travel in the city. Charlotte invited George and the boys to share supper from her food basket and to spend the night.

Going into the dining room, she placed the food basket on the dining table and uncovered four plates from the buffet. Opening the basket, she placed ham biscuits, apple slices, and a piece of walnut cake on each plate. George pumped a bucket of well water at the back door for them to drink.

After eating, George told her that he and the boys would sleep in the carriage house.

"Oh, no," she said. "There is plenty of room in the house for the three of you, and I have no idea the condition of the carriage house."

She sent George to the downstairs guest room and insisted that the boys sleep in the spare bedroom upstairs. Instead they asked to go to the slave quarters behind the kitchen.

Feeling tired, Charlotte climbed the staircase to her bedroom, her mind muddled. With the slaves free and no longer servants, just where should free slaves sleep?

Finally in her chamber, she shook the silk curtains of the canopy and climbed into her rice bed. The curtains were not as dusty as she thought they would be, despite the fact that no one had slept here for over two years. She smiled as she snuggled in the soft covers. It felt great to be in Charleston and in her own bed. The mattress was harder than the feather bed at Heartland, but she would get used to it.

Before she blew the lantern out, she looked around the room. Everything looked the same as it had when she left in 1863.

She had left the city in November, 1863, to observe Thanksgiving at the Grimball family's plantation, Heartland, on John's Island. She was never able to return home until now. At that time she packed her personal things to take with her, as she'd planned to stay for an extended time. She was happy to stay longer as it was not safe so near the Charleston's block-aded harbor. [1]

Without house servants and with the deplorable conditions in the city, the time on the plantation had turned into years. With her husband James in the army, and the slave situation, the John's Island plantation needed help. Charlotte remained to assist overseer Owens in running the plantation and see that all the slaves were accounted for, and to secure the land.

With the war over in April, Charlotte had spent the last month signing documents for the slaves who desired papers upon leaving. Some of them wanted money, and since Charlotte had none to give, she offered free housing to families that wished to stay. With the exception of Big John's family, all the former slaves left. The word freedom meant more to them than a roof over their heads.

By May, 1865, seventy-eight former slaves had left Heartland Plantation as freedmen. Only Big John, his wife, and their boys, Pug and Ham, stayed. Charlotte paid John wages and provided housing for his family. But with the upheaval of the war now over and the slaves freed from the plantation, she'd thought it was time for her to return to Charleston to prepare for her husband James Grimball's homecoming.

Last week she had telegraphed James' brother, George, asking for help to get home to Charleston. George owned a saw mill north of the city, and kept mules and wagons. She knew he would provide her transportation to Charleston.

Early yesterday morning, George Grimball had met her at the Stono River Ferry with a mule-driven wagon. With the help of Pug and Ham, George was able to get her across the river and safely to Charleston. She was thrilled to be home and thankful it had been spared. Before sleeping, she whispered a prayer of thanksgiving. "Dear God, thank you for the safe trip home. Thank you for sparing my house. Take care of James and bring him home soon. Please, let me soon hear from Jimmy. Amen." Her voice quivered as a tear ran down her cheek. She rolled over, burying her face in a pillow and shed a few tears for her missing son, Jimmy.

Sitting up, she wiped her eyes and blew out the lantern. Even after this tiring day, the task of getting home gave her a contented feeling, and with George and the two boys asleep in the house, she felt safe.

Early the next morning, George awoke at his usual time. Last night he had fallen asleep immediately due to the fatigue of the long journey to Johns Island and back to Charleston. Now he was ready to go home. He would take Pug and Ham back as far as Fleming's Ferry, and then head to the neck of the city to his saw mill. He dressed himself and went to the slave quarters. He woke the two boys and stopped in the kitchen to start a small fire to brew coffee. He wouldn't take time to cook breakfast, coffee would do.

The rations that George had brought from home were still on the kitchen table. Among the foods were two loaves of homemade bread that his wife, Caroline, had sent. He rummaged in the pantry and found a jar of Charlotte's fig preserves. He made Ham and Pug fig preserve sandwiches. They ate while he drank coffee. The fig preserves looked so tasty, he reached for the bread and made himself a sandwich, too.

When he finished eating, he wiped off the table and said, "I will meet you at the back entrance. I must tell Charlotte we are leaving."

Charlotte was still asleep when George knocked on her bedroom door and said softly, "Charlotte, we are leaving now, thanks for everything. I will check on you next week."

Charlotte knew she should get up and give George and the lads a proper send off, but her body would not move. Instead, she managed to say, "Thank you for your help, and be careful."

As George went out the back door, Charlotte rolled over and thought, George did need to get home. With the war over his lumber was in great demand. Within minutes, she drifted back to sleep.

# CHAPTER 2

# THE LETTER

At eleven o'clock, Charlotte was awakened by the beams of the sunshine shining brightly through the curtains. She looked at the clock and couldn't believe it was so late. Hopping quickly out of bed, she put on her robe. There was so much she must do now that she was home in the city.

Sliding into her slippers, she walked to the staircase and hurried down the steps to the kitchen. Pleased that George had built a fire earlier, she stirred the smoldering ashes in the fireplace and hung a pot of water to make tea. She sat down at the butcher table, checking the rations George brought from home. There were eggs, flour, cornmeal, lard, carrots, yams, white potatoes, sugar, spring onions, coffee, and a small bag of imported tea. His wife Caroline had sent two loaves of her delicious homemade bread.

Charlotte opened the bag of tea and waited for the water to boil. It was wonderful to have imported tea once again. It had been over three years since her last cup. While waiting, she sorted the rations on the table. After breakfast, she would take part of them down to the cellar. With just one person to cook for, they should last a long time.

Noticing that George had cut one loaf of bread, she cut two slices to eat. Delighted to see the jar of fig preserves, she dipped a spoon into the jar and spread preserves on the bread. It was the last jar of the batch she had made in the spring of the year the war began. She licked the sticky syrup off the spoon and reached for the hot water to make a cup of tea.

Sitting down in a chair, she savored the fig preserves and ate the slices of bread. Eating in her own kitchen gave her a warm feeling. The war was truly over and James would soon be home to stay. She finished her tea and wanted another cup, but knew she would need one later in the day and she must use it sparingly.

Standing up, she put the rations into a basket. She must take them to the cellar later, but for now there was a more important thing to do. She must write to James. With the war over, it would be the last letter she would send to the field hospital. No longer needed, the field hospitals would come down. She washed the few breakfast dishes and walked to her writing desk in the hallway. Picking up her ink pen and some paper, she began to write.

*May 25, 1865*
*Charleston, SC*


*My Dear James,*

*This is a happy day. I retreated from John's Island to the city yesterday. Our beloved Heartland Plantation is now a lonely place. Most of the slaves have left. Big John and his wife, Sarah, plan to stay for now. Overseer Owens and his wife, Jennie, will continue to look after the place. They will take care of the cow and the pig. The Yankees took the horses.*

*Nothing much is left in the plantation house except the furniture, the dishware, and my piano. I told Big John and his family to move into the big house with Owens for safety's sake. Big John and his family will have the upstairs rooms, and Owens and Jennie will live* downstairs. Sarah will do the cooking and cleaning, and Jennie will do the laundry and the gardening. I hope the arrangement works out.

Big John and his two sons, Pug and Ham, helped me get home to Charleston. They put my things in a small fishing boat and took me as far as Stono landing to meet George. I carefully chose the things I cherish most, and the things I would use in the city. I put clothes in our large trunk, and your mother's china in among the clothes. I managed to put family pictures between the quilts. Young Ham dug up the silver buried under the house and fit it in and around the quilts. I put my jewelry and your coin collection in my purse. I brought one pistol and left the others with Owens and Big John. They may need them more than I will.

We arrived at Stono Crossing at noon. Your brother George met us there with his biggest wagon. The ride through the city disturbed me. Freed slaves ran along the streets and colored families huddled on roadsides. Children were crying and a stench filled the air.

Our house on South Bay survived well. Only two chimneys lost bricks, and there was some water damage to the windows in the drawing room. God is good. I am so thankful. I shouted for joy when I saw it.

I am here alone. Liza planned to come back to the city and work for me, but her man, Big Tom, decided to leave the plantation in February, 1863, after hearing that Lincoln had signed the Emancipation Proclamation. George and I tried to reason with him. Tom would not take no for an answer. George knew Tom would be no help at Heartland thinking he was free, so George let him go. Tom did not take into account the battlegrounds all through our state and on through Virginia. He would legally be considered a runaway slave, and, worst of all, he took Liza and baby Lilly with him. Poor little Lilly, hardly big enough to walk, having to endure such a journey. I pray they made it.

Still no word from Jimmy. The Gibbs' son said he saw him before a battle in Virginia.

Charlotte put down her ink pen and ran her hands through her uncombed hair. Home again in Charleston, and yet she could never remember a harder day than yesterday. Technically the war was over, but in her mind, the ills of the past four years resounded again and again. Her husband, James, was recuperating in a field hospital near a battlefield at Petersburg, Virginia. He'd said his wound was not life-threatening, but he had been there since Christmas. To what extent was he wounded? His letters sounded cheerful enough, but she wondered how he really felt. Would he be able to run the plantation when he got home?

Then there was Jimmy, her only child, missing somewhere in Virginia. No news from him since November 1864. Why did he stop writing? Was he unable to write? The situation made her jittery.

Suddenly, tears ran down her face. With all that she had suffered through in the past four years, she had done her best to stay strong. Now the strains of war were taking hold emotionally. More tears fell. She had not cried like this since the war began. "Why, God, why? I can't keep our houses up without my men."

With her head in her hands, she continued to weep, not so much for her son and James, but from pure exhaustion. Wiping her eyes, she picked up the pen and continued writing again.

> *This is the last letter I will send to the field hospital. Hope you will be home soon. Your most devoted wife, with all my love,*
> *Charlotte*

> *P.S. Had a note from your brother, Frederick. Freddie is home from the Union Cavalry. They are all well and at home in Baltimore.*

# CHAPTER 3

# NO HELP

Charlotte placed the letter into an envelope and addressed it to Lieutenant James Grimball, Field Hospital, Petersburg, Virginia. She wiped her eyes and stood up from the writing desk. More tears fell. This was so unlike her. It was an embarrassment.

Needing air, she walked through the entrance hall to the front door. Unlocking the door, she stepped onto the piazza. The hot and humid Charleston air greeted her. To her wonderment, the shadows seemed long. Had it taken all day to write her letter? The trip home and the conditions of the city had taken her energy. How long had she cried? How long had she sat at the writing desk? More tears came, but why? Her house seemed the same, but the city had changed. Houses and churches were gone. Rubble lay everywhere. Water ran in the streets from crumbling spots on the sea wall.

She sobbed loudly and sat down on a damaged chair on the porch and continued to weep. Four years of tears were long overdue. As sunset took over, she rose and stumbled into the house. No more tears for today, she thought. She walked down the hall to the shelf that held lanterns and supplies. Taking a lantern and matches, she went into the kitchen to start supper.

She thought of Liza, the household slave who usually came to the city with her when Charlotte came home. Liza had cooked for the Grimballs for eleven years. Charlotte wished she was here today. Liza's man, Big Tom, should have left Liza and Lilly at the plantation. Crazy fellow. But when he thought that the bonds of slavery no longer restrained him, he'd headed north, taking Liza and baby Lilly with him.

Charlotte broke two eggs into a frying pan. She held the pan over the flames and stirred the eggs until fluffy. Slicing two pieces of bread from the loaf, she placed the eggs and bread on a pottery plate. She poured herself a cup of tea and sat down at the butcher table, too tired to go into the dining room. She blessed the food with a short prayer, picked up her cup, and slowly drank the imported tea, savoring every drop. Placing the empty cup on the table, she heard a noise. It seemed to come from the hallway.

Startled, she peered down the hall. She only saw shadows from the sunset. She sat back in the chair and finished her eggs and bread. How wonderful it was to taste homemade bread and imported tea once more! With the water that George had brought in from the well, she washed her plate and cup. She picked up the lantern and started up the stairs. When she reached the landing, she heard the noise again. This time, it sounded as if it was coming through the floor.

She murmured, "A raccoon must have gotten into the cellar. It'll have to wait until morning. I am not going out in the night to release a wild animal."

# CHAPTER 4

# THE CELLAR

Charlotte woke early. She would not waste this morning as she had yesterday. There was much to do in preparation for James' homecoming. After a few minutes, she rose from her bed and walked to the window, a habit she had when at home in Charleston. She pulled back the curtains and looked at the Gibb's house. She gasped. Her neighbor's house was completely gutted from fire, probably by the Union ships that had barricaded the harbor. Only the carriage house stood, every window broken. She felt faint and fell back onto the bed.

"How horrible," she lamented. "I was so busy looking at my own house that I failed to notice my neighbor's home. Where are the Gibbs, with their home completely destroyed?"

Tears ran down Charlotte's face. "Why did I come home alone? Why didn't I wait until someone could come with me? All this could make a person go mad."

New tears flowed again. "I can't go on like this. I will send George a message. Maybe Caroline or one of their daughters could come stay with me for a while."

Gaining control of herself, she dressed in the same clothes she wore yesterday and coming home. Today she would go to the attic to see whether her summer clothes were still where George had stored them last fall.

Still shaking from the shock of the neighbor's house, she went downstairs to the kitchen. Seeing the basket of rations still on the table, she remembered the noise from last night. "I must take these rations to the cellar and see what varmint is there."

She stirred the banked fire and put on a pot of water for coffee. She picked up the basket of rations and headed to the backdoor. Holding up her long skirt, she went down the narrow steps to the backyard. She walked toward the cellar doors near the wall of the terrace.

Approaching the doors, she noticed they were unlocked. Why? George would never have left the doors unlocked, not with the city full of homeless people. Fear swept over her. Was there something more than a raccoon in the cellar?

Putting down the basket, she walked past the terrace wall and picked up a broken tree limb. Holding the limb with one hand, she pulled open a cellar door with the other. The sun cast enough light that she could see the floor of the dark cellar.

Stepping inside, she heard a movement. A light shone from a lantern sitting on a small table near the south chimney. Her mind raced. A Yankee soldier, a Northern raider? Who was in the cellar?

Holding the tree limb with trembling hands, she shrieked, "Who goes there? This is private property!" As if that mattered now in Charleston.

From the shadows in the back of the cellar, a voice called out, "Miss Charlotte, it's me, Elijah, from the plantation. I ain't here for to harm you." His familiar voice in the Gullah [2] dialect set a wave of relief through her body.

"Elijah, you scared me half to death. What are you doing here? Where is Jed? Didn't he leave with you to join the army? Are you a soldier?"

Elijah answered, "No, ma'am, I ain't fight de war. Jed left me at the Stono. He headed for de Yankee army. Me, I ain't want 'a fight nobody. When I get to town, I 'membered your place an I been here ev'r since."

"You've been here almost two years, and George never saw you?"

"He came one time at dayclean before I git out. He scared me. I hid the lantern and lay low under de house lest he sees me. I ain't bothered things but for cover. I did get a pair of Massa James' old boots. I's still wearing dem. I's pay you fuh 'em. I's working at de wharf. I sleep here or in the attic, 'cep' when it is cold I stay on the ship. Cap'n ain't mind."

"Well, it's good to see a familiar face. Come on out and help me with this basket of rations," Charlotte replied, not really knowing what else to say. A former slave living in her house? She didn't mind, but digesting all that Elijah said would take a while.

She moved to the door of the cellar, and Elijah followed. Stepping out to the yard, he picked up the basket and returned to her in the cellar.

"Thank you, Elijah. It is nice to have a man around. Show me the best place to put these vittles. Liza always did this job. You can help me learn."

"I can hep you if you let me stay. I's free now an' I gets a little money. I can pay my way," Elijah said in a pleading voice.

"We'll talk about that later, Elijah. "Now I need a cup of coffee. Come on to the kitchen. I am glad to have someone to talk to. The silence here is deafening."

He followed her up the back steps to the kitchen. He stood erect at the door until she invited him in and pointed to a chair. He slowly sat down. No white woman had ever invited him to sit as a guest. It was somewhat baffling.

She strained the coffee grounds and poured two cups of coffee. Elijah waited. When she took her cup, he sat down. "Would you like breakfast?" she asked.

"No t'ank you. I eats when I get to de ship. De cap'n always cooks up eats for breakfast. Dat de way I survived being here."

Elijah sat quietly while she finished her coffee.

"Elijah, tell me about you and Jed leaving the plantation. When did you run into the Yankees? I remember the day you left. It was the same day six Union soldiers came to the house and demanded food and blankets. I let them take whatever they wanted. They took all the chickens they could catch. From the house, they gathered blankets and quilts before Owens and Big John came out with rifles. They left as quickly as they came. It petrified me. We'd heard so many horror stories of what the Yankees did on many plantations. I got down on my knees and thanked the Lord for sparing us from danger."

"So sorry, Miss Charlotte. Jed and me ran into Yankees 'fore we get off de island. We's gwing up de rivuh when we seed a boat tied to a landin'. Union soldiers were over on da Jenkins property, shooting at a target drawn on de side of de barn. [3] We hide in de bulrush, afraid dey would see us. We waited. When dey went to de otter side of de barn, we ran as fast as we could to de landing.

"Old Mr. Seabrook sat dere with de cutter. He knowed us and didn't ask any questions while rowing us to Jim Island. Dat was good, as dere was lot of Rebel soldiers encamped near the Stono Rivuh on the Jim Island side. They waz ready to fight and didn't even notice we.

"Mr. Seabrook say something about a battle on Jim Island soon, and dat de Yankees were on Folly Island. Seeing all dem soldiers with guns, I git real scared and decide I didn't want 'a fight. I told Jed to go to Folly Island, I'd be okay. The last I seed of Jed, he headed across the island to find the Union Army. I reckon dey let him be a Yankee."

Elijah took a drink of his coffee and continued, "I stay near Jim Island Creek until some folk were gwing 'cross to Charleston. Dey say I can ride in de boat, too. When we got to de harbor I ain't never seen so many ships. Dey called it a blockade. Dem Yankee sailors kep' de harbor blocked so dat no shipping goods could come to de city. De ships stay a long time. Dat's why it waz hard to git tea and coffee, dey say."

"That is true, Elijah. George got this coffee after the blockade lifted. It surely tastes better than that awful weed–root stuff we drank for the past four years."

Elijah stood up. "T'ank yuh fuh de coffee. I go to de ship now. Can I come back dis evenin'?"

Charlotte said, "Why, yes, come on back. It would be good to know that someone's here if I need help. You can sleep in Liza's old room on the porch. The attic and cellar are mighty dusty."

Elijah smiled a big smile and said, "I be back 'bout dusk dark. T'anky ma'am!" He hurried out the back door.

Charlotte noticed how responsible Elijah had become since leaving the plantation. She let out cheerful sigh. She didn't know if Elijah's being here was proper or not, but she knew that she would sleep better knowing he was in the house. She would decide later what to do about him, but for now, she was going to have another cup of coffee.

# CHAPTER 5

# THE ATTIC

Charlotte finished putting the breakfast dishes away and thought of Elijah living in her house all this time. At least he had taken care of things. She was sure he was the one who had dusted the house, but she would remember to ask him about it.

Thinking back, she remembered him as a small boy on the plantation. His momma, Lola, worked in the laundry house. Lola died from the fever in the 1850. After her death, Elijah's pa ran away from the plantation, leaving Elijah with Jed's momma. While Lola lived, Elijah stayed near the laundry house playing games with the other enslaved children his age. Even though Elijah was older than Jimmy, he sometimes asked Jimmy to join in a game of marbles or roll-the-hoop. For some reason, games with the colored boys seemed to fascinate Jimmy.

On the days Charlotte went to the laundry, Jimmy used to play with Elijah while they waited for Lola to iron James' shirts. In Charlotte's mind she could still see the pressing irons heating on the old wood stove in the small laundry house. The heat from the stove made the room extremely hot. She wondered how Lola stood the heat all day. Lola was the best shirt presser ever at Heartland. No one had pressed James' shirts to please him since her death.

Elijah still looked very much as he had as a child. Taller of course, with handsome black hair and bronze skin. Folks around the plantation said his mom came from the island of Barbados, not from Africa. Charlotte never asked James if that was true or not.

She never really knew the slaves well, only the household ones. Most worked on the land, doing field work and helping to harvest the rice. James and Overseer Owens usually looked after them. James treated them with fairness and consideration. However, Overseer Owens was sometimes harsh and too rough on them, especially when James was absent from the plantation.

She recalled a time when James went away on business and a slave escaped. Owens sent men with dogs to chase him down. They found him near the Stono River hiding in an old corn crib. When the men brought him back to the plantation, Owens beat him unmercifully, leaving stripes on his back.

Charlotte remembered the sick feeling that came over her as she watched the beating. It nauseated her so, she'd taken to her bed. When James returned, he reprimanded Owens for his cruelty. Owens got upset but did not retaliate. He knew that on other plantations, slaves were often beaten, but he must do what the master would have him do. He liked his job and wanted to keep it.

Charlotte knew the household slaves well. Big Momma and Liza had taught her how to keep house and cook. Liza knew more about cooking and cleaning at age fifteen than Charlotte knew at twenty-five. Living below Broad Street in Charleston, a white girl child was usually not allowed in the kitchen. Slaves did the cooking and serving of the meals. Charlotte's chores centered on good manners and looking pretty. She did not like the frilly dresses her mother made her wear, but later understood a mother's duty was to train a daughter in the ways of a Southern lady, especially in Charleston. Charlotte depended on Big Momma and Liza to teach her the skills to become an acceptable hostess in the city.

When Charlotte married and moved to Heartland, it was a rude awakening. She'd had no idea how to run a plantation. If it hadn't been for Liza and Big Momma, James would have starved.

Big Momma could cook up a meal in no time flat. Liza worked right along with her. They taught Charlotte to cook bread and cakes, but that was about all the cooking she did as long as the slaves had been there. Big Momma died right before little Lilly was born, never to know her precious grandchild.

Remembering, Charlotte's tears began to flow. No, not today. She would not cry. There was no time for sadness, there was too much to do. She must get to the attic while there was a little breeze coming up from the water.

Up the staircase she hurried, and on to the attic door. She turned the key in the lock, unlocking it. To her surprise, she found the attic extremely clean. The big trunks were now located near the side walls. A small bedroll rested under the west window. No spiderwebs blocked her way, relieving her of the usual fight.

To see things so tidy pleased her. She could easily go through the trunks, now that they were not piled high on top of each other.

The summer heat had already warmed up the place. She opened a small window on the east side to let in a little breeze from the water. She located her old trunk and stooped down to open it. To her amazement, she found her summer clothes neatly folded, the outfits still together. Elijah must have learned to fold clothes from his mother in the laundry house so many years ago. What a splendid skill to have.

Charlotte took only the clothes she knew she would wear and replaced the rest in the trunk, then stood up to close the window. As she left the attic, she locked the door and headed down the stairs. Reaching the ground floor, she heard a knock on the front door.

Peeping through a side curtain, she saw a telegram messenger. Terror seized her and she wondered who was dead, Jimmy or James? She hurriedly unlocked the door to the foyer, and opened the front door.

"Good morning, madam. Are you Mrs. James Grimball?"

Charlotte tried not to show her fears, and said, "Yes, sir."

Handing a yellow envelope to Charlotte, the messenger said, "This telegram is for you."

With shaking hands, she took the telegram. Her voice quivered and she managed to say, "Thank you."

As the man left, she leaned heavily on the door, feeling faint. What if the telegram contained bad news? What would she do? She fumbled with the envelope, finally getting it open, and read the message.

*Discharged today. Leg well. Coming home soon. I love you, James.*

As she read the short message, tears of joy ran down her cheeks. Holding the telegram to her breast, she prayed, "Thank you, Lord, thank you. Now, please let me hear from Jimmy."

With her prayers for James answered, she still needed to learn Jimmy's location and his condition.

Gratified and relieved by the good news, she headed to the parlor and sat down on the settee. Reading the telegram again, she felt a new calmness. Her husband was coming home. What joy! Shedding tears of bliss, she closed her eyes. The telegram dropped to the floor. She relaxed, and before she knew it, she drifted off to sleep.

# CHAPTER 6

# SUPPER WITH A FREED SLAVE

Four tolls of the old grandfather clock in the hall woke Charlotte with a start. Four o'clock? Was the clock wrong, she wondered?

After retrieving her summer clothes from the attic and receiving James' telegram, she'd sat down on the settee to relax. Before she knew it, she'd gone to sleep. That was hours ago. Now it was almost supper time.

Jumping up from the settee, she spied the fallen telegram and picked it up. She put it safely into her apron pocket. She would read it again after supper, but now she must cook supper for Elijah.

In the kitchen, she reached into the smoldering ashes in the fireplace and took out two yams she placed there last night. She put water on for tea and coffee, and hurried to the pantry for cornmeal, lard, onions, and eggs. Mixing the eggs with the corn meal, she added a chopped onion to the mixture. In a hot skillet, she dropped several spoons of the mixture into the sizzling grease. Holding the pan over the fire, she watched the mixture turn into golden brown hoecakes.

The aroma of onions and cornmeal filled the kitchen. Pouring off the grease into a bowl, she forked the hoecakes into a small basket and placed the basket into the warming oven over the fireplace.

She felt satisfied with her cooking. Her hoecakes looked as good as Liza's. It was a good feeling to have someone to cook for again.

She set two plates on the butcher table and went back to the pantry to get scallions to eat with the hoecakes. The meal was small, but at least she had supper on the table.

As she poured herself a cup of tea, she heard the back door open.

"Miss Charlotte, it's Elijah. Can I come in?" he called.

"Come on in, you are just in time for supper," she called back.

He came into the kitchen with a grin on his face and a poke-sack in his hand. "It's nice dat supper be ready to eat. It smell good," he said. He put the sack on the table and began taking out its contents. "I been to de market place and get some snap beans, t'matoes an' fresh milk," he said.

"Wonderful," she said, clapping her hands. "The milk will taste delicious with the hoecakes I cooked."

"How ye know I likes hoecakes?" he asked.

"I did not know, but I like them. Go wash up so we can eat before the food gets cold," she told him.

Elijah went to the pump at the back door and washed his hands. As he was coming back up the steps, it dawned on her that he was no longer her slave, and she had no right to tell him to wash up. He hadn't seemed to notice her blunder, or at least he did not react any differently. She would have to think before speaking next time.

She pulled out her chair and asked, "Shall we eat now?"

"Yes 'um, I's hungry," he answered, sitting down at the table.

She bowed her head to say grace. Elijah bowed his head, too. He surely was thankful that Miss Charlotte had cooked supper for him. Her hot food tasted better than the cold soup he usually ate for supper.

"I have news about James. He is on his way home," Charlotte said. "He is out of the hospital and discharged from the army. He is still in Virginia and did not say how he was getting home or when. But I am happy to know he is well enough to come home."

"Dat's good, Miss Charlotte. I know yuh's miss'n he. I hope he let me be here when he gits home. I likes it here," Elijah said. "Dis is mighty good eat'n for supper. You's a good cook."

"Thank you," Charlotte replied. "It is good to have someone to eat with. This house gets mighty lonely when there is no one to talk with. I wanted to tell you how pleased I was when I found the attic so neat and clean with my summer clothes folded carefully."

"Yes'um. That's one t'ing I ain't forget about. Momma, she teach me dat fore I be five year old. I try to keep t'ings neat and clean, and folded up," he replied.

"Very good habits," Charlotte said. "You used her good training to keep this house neat and clean since you've been here. Thank you. It is greatly appreciated." ·

"It was the least I could do for having such a good place to sleep at night," he said, grinning. "I likes being here. It's close to de ship."

Then he sat quietly eating his supper. When he finished eating, he stood up and said, "T'anky ma'am for supper eats. If is still all right, I go to Liza's room. It's a good room. I seed it when I first be here."

"I changed the sheets today and put a pair of Jim's pajamas on the bed that are probably too short for him. If they fit, you are welcome to them," Charlotte said.

"You's mighty good to me. T'anky ma'am. I can use dem. Later, I'll snap de beans for you," he said as he reached for a lantern.

She said, "Before you go, Elijah, I've been wondering where you got food to eat for the time you've been here?"

# CHAPTER 7

# FOOD FROM THE CAPTAIN

Elijah put the lantern on the table, sat down, and began telling his story.
"I's told you 'bout working fuh de cap'n. He's a Yankee and his small ship was part of the big blockade in the harbor. His ship is anchored near Atlantic Wharf at the end of Broad Street. He hired sev'ral freed slaves to work fuh him. One of the slaves belonged to the Heyward family dat live on Montague Street. I knows you 'member dem. De missus use to come here fuh tea. Well, the Heyward family moved to Flat Rock, North Carolina, to live out the war. Before dey lef' the Low Country, they hired der slave, Isaac, to stay in their house on Montague Street. Isaac knowed how to read and write, so he could let dem know about de war in Charleston. My cap'n is Missus Heyward's second cousin from Pennsylvania. Da family paid him to feed Isaac.

"When I first come to Charleston, I start lookin' for food and I met Isaac at de wharf. He took we to de captain to git work and vittles. I got a job working fuh de cap'n fuh food. He gave me de leftovers to bring back here. Dat's why I eat cold soup at night. De cap'n and his ship stay here to hep his cousins and de freed slaves. The Heywards are back in Charleston, and Isaac still work for dem. Dey's good folk. Dey save my life."

Charlotte said, "Such a warming story. I am glad someone took care of you in such hard times or you would have starved to death. Sounds like your captain is a generous person. I would like to meet him someday."

"He'd like dat. I's been tell'n' him 'bout you and de plantation. He knows 'bout me staying here," Elijah said, rising to his feet. He picked up the lantern and walked headed to Liza's room.

Charlotte finished cleaning up the kitchen. It wasn't yet dark, so she went upstairs to her bedroom. Sitting down at the dresser, she let down her hair and began brushing.

It was hard to know how to respond to Elijah, she thought. He was a helpful young man, and she was fortunate to have someone in the house, what with the city filled with carpetbaggers and misplaced freed slaves. It was still perplexing to her. She hoped George would come to visit and talk to her about Elijah's situation. But with his sawmill business he couldn't take a day off unless it was an emergency. Even with the war over, it has created problems for everyone. Not just problems for the North and South, but for the Union. The death of President Lincoln added even more turbulence. She would be so glad when James got home. He was the wise one.

She opened her bedroom door and looked down to the first floor. She could see a lantern light coming from the kitchen, and Elijah was sitting at the table snapping beans. She smiled and closed the door softly. Getting ready for bed, she smiled again. It had been a long day, but good things were beginning to happen. James was coming home, and she had a house guest who was snapping the beans.

# CHAPTER 8

# A SLEEPLESS NIGHT OF MEMORIES

As Charlotte lay sleepless in her bed, she thought, yes, good things were beginning to happen. But what about Jimmy? If only she knew if he was dead or alive, she would be able to handle his absence with less anxiety. His letters had come once a week for his first two years in the army. Why had they suddenly stopped in November of last year?

She remembered her life before the war. Her mind went back to 1840, the summer she and James had married at St. Michael's Church in the city. James graduated from West Point that spring, and she had begun to plan their wedding. They had courted for four years, but waited until he graduated before thinking about marriage.

She smiled as she thought of her first night in this house as Mrs. James Fenwick Grimball. There had been a great party after the wedding. The parlor had been beautifully decorated, with candles and flowers everywhere. Big Momma and Liza baked wonderful pies and cookies, and also a three-tiered wedding cake. The cake was fabulous in looks and in taste. It had been such a joyful party.

After everyone left, James picked her up and brought her up the staircase to this very room. It had been a night to remember.

After he graduated, his father had brought him on as Heartland's financial administrator, inviting them to come live on the plantation. James liked the idea, but Charlotte had wanted to stay in the city.

She remembered how she felt when she saw the plantation for the first time. It was a beautiful place, but too far in the country for a city girl. The carriage lane with the big oak trees was impressive, but when she thought about taking care of eighty slaves, she knew was not ready for that responsibility.

Charlotte lost her father in 1850. Her family had only owned six slaves, and Charlotte did not know them well, with the exception of Anna, the household cook. Anna had taken care of her as a child, and stayed until Charlotte's mother's death in 1855. Anna was sold to the Master of Magnolia Plantation that same year.

After much discussion, James had agreed to stay in the city. He brought Big Momma and Liza from the plantation to be their household servants.

It was a year later that Jimmy was born in this very bed. Charlotte still remembered the emotion she'd felt holding her newborn baby boy. When Jimmy was six months old, they moved to the plantation. Liza and Big Momma moved with them. Not only did they do the cooking, but Big Momma raised Jimmy.

Charlotte sighed, "I must get some sleep. I must stop thinking about Jimmy." She paused, and prayed, "Dear God, please bring him back to me."

She turned over and closed her eyes. No sleep came. She could not get Jimmy off her mind. As she fretted over going to sleep, she heard the grandfather clock strike one o'clock. She sat up in bed, but more memories of Jimmy's childhood filled her head. He had been such a good child, always wanting to please. Tears began to fall as she continued to think of her missing son. This was the worst night she'd had since Jimmy's letters stopped coming.

What a nightmare, she thought, reaching for the lantern on the bedside table. In the darkness, she searched the table for matches, and was able to turn up the wick and light the lantern.

She climbed out of bed, went out of the bedroom, and down the dark hall to Jimmy's room. She had not been there since coming back from the plantation.

Opening the door, she could smell the dust that had accumulated since he left. Evidently, Elijah had not touched this room.

She placed the lantern on a small marble-topped table and stood in the middle of the floor. She was able to catch a scent of Jimmy, and smiled. The room was just as he'd left it. A pendant from the military school hung on the wall over his bed. A school uniform hung on a wooden peg on the wall, pressed and ready to wear. A pair of black military shoes sat on the floor beneath the uniform. Dust covered the blue uniform and the once-shiny shoes.

She remembered how grand Jimmy had looked when wearing this uniform. But he'd looked grander in his grey Confederate uniform. She saw him in that uniform on his last trip home.

She walked around the room touching things that he'd used in the past--books, an inkwell, a whistle made from a block of wood, a small pocket knife, his favorite fishing rod, and several bags of marbles. He'd spent much time playing marbles with the slave children. She touched his things as if they were made of gold, and, at that moment, they were.

When she heard the clock strike two o'clock, she picked up the lantern and walked back to her own room. She blew out the lamp and crawled back into bed. She closed her eyes tightly and began singing a lullaby she'd once sung to Jimmy. In the middle of the second verse, she fell asleep with a smile on her face.

# CHAPTER 9

# YOUNG JIMMY

James Fenwick Grimball, IV at age 19 completed his second year at the South Carolina Military College in Charleston, known as the Citadel, just as the war began. His father, James Fenwick Grimball, III, a graduate of West Point, class of 1840, insisted Jimmy attend a military college. As long as Jimmy could remember, his father talked about the military training he'd received at West Point. He often lamented the fact that he never served in a military setting, and gave Jimmy no choice in the matter of higher education. When Jimmy came of age, his father thought a career in the military was best for his son. Even if Jimmy never went to war, military training would prepare him to be more organized and self-disciplined, and give him survival skills for life.

In 1836, Jimmy's father and uncles had inherited the family plantation, Heartland, located on John's Island, South Carolina, which had eighty-two slaves. It was where Jimmy grew up.

Jimmy's early education came from private tutors. Some stayed at Heartland, while others commuted each day. Jimmy was considered accomplished in book learning among his peers, but showed little interest in the running of the plantation. He preferred reading and his studies to hard labor. In 1859, Jimmy started college at the Citadel, and finished two years there.

He wanted to go on to his third year at the college, but things changed when his father enlisted in the army in January 1862. There was no time for more schooling during the war. Therefore, in 1862, Jimmy joined the 23rd Regiment of the First Military District of South Carolina. He soon found himself encamped in the village of Secessionville on James Island, not far from Heartland Plantation. He thought it was great being stationed so near home. He did not know that James Island would soon be the site of a decisive battle in the defense of Charleston.

The Union troops had planned to land on the southeastern end of James Island and make a surprise assault onto the Charleston Peninsula. Meanwhile, Major General John C. Pemberton, [4] seeing Union preparations for advancement on James Island were underway, placed Brigadier General Nathan George Evans, a South Carolinian, in command of the James Island defenses [5] and in charge of Jimmy's regiment. Jimmy spent his first few days as a soldier building earthworks to help defend the island.

Only a few days after Evans took command, the battle of Secessionville took place. [6] Stationed less than four miles from the Yankee's target Fort Lamar, Jimmy's regiment was one of the first battalions to face the firing line. General Evans hauled Jimmy and the other foot soldiers out of bed at four a.m. on July 16 to defend against the Union lines fighting at Fort Lamar.

Jimmy's regiment watched the battle from afar until the Union troops began retreating. The Yankees hid between trees and on the borders of the furrows in a cotton field near Jimmy's encampment. It was Jimmy's first battle, and he was fearful knowing the battlefield was so near his childhood home. Too close for comfort.

For some reason, Evans did not rush his troops into the fighting, so by the time they arrived, the battle was over. Evans was reprimanded for his tardiness, but Jimmy was glad he did not have to fight that day. Later in the year, Evans received orders to take his regiments to Northern Virginia to fight in the Petersburg Campaign. Before he could move his troops, he received injuries from a buggy fall in Charleston. He was replaced by Brigadier General Stephen Elliott. [7]

Under Elliott's command, Jimmy's regiment left for Northern Virginia in late 1863, and for the next eight months found themselves in trenches fighting Union soldiers in the Petersburg Campaign.

Between battles, Jimmy wrote home. Charlotte received letters from him weekly until November 1864, when the letters stopped coming.

Under the command of General Elliott at the battle of Boydton, [8] near Petersburg, Virginia, in October 1864, Jimmy engaged in one of the battles of the Petersburg Campaign. It had been organized by the Confederacy to save their food supply from being captured by the Union Army. General Grant's troops were guarding the railroads to try to cut off the Confederate Army and take their ration supplies.

In the battle, Elliott's regiment planned to apprehend Grant's troops by surrounding the guards to capture them. The soldiers fought fiercely, leading to a Confederate victory.

Near the end of the battle, Jimmy turned to face two Union soldiers. One held him at bay with a bayonet, the second soldier grabbed his rifle. Jimmy fought the officer, but with a rifle and a bayonet in his face, there was nothing to do but give in or be killed. Without further struggle, he surrendered and became a prisoner of war of the Union Army.

The officers roughly led him to a place where other captive Confederate soldiers stood. Though it was late in the day, the prisoners were given no supper and told to sleep on the ground for the night. If anyone tried to escape he would be shot on the spot. Jimmy could not believe that he was a prisoner of the Union Army, a situation that had never occurred to him.

The next morning the prisoners began a march to Petersburg, Virginia. When they arrived at City Point, they ate a small amount of meat and crackers for breakfast. After breakfast, they were marched to the river where several transport steamers waited to take them to Point Lookout Prison Camp in the state of Maryland. [9]

Packed in like cattle going to market, there were at least five hundred prisoners on each boat. The stench of human bodies and dried blood gave Jimmy a sickly feeling in the pit of his stomach. Many of the men vomited.

The boat arrived at Point Lookout Prison the next morning at sunrise. Unloading at the dock, the prisoners were commanded to form a line for inspection. In doing so, it did not take Jimmy long to realize the terrible situation he now faced. All prisoners were ordered to empty their pockets and put their baggage on the ground in front of them. Jimmy quickly hid his gold coins in a boot. The Yankee guards confiscated anything of value if found. They took Jimmy's gun and his blanket, but did not check his boots.

What happened next shook Jimmy to the point of despair. A prison officer ordered them into formation and marched them into a "bullpen" which led into Point Lookout Prison Camp. It reminded Jimmy of how cows were led to slaughter on the plantation.

Point Lookout Prison Camp covered forty acres of land between the Potomac River and the Chesapeake Bay. Later on, records reported it was deemed the largest and worst Northern prison camp of the war.

A fourteen-foot-high wooden fence surrounded the camp with a wooden platform built inside the fence for the guards to walk upon. Jimmy found that most of the guards had been enslaved, who often took the hostility of their former lives out on the Southern prisoners. They delighted in provoking them. Their authority over the defenseless prisoners was the thing Jimmy first noticed. It gave him a sick feeling, along with a new fear...a fear of the guards.

Inside the gates, there was a ditch called the "dead line." If a prisoner crossed the ditch, a sentry immediately fired at the prisoner to kill him.

Regular rows of small tents divided the camp into ten companies with two hundred men each. Latrines were pits called sinks. When a sink overflowed, dirt was used to fill it up and another pit was dug. A lagoon of stagnant water within the compound also served as a latrine and a dump, which led to many diseases.

With no roof over the prison, shallow ditches were dug in front of each tent to hold rainwater and water that overflowed from the Chesapeake Bay. The water, saturated with green copper, tasted salty. It was the only water for the prisoners to drink and use for bathing. Clean water was never provided.

Jimmy was assigned to a tent large enough for twenty, with forty prisoners inhabiting it. He learned there were some twenty-thousand prisoners being housed in a camp with a ten-thousand-person capacity. The overcrowded conditions, plus the lack of food and clean water, led to prisoners dying daily from disease and starvation. Rations being in such short supply caused some men to eat roaches, raw fish, and rats.

Jimmy kept his coins hidden, but when he was starving, he pulled out a gold coin. He knew this was morally wrong, but it could help him survive. The coins quickly made him friends with the mess chef, a former slave. Jimmy received extra rations whenever the chef managed to add food without fear of being shot. Jimmy was careful not to spend all the coins. He would need some cash if he ever got out of this hellhole.

He suffered from dysentery from the unclean water, and bilious attacks from the food. With soldiers stacked like sandbags in each tent, it was hard to get a good night's sleep. Some men dug holes in the ground for a place to sleep. The holes were warmer than the tents on cold nights. However, many prisoners died during the winter months from sleeping on the frozen ground.

Jimmy lay awake some nights and imagined being at home in Charleston and eating until he was full. Even though he sometimes had more food than his mates, he had lost thirty pounds since he was imprisoned.

Although he missed his mother and father, he had not written home since becoming a prisoner. It was wrong, but he could not bring himself to tell his mother he'd worn the same shirt for six months. Neither could he tell her that the coat he was wearing came from a prisoner who'd died of starvation. His boots belonged to a soldier shot by a guard for eating food from another man's plate. How could he tell her that he suffered from head and skin lice and had no blanket to cover himself? Things were too horrible to write about. It would break her heart.

Nightly he prayed, "Please Lord, let this barbaric war be over soon, and let me survive."

He prayed for his father's safety on the battlefield, and for his mother at home in Charleston. Sometimes he prayed and read the Bible all night to block out the groaning of the suffering prisoners. When things got too bad, tears flowed down his face. His father had sent him to military school to develop survival skills, but had it really helped? He didn't think so.

Some evenings, prisoners would begin to sing. At first, they would sing sad, lonely songs, but as more prisoners joined in, the songs became livelier. Jimmy loved music and loved to sing. These were the nights he actually looked forward to. It was the only activity that ever gave him hope.

The prisoners would sit together around a camp fire and sing familiar songs, from Amazing Grace to Goober Peas. Dixieland was a favorite. However, sometimes guards would shoot their guns in the air to show their hatred of the South. Other favorites were Bonnie Blue Flag, John Brown's Body, and The Girl I Left Behind. Jimmy's favorite song was Jesus Loves Me. It conjured memories of his mother singing to him as a child. It gave him a warm feeling of home. He always slept well on music night.

However, he hated rainy nights. Without a roof over the camp, the prisoners slept in pools of water, often causing already weakened soldiers to sicken.

With so many prisoners packed together, it was difficult to get any exercise. Sometimes a game of baseball would give him a chance to run a little. Most of the men played cards to pass the time. Jimmy became the best poker player in his tent. If only he could play for money. It was tempting, but his coins remained firmly in his boot.

In April 1865, a few days after Lee's surrender at Appomattox Courthouse, the prisoners woke to the sounds of people yelling and horns blowing.

"The war is over. Lee surrendered!" was yelled throughout the prison. Everyone began to shout, even the staff. It was a victorious sound.

Jimmy shouted, too, then silently said, "Thank you, God. Thank you."

# CHAPTER 10

# HOME REPAIRS

Three weeks had passed since Charlotte returned to Charleston. In some ways, it seemed longer. So much had happened since that day. Eternally thankful that her house on South Bay stood with minor damage, she could not complain.

Elijah now stayed under her roof. No longer a slave, he worked for room and board. Charlotte felt safer in her home with him there. Best of all, she had heard from her husband, James. He was now discharged from the army and on his way home.

In her morning meditations, Charlotte thanked God for the things that had come to pass in such a short time. She prayed for James' safe travel as he began his journey home. And she made a special plea to hear from Jimmy.

Closing her prayer book, she lifted her freshly ironed skirt and headed down the curved staircase toward the kitchen. To her surprise, she found Elijah already stirring the fire and putting water on for coffee.

"Good morning, Miss Charlotte. I's been up fuh 'while and I thought I would start de coffee. Hope you don't mind?"

"Not a bit, you can start breakfast anytime you want to. This is a beautiful day in Charleston. I am going to rejoice in it," she said cheerfully.

"Yu's mighty happy because your man is coming home. I's glad fuh you. But 'fore he gits here, I be fixin' the chimneys," Elijah said.

"You don't have to do that. We won't need the chimneys until winter," she replied.

"I know dat, but I's want de place to look like it did 'fore he left," Elijah explained.

"He will be pleased, and so will I," she said. "But I do not want you to miss time from your job. It might upset the captain."

"I talked to de cap'n, and he say dat I be off fuh a week to help you. T'ings at de harbor are slow at dis time." Elijah said with a big smile, "Working fuh you will be like de plantation days."

Charlotte didn't know how to respond to that. He was free and she didn't want him to feel like a slave again. "No, Elijah, not working on the plantation, but like friends helping each other."

"Dat's what I mean," he said. "Where do we start?"

She knew she must choose her words carefully. She realized that he did not understand the true meaning of freedom. In some way, she would have to explain to Elijah that he was no longer owned by the Grimball family, but free to go wherever he pleased, without obligation to James or herself.

After breakfast of biscuits and eggs, she untied her apron and said to Elijah, "This morning, can you help me put another bucket on the rope at the well? A Yankee bullet left a hole in the side of the old one. Then we will pick the figs that are ripe on the bushes near the terrace. That should take us all morning. At lunch, we will figure out what we can do next to make this place look as good as it did before the war."

Grinning from ear to ear, Elijah said, "Dat sounds a good t'ing we do fuh Massa James."

She led the way to the back door and outside. As they walked to the well, she wondered how she could clarify the true meaning of freedom to Elijah. The task was a serious one, and it was going to be a long, hard road to explain it to a former slave. Somehow she would have to explain to him that he was now a freedman, free to go and do whatever he wanted to do. She didn't want him to feel like a slave again by doing repairs for her.

# CHAPTER 11

# WASH DAY

Yesterday had been a very busy day for Charlotte and Elijah. The needed repairs had been completed and they were able to pick two buckets of figs. This morning, she was up at sunrise, and was surprised to find Elijah in the kitchen washing the figs.

She couldn't believe what she was seeing. "Elijah, what are you doing?"

"Last night you say you need to make preserves with de figs we picked," he responded. "I was gettin' dem ready for you to cook. I did somebin wrong?"

"Oh, no. It's not wrong. I had planned to do some laundry this morning and work on the figs in the afternoon," she said. "But it's all right. We can let the figs soak in sugar this morning and I can cook them this afternoon. It is good that George brought me sugar on his way to Heartland. It was so scarce during the war."

Charlotte went to the pantry and brought out the bag. She put the figs in a large pot and poured sugar over them. While she prepared the figs, Elijah asked if there was anything he could do.

"Why, yes," she said. "If you don't mind, would you go to the cellar and get the big iron wash-pot? I am washing the bed linens today, and will need to boil them for a while. Would you mind also starting the fire? I'm not used to starting a fire that large. Big Momma used to do that for me. I hope that's not too much to ask of you. You know you are no longer obliged to do the work unless you want to, right? I will pay you extra for helping."

"I don't want no pay for helping you, Miss Charlotte. I am t'ankful for a roof over my head. Instead I should pay you. You too good to me," Elijah said. "I's glad I can be useful to yuh in any way. I's headed to the cellar and will built the fire and pump the water."

As he closed the back door, she sighed. She hoped it was the right thing to ask for help from Elijah. She didn't like to admit it, but she did miss the slave help. It was a whole new way of life for a Southern woman. Hopefully things would be easier when James got home.

She covered the fig pot with cheesecloth and walked into the hall. There she picked up her overly loaded laundry basket and headed toward the back door. It would be nice to sleep on clean sheets tonight, and she'd also have a clean set waiting when James got home. She would tell Elijah he could wash his sheets, too, while there was still a fire.

In the backyard near the terrace, the water in the iron wash pot began to boil. Elijah added lye soap to the water. The soap was probably made at Heartland. He remembered helping Master James make soap several times, years ago. Elijah brought the scrub board up from the cellar in case it was needed.

This was only the second big wash day Charlotte had had since coming back from Heartland. Her brother George had helped her last time, as Elijah had been working for the captain. She usually washed a personal garment or two every day, but when the iron pot was brought out, it was a serious laundry day, usually with curtains and bed linens.

When Elijah saw her struggling with the weight of the laundry basket, he ran to help, taking it from her.

"Thank you, Elijah. I didn't know if I would make it or not," she said, laughing as she began putting the dirty linens into the water. She made sure the linens were covered with water before stirring them with the hand-made wooden paddle. "Elijah, why don't you go strip the linens from your bed. You can use the same fire to do your laundry."

"T'ank you, Miss Charlotte. I'll get dem now while you stir awhile," he said, turning toward the house.

There were four sets of bed linens in the pot, along with pillow cases and two light blankets. They must be boiled for a half hour or so. It would depend on how soiled the things were. Next, another large vessel was filled with cold water and placed by the hot fire. Using the wooden paddle, each garment was lifted and dropped into the pot of cold water. As the items cooled, it usually took two people to reach into the vessel and together wring the water from it. If the linen looked clean, it would be hung over the clotheslines which were strung from post to post in the backyard. Sometimes clotheslines were attached to trees. If the item had dirty spots that the boiling did not remove, it was rubbed on the scrub board then put back into the boiling water.

Elijah quickly returned with his dirty laundry to the assist with the wash. He worked with Charlotte for several hours, getting it all clean and hung on the clotheslines. It was only after finishing the household things that he changed the wash water and rekindled the fire to do his own laundry.

By noon all of the washing was completed, but Elijah's laundry could not be hung on the lines until the rest was completely dry. Charlotte invited him to come into the kitchen and have dinner while they waited.

After eating ham biscuits and drinking sweet tea, she got empty jelly jars from the pantry for the fig preserves. She boiled the jars until sterile and placed them on the table, then stirred the figs in the pot and tasted them. They were wonderfully sweet and ready to go into the jars. With a wooden spoon, she dipped up figs and filled each jar.

Licking the spoon, she said to Elijah, "Please go to the pantry and bring me a block of wax. When the jars cool, I will seal them with it to preserve them. I'll have figs at Christmas time to make my famous figgy pudding, one of James' favorites."

"I's like it, too. My momma used to make figgy pudding when I was little, but I ain't had any since she passed."

"I hope you are still here to enjoy mine at Christmas," Charlotte told him.

"I hope Massa James will keep me. I likes working here," Elijah said.

"I think he will. He'll need someone for sure, and I can put a good word in for you. I couldn't have gotten this place looking as great as it does without your help. I appreciate all the hard work you've done this month, and I am sure he will be so pleased," she said.

"T'ank you. I's proud of making everything look new, and I hope Massa James will also be satisfied."

Charlotte wiped her hands on the cheesecloth and reached for the melted wax in a pan on the stove. "Elijah, I'll finish the figs while you go check on the wash. You should be able to hang your laundry now. There is still enough sunshine to get it dried before supper."

"I was just thinking about doing that. T'ank you," Elijah said, and headed down the back stairs.

# CHAPTER 12

# FREEDOM FOR BIG TOM

In early 1863 when President Lincoln wrote the Emancipation Proclamation, [10] Big Tom, who was a dependable slave belonging to James Fenwick Grimball, thought that Lincoln had given slaves their freedom, so he decided to leave the plantation, taking his woman, Liza, and their child, Lilly, with him.

Charlotte and Owen had tried to reason with him, but no, he was bound north to get rich. Big Tom didn't stop to think about the battlefields he would have to cross, nor did he think about how he could survive in the war-torn states along the way. He would be treated as a runaway slave if caught, but freedom was all he'd wanted. Charlotte knew that Big Tom would never again be content at Heartland, so she and George let him go. Charlotte was brokenhearted when she found that he was taking Liza and Lilly with him. Traveling with a three-year-old would not be easy.

Tom was given James's small cargo boat to start the journey north. He rigged it with a homemade sail and attached a wooden oar to the stern to steer the boat and propel it with a sculling motion. He decided to wait until a full moon week to begin the journey down the river on an outgoing tide.

Liza baked three pans of biscuits before leaving, and placed them in a basket with the ham Tom took from the smokehouse. A jar of molasses, some apples, and boiled eggs filled the extra space in the basket. Those rations would not last long, but it was all she could get from the big house without upsetting Miss Charlotte. Liza thought this was to be a great adventure for Lilly and herself. At least, that was what Big Tom made her believe.

Packing lightly, Tom, Liza, and Lilly set off from the pier at the plantation one late afternoon in March 1863, hoping to get into the Atlantic Ocean by dark. Liza saw many manned batteries along the Stono River as they left on the outgoing tide that brought them into the Atlantic Ocean. Big Tom saw the troops but gave them no thought. He thought a freed slave could go wherever he pleased.

As they passed a Union encampment on Little Folly Island, a Yankee soldier fired a shot that missed the boat but went through the sail. Big Tom laughed and hollered, "You missed us," but it frightened Liza and Lilly.

Lilly began to cry. "I want to go home," she sobbed.

"Keep dat young'un quiet," Tom bellowed.

Right away, Liza knew she should have stayed on the plantation. It was impossible to keep a three-year old quiet.

As Tom steered the boat, he tried to stay within seeing distance of land, which made it harder. The undercurrent kept pulling the boat in different directions. As the sun began to go down, he turned the boat toward the open sea. Soon the small boat with its makeshift sail was just a dot on the huge Atlantic Ocean.

As the sun slid into the horizon and the darkness began to fall, Lilly began to cry. "It's dark. I's scared," she said grabbing onto Liza's apron.

"Hush, my little one, we is waiting for Mr. Moon's light to come, then it will be light again," Liza said, trying to comfort her. But she was beginning to feel anxious herself.

She opened the food basket and took out four biscuits and the ham. Cutting the meat with a knife, she handed a ham biscuit to Lilly. She would feed Lilly and then take Tom his supper later. He was excited about the boat and was travelling much faster than Liza thought possible, so supper could wait.

Tom was the best navigator of the rice boats when it was harvest time at Heartland. Massa James had depended on him, back then.

Pulling Lilly closer, Liza ate a ham biscuit. Lilly was satisfied after eating, knowing she would have milk later. Liza always nursed Lilly before bedtime. [11]

Suddenly, the sky began to get lighter as the moon came out from behind a cloud. "I see Mr. Moon," an excited Lilly shouted. "He did come. Now we can ride by Mr. Moon's light."

"You are right, Lilly," Liza said, pulling the child into her lap. "I see the moon, the moon sees me." She paused, and Lilly finished the poem.

"God bless the moon, and God bless me."

"Good girl," Liza exclaimed. "You remembuh'd." She gave Lilly a big hug. "Now I think it is your bedtime. You can sleep while Mr. Moon's light is shining."

Liza unbuttoned her shirt and Lilly began her bedtime nursing as Liza sang a child's lullaby, part of their nightly ritual. Soon, the tired three-year-old was fast asleep.

Liza took a blanket and wrapped it around her baby's small body and gently placed her on the pillow that Tom had made for Lilly to sleep upon. It was the one thoughtful thing he'd done for her in preparing for this journey.

As soon as Lilly was asleep, Liza stood up. It was her first time standing since they started the trip. Her body felt wobbly. She always felt insecure in a boat on the deep water. After standing still for a few seconds, she picked up the food basket and walked to the stern. "Tom, is you hungry? Do you want to eat now?"

Tom stopped what he was doing and said, "I could eat a whole ham."

On a piece of scrap cloth, she placed two ham biscuits and an apple, and handed the food to Tom.

As soon as he saw the food, he bellowed, "What is you trying to do to me, dis ain't enough food to keep a cat alive, let alone feed a hardworking cap'n of a sailboat. I need mo food."

"Too bad," she said, "Dat's all you get tonight. Dis food mus' last us a couple more days and dat's it for tonight."

He snatched the food basket from her, and grabbed the jar of molasses and two eggs. He began pouring the molasses over his biscuits, letting some of the syrup drip to the bottom of the boat.

Liza hurriedly began to wipe up the syrup with her apron, saying, "Tom, yuh going to be sorry when de food be gone in de middle of de ocean."

He threw the food basket down and turned back to the stern of the boat, eating his second egg. Liza felt like crying. She knew this was going to be a long and dangerous trip if he was going to act like this. For the second time since leaving land, she wished to be back at Heartland.

She closed the food basket and placed it out of Tom's reach. After checking on Lilly, she removed her apron and hung it over the side of the boat to dry. She sipped water from the canteen and lay down next to Lilly, covering herself with part of the blanket. She said her usual nighttime prayer, and added, "Lawd, keep us safe on dis boat while we trabble." Shading her eyes from the moon-light she drifted to sleep.

———

Just at sunrise, Lilly began to move around on her pillow, waking Liza.

"Go to sleep, baby. It ain't time to git up," Liza said, thinking that the longer Lilly slept, the less she would bother Tom. The child turned over and was soon sleeping again, but Liza wasn't able to do the same. Even though it was daybreak, she lay wondering just how far the boat had sailed during the night. How many more nights would they be sleeping in the moonlight? What if it rained? What if they ran out of food? Before the trip began, she did not think to ask these questions. Now she wondered if Big Tom even knew the answers.

Soon the sun began to rise in the east, casting new rays of light through the gray sky. At least today's weather was clear and the sun was bright. The only sound she could hear was the sloshing of the water against the back of the boat.

"Tom? Tom, is you awake?"

There was no answer.

Sitting up, she looked to the stern of the boat and could see Tom slumped over the small stool he sat upon to guide the boat. She jumped up from where she lay and hastened back to him.

"Tom! Tom, wake up! Is you okay? Wuh happened? Why you sleep? Weh is we?"

He rose quickly, stunned to see the sunrise. "I's okay. I guess I jus' went to sleep while the boat been sailin'. We's fine."

"But de boat's not moving," she said.

Big Tom realized that the sloshing of water was only coming from the rear of the boat. From the stern, he stepped over the side of the boat, and his feet landed on soft beach sand. "We's okay, we is on a beach."

"A beach!" Liza exclaimed. "What beach, weh's about?"

He said, "We must be in North Carolina by now." Little did he know that they were only about fifteen miles above Charleston at Breach Inlet, between Sullivan's Island and the Isle of Palms.

"Now that the sun is up, I's go walking to see weh we be. I might can find some food," he crowed. "You'en stay right hea. Don't get out of de boat. I's be right back."

"Here, Tom, tek the canteen. See if you can find drinking water. It be almos' empty," she said, handing it to Tom.

Leaving the boat, he started walking inland, only to find that the beach sand did not reach far and the rest of the soil was crusted with oyster shells. He spied a large oyster bed. He knew good eating when he saw it. He lumbered to the oysters and reached down to gather some for breakfast. On the first try, he cut his hand on an oyster shell and came back to the boat yelling and bleeding.

"I ain't gwing waste my time getting cut from oyster shells. Dey ain't worth it," he said, wrapped his hand with his handkerchief, and climbed back into the boat.

"Did you git water? Liza asked.

"No, I forgit when I cut myself. I's git it later. There is still a little in the canteen. We's got to get gwing," he said.

"Not before breakfast," she replied, and reached for the food basket.

Lilly raised her sleepy head and Liza picked her up. "Are we der yet?" the girl asked.

"No honey, we must ride some more, but first we will eat breakfast," Liza said, opening the basket. "There's only ham, biscuits, and eggs left."

"I's tired of biscuits and boiled eggs," Tom grumbled. "We need better food dan dat. I's get oysters next time even if I git cut doing it."

Liza and Lilly ate quietly, listening to him complain about the food. Liza drank a small amount of water from the canteen and gave Lilly a drink.

Turning to him, she said boldly, "Tom, I's tired of you fussing and grumbling about the food I brought. It was all I could get from the plantation's kitchen that would las' more den two days. You might as well enjoy it 'cause after it be gone, you'll be gitten us food and it won' be easy."

He looked at her and said nothing aloud, but under his breath she heard him whisper, "When I get north, I's eat anything I want to eat."

He finished two biscuits, an apple, and drank the remaining water from the canteen. Then he said, "Time is wasting, got to get de boat headed north."

Liza was glad the weather was warm and clear. It had been cold during the night. She put another blanket in the bow of the boat, in case it was needed later today.

Tom looked around the inlet, and grasping the sculling oar, began to move the boat out to sea. The undercurrent seemed better today, and the wind felt stronger.

"I ain't going to wait 'til nighttime to sail. De wind is jus' right. You and Lilly get in ya seats. I's starting de boat now. North, here we come," he said proudly.

Liza picked up Lilly and sat down in the bow of the boat just as the wind began to flap the sails and the boat moved in a northerly direction.

She thought Tom was making a mistake by sailing in the broad day-light. There were still Yankees in these waters, but Tom thought he was the only one who could make decisions on this trip. Now her biggest question was, how was she going to entertain a three-year-old for a whole day on a sailboat? At least at night, Lilly slept.

Liza had brought along the ragdoll that Big Momma had made for Lilly before her death. And from Charlotte's rag bag, she'd brought scrapes of cloth, some needles, buttons, and thread to help Lilly make church dolls. Liza had also put several empty thread spools in her bag, as Lilly pretended they were dolls. The scraps of cloth could be used for napkins or towels.

While Liza was busy entertaining Lilly, Tom waited for mild wind to push them in the right direction to begin their day of travel. Soon the sails caught the north winds and the small boat began to go faster.

"Look, Liza, we's sailing," he yelled and sat down.

"Good, Tom. I's proud of you. Did you get water for de canteen?" she asked.

"I told you I forgit. You can take your cup and get water from the ocean anytime," he said, turning back to the stern.

"No, dat's sea water. It can make you sick, you know dat," she said in disgust. "I ain't want seasickness in des boat."

"Ah, one or two cups won't hurt you. I've done it and I ain't sick," Tom boasted, and began steering the boat.

As the sun climbed higher, the heat began to take over the nice breeze. Liza needed water. She'd been taught as a child not to drink the salt water, and she remembered seeing one of the slaves get sick from the water in the rice field. She didn't want to be dat sick in this small boat.

"I's thirsty," Lilly said, wiping the sweat from her tiny face.

"I know, dear, so am I, but the canteen is empty and the ocean water isn't good for us to drink. Come sit in my lap and see if I have any milk. Dat will help your thirst."

Lilly climbed into Liza's arms and was able to nurse a small bit of milk, which seemed to satisfy her enough, for she returned to her doll without whining.

But Liza needed water. She knew there would be no milk for Lilly tonight if she did not have water. She picked up the tin cup, leaned over the side of the boat, and filled the cup with ocean water. If it didn't make Tom sick, hopefully it wouldn't make her sick.

The water was very salty and she ended up throwing half of it overboard. She hoped the water wouldn't harm her. However, the movement of the boat was making her stomach feel queasy. Seasickness could be terrible. You couldn't stop the waves from tossing. It was near noon, and Lilly was tired of playing with the spool dolls. She began to whine, "Let's stop, Mama. I want to play in the water."

"We can't stop, my dear. Not until Tom want to. Besides, de water is too deep to play in," Liza said, trying to appease her little one.

"I's tired of riding on de water and de wind is blowing water into de boat. My feet is wet," Lilly complained.

"Yes, I know, but dat helps us stay cool. Come, sit in my lap, I will dry you off with a blanket," Liza said, reaching for one from under the seat. To her surprise, the blankets felt wetter than her apron. Shaking one of them in the wind, she wrapped it around Lilly.

"The blanket is cold, but feels good in de hot sun," the child said, leaning back into Liza's arms.

She began singing to Lilly, who soon fell asleep. It was near noon, but she would let Lilly sleep for a while. It would give her some alone time. She felt like Lilly, tired of sailing and the getting wet from the water. Maybe she would feel better if she walked to the stern of the boat. She could stretch her legs a little.

As she approached the stern, Tom said, "I's very tired, and feel like I will go to sleep if I stand here much longer. Do you think you could steer de boat and let me rest a few minutes?"

She was amazed and pleased that he thought she could navigate his sailboat. "Of course, I can," she said, giving Tom her first smile since the beginning of the trip.

If Big Tom could make the oar move the boat back and forth, she surely could do it, too. It couldn't be too difficult.

"I don't know anything about sailing a boat, but you need to rest, so I will do it to help."

Tom stood beside Liza and said, "All you do is hold on to de long oar attached to the boat. Watch me. If I turn left, de boat goes right, and if I turn it right, de boat goes left. Just hold it still and it goes straight ahead. Dat is the way we want to go. Try it Liza. You can do it. I need to rest."

# CHAPTER 13

# WIND AND MORE WATER

Liza took the oar from Tom and found it easy to move the rudder to the correct direction.

Tom walked to a seat and quickly lay down. "If you get in any trouble, I's right hea."

Liza was excited to have been asked to steer. It made her feel important. Suddenly, a big wave sloshed over the side, pouring at least a gallon of water into the boat. The water gave her a fright and she let go of the oar, but grabbed it back before the boat changed direction. She feared that Tom would start hollering at her, but thank goodness he was already asleep.

She calmed down and got the rudder back on path. The water seemed very rough, and she hoped no more big waves would come while she was steering. It was scary.

Should she wake Tom? Just as she had that thought, a large wave came crashing into the boat. This time she let go of the guiding oar and lost complete control. The sound of the wave woke Lilly and Tom. The frightened child started screaming, and Tom started hollering angrily. Liza ran to Lilly, and Big Tom ran to the stern. He grabbed the control oar, but it was too late. The boat was going around and around in the ocean.

Tom was able to stop the boat from turning, but it had nearly filled with water. Lilly's rag doll was floating with her other toys on top. The blankets, completely soaked, had settled to the bottom of the boat. The food basket was filled with water, covering the biscuits. Two apples floated on top.

"You dumb, ooman!" [12] Tom shouted. "I told you not to let go of de oar. Dis is big trouble. The boat is too heavy to sail far like dis. We's got to head for land and empty de water."

Liza, holding a frightened Lilly, was in tears. Tom's shouting wasn't helping. Through her sobs, she said, "We needs to start bailing now or we's never get to land."

Placing Lilly on the stool in the stern, Liza grabbed her drinking cup and began bailing water, but the cup did not hold enough to do any good. She took off a boot and tried that instead. Success!

Tom was so dumbfounded that he just watched as she worked at bailing water. Coming to his senses, he removed a boot, too, and began bailing.

Baby Lilly stood in water up to her knees and cried, "I want to go home."

Liza stopped bailing and took the child into her arms. "Lilly, you gotta stop crying. We's okay. The wind makes the water come into de boat, and it will keep the boat from going. As soon as we can get de water out, we can go to land. Understand?"

Lilly stopped crying and placed her head against Liza's chest, sniffing. "I try, but I's scared."

"Dat's all right. I was scared when de big wave came, but now much of the water is gone and things be better," Liza said.

Lilly smiled and wiggled out of her mother's arms. "Can I play in de water?"

Liza laughed. "Yes. Seeing you are already wet, you play 'til the water is gone from de boat." She hoped that would calm Lilly long enough to finish bailing.

Tom was still working quietly. Finally, he stopped bailing and said, "Most of de water is gone. De boat's movin' with de waves. I thinks we can start sailing west to find land."

"Good idea. But part of de sail is missing," she said.

"Dat ain't a problem, we just won't go so fast. De sculling oar still be attached, an' with de water gone, de boat should sail again."

"We better get going and pray de waves stay in de ocean. It already noon and we needs to get to land before sunset to find food and fresh water," she said.

He nodded and returned to the stern of the boat, and begin working with the sculling oar.

She picked up a wet blanket and tried to wring it out, holding it over the sea. She certainly didn't want any more water in the boat. Then she picked up the two floating apples and put them in her apron pocket. There was no telling when they would find food again.

Lilly rescued her ragdoll and busied herself trying to get the doll dry. She showed no fear from the earlier trauma.

Everything was silent for a change, but suddenly Tom called joyfully, "The oar is working. We's okay and headed to land."

Liza picked up Lilly and swung her around. "We soon will be on land again." She was relieved the boat was moving, but she was still worried about where their next meal would be coming from. The water had ruined the food basket.

Lilly said, "Momma, I's hungry."

"I know, but we must reach land before we can eat. You can try and see if I have any milk, and wait to eat later."

Lilly crawled into Liza lap and began to nurse. She quickly lifted her head and said, "The milk went away, too."

"I was afraid of that. The canteen's also empty." Reaching into her pocket, Liza handed Lilly an apple. "We can eat apples while we sail to land."

Eating the apple, Lilly snuggling closer to her mom. When Liza finished her apple she started singing, "Michael, row the boat ashore, halleluiah…"

Lilly sang along awhile and soon fell asleep, and so did Liza.

She didn't know how long she had slept, but was awakened abruptly. The boat had hit something. She jumped up and called to Tom, "Weh is we? Wot did we hit?"

Still at the stern, he said, "No problem, just a small sandbar. We's near land. We may have to push de boat to shore."

She stood up, looking up at the shore. To the far right beyond an inlet she could see two tall spiral cone-shaped chimney-looking buildings. She recognized the tallest as a lighthouse. Its lantern room was painted black due to the war. There was a small cottage near the lighthouse, and a fishing pier.

With her help, Tom maneuvered the boat to the sandy shore across from the lighthouse. A well-traveled path led inland from where the boat docked.

Lilly woke up crying for her momma. Liza reached into the boat and took Lilly in her arms saying, "Look, little one, we are back on land."

She put Lilly on the ground. They were on land with no shelter, or fresh water, or food, but it could be worse. They could still be in the middle of the ocean!

Tom was really tired after getting the boat back to land. There were several moments that he'd been afraid they would never make it. They were badly in need of water and food. He knew they must find both before darkness fell.

Liza picked up Lilly and said to Tom, "There is a cottage beyond that inlet, but I think we can find another house if we follow de path behind where de boat is docked.

He joined them and they went down the path going inland. It was easy walking, so she put Lilly down to walk beside her. The sun felt good on her face, and Lilly ran ahead, talking to herself. Big Tom was far ahead of them. He was running, hurrying to get north.

Off in the distance, Liza saw a house that looked much like the house at Heartland plantation. She called to Big Tom, "Dere's a house. Let's stop and see if we can git food."

He stopped and turned around. "We ain't gone far enough."

"Lilly and I is stopping, cause I am not lettin' her starve," Liza said, taking Lilly's hand. "We be gwing wit'out you if you do not come with us."

He walked back to Liza and Lilly. "But we not stay der long," he muttered.

The road leading to the house was well-travelled, yet the place seemed deserted. As they walked closer, they saw a white woman sitting in a porch swing.

"Howdy," Big Tom said. "Can we have water from de well? We be walking for a while."

"Help yourself," she said, standing up and moving to the steps.

Liza noticed that the woman limped as she walked. "Do you need any help around here?" Liza asked. "I be glad to work for room and board."

"That's a nice thought, but I must talk to my husband about it. All of our servants and field hands left, and I surely miss them."

Tom drank water from the well and walked to the steps beside Liza. "What's gwing on here?" he asked. "We can't stay here. We's gwing north."

Liza turned to him and said forcefully, "You may be gwing north, but Lilly and me's staying right here 'til we can get back to Charleston."

"No ooman's going to talk like that to me," Tom roared.

"You is coming with me, hear?" He grabbed her arm, pulling her toward the road.

Lilly ran behind, crying, "Don't hurt Momma!"

Liza jerked away from his grip and ran to her daughter. Picking her up, she ran past the well just as the master of the house came out the front door with a shotgun. Walking in front of the woman on the steps, he shouted, "What's all this racket?" He pointed the gun at Big Tom's head. "Get off my land, or I'll shoot."

"But, dat's my woman and child," he protested, pointing to Liza and Lilly. "Dey coming with me."

Liza came out from behind the well and said, "Go on, Tom. Lilly and I are staying. At least for today. Go on, we's be okay. Dis trip be too hard on us."

"You heard the woman. Now, get," the man commanded.

Tom started running. Liza watched him until he got to the trees on the beach. She turned to the couple on the porch. "So sorry. I made a mistake leavin' wit' him. Can we stay here until morning? Den we start back home." Remembering her Big House manners, she said, "I be Liza Grimball from Heartland Plantation near Charleston. Dis here my baby, Lilly. We obliged if we can sleep in your barn for de night. Den we be gone."

The man put down his rifle and walked down the steps to where Liza stood. "I am Will Willard, and this is Mrs. Willard. Come in and rest awhile. You have come a long way. Where are you headed?" he asked.

"Big Tom headed north to get rich," Liza said. "I not know it so far away. Lilly and I been mighty tired, and Tom will not stop. He ain't treated Lilly good since we left home, so I's glad he is gone. We's goin' back to Charleston."

"You are welcome to stay, and you can sleep in one of the slave cabins instead of the barn. They are empty. All twenty of our men left to join the Union Army," Mr. Willard said. "And they took their women with them."

Liza and Lilly chose a slave cabin near the big house. Mrs. Willard brought bed linens and a bucket of water to the cabin. She took to Lilly right away. Lilly, shy at first, didn't take long to warm up to the nice lady.

"I'll bring you some supper as soon as the bread finishes baking. We are having fried chicken. We were able to keep our chickens when the Yankees came through. I hid them under the house. The troops took our horses, and the hams from the smoke house. The cow is in the barn. You can get milk for the baby, if needed."

# CHAPTER 14

# THE WILLARDS

Liza arrived at the Willards during the summer of 1863. She became their cook after the first week there. Within a month, she and Lilly had moved upstairs in the big house.

Mrs. Willard had once injured her hip in a carriage accident and was left with a limp and some arthritic pain. She was happy to have Liza to stay and work for room and board. When she was young, Miss Willard had taught school. When Liza heard the missus was a teacher, she was eager to learn to read and write.

To Mrs. Willard's delight, Lilly also wanted to learn. She taught the little girl to count to one hundred and to say the ABCs before her fourth birthday. Lilly could read by her fifth birthday.

Mr. Willard was a deep sea fisherman by trade, working in the small fishing village of McClellanville, South Carolina, a few miles from his home. However, fishing had been slow since the war began, with the many war ships patrolling the coastal waters. Mr. Willard spent most of his time catching river and creek fish to sell to local folks around town. He'd wanted to join the army, but could not leave Mrs.

Willard due to her injury. However, he paid his nephew to go as his substitute soldier. [13]

Liza liked it at the Willard's, but still pined after Charleston and cooking for Miss Charlotte. But with the war still nearby, she would not travel until after the war ended. In April 1865, when Lee surrendered to the Union Forces, Liza made plans to go home to Charleston. Since she could now read and write, she wrote Miss Charlotte, asking if she and Lilly could come home. Although very attached to the Willards and appreciative of all they had done for Lilly and herself, she still longed to go home to Heartland. By June of 1865, Liza had not heard back from Miss Charlotte, but decided it was time to start home, anyway.

The Willards were heartbroken when they learned of her plans to leave, but they understood. She and Lilly had become family to the lonely and childless couple. Lilly was like a grandchild.

With a heavy heart, Mr. Willard loaded Liza's belongings and a food basket into his mule-drawn wagon.

Mrs. Willard hugged Lilly and placed her in the wagon, saying, "Goodbye, my little one. I love you. Take care of your momma."

"Bye-bye," Lilly said. "Love you, too."

Mrs. Willard was sad but proud. Lilly and Liza both now spoke standard English instead of Gullah, the Creole language spoken by slaves on the plantations.

Liza climbed into the wagon and sat next to Mr. Willard. Lilly climbed into the back. They rode in silence. Liza knew if she spoke she would cry, and she didn't want Lilly upset.

Mr. Willard took them as far as the Sewee Beach, having stopped once to water the mules. He halted the wagon and said, "Since it is not safe for a woman to travel alone on the King's Highway, [14] it's best if you and Lilly walk along the beach. I think it will be safer than the road. At night, make camp near trees and bushes, not in open spaces."

Liza managed to say, "Yes, sir. Thank you for everything. Take care of the missus." She lifted a sleepy Lilly from the wagon.

Mr. Willard put Liza's bag and food basket on the ground near where she stood. He said goodbye to Liza and picked up Lilly. He hugged her tightly. Wide awake now, she laughed and gave him a bear hug. Mr. Willard did not speak, but placed Lilly back on her feet. He felt his heart was breaking saying farewell to her. She was the only child the Willards would ever hold so dearly.

"Bye, now. Take care and be safe, God bless." Choking back tears, he guided the mules and turned the wagon around to head for home.

"Where's Mr. Willard going?" Lilly asked.

"He is going home to Miss Willard," Liza answered in a hushed voice. For the first time, she wondered if she was doing the right thing by leaving such good people.

They crossed King's Highway and followed a sign that pointed to Sewee Beach. Holding her food basket in one hand and her bag of belongings in the other, Liza headed down the narrow path to the beach with Lilly. Here they would begin their walk to Charleston, back to Heartland and Miss Charlotte.

CHAPTER 15

# DISCHARGED

T he war was over and James Grimball would soon be examined by the chief medical doctor in hopes of finally being discharged from the army. Soldiers like James who could walk went first and were transported from the field hospital in City Point, Virginia, to the Chimborazo Hospital [15] in Richmond, Virginia, by wagon.

James' right leg had been injured in 1864 during a battle south-west of Petersburg, Virginia, some twenty miles below Richmond. The Confederate Army triumphed, but with many wounded, including James. He was fortunate to have been rescued by his own regiment and carried to a nearby Confederate field hospital.

At the Richmond hospital, the patients seeking discharge stood in line until their names were called. Names were in alphabetical order. James was thankful his name began with G and not Y. Some of the men fainted while waiting in the hot sun.

"Grimball," the doctor called.

James walked to the head of the line and stood at attention, "Here, sir!"

"Relax, soldier, the war is over," the doctor said. "I am Dr. Holden, here to check if you are well enough to be discharged."

"Yes, sir," James said, relaxing his posture.

Dr. Holden continued, "I see in your record that you received your wound in the Petersburg Campaign, October 1864, and have recuperated in the field hospital for the past six months.

"Yes, sir," James replied. A bullet had hit him in his right leg during the battle, damaging his hamstring. At the Confederate City Point field hospital, at first the doctors had wanted to amputate, but James persuaded them to let the wound heal on its own. It had finally healed, but had taken longer than he'd hoped, due to an infection.

"Leg better?" the doctor asked.

"Yes, sir, but I still use the cane."

Doctor Holden pressed on James' knee cap. "Any pain?"

"No, sir."

"Get rid of the cane as soon as possible, or it will become a crutch," the doc ordered. "Seeing that you are in good physical condition and can walk again, the army is giving you an honorable discharge. You can go home now, Grimball. Good luck."

James turned from the hospital line, thinking, good luck? Was that all he had to say? Luck wouldn't get James back to Charleston. His Confederate money was no good, and he only had two gold coins in his pocket. It was going to take more than luck to get him home.

Disgruntled, he picked up his haversack, his bedroll, and rifle. He should send a telegram to Charlotte to tell her he was coming home. A letter would take too long with the good news.

After leaving the hospital, he had no idea where to go. He was in Richmond, [16] but did not know which way to turn to go south.

He looked around. The scars of war were everywhere. Piles of debris lay in the streets. Many houses had been struck by shell fire, and chimneys were gone from others. Railroad ties were missing from the tracks. The city had been terribly torn up by the exploding fragments of the conflict. It was hard to believe that the capital of the Confederacy had come to this. Seeing the devastation gave him an uneasy feeling, almost to queasiness.

He spied a small general store across the railroad tracks. Holding his cane, he walked toward the store. He could walk without the cane, but how far? He did not know.

The store was clearly damaged, missing bricks, broken steps, and had only a partial chimney, but it was open for business.

Using his cane to go up the steps, he ascended to the porch. It was crowded with idle soldiers and freed slaves, all wanting a handout. He managed to push his way to the door.

"Not another one," scoffed the clerk. "What can I do for you?"

"Do you have telegraph service?" James asked.

"Sure, cost you a dollar, and no Confederate money, hear?" the clerk said.

James pulled out a gold piece, and asked, "Will this do?"

"Just right. What do you want to say?" the clerk asked.

James dictated his message. "*Discharged today. Leg well. Coming home soon. I love you. James.* Send it to Mrs. James Grimball, 10 South Bay, Charleston, South Carolina."

"What else can I do for you?" the clerk asked. The gold coin had made him amenable.

"Are the trains running?" James asked.

"Only a few going west. Since President Lincoln's death, the trains from North to South have stopped. I've not heard if they are back on track. The man at the depot would know."

"Where is the depot?" James asked.

The clerk pointed. "Just follow the track that way. The station was practically destroyed by cannon fire. A tent is there for the business office. Someone will be glad to help a Reb."

"Thank you, sir," James said, nodding to the clerk as he walked to the door.

"Anytime, soldier boy, anytime," the clerk said. "Be careful."

James left the store and followed the track about two blocks. The station stood in the middle of city. Formerly a stately building, it was now a large area of bricks and rubble. Walking past the destruction, he found the office tent.

A man dressed in a conductor's uniform sat at a table. "Good morning, soldier. Going home?" he asked.

"Trying to get there," James said, "Is there a train running south?"

"How far south?" the official asked.

"To South Carolina," James said hopefully.

"I will check the schedule." The official fumbled through some papers on his desk and said, "Seems to me, the Richmond-Danville Railroad is back running. The day after General Lee surrendered, the Union state treasurer took over the railroad lines, saying they belonged to the Union, but Congress declared it unlawful to stop the lines as soldiers needed transportation home."

"Thank goodness."

Finding the schedule, the official said, "Yes, sir, the train will leave Richmond on Saturday at eleven sharp. Is that the one you want to take?"

"Yes, sir. Only one problem. I do not have enough money for a ticket. All I have is Confederate money," James replied with a frown.

"Confederate money is no longer of any value. Sorry, it's not my regulation. Do you have spoils?" the official asked.

"No spoils, only my Confederate rifle and my pistol. But I do have my grandfather's eighteen karat gold watch. Will that help?"

"Indeed, that watch should take you all the way to South Carolina," the official said with a smile. "The ticket takes you to Danville, on to Greensboro, North Carolina, to Charlotte, and then to Columbia, South Carolina."

The official took the watch and stamped an official USA on a ticket. He handed it to James and said, "You must be here before eleven a.m. Those trains leave on time."

"Thank you, sir. You have been very helpful. How long should it take to reach South Carolina?" James asked.

"The trains go about twenty miles per hour, sometimes faster, but with the destruction to parts of the tracks, the engineers fear going fast. I guess it will take you at least ten days or two weeks, possibly even longer, to get home. Good luck and Godspeed."

James thanked the official again, picked up his bedroll, haversack, and rifle, and walked out into the sunshine. Clutching the train ticket, a tear ran down his face.

He was going home to his darling Charlotte, home to Charleston, home to his beloved state of South Carolina.

# CHAPTER 16

# SMALL WORLD

It was Friday morning, twenty-four hours before the train would depart from Richmond. James was so excited that butterflies fluttered in his stomach. With a railroad ticket in his pocket, he felt some contentment. The ticket would take him to Columbia, South Carolina. Conceivably he could get a horse there to Charleston, even though he had heard about Sherman's troops destroying much of the city and confiscating the horses and other livestock.

With a whole day to wait for the train, he took time to look around Richmond. With the tall buildings reduced to rubble, the city showed no element of government. The stately buildings no longer met the sky. One could only see trash and broken bricks along the streets.

James pondered, did Charleston look like this? In Charlotte's last letter, she'd written of much destruction in the city. He felt blessed that the house on South Bay received little damage.

He walked until he found a park bench. It had seen rough times but still stood. Sitting down on the battered bench, he took his canteen out of his haversack and drank some water. His stomach growled. Without his grandfather's watch he didn't know the correct time. He'd treasured that watch, but had needed to trade it for a train ticket home.

He couldn't wait to see Charlotte again. So many nights in the hospital he dreamed of home and his beloved wife. Most of his dreams were filled with her presence. He missed her sweet smile and the sound of her laughter. He longed to hold her once again. It had been so long. They would celebrate their twenty-fifth anniversary in September. Surely, he would be home in time to commemorate the day. He loved her so much.

While in the field hospital, he'd spent much time thinking about his life with Charlotte. His life in the military had paled as the adventure he'd once thought it would be. He did not regret being in the army, but he did regret leaving the total responsibility of running the plantation to Charlotte. His brother George had done what he could to help her, but lived too far away to take the heavy load from her shoulders.

The Grimball family had inherited Heartland Plantation in 1780, and it passed from one generation to the next. James' father, James Fenwick Grimball II, died in 1839, leaving the Plantation to his three sons, George, James, and Frederick.

George, the oldest son, had established a saw mill business north of the city before his father's death and had no desire to run the plantation. Frederick, called Fred by the family, had studied law at West Point. Upon graduation, he married Jane Foster, his roommate's sister from Baltimore, Maryland. Jane wanted to stay in Maryland, so Fred had agreed and opened a law firm there. That left James in charge of Heartland Plantation.

James remembered Charlotte's reaction when she found out that he would run the plantation. No way did she plan to live on John's Island, the largest sea island off the coast of South Carolina. The thought of directing slaves frightened her. Plus, she knew nothing about growing rice and didn't care to learn. Being a Charlestonian, in the city she would stay, and that was that.

James laughed to himself. That had been their first fight, but things turned out well. For four years, he commuted back and forth to Johns Island by boat while he and Charlotte remained in their house on South Bay.

In 1844, James Fenwick Grimball IV entered the world. James still remembered how proud he'd felt to have an heir, a son to carry on the Grimball name and possibly to operate Heartland during the next generation.

When Jimmy was six months old, the family moved from Charleston to Heartland Plantation. Charlotte became a strong mistress of the plantation and a desired hostess on John's Island. The thought of life on the plantation brought a smile to his face.

Suddenly, three colored men walking on the road distracted James' thoughts. Their laughter and jokes interrupted his reminiscing. He particularly noticed the tallest man in the group, who reminded him of a former slave at Heartland, Big Tom. Listening closer to his laughter, he knew it was Big Tom.

Standing up, James walked toward the men. Getting near enough, he said, "Big Tom, is that you?

The men turned to look at James. The tallest man spoke. "Why, Massa James, is dat you? Why is you in dis place?"

James reached to shake Tom's hand and said, "I am on my way home from the war. I have been in a field hospital for six months, but tomorrow I head for Charleston."

"Is you okay?" Big Tom asked. His companions walked on, leaving him to talk to James.

"My leg is still a little stiff, but I'm good. How are Liza and Lilly?" James asked.

Big Tom hung his head and slowly answered, "I ain't knowed. I lef' dem in McClellanville when Liza say she ain't gwing any farther. We stopped at a farm house and the woman der say dey can stay, so I left. I's got me a clean-up job here in Richmond and is mak'ng money. I's gwing to get rich."

"Good for you," James said, glad he'd treated his slaves well all these years, so this one held no animosity toward his former master. "I wish you luck."

"I's best be gwing for I's late for work," Big Tom said. "I's glad to sees you made it throu' the war. Tells de folk back home hello fuh me."

James stood watching Big Tom run to catch up with his buddies. It was truly a small world. It seemed impossible that he should meet one of his former slaves this far from home. Charlotte would never believe it, but she would be glad to know what happened to Liza and Lilly.

# CHAPTER 17

# JAKE

James continued to sit on the bench in Richmond, killing time until tomorrow. The midday sun blazed hot and his stomach grumbled. He wondered how much food he could get for one gold piece.

Leaving the park bench, he walked toward the store. Reaching it, he found only a few freed slaves on the porch. He nodded to them and crossed the porch to the door.

Inside, the clerk recognized him at once. "Did you find the depot?"

"I surely did," answered James, "I bought a ticket for a train that leaves in the morning. Hopefully it will get me to South Carolina in a week or two."

Placing his rifle on the counter, he asked, "Do you want to buy a rifle? It's an 1861 Sheffield. [17] It'll cost you fifteen dollars and I will throw in the bullets."

"It's a mighty good looking gun. Sure you want to sell it?" the clerk asked.

"Need the money," James explained. "My army pay is in Confederate bills, no good for currency now."

"I sure like the rifle, but I can't pay that much for it," the clerk said. "Would you take ten?"

"Sold to the honorable clerk," James replied with a laugh, handing the rifle and bullets to him. "Now, can you fix me something to eat? I give you a gold piece."

"Deal," the clerk said. "And I will give you ten dollars in change."

They both laughed, and James breathed a sigh of relief. He might be sorry giving up his gun, but he needed money for food on the long trip to South Carolina. He still had his pistol for protection.

The clerk took the rifle and stood proudly at attention like a soldier. "I couldn't go to war due to poor eyesight and flat feet. I would have made a good gun bearer. Don't you think so?" he asked.

James smiled and said, "You would have been the best."

The clerk put down the gun to wait on another customer, then fixed James two ham biscuits and gave him a cup of coffee. Placing the lunch on the counter, he opened the cash register and took ten gold pieces and handed them to James.

"Thank you," he said, finishing his biscuits and coffee. He put the ten dollars into his haversack for safe keeping. Standing up, he realized that the sun would soon be setting, and he must find someplace to sleep. He said to the clerk, "Thanks for your help. I will leave now."

Grinning, the clerk said, "Anytime, Reb, anytime. Good luck!"

As James left the store, his wounded leg throbbed. He must have walked too far today. He sat down in a rocking chair on the porch and contemplated what to do next. While sitting on the now empty porch, he wondered what time the store closed at night. Using his cane, he stood and headed back into the door of the store.

The clerk sat at the checkout counter examining his newly purchased rifle. Seeing James, he smiled and greeted him. "Well friend, you're here again. Hope it's not to renege on the gun sale. It's a real Confederate Army rifle. I'm really proud to own it."

"No, no reneging. I wanted to ask if you know anyplace around here where a Reb could stay the night." James asked.

Without hesitation, the clerk said, "You can sleep here if you like. I have an extra bedroom in back with a cot. My brother sleeps there when he is in town. You can call me Jake. It will be good to have the company. Thanks to you, I have a rifle for our protection from drifters."

"Thank you, Jake, I am James Grimball from Charleston, South Carolina," James said, shaking Jake's hand.

"Glad to meet you," Jake said. "I am Jacob Thomas from Richmond, Virginia. They call me Jake."

James delighted to have a place to sleep tonight asked, "Are all Virginians as friendly and cordial as you?"

"I reckon so. At least my buddies are," Jake answered. "Most went to war. Several are back home, but they are not the same. War changed them. I can't rightly say how, but they have changed."

"War can change men in many ways," James said. "I've changed, myself. I've developed a greater empathy for people and their problems, and I appreciate my family more than ever. War works on the mind as well as the body, stressing many to an emotional breaking point. Many of my comrades showed those signs. It may take a while for your buddies to return to their old selves. Give them time. Hopefully, they will come around."

"Well put. You sound like a preacher," Jake said. "I do not hear men talk like that around here except at church. Are you a preacher?"

"No, not a preacher. Just one of God's children," James said. "How about you?"

"Not me," Jake said. "My Grandfather is preacher at a small church on the other side of Richmond. The church building was destroyed by cannon fire. The people are meeting in Grandpa's house for now. I try to go there every Sunday."

"Very good," James replied. "We all need to hear words from the Good Book as often as possible. They have brought me this far, and hopefully will get me home."

"I'm sure they will," Jake said, reaching for the coffee pot. Let's have a piece of cake and some coffee before we turn in. My grandmother makes my cakes, and they are delicious." Jake cut two big slices of a freshly home-made black walnut cake.

Tasting the cake gave James more memories of Charlotte. Her black walnut cake tasted even better than this luscious piece, or so he remembered.

He slept well on the cot, but morning came quickly. The mattress, firmer than the hospital one, felt good to his tired body. His leg did not throb this morning, but still felt sore. At least he would not have to do much walking to the train. He dressed in haste and picked up his haversack and cane. He missed his rifle, but he'd needed the money more.

Jake was already in the store stirring the fire and making coffee. The aroma gave James an urge to move into the store.

Jake arose from the fireplace and greeted him. "Good morning, Reb. I hope you don't mind me calling you that?"

"It's fine with me. I was a Reb for almost four years. Just glad I don't have to see anymore battles," James said, reaching for the cup of coffee Jake offered him.

"I made hominy grits and eggs for breakfast. Here, have some," Jake offered, handing James a plate.

"Sounds great, and smells good, too. Haven't had hominy grits since I left Charleston," James said. "By the way, what time is it? I don't want to miss my train."

Jake laughed and sat down at the table across from James. "It is only seven-thirty a.m. You've got plenty of time to enjoy your breakfast and sit awhile before that train gets here. The walk to the depot will take you about fifteen minutes. I will let you know when you should leave to get there early enough."

"I am anxious to get on the way home. Forgive my haste," James said.

"I understand, and I am going to miss you. You are a great man to know. I am glad you came my way," Jake replied.

"I am glad I came this way, too. I appreciate your friendliness and hospitality. If you ever get to Charleston, you will always have a home away from home," James said with all sincerity. "It feels like we've been friends forever."

"And that's a good feeling," Jake responded. "I just might show up in Charleston one of these days. I have always wanted to travel south."

They sat quietly drinking coffee. The bell on the front door rang.

"This is nice, but the store opens at eight a.m. and my people are already here," Jake said, jumping to his feet. "Another day, another dollar, as my pa used to say. I best put my apron on and get to the counter. When you leave, take this poke-bag with you. It's some vittles you might need later. See you when you finish eating. I'll keep up with the time."

What a thoughtful person, James thought. He continued to sit and drink coffee, watching Jake wait on the first customer. It was a gorgeous day in the state of Virginia. He'd made a new friend, eaten good food, and enjoyed hot coffee. Best of all, at eleven, he would head for home.

It felt as if the butterflies in his stomach turned over. He had so much to thank God for, yet an element of fear persisted as he thought of the long ride home.

He bowed his head and prayed, "Lord, give me traveling grace. Amen."

He cut himself a piece of walnut cake, wrapped it in paper, and put it in his haversack. He picked up the poke-bag and walked across the store.

Jake stood behind the counter counting money.

James put his hand out to shake. "I think I will walk on to the depot, my friend. I want to thank you again for your cordiality and for the accommodations for the night. I will always remember my days in Richmond. May you continue to unselfishly help others. God bless."

Without another word, they gave each other a bear hug.

Jake wiped his eyes and said, "May God hold you in the palm of His hand. Be careful."

"Thank you. He will," James said, and walked out of the store.

# CHAPTER 18

# THE TRAIN

James used his cane as he walked to the depot. His leg did not hurt and he wanted it to stay that way for the trip home. Arriving at the station, he found another six discharged Confederate soldiers waiting for the train. A colored couple also waited. They all stood outside the tent in silence.

At ten-forty, the train came roaring into Richmond. As it stopped, the train official rose from the tent and went to the platform. Five Union soldiers followed by four Confederate soldiers stepped from the train.

Before James could see where the soldiers went, the conductor called, "All aboard!"

James used his cane to boost himself into the train. To his surprise, the coach overflowed with Confederate soldiers. They gave a welcoming cheer as James entered. Although ragged and dirty, all the passengers seemed happy. They all talked at once, which made it hard to understand what was being said. He assumed they were all on their way home. He joined in a yell as other soldiers entered the coach.

At exactly eleven o'clock, the engine left Richmond and headed south. He gave a whoop and a holler as the train's whistle blew. There were very few seats to choose from in the coach. Suddenly, the train lunged forward, and he fell into a seat beside a blond-headed soldier about Jimmy's age.

James laughed and said, "Is it okay to sit here?"

"Sure, glad to have you. How far you going?" the man asked.

"All the way to South Carolina," James said with pride.

"Me, too," said the soldier. "I'm from Orangeburg. What about you?"

James perked up and answered proudly, "Charleston. What a coincidence. My name is James Grimball. It's a real pleasure to find another soldier from South Carolina."

The young soldier held out his hand and said, "My name is Daniel Jeffcoat. Yes, it makes me know I am really headed home."

"Me, too," James said. At least there would be someone else getting off in Columbia with him. "How do you plan to get from Columbia to Orangeburg?" he asked.

"Don't have an answer. If push comes to shove, I suppose I could walk," Daniel replied.

"I was thinking of trying to get a horse. My wound is in my knee and leg. I can walk, but not that far," James said.

"Hopefully, my sister will meet me with a horse and buggy," Daniel said. "However, in a letter she said that Sherman took most of the horses. It may be difficult to find one. I guess we'll have to wait and see."

Daniel had a stack of letters from his sister. She had written him often. He told James he'd read them over and over. From her letters, he'd learned that Orangeburg survived direct impact from Sherman's March to the Sea. There had been a battle along the banks of the Edisto River, where the Union troops had set fire to a large store. Heavy winds carried the blaze to many houses near the river. Before leaving Orangeburg, Sherman's troops destroyed the railroad depot and many miles of track. The Russell Street Courthouse had been demolished by artillery fire from Sherman's troops as they left the city, headed to Columbia.

James and Daniel spent the next few hours talking about their war experiences and their homes in South Carolina. They'd both fought in the Petersburg Campaign, but in different battles.

Around three o'clock, James opened Jake's bag of vittles. It contained ham biscuits, boiled eggs, and a jar of homemade strawberry jelly. He shared with Daniel and still had some left for supper. For dessert, they divided the slice of walnut cake.

About four-thirty p.m. the train came to a stop at a strange-looking depot. Many of the soldiers ran out the doors, some pushing and shoving. James and Daniel did not understand the rush. A conductor, seeing their confusion, explained that this was a food depot, and for twenty-five cents one could get a decent meal. The train stopped twice a day. Some railroads had more food stops than others. Many of them had been damaged and destroyed during the war.

The conductor suggested that at the next food stop they should try to get out fast and take their tin plates with them. "You can put your meal on the tin plates and bring it back to the train to eat at your leisure."

There was little to do on the long train ride. A few old newspapers were passed around for reading until they were in shreds. James read and reread parts of the Bible and his prayer book. At one depot he bought stationery paper for five cents. He began to write notes about the trip home.

Daniel had brought stationery of his own, and used pages to sketch pictures of soldiers and landscapes. Daniel, an artist for sure, captivated James with his artwork, so he tried drawing a picture himself. He drew a tree but it looked more like a fishing pole than a tree. The other soldiers had a good laugh at it. James decided to stick with note-taking.

On the fourteenth day of travel, the conductor said they would soon be in Charlotte, North Carolina. The train would have been there sooner, but there had been several stops to fix railroad ties. Once the train had stopped for two days due to a bridge washout.

By now, James's clothes were filthy. What he wouldn't do to get a bath and a haircut. The train never stopped at a station long enough but to wash his face and comb his hair. Maybe he could get a bath in Columbia before heading to Charleston.

Many soldiers left the train at stops throughout North Carolina. Those remaining in the coach were James, Daniel, and five other people-a man and wife with a child, and two other discharged Confederate soldiers. The family of three would get off in Charlotte where their summer home was located. The war had kept them from visiting it for the past four years. They'd come to survey the damage, if any. The other soldiers were going to Georgia by way of Columbia, South Carolina.

As the train stopped in Charlotte, two more Confederate soldiers boarded the coach. One walked with crutches due to a wound received in the battle of Belle Plain, Virginia. [18] His buddy in the same battle had survived uninjured. Both were concerned what condition they would find the city of Columbia in, after Sherman's march.

Daniel and James ate a big meal in Charlotte. The next stop would be Columbia, South Carolina. James' biggest problem was to find a way home. He wondered how far the ten dollars from his rifle money would get him. If he could sell his pistol and his ivory-handled knife it could help, but he would keep the gold locket he'd purchased for Charlotte while at Tent City Hospital. It was carefully hidden in the side pocket of his haversack.

The conductor told James they would get to Columbia the next day. One more night on the train. James gathered his belongings and placed them near himself as to make a quick exit off the train.

Before he said goodnight to Daniel, he expressed his appreciations of their meeting and how much he'd enjoyed his company on the train. "Next time you come to Charleston, look me up. Our house is easy to find. It's on the waterfront in the city, 10 South Bay," James said.

"I may do that. I love Charleston, and now my buddy James lives there," a cheerful Daniel replied.

"Glad you feel that way. We've shared a lot on this trip. Buddies we are, for sure."

To James the sound of the train wheels seemed to chant, *going home, going home, going home*. Closing his eyes, he fell into a light sleep, thinking of Charlotte and South Bay.

# CHAPTER 19

# THE HORSE

With night beginning to fall, the train was going at a very low speed. During night travel, the engineers slowed the speed to keep the train from running into trouble on the tracks. At times, it would completely stop and the tracks were inspected, especially near a trestle or bridge.

While James and Daniel were fast asleep, the train stopped abruptly, awakening them. They watched as an engineer took a lantern and got off to inspect the track. He came back in a hurry, reporting there was something brown a few feet ahead of the engine. He returned to the track and walked toward the object, discovering it was a piece of a horse's saddlebag.

Hurrying back to the train, he reported to the chief engineer. "This could mean a horseman was thrown from a horse and could be stranded or possibly injured," he told the officials.

The chief replied that the train officials must try to find the rider before traveling on. But it was too dark to do it now. They must wait until daylight to complete the investigation.

James rallied from his sleep as an engineer came to the coach and announced, "Attention passengers, the train will delay until sunrise. Evidence of an accident was found on the track. We must investigate before moving on. Thanks for your patience."

James shuffled from one side to the other and went back to sleep, wondering if he would ever get to Columbia.

As the sun rose, Daniel shook James. "Wake up, let's see what the engineers are up to."

Looking out the windows, they could see an open field and a black horse standing near a small brook eating grass. A portion of a saddlebag dangled from the left stirrup. It looked as if the horse had lost its rider. No house or barn were in sight, only miles of grass and small trees. Here and there were traces of campfires, possibly vacated army encampments. Daniel and James thought this place may have been on Sherman's trail, but that had been months ago. Where did the horse come from? Where was the rider?

They watched as an engineer walked to the grazing animal and grasped its reigns. The horse did not object, indicating that its owner was a true horseman.

Two train employees looked for the rider. Dead or alive, they would give him a lift on the train. After two hours, the engineers gave up the search. By this time, all the soldiers were outside helping with the search. James picked up a few Yankee mini balls. Sherman had indeed traveled that way.

At ten a.m., someone sounded the train whistle, and everyone climbed onboard. The horse, which had been tied to the side of the engine, showed no signs of distress, mystifying everyone at its calmness.

The chief engineer said, "I am putting the horse in the cattle car. We will take it to Columbia since the owner is unaccounted for. Please return to your seats. We will be on our way in a matter of minutes. Thank you all for your help in the search."

James and Daniel boarded the train, and James asked, "What will happen to the horse? I wish they would sell it to me. I would ride it to Charleston."

"Good idea," Daniel said. "Won't hurt to ask."

"I probably don't have enough money," James lamented.

"What about your pistol and bone-handled knife?" Daniel asked.

James replied, "They are not worth much, but they may be the answer to how I get home. I can only wait and see what the railroad plans to do with the horse."

The two settled in the coach and waited. Through the windows, they could see several engineers still outside. It seemed they were discussing the matter further. James thought maybe he could buy the horse. If he didn't have money enough, I could send for it from Charleston. He didn't rightly know his true financial status since the war, but he did know that for the past four years, little or no profit had come from crops, and none from sales of Heartland's rice.

The sudden thought of poverty jogged James back to reality. There was no way he could buy a horse. Fear seized him for the first time since the battlefield. If there was no money, there could be no horse. How would he ever get home?

The excitement of the nearing Columbia waned. He began to rethink the problem of how he would get to Charleston.

Daniel recognized James' sudden change of demeanor and said, "My sister may meet me in the buggy. If she does, you can ride with us to Orangeburg and see about getting a horse there."

Daniel's words gave James hope, and lessened his fears a bit. It wasn't just the thought of not getting home, but for the first time since joining the army, James realized that money might be in short supply in Charleston and at Heartland.

At that moment, an engineer came into the coach. "Attention, we are only ten miles from Columbia. Prepare for leaving the train. For your information, the Gervais Street station in Columbia was destroyed by fire during Sherman's march. A makeshift platform is being used as the station at this time. Please be careful as you leave the coach for your own safety. Thank you for traveling Richmond-Danville Railroad. May God be with you."

As soon as the engineer turned to leave the coach, James jumped up and in a loud voice asked, "Please sir, what will happen to the horse? I need a way home. Will the railroad sell it to me?"

The engineer was caught off guard and said, "I have no idea. Let me talk to the chief and get that information. I do know the railroad cannot keep the horse. I'll go see what I can find out and be back shortly."

Soon as the engineer left, Daniel said, "I told you it would not hurt to ask. You may get a horse, after all."

"I cannot believe I spoke up, but I am desperately in need of a way home," James said, sitting down again. "Thanks, Daniel. You gave me the courage."

"No, you would have done it without my help," Daniel said. "You need that horse."

"I suppose you are right. I am anxious to get home," James replied.

Before long, two engineers came into the coach and walked directly to James. The chief engineer said, "So, you need a horse?"

"Yes, sir," James replied. "I have no way to get to Charleston without one."

"The railroad officials have discussed what to do with the horse. We cannot keep the horse as all the cattle barns in Columbia were destroyed in the war. And since we are unable to find its owner, you are the lucky one. The horse is yours."

James and Daniel both shouted, "Hurray!"

James shook the chief's hand and thanked him over and over. "How much do I owe you?" he asked.

"Only a half-dollar for the horse's board," the grinning chief said.

"Wow, only a half-dollar? I will give you a whole dollar," James said, hurrying to get the money from his haversack.

"Come to the cattle car when we arrive in Columbia. I will have him ready for you. You will need a saddle," the chief engineer said. "Godspeed as you travel home."

As the engineer left, James whooped and hollered again. His prayers had been answered. Daniel and the other soldiers clapped and laughed. It was good to see them all so happy.

James and Daniel fell back into their seats, beside themselves with joy. Two jubilant soldiers ready to go home.

# CHAPTER 20

# A SHOCK TO ALL

The men settled down as the train slowly entered the capital city of South Carolina. [19] The train stopped at an empty lot on Gervais Street, not far from the capital building.

Through the train windows, the passengers looked toward the main street of the city. To their despair, the city was not there. They saw only destroyed buildings, burnt trees, and scattered bricks and mortar on the ground. No one spoke. All were in shock.

James turned around to see the damage to the state capital building. The building was still standing but looked darkened from effects of artillery shelling. Part of the building was lost to fire. Some windows were broken and steps cracked from military guns.

It was so hard to believe this was the same city they'd left in 1863.

The young soldier with the crutches began to cry. Hearing his sobs brought tears to the others. Everyone stood weeping in silence.

Daniel broke the silence and said, "Let's all get off the train. My sister may be waiting for me."

With that, the soldiers from Georgia led the way. Everyone hurried to the makeshift platform, eager to get off.

The chief engineer stood on the platform to give assistance, if needed.

Still stunned by the condition of the city, James asked him, "Did Sherman do all this?"

"Sherman's guns and cannons caused much damage and set off many fires. However, drunken and abusive soldiers caused many other fires. It was a terrible time. Many people evacuated to Charlotte, on this very train," the engineer explained. "Sherman's troops took most of the livestock from the city. It is good that you have a horse to get you home."

"Thank you, sir. I need to fetch it now."

"Yes, I know. One of my men is waiting for you at the cattle car. It is the last car before the caboose. Good luck to you, soldier, and thank you for fighting for the Cause."

James turned toward the back of the train. His wounded leg felt stiff. He stood, trying to decide if he should use his cane or walk without it.

Daniel joined him, saying, "I've looked all around and my sister isn't here. I'll walk with you to the cattle car."

"Good. I want you to see my lucky horse," James said.

The two walked toward the cattle car. It was a beautiful day, but the environment around the station gave James a bad feeling. An engineer stood beside the train holding the reins of the horse.

Recognizing James, he said, "You got yourself a real prize, a whopper of a good horse. He's all yours. This horse should have no problem getting you home to Charleston. Be careful, though. There is still a lot of hostility out there, even with the war over. Good luck to both of you."

"Thank you, sir, I'll take good care of him," James replied. He took the reins and patted the horse's head. "I will call him Lucky."

"Great name for this horse, for sure," Daniel said, scratching Lucky's mane. "He's a handsome one."

"In my last telegram to my sister, I told her we would get here today or tomorrow. Since she is not here, will you stay with me until she comes, even if it is tomorrow?" Daniel asked.

"Sure. That's what friends are for. And after our weeks on that rocky train, one more day before traveling will let me rest a little before getting on the horse."

They walked with the horse back to the tent office and asked the railroad official about a place to stay the night.

The official said, "That can be a problem. Many people are having a hard time finding a place to sleep. However, my aunt runs a boarding house at 48 Bull Street. She may have a room for rent, and if not, she will find a place for you to sleep even if it is in a barn. Her name is Mrs. Bates. Tell her I sent you. There is a stable for horses in the back of her place."

James said, "Thank you for your help. We will stay here until three to see if Daniel's sister, Miss Jeffcoat, arrives from Orangeburg. She will be driving a buggy. If she comes after we leave, please tell her where we are staying."

"Be glad to. And I suggest that you go on over to Mrs. Bates' now as the place fills up fast. I will tell the sister where you are."

"Thank you, sir," Daniel said, turning to James. "Do you think we could ride Lucky bare-back to Bull Street?"

"I am sure he is up to it, but are we?" James laughed. "I doubt I can even get on him without help."

Daniel joined in the laughter, "If you plan to ride Lucky to Charleston, you'd best practice getting on him. I know your leg is stiff, so why don't you get on the platform and I will lead him up to it so you can get on his back from there."

"Smart idea. Let's try it," James said, walking up the steps.

Daniel guided the horse to the side of the platform and had Lucky to stop. James handed Daniel his cane and threw his good leg over the horse's hindquarters. With a little adjustment, he was able to bring his wounded leg up and settle on his back without discomfort.

"You did it!" Daniel cried. "Now hold Lucky still while I climb on." He quickly placed James' cane under the bench on the platform, and in a matter of seconds was seated on the horse behind James.

The engineer at the tent door shouted, "You two are some fine horse-men. I didn't think you would make it. Be careful, there is ash and rubble on the streets. It is good that you are riding while it is still daylight."

James felt like a kid with a new toy, or like a king, riding his own horse. Daniel held his arms tightly around James' waist.

"Giddy up," told Lucky, and the horse began moving away from the platform. Guiding the reins, James headed toward Gervais Street and continued on to Bull Street.

"You are quite good at riding," Daniel said. "It has been a very long time since I have ridden one. Our horse at home is only used for the buggy and plowing."

James proudly said, "On the plantation, I rode every day. Riding a horse made it easier to get from one rice field to another. I learned to ride bareback by the time I was ten. Actually, Nehemiah, a slave, taught me to ride. Father gave me a horse for my twelfth birthday. I named him Shadow. Father and I would go fox hunting together. Shadow had a special way of spoofing out the foxes. One year he fell, jumping a fallen tree. It sent me sailing into pluff mud [20] in the marsh and broke Shadow's leg. Father had to put him down with his rifle. I was physically unharmed, but my heart pained for a long time from losing Shadow."

"That such a sad story. But you have good memories, and that's what counts," Daniel said.

James slowed Lucky's gait and looked around. "This is Bull Street. Keep your eye out for number forty-eight. With so much damage to the houses, it could be hard to find," James said.

They passed the South Carolina Mental Hospital and traveled one more block.

"There it is, number forty-eight. It's the house on the corner," Daniel said. "I will get off Lucky first and help you get down."

Daniel slid off the horse's rear end and led Lucky to a large hitching stone. This enabled James to climb down without bothering his leg.

As James reached the ground, he said," That was not bad. I think I can make it to Charleston on this lucky horse."

"You sure are a great horseman. There is no doubt you will make it home," Daniel said, rubbing Lucky's back.

They walked to the front of the house and knocked.

A short, rosy-cheeked woman opened the door. "May I help you?"

"Mrs. Bates, your engineer nephew told us you might have a room for the two of us to spend the night at your place. We can pay," James said.

"Come in, and I will see what I can find for you," she said, taking a book from the table by the door. She turned a few pages and asked, "Must you be together?"

"Oh, no. Just a place to sleep, is all," James answered.

Mrs. Bates said, "I have a cot on the porch and a sofa in the big room. I am sorry but that is the best I can do today. Will that be suitable?"

"Yes, that is plenty. We only want a night's rest before we leave town in the morning," James said. "I will sleep on the sofa and my friend, here, will sleep on the cot."

"No," Daniel said. "I will sleep on the sofa and he will sleep on the cot. His wounded leg will fare better on the cot."

"That's fine with me. Make yourselves at home. Supper will be at six in the dining room. Take your horse to the stable around back. It will be safe there. See you at supper," Mrs. Bates said, and turned toward the kitchen.

"Nice woman, and nice place," Daniel said. "We will have plenty of time to take Lucky to the stable and rest before supper."

James did not hear what Daniel had said. He was busy looking for his cane. "Where did I put my cane?" he asked frantically. "I need my cane!"

"I left it at the train tent. I put it under the bench there while we were getting on Lucky. We can get it in the morning. It's too dangerous to go back now," Daniel said.

"Yes, but I need it," James said.

"Do you really need it, or just think you do?" Daniel asked. "You will just have to do without it tonight. Come on, we need to put Lucky in the stable."

James took the reins of the horse and walked to the backyard of the house in total silence.

Daniel walked quietly beside him. Without any conversation, the two guided Lucky into the stable, curried, and fed him. Afterward, James led him to a stall for the night.

Walking back to the house, Daniel said, "Didn't you tell me that the doctor told you to do away with the cane?"

"He did, but I am afraid of falling and injuring my leg again," James confessed. "I still need it."

"Maybe this is a good time for you to try to do without it. You won't know unless you try. You did great getting on Lucky's back without the cane," Daniel said.

"You are right, my friend. Let's go to supper and then to bed. The problem will seem smaller in the morning, or so my mother used to say."

"That sounds like a good idea," Daniel said, and they headed to the kitchen.

James ate in silence and only spoke after eating bread pudding for dessert. "Charlotte's bread pudding is much sweeter. Good night."

James found the cot on the porch and closed his eyes. Tomorrow was another day. But he had to find his cane.

# CHAPTER 21

# ABIGAIL

The singing of birds in a tree near the porch of the boarding house woke James from a deep sleep. At first, he couldn't remember why he was in this strange place. Looking around and seeing the many sleeping people, it dawned on him that, at last, he was in Columbia, South Carolina. While on the train he'd often wondered if he would ever see his home state again.

Without his grandfather's watch, he had no idea of the time. He quietly raised himself from the cot and let his feet touch the floor. He smiled to himself. He had not used his cane. Maybe Daniel was right and it was time for James to be rid of it, even if he found it again. It had become a crutch, both literally and figuratively, just as the doctor said it would.

He gathered his pistol and haversack, then tiptoed across the porch. The smell of bacon frying and voices from the kitchen led him to the dining room. Daniel would meet him at the stables at seven o'clock.

Mrs. Bates greeted him in a cheerful voice. "Did you sleep well?"

"I certainly did. Thank you for the lodging. I will pay you now. My friend and I need to leave after breakfast," James said, handing Mrs. Bates two gold coins.

Mrs. Bates said, "Thank you, and please come again," as she put the coins into her apron pocket. "May God be with you as you travel. Be careful."

"Thank you," James replied. He would certainly feel more secure if he could find his cane. He probably should go home without it, but not knowing what he might encounter on the trip, he would feel much better having it along.

He picked up a tin cup from the table and poured himself a cup of coffee. Sitting down, he reached for a hot homemade biscuit. Loading it with butter, he added homemade strawberry jam and smacked his lips after the first bite. South Carolina cooking and homemade strawberry jam were the best!

After eating, James met Daniel at the stables.

"Good morning," Daniel said. "Did you have breakfast?"

"Yes, indeed. The homemade biscuits were grand," James replied. "I ate three."

"So did I," Daniel laughed. "I could have eaten more, but I didn't want to wear out my welcome. How's your leg doing without the cane?"

"It is fine. I really can walk without it," James admitted. "But I'd like to have it going home. Sorry I sounded so grim about it last night. The fear of falling isn't pleasant."

"I understand. I would probably feel the same way. Come on, we must feed Lucky and then go back to the station. It's the best place to wait for Abigail. And I hope your cane is still there."

"Abigail is a nice name," James said as he entered the stable to get Lucky.

"Mother named her from the Bible. Abigail was one of King David's wives. She also named me after the prophet Daniel," Daniel said.

"Good names for good people," James said. "James is a Bible name, too, but I was really named after my grandfather, James Fenwick Grimball Sr., which makes me James Fenwick Grimball III. We named our son James IV. It's getting a bit complicated. Maybe it's time to start using other names. At least Jimmy will be the last boy named James in my house."

James mounted Lucky with Daniel, and they headed back to the railroad tent. It was a sad and dreary ride, seeing so many homeless people along the roadside. He couldn't believe the many forlorn children who appeared lost in the rubble of the city.

Softly, he said, "Never before have I felt so distressed and helpless, seeing all the need at this time. Columbia will never be the same."

"True. Recovery will take a long time," Daniel said.

"You certainly are a bright young man for your age. I hope my son Jimmy has come through the war with your kind of attitude. I am older, but you are the one with a positive outlook for the future. You are truly gifted, and have been a blessing to me," James said in all sincerity, "I am anxious to meet Abigail. Is she older or younger than you?"

"I am two years older. She will be twenty-two in October. We have always been close. Her letters kept me going when I was in the army. I will be so happy to see her again."

———————

Meanwhile, across town, Abigail Jeffcoat drank the last drop of coffee in her cup. She had gotten to Columbia last night just as the sun was setting. Knowing she would not find the make-shift train station in the dark, she had stopped at a family friends' place on the outskirts of the city near Lexington County. The friends, Betsy and Walter Taylor, were once neighbors of the Jeffcoats in Orangeburg. They'd moved to Columbia before the war. The Taylor's daughter, Emily, was Abigail's best friend. She had written Emily that she was coming to Columbia to meet Daniel, and her friend had invited Abigail to visit while in town. They had not seen each other since before the war began. Once wild, skinny teenagers, the two women had grown up to be beautiful ladies, and had a lot of catching up to do.

Emily reached for the coffee pot, and refilled Abigail's cup.

"Thank you," Abigail said, "I can't believe we are finally together again. The war years have been terrible, but I am thankful we endured no real harm."

"Daniel wrote in several of his letters that he came very near death in several battles. He was a good soldier. My family will be glad to see him home uninjured," Abigail said.

"I bet he is even more good-looking. You know, I've had my eye on him since I was fourteen," Emily said, her face blushing, "Can I go with you to meet him?"

"Sure you can. That will give us more time together," Abigail said gleefully.

After more girl talk and chatter, Emily asked Abigail about the damage Sherman's March did in Orangeburg.

"We were fortunate that his troops did as little damage as they did, especially considering what they did to Columbia. They came up the Edisto River to Orangeburg and defeated a Confederate regiment in a battle along the banks. The troops set fire there and the wind carried the blaze through the buildings and houses along the river. They set fires at the railroad depot and damaged miles and miles of track. "

"That's awful."

"On their way out of town, they destroyed the Russell Street Courthouse. We were fortunate. Our house is southwest of the city and survived without damage. We were thankful we had a horse left to use— the same horse that brought me to Columbia in the buggy."

Abigail finished eating just as Emily's mother entered the room. "Did you have enough to eat?" Betsy Taylor asked.

"Yes, thank you. It was good to taste your homemade strawberry jam again. I remember Emily and me picking strawberries to make jam when we were about twelve. We ate as many as we put into the bucket, right Emily?" Abigail said. "Such wonderful memories of our childhood."

"Do you remember when we ate too many green apples and got stomachaches?" asked Emily.

"Of course I remember. I haven't eaten a green apple since," Abigail said, picking up her purse, "Reminiscing is great, but it is time for us to go to the railroad station. Thanks for breakfast, Mrs. Taylor. I hope Daniel will be waiting for us. Hopefully we will be back by mid-afternoon. I would like to get back to Orangeburg before dark."

Emily grabbed her bonnet and followed Abigail to the buggy parked in front of the house. Her father had already hitched it to the horse.

Abigail climbed into the driver's seat, took the reins, and called, "Giddy up, Big Boy, we are off to get Daniel."

Back in town, James and Daniel had ridden Lucky from the boarding house on Bull Street to the railroad tent. Daniel jumped off quickly to look for James' cane. It was still under the bench where he'd left it.

James pulled up alongside of the platform to get off Lucky without pain. It was easier this time. As his feet touched the floor, he saw Daniel with the cane. "You found it!" he said, elated. "I am doing pretty well walking without it, but I feel safer having it along. I may need it to fight off a wild animal on my way home."

"Yes, sure. Maybe a hound dog," Daniel said gleefully.

It was a clear day, but a hot one. James had almost forgotten how hot it got in a South Carolina summer. He walked up the steps of the platform and sat down on the bench under the shade of the tent. Daniel went inside the office to see if they'd had any word from his sister. As he came out, he spied a buggy with two young women turning into the empty lot next to the tent.

James noticed the buggy, too, and wondered if a train was arriving. The driver of the buggy had shining red hair. She stepped down and looked around. The second woman who was wearing a bonnet stepped down on the other side of the buggy. They were chattering cheerfully to each other.

Daniel looked at them and then took a second look. Jumping off the platform, he began running toward the redhead, calling loudly, "Abigail! Here I am!"

"Daniel!" Abigail screamed happily, and ran into his arms.

The young woman with the bonnet stood close, smiling from ear to ear.

James smiled, too. What a wonderful homecoming, brother and sister hugging, crying, and laughing at the same time. The love of family showed through their emotions instead of words.

Daniel was first to speak. "I didn't recognize you at first. You are no longer my skinny little sister, you are all grown up. It was the red hair that let me know it was you. It is still so beautiful. At night when I couldn't sleep, I could see you running across the yard with your red hair in pigtails."

"No more pigtails," Abigail said, grinning. "They are now curly locks."

The other woman moved to his side and asked, "Do you remember my blond pigtails, Daniel?"

He stared at the gorgeous woman. Turning to his sister, he asked, a bit embarrassed, "Should I remember your friend?"

The two women giggled. "Daniel, this is Emily Taylor. You should definitely remember her pigtails, too."

"Emily!" he cried. "You've turned into a ravishingly beautiful woman." He reached out to hug her, and her bonnet fell from her head. Her long golden hair shone as bright as the sunshine as it cascaded from her bonnet.

He was utterly tongue-tied. Suddenly, his heart began to beat very fast. How could this magnificent woman be the same scraggly little girl he knew before the war? A woman like Emily could steal his heart in a minute, and Daniel wasn't quite ready for what he felt when he looked at her.

He should not have the thoughts he was thinking about her, but it had been a very long time since he had seen a young woman, let alone one so pretty.

Trying not to blush, he turned to James. "Come and meet my sister, Abigail, and her friend, Emily," he said. "Then we must get this show on the road."

James stepped from the platform carrying his cane.

"Ladies, this is my friend, James Grimball from Charleston. We traveled on the train together all the way from Richmond."

They all shook hands and chitchatted for a few minutes.

Daniel then said, "I think we should get going if we want to get to Orangeburg before dark. It is already ten o'clock."

"I was thinking the same thing," James said. "I am not sure of my plans. I can't make it to Charleston in one day. I might just stay here another night and start home early tomorrow morning."

"Hold it right there, friend," Daniel said. "I've figured it all out. We will hitch Lucky to our buggy alongside of Big Boy. You can ride with us as far as Orangeburg, then stay the night at our house and get an early start in the morning. Maybe two horses are better than one, who knows? What do you say to that?"

"Good thinking, my boy. Thank you. You've helped this old man in many ways, and now you are doing it again. I will go fetch my horse. He is tied behind the tent."

While James went to get Lucky, Daniel unhitched Big Boy from the one-horse position, changing the buggy to a two horse position. He had to stay busy to keep from looking at Emily. His heart was still beating fast from their first meeting.

This was crazy! He'd never had a woman affect him this way. He wished he could talk to James about his reaction to Emily. James was older and more experienced. He'd know what it all meant.

But first they must take Emily home, and start for Orangeburg.

# CHAPTER 22

# WOMAN DRIVER

"I will drive," Abigail said. "I don't think a second horse will give me trouble."

James and Daniel climbed into the back seat. It was a little crowded, but James could move to the front seat when Emily got out. That would give more leg room. Daniel sat quietly as Abigail gave commands to the horses and turned the buggy left on Gervais Street, heading them toward Lexington County where Emily lived.

Abigail's driving impressed James. She was excellent for her age and for a woman. To make conversation, he complimented her on her driving.

She laughed and said, "With Daniel away, I had to learn if I wanted to go anywhere. Mother never drove a buggy and father was often too busy to go me. With the house slaves leaving or hesitant, I taught myself."

"You taught yourself well. Not many women drive a buggy. My Charlotte can, but she prefers to be a passenger," James continued.

Emily said, "My father will not let me drive a buggy. He says is a man's job, but I think women should learn, especially now that the enslaved servants have left."

"Did you have many slaves?" James asked.

"Just seven, and only one stayed. They are sorely missed," she replied. "Thank goodness Clara, the cook, stayed. I don't know what mother would do without her."

Turning to Abigail, he asked "How many slaves did the Jeffcoats own?"

"Father owned five at one time, but in 1863, Sara, a house servant, ran off with a slave named Big Joe from a nearby plantation. They thought they were freed after Lincoln's proclamation. That was when Mother taught me to cook. Now, I do most of the cooking. Especially on days Mother helps Father at the store."

Daniel had not spoken since they left Columbia. All he could do was look longingly at Emily. Now he asked her, "Have all of your father's slaves left?"

"No," she said. "Our cook, Mamie, is staying to help Mother. Father pays her a small wage with room and board. She seems happy with the situation. Mother would have a hard time doing all the cooking on her own. Mamie's been our house servant since before I was born. We are the only family she's ever known."

Abigail said, "Hank, our grounds keeper, is the only one still at home. He is getting older and said he was free enough with the Jeffcoats. Cook and her man are still in town. Mother tried to get her to stay for pay, but they wouldn't. I am afraid they will see hard times now with all the confusion in our city and state."

James said, "I am afraid we all will continue to see hard times for quite a while. The shooting is over and the South not only lost the war but lost its Confederate money. That bothers me the most. We must reconstruct, but with what?"

"Let's talk about something else. All this pessimism about the future scares me," Emily said seriously.

"It scares us all," he said. "Sorry to have brought it up. We will need to pray for understanding and faith to take us through whatever is ahead."

"May God be with us all," Abigail said as she turned the horses into a narrow lane that led to the Taylor's farm.

Daniel found his tongue again and said to Emily, "It was good to see you again. I do hope you can come down to visit us in the near future. When Abigail can get us back to Columbia, may we come calling?"

"You know you are always welcome in my home. I'd like that very much. Come as often as you like," she said, batting her eyes at Daniel.

James smiled. Trips to Columbia would become more frequent judging by the chemistry between Daniel and Emily.

Going down a row of oak trees that led to the two-story farm house, Abigail said to Emily, "Unfortunately we can only stop long enough to let you out and James to get into the front seat. It was great to be with you again. Give your parents my regards and thank them for the night's stay. I will write soon."

Abigail stopped at the steps of the stately house. Daniel jumped out and took Emily's hand to help her down from the buggy. He walked with her to the front door, still holding her hand.

"She's always loved Daniel," Abigail said, laughing. "Maybe something will come of it now they are older."

"I think you could be right," James said, seating himself in front next to Abigail.

"Daniel, we are leaving," Abigail called.

He jumped two steps at a time getting back to the buggy. "She didn't want me to leave," he said, blushing.

"She didn't want you to leave, or you didn't want to leave?" Abigail asked teasingly as she turned the buggy toward home.

"She has grown into a lovely young woman. I can't believe she is the same girl who used to climb trees with us," he said. "I would like to know her better."

"Maybe you can. After all, she is my best friend, and she loves coming to Orangeburg," Abigail said. Daniel needed a girlfriend, and Emily needed a boyfriend. They would be great together.

The buggy rocked along the road and Daniel sat quietly as if in a daze. James dozed off in the front seat.

Abigail began to sing *Dixieland*.

Daniel joined in and sang with her. "We used to sing this song between battles. Being back in Dixie makes that wish come true. Even though things look bad around here, I am glad to be home to stay. I missed you, Abigail. You, too, have grown into a charming young woman. Do you have a suitor?" he asked.

"No, not really. I go to the church picnics with Thomas Williams sometimes. But I am not interested in him to come a-courting," she said.

"Good ole, Tom," Daniel said. "Unless his personality has changed since I left home, he is about as interesting as a shoebox."

They both laughed. Abigail said, "He is a nice young man, but he could bore a hole through a fencepost. At that, their laughter became loud enough to wake up James.

"Am I missing the fun?" he asked.

"Not really," Abigail said. "Laughter is medicine to my soul."

It was dusk dark when the buggy got to Orangeburg. Abigail could barely see the road. They had made good time. Indeed, having two horses had added speed to the buggy.

Daniel's mother and father were sitting on the large front porch anxiously awaiting their son's homecoming.

Mr. Jeffcoat heard the horses coming up the tree lined lane. He jumped up and hurried down the steps, turning to his wife, saying, "Here they come. Light the lantern."

She lit a lantern and followed him to the bottom step to wait. Tears of joy were already on her cheeks. It had been a long four years. Now her firstborn was home again.

# CHAPTER 23

# HOME FROM THE WAR

Abigail slowed the horses as they reached the sandy drive leading to the steps. Daniel stood up in the buggy and shouted, "I'm home. Thank God, I am home again!"

As they came to a complete stop, he jumped out and ran into his mother's arms. His father hugged them both as they cried and laughed and cried some more.

James took his time getting out of the buggy. He wanted Daniel to have this private moment with his family. He turned to Abigail and said, "Go to your family. I will see to the horses."

"Thank you, Mr. Grimball. I really didn't give Daniel a proper welcome in Columbia and would like to do so now. Just tie the horses to the hitching post. Hank will put them in the stable. Go on into the house. We'll be there shortly." She hastened to where her parents and Daniel were embracing. With happy tears, she joined them in welcome hugs for Daniel.

The homecoming scene touched James and a tear rolled down his face. Hopefully, he would soon have his own homecoming with his dear, sweet Charlotte. At this moment, he missed Charlotte more than he ever had. His whole body ached with the thought of holding her again.

As he started up the front steps, Mr. Jeffcoat called to him, "Welcome to Orangeburg. Forgive our manners, but we have been waiting for four years for our son's return from the war. Any friend of Daniel's is a friend of ours. Make yourself at home. Mrs. Jeffcoat will be with you shortly. Supper is all ready. She's been cooking Daniel's favorite foods all day."

"Thank you, sir. I would not want to interrupt a homecoming. I am anticipating my own very soon. It's been a long time since I've seen Charleston."

Mr. Jeffcoat reached James and shook his hand. "So, you are from Charleston? Nice city, but I hear the Yankees messed things up a bit. Did your home have damage?"

"Our plantation on John's Island missed the line of fire from the Yankees that surrounded us for two years, though the Union soldiers looted the place several times. But no one was harmed. Praise God! My wife has been staying at the plantation, so I am not sure about the situation of our house in the city. My brother wrote saying it had survived with little damage. I figure he meant the house is still standing. From what I hear, the city endured heavy destruction. Many valuable buildings were struck by shells, others destroyed by fire. I am not anxious to see the ruins of our beautiful city," James admitted.

"Our prayers were answered here in Orangeburg by being spared from Sherman's unbelievable march through our city," Mr. Jeffcoat said. "Many friends lost their horses to his troops. Houses were burned near the river. That was one time I was glad we did not live near the Edisto River. The fishing pier where Daniel and I used to go fishing was completely destroyed by fire, and some of our friends near there were left homeless."

"That's such a shame."

"Let's sit down to wait for the missus. You know how women are with time," Mr. Jeffcoat said, sitting down in one of the rocking chairs on the porch.

James followed suit, saying, "You have a nice place here. How far is your business from your home?"

"Less than a mile. I can walk there in fifteen minutes. When I had more than one horse, I would often ride there, but walking is better for my health and I enjoy the walk," Mr. Jeffcoat said.

Just then, Daniel and his mother came up the steps, and Daniel was saying, "Yes, ma'am, I am ready for supper. Can't wait to eat your home-made cooking. It smells so inviting. I have missed it for too long."

Reaching the top step, Mrs. Jeffcoat grinned and said, "Come on in for supper, y'all. My boy is hungry."

James and Mr. Jeffcoat followed them into the dining room where Abigail was already bringing in hot dishes from the kitchen.

When everyone was seated at the table, Mr. Jeffcoat bowed his head and said a special blessing. "Dear Heavenly Father, we thank you for bringing our son home to us uninjured and in good health. Thank you for this food before us. Use it for our good, and our lives for Thy service. Bless Mr. Grimball and give him a safe journey home. In Thy name we pray. Amen."

# CHAPTER 24

# HEADING TO CHARLESTON

The sun was rising in the east when James came down the steps of the Jeffcoat's home. The family was still asleep. He had said his farewells to Daniel and his parents last night. He was anxious to start his journey to Charleston while there was still a morning breeze. By noon, it would be very hot for the horse and for himself.

Mrs. Jeffcoat had left food on the kitchen table for breakfast. James enjoyed two ham biscuits and two boiled eggs which he devoured quickly. The only thing he missed was a cup of coffee, but he drank water instead. Refilling his canteen, he picked up the poke-bag of vittles with his name written on it that Mrs. Jeffcoat had thoughtfully prepared for his journey.

He left the kitchen quietly and walked out the front door. At the foot of the high porch steps stood his horse, Lucky, already saddled. Hank, the gardener, had saddled him earlier, which would give James a little head start. Using his cane, he boosted his wounded leg into the left stirrup and threw his body over Lucky's. He quickly made it without pain. Good thing he'd told Daniel he would need his cane, he thought, placing the cane across the front of the saddle—the place where men usually put their guns.

He lightly kicked Lucky's sides and said, "Well, boy, it is time to go. Giddy up." As Lucky began to trot, he guided the horse west toward the Edisto River. There, he found a well-used path heading south toward the coast. He knew it was the way home. As he rode, he began to see scarred timbers left from fires, probably set by Yankee troops. If he followed the path of burned timber, he would be heading toward the Lowcountry of South Carolina, for sure.

Seeing more and more remnants of war along the path, he thought surely this had been Sherman's route into Orangeburg. He was glad he had never met the general and his troops. It sounded as if Sherman killed just to be killing, and destroyed plantation homes as vengeance over the South. How could one man carry so much hate within?

James was glad he had left early. He was making good time. He had almost forgotten how free he felt when riding a horse. He fondly remembered the many rides on the plantation, and sadly recalled the day his horse, Shadow, had to be put down. How unhappy that experience had made him! He certainly didn't want anything to happen to Lucky. This horse was God sent. It truly was an answer to his prayers. Otherwise he'd be walking home, and with his wounded leg he probably would never have made it. Or it would have taken him a month.

Suddenly, Lucky slowed his gait, bringing him mind back to the present. There was nothing in sight.

"Well, old fellow, I suppose you need a drink. The Edisto is a wide river, so let me find a place where we can get nearer the water." James slid off Lucky's back. Taking the reins, he walked toward the river until they were at the water's edge.

Lucky began to drink. He was really thirsty. James had been so deep in thought that he had not realized the sun was so high in the sky. Without his grandfather's watch, he had forgotten all about the time. From now on, he would use the sun as his timepiece. He led Lucky up the riverbank back to the path while looking for a shady spot to let the horse rest, and to get water for himself.

He saw a cluster of trees down the river a piece and walked beside Lucky until they were both under the shade of a large oak tree. He tied Lucky to a limb of the tree, found a small stump, and sat down.

Taking out his canteen, he began to drink. He needed water as much as Lucky, and was also grateful to take a break. While the animal grazed on the grass beneath the tree, he sat back and rested for a while. Then he got up and walked along the river bank to exercise his leg. He must do whatever it took to avoid any discomfort on the trip home. He wanted to be able to walk into Charlotte's arms without his cane.

Rested, he untied Lucky and led him back to the path. He could feel the sun getting hotter and hotter. He was making good time but he had to remember not to ride too fast for Lucky's sake. He surely didn't want to be left alone in this forlorn place. Mounting up, he began his journey again, but this time at a slower pace, to keep Lucky from getting overheated.

After traveling some distance, he noticed the sun was directly over-head. It was time to stop again for water and food, so he looked for a place in the shade near the water.

He came to a narrow road going southwest, but it actually looked more like a carriage lane than a main road. He rode slowly on the lane until he came to a row of live oak trees. That indicated it was, indeed, a carriage lane and he should soon see a house. Hopefully a good place to get water and rest awhile.

## CHAPTER 25

# BOWMAN PLANTATION

In the lane before him, James saw the broken remains of a plantation gate with the initial "B" still intact in the iron. Pulling Lucky's reins slow to a trot, he entered the property beyond the gate. To his disappointment, he did not see a house, but only saw four brick chimneys amid blackened and burned timbers and scattered bricks where once a great house had stood. Beyond the chimneys were the remains of a large barn, also mostly destroyed by fire.

"Whoa," James said to Lucky, and quickly dismounted. He took his pistol from the saddlebag and reached for his cane. He hurriedly hitched Lucky to a blackened hitching post and walked toward the chimneys.

Burned timbers were piled high, making a path to the middle of the outline of the destroyed house. He followed the scarred timbers and suddenly came upon five graves, each marked with a wooden cross. He leaned down and examined one of the crosses. Someone had carefully carved it from a piece of wood. All five crosses were beautifully hand-carved and were not weathered with age.

He stood in wonder. He knew he must eat, but this place had made him curious. He was thinking fast. There must have been a survivor who had carved the crosses and buried the five people. Who were they, and where was the survivor?

Forgetting about food, he walked the length of the destroyed house. Near the front chimney, he found the cornerstone. The name read Bowman. It was obvious this had once been a stately plantation belonging to the Bowman family. How sad, he thought. No headstones to identify them, but at least they had been put into graves. By whom, was still a question.

He walked back to Lucky and took his food basket from the saddle. Sitting in the shade of a live oak tree, he ate two ham biscuits and a couple of boiled eggs. The ham would be good for several more days, but he must not keep the eggs too long. He drank water from his canteen and remembered he needed to get Lucky back to the river before they started off again. Or maybe if he looked around he could find a watering trough or a well nearby.

He loaded his food basket back on Lucky, then looked beyond the chimneys to the remains of the barn. There he could see a watering trough for cattle. He couldn't tell if there was water in it or not, so he mounted up and headed to the trough. He found it half full of clean water. There was a small pump at the end of the trough. Dismounting, he worked the handle and water gushed out.

"Would you look at that?" he said. "Water for everyone. Your turn, Lucky. Enjoy."

While Lucky drank, James took both canteens from the saddle bags and pumped fresh water into them. He looked closer at the pump and noticed there was no rust or grit on the handle, and no trash in the trough. He was sure the pump was used regularly by someone, possibly the survivor.

Patting Lucky on the head, he said, "I know we must get on our way while the sun is still up, but the mystery of the missing survivor is haunting me. I am sure there is someone watching us from out there. I want to ride around this place once more before we hit the road."

He hung both canteens on his saddle and climbed onto Lucky's back. "Giddy up!" he said and headed toward the back of the destroyed house where he could see the Edisto River. There was a well-worn footpath leading to the river. Even though it wasn't for riding, he urged Lucky down the path.

Suddenly, from out of the weeds two billy goats ran into the path in front of Lucky, frightening him. Lucky took off running.

James quickly pulled on the reins. "Just take it easy, they are only goats. They won't hurt you," he said, gaining control of Lucky. He slowed for a second or two, then continued on until he could see the river. Tall grass kept him from actually seeing the water, but he could see a footpath leading through the weeds the way the goats had gone.

James dismounted Lucky and said. "Stay here, boy. I want to see what's down there. I'll be right back."

Taking his pistol, he headed down the path through the weeds. A large oak tree was growing beside the river at the end of the path. Beside the tree, there was a small lean-to built against it. The goats were eating from a broken dish in front of a makeshift door.

James walked softly, not wanting to frighten the person or persons in the small place. When the goats saw him, they bleated and ran away through the tall weeds. The door to the lean-to opened and out stepped a young colored boy holding a large bow and arrow, ready to shoot.

Seeing James so close, he shouted loudly, "Get out of hea or I'll kill yuh." He aimed the arrow and pulling back the bow.

James pointed his pistol at the ground. "Put down the bow and arrow. I am not an enemy. I just want some information concerning the big house and the graves."

"Are you a Reb?" the lad asked, still pointing the arrow at James.

"Been a Reb for four years and I'm on my way home to Charleston. I just want to know about the graves," James answered.

The lad lowered the bow and said in a quivering voice, "I ain't kill 'em, the Yankees did. I hide in the tall grasses across the ribbuh. Dey killed the massa, missus, my ma and pa, and little brodduh. Dey took the house t'ings and the hawss. Den they set the house on fire. After dey left, I burry dem. Me and my goats are all dat waz left."

James felt terrible for the boy. "My name is James Grimball. What's yours? You did a good job with the graves. I'd like to help make headstones for them, if you like."

The lad slowly put down the bow and arrow. "That's good, cause I can't write. Name's Noah. Ma name me from de Good Book."

"Did you carve the crosses that are on the graves?" James asked.

"Yes suh. My pa teach me to carve wood dat way," the lad answered. "De massa used to sell 'em, but he be gone so I ain't carved since the cross."

"Why are you still here all alone? Isn't there a town nearby?" James asked.

"I ain't leave 'til Master Tim comes home. He won' know wuh happen to his folk, 'less'n I stay."

"Master Tim is the Bowman's son?" James asked.

"Yes suh. He fight in the war since de start. Don' know if he dead or alive. The missus used to go to town and get letters, but me, I don't know weh to go."

"Where is the town?" James asked.

"On de odduh side de ribbuh. I us'ta ride in de wagon but I ain't tried to go dere since the Yankees burnt the bridge. Didn't want to leabe my goats."

"How have you survived by yourself?" James asked.

"I use my bow and arrow to shoot rabbits, squirrels, wild pigs, and big birds. I's go fishing in the ribbuh. Der's big fish in der. Nanny goat gibs me milk."

"Noah, you are certainly a smart young man. I just wish you could get to town and find out about the Bowman's son. You could also take your woodworking and sell them there, and make a little money," James suggested.

"Why?" Noah asked. "I ain't need no money hea. I like it jus like it is."

"You can't stay here forever," James said. "It will be hard on you come winter."

"I's need to t'ink about dat, but I am not leaving 'fore Master Tim gits home," Noah said.

"I wish I had the time to go with you to the town across the river. The post office there could possibly give you information on Tim's whereabouts."

"Dat would be a good t'ing to know," Noah said. "But before you leabe, would you mark de graves for Massa Bowman, Missus Bowman, Ma, Pa, and little Teddy?"

Noah went into his lean-to and brought out five pieces of old lumber and a small piece of charred wood. "You mark 'em with des," he said to James.

James was amazed at Noah's knowledge without book learning. He was, indeed, a survivor.

"Do you know Mr. Bowman's name? What did the missus call him?" James asked.

"Sometimes she call him Bow, and sometime she call him Timothy, like Master Tim."

"So, his name was probably Timothy Bowman, Sr." James said. "What did he call the missus?"

"Her name was Nellie. Sometimes he called her Mom, but she wurnt his mama," Noah replied.

"That is not unusual. A lot of men call their wives Mom," James said.

He wrote on the first piece of board *Timothy Bowman, Sr.* using the charred wood. Beneath it, he wrote, *d. 1865, Husband & Father.* Taking a second piece of wood, he wrote the name *Nellie Bowman,* and added the date and the words, *d. 1865, Wife & Mother.*

He walked to the Bowman's graves and used his boot to hammer the boards into the head of the graves.

Turning to Noah he said, "Now tell me your Ma and Pa's names."

"I ain't knowin' for sure. Ma always called him Andrew, or Andy. He called her Mattie, or Ma. My broddah was Teddy. Ma said he was named for our grandpa who died 'fore I was born," Noah said sadly. "I miss Teddy.

He my best friend." He was quiet for a moment and then handed the last three boards to James.

Using a second piece of charred wood, James wrote the name *Slave Mattie d. 1865, Wife & Mother*, on the third board. On the forth piece he wrote *Slave Andrew d. 1865, Husband & Father*. James found the task of writing Mattie and Andrew's names difficult. It seemed to him something more than slave should be written, but he knew slaves didn't usually have last names. On the fifth board, he wrote, *Slave Teddy, age 7, 1865*. He handed the marker for Little Teddy's grave to Noah, and said, "You can hammer this one for your best friend. I'm sure he would like that."

Noah burst into tears. Quickly taking the marker, he raced to the grave and with tears falling, he hammered the marker into the ground with a rock.

James said nothing. This was probably the first time Noah had let himself cry for his parents and little brother. While Noah continued to weep, James hammered a marker for his parents on each grave.

When he was done, James walked over to where Noah was sitting. In a fatherly way, he knelt down and took the young man into his arms. James found he also had tears in his eyes, for the injustice of war, and for Sherman's merciless destruction of this plantation.

James didn't know how long he held Noah, but he knew he had another hour or so to travel before sunset. Noah's tears had stopped, but he was still clinging to James. He whispered, "Noah, I must be on my way to Charleston. We must get up now."

"I know," Noah said, giving James a warm hug before standing up. "T'ank you."

In silence, James walked to where Lucky was hitched and reached into a saddle bag, taking out two sheets of writing paper and began to write.

*To Whom It May Concern:*

*My name is Noah from the Bowman plantation. I am looking for information about soldier Timothy Bowman Jr., who was in the war but has not yet returned home. I am the only survivor on the Bowman plantation and I want to find Master Timothy in order to give him information concerning the destruction of his home and the burial place of his parents. Since I can't write, this letter was written by a soldier friend, James Grimball, 10 South Bay, Charleston, South Carolina. I thank you.*

*Noah, freed slave from the Bowman Plantation*

Noah walked to where James was sitting and asked, "What's you writing? I can't read."

"Right," James answered. "But other folks can. I want you to take this letter to the town on the other side of the river. You can swim across and walk in the direction you remember Mr. Bowman driving the wagon. Go until you find a house with people. Do not be afraid to talk to a white man or woman. You are no longer a slave. You are free now, so you can talk to anyone and ask directions to the nearest town and post office. You might tie old cloth strips on trees along the way so you can find your way back here, if you're unsure. Don't worry about the goats. They will take care of themselves. You should leave when they are asleep so they don't follow you."

"Yes suh!"

James folded the sheet of paper and handed it to Noah. "I advise you to go while it is still summer and the days are longer. One last thing, Noah. You should begin carving again. You have a great talent for carving objects from wood. If you ever need money, it will be easy to sell your carvings."

"Okay, suh."

James reached to shake Noah's hand, "I will never forget you, Noah, and I hope and pray you will find Mr. Tim."

As James mounted Lucky, tears welled in Noah's eyes. "I ain't forgit neith'r. T'ank you."

As James turned Lucky toward the carriage lane, his heart ached for this lonely lad. If only he could take him to Heartland.

# CHAPTER 26

# THE WIMBERLEYS

James realized he must make up some travelling time due to his stop at the Bowman Plantation. He would have liked to stay longer. Noah needed the help. Hopefully, the letter would help him find Master Timothy.

As James turned Lucky southeast, he saw a railroad track running parallel to the river. Riding closer to the tracks, he saw that the tracks were broken and some of the rails had been heated and twisted into loops, a telltale sign of Sherman's troops. They were called Sherman's neckties.

James had heard of this type of destruction but had never seen it before. Now he knew for sure he was travelling Sherman's route from the coast to Columbia. However, continuing on this same path would take him south of Charleston. He wished he could find a town or a house to get better information.

After a few more miles of travel, he came to a crossroad. He turned onto a well-traveled road heading away from the Edisto River. Possibly this would take him to a town. He hoped so. The sun was getting lower in the west. He needed to find water for Lucky and a place to bunk for the night. Thankfully, he still had water in his canteen for himself, and two ham biscuits in his sack, along with several apples.

Soon, he began seeing seabirds in the air and noticed swamp grass along the sides of the road. He knew water must be near. Within a half mile, he came to a cypress swamp. The shade from the trees helped cool the afternoon sun, sheltering a great watering hole for Lucky. The drape of Spanish moss on the trees told him he was nearing the Lowcountry of South Carolina, getting closer to Charleston.

After a short rest, he mounted Lucky again. Again, there was no pain in his recovering wound. The exercise of getting on and off Lucky was proving to be good for his knee.

In the distance ahead, he began to see small buildings, and a house or two. Crossing a railroad track, he suddenly found himself in a small settlement. A railroad sign said Ridgeville. He couldn't believe he was so close to Charleston. His grandfather had talked about traveling to Givhans Ferry near Ridgeville, to a family reunion, back when he was a boy. James hadn't known back then where Ridgeville was located, but his family members had traveled to this very place in a horse-drawn wagon. For his grandfather, it had been a wonderful childhood memory, probably one of the longest trips he took as a boy.

Seeing a general store across the tracks, James pulled Lucky's reins and steered him to the store. "Good boy, I am sure we can find water at this place," he said, slowing down.

Two elderly men were sitting in rocking chairs on the porch of the store. They sat staring at James. "Howdy, fellow. What bring you to Ridgeville?" one man asked.

"I am James Grimball from Charleston. I've been to war. Just trying to get home to my family."

"Where did you fight?" the second man asked.

"Mostly in western Virginia," James replied. "Was wounded in the Petersburg Campaign. Stayed in a field hospital for near six months. I'm doing fine now, and hoping to get to Charleston. Is there a well or watering hole around here? My horse needs water, and so do I."

The first man stood up and walked toward James with his hand out. "Welcome to Ridgeville. It ain't big, but it's home. I am Lum Wimberly, and this here is Troy Stone. I am the store owner, and there's a well to the right of this porch. Drink as much as you like. There's a trough for animals on the side."

James shook hands with both men. "Glad to see people. I have been riding since sunrise and have only encountered three people, including you two. Before I water up, I'm wondering, is there a place I could stay the night?"

Lum stood and said, "Sure, soldier. That's my house on the other side of the well. We got an extra bedroom, and you are welcome to sleep there if you'd like."

"Your family won't mind?" James asked.

"Ain't but me and the wife. Our daughter lives on Ferry Road. Her husband just returned from fighting in Georgia. He made it through fine—a little skinny, but we are glad he is home. Four years was a long time."

"I will be glad to pay for the board," James said, remembering Jake in Richmond.

Lum said, "I tell you what. I will lock up the store and head on home to let the missus know you are coming. Go water your horse and fill your canteen, then come on over."

"Please, don't go to any trouble. I just need a spot to rest my body," James said.

Mr. Stone stood up and extended his hand. "Glad to meet you. I'll be going on home. The wife will have supper about done. Good night, Lum. Mr. Grimball, see you in the morning."

James felt very welcomed by both gentlemen. He could hardly believe how fortunate he was to be in such a friendly place. At the well, he filled his canteens with fresh water and allowed Lucky to drink as long as he wanted. From the well, he could see the lantern light in the Wimberley's kitchen and the missus busy setting the table.

He been very blessed by so many people while traveling from Virginia. He remembered what Jake had said as he left. "May the good Lord hold you in the palm of His hand."

After Lucky was watered, James wet his handkerchief and washed his face and hands. He took Lucky's reins and they walked to the house next door. He tied Lucky to the hitching post near the front steps just as Lum opened the door.

"Come on in. The wife and I are glad to have you. She made some spoon bread, my favorite."

"Thank you. All home cooking smells like heaven to me after that hospital food I ate for six months."

"This is my wife, Esther," Lum said. "Sit down at the table. Everything is ready except the spoon bread."

"I hope I am not intruding, ma'am," James said. "Everything smells wonderful."

Esther smiled. "We are glad for the company. We don't see many new people in this small town, but they are always welcome, especially our soldiers." Taking the spoon bread out of the oven, she joined them at the table.

Lum bowed his head and said a blessing, "Dear Lord, thank You for our guest. Give him traveling grace. Thank You for this food, and for the hands that prepared it. In Thy name we pray. Amen."

"Thank you," James said, "I certainly have had God's grace on this trip so far, and I believe it will get me home." He took a piece of spoon bread and smothered it with butter. It melted in his mouth. It tasted so good he asked for another one.

Esther laughed. "I'll give you two, while I am at it. If you don't take them now, Lum will eat them all. They are his favorite. He sometimes eats a whole plateful, unless I grab first."

Lum blushed and said, laughing, "Mother, I am not really that bad, but I do love your cooking."

"Everything is delicious," James exclaimed. "Even fried watermelon would taste good to me now."

They all laughed as Esther cut slices of the homemade chocolate cake that sat in the middle of the table. She served the cake and said, "I baked it this morning. I felt I might need it before the weekend."

James thanked her again for the wonderful meal, and said how much he appreciated the warm welcome in Ridgeville. His grandfather's memory of the town had become a family story long ago. Now he would have his own tale to share with his family.

After they finished eating, Lum stood up and said, "Come. I will take you to the guest room. There is a chamber pot under the bed. The outhouse is near the back fence, but it is too dark to go there now. Sleep well!"

"Thank you for your kindness. Good night, God bless," James said.

He slept soundly, dreaming of being home at Heartland. A rooster crowing under the window woke him at sunrise. The smell of bacon frying met his nose, letting him know that the Wimberleys were already in the kitchen. He made up the bed, picked up his haversack, and walked down the hall to join them.

Lum was sitting at the kitchen table reading a newspaper, drinking coffee. "Good morning, Grimball! Hope you slept well. It's a beautiful day." He reached for the coffee pot and poured a cup for James. "Sit down. Esther will have breakfast soon."

Esther turned from the stove, smiling. "Hope you like eggs and grits. I also made biscuits."

"It all sounds marvelous. I've eaten so much hard tack, biscuits taste like candy bars," James said, sitting down at the table.

Lum poured himself a second cup of coffee and said, "This is the first real coffee we've been able to get since the war. I almost forgot how good it tasted."

Esther said, "It certainly is a beautiful day for traveling to Charleston. You should reach Plantation Road by late afternoon. Will you go through the city of Charleston on your way?"

Turning to Lum, James asked, "Which way would be faster?"

"I'd follow Bee's Ferry Road until you cross over the Ashley River, then on to Chaplin Landing on King's Highway, going south. You will come to the main road leading to John's Island. You probably know your way from there."

"Sure, I know my way home from the King's Highway. I used to take bags of rice to Edisto Island that way. Thanks for reminding me of that route. I can't believe I am that close to home." James stood up from the table. "It makes me want to get started on this last leg of my journey. Thank you for your kindness and the room and board. I wish you would let me pay you for your graciousness."

"No way. We are glad you came," Lum said, shaking James' hand. "Be careful, and now that you know where our place is, come visit us again. We can go fishing on the Edisto."

Esther was wrapping up bacon biscuits and cake as James and Lum said farewell. "Mr. Grimball, here's a little food you may need on your way. May God guide you home. Our prayers go with you," she said, and they walked him to the door.

Before leaving, James watered Lucky and checked his canteens. Climbing on Lucky's back, he waved goodbye to the Wimberleys as they stood smiling on their front porch.

As he took the road going parallel to the railroad tracks, he said to Lucky, "Such good folk. I should have told them my grandfather's story. We could be related."

# CHAPTER 27

# POW FREEDOM

The prisoners cheered inside Point Lookout Prison Camp at the announcement that the war was over. They could finally leave the miserable place!

They began climbing and scrambling over each other, trying to get out the front gates. The Union officers shouted orders to no avail. Their voices could not be heard through all the commotion. The prisoners healthy enough to walk didn't wait; they ran. The guards opened fire, killing several on the spot. But many escaped before the gates were secured.

Once outside, the prisoners ran for their lives. Jimmy ran, too. However, he soon realized his body would not make it far running. He breathed heavily. High adrenaline had given him his initial start, but in slowing his pace, he began thinking with his head and not his heart.

Where was he headed? How would he get home? Will his gold pieces be of any value?

Seeing a pile of twisted railroad ties, he stopped and sat down. As he watched his fellow inmates scattering, he wondered how many had survived the many months in Point Lookout. For five months, he'd prayed daily for this war to be over, and his prayers had finally been answered.

Free at last!

But what next? He needed a plan.

He pulled off his boot and dumped out the precious coins hidden there. With only twelve coins left, he wondered how and where he should go from here. He put the coins back into his boot and stood up.

Food and cool clean water came first.

Looking ahead on the road, Jimmy could see a small farmhouse in the distance. A house with a well meant pure, clean water, for sure. If he could make it that far.

Trying to hurry along with the other escaped prisoners made it rough. Now and then a man would fall to the ground from exhaustion, perhaps to die. He didn't dare stay to find out. When he arrived at the well, many of his comrades were taking turns sharing a taste of cool, clear, drinking water. They welcomed him and passed the bucket. The water tasted heavenly. It had been so long.

More and more men joined them, until the greed for more water reared its head. At this point Jimmy left. This pointless fighting was too much to handle after all he had been through. But at least he'd tasted good water for the first time in five months.

Eventually, he slowed almost to a stop. "Where am I going?" he asked aloud.

He was in the north, in the state of Maryland, far from home. Then he remembered his Uncle Fred lived in Baltimore. If Jimmy could get there, his uncle would help. But how far was Baltimore from here?

Barely walking now, he felt the heat of the sun scorching down on his arms and face. "If only I could get to Baltimore," he murmured. Without warning, his head and stomach began to hurt, and he felt dizzy, and he tumbled to the ground.

He needed food, but where to get it?

Not far from where Jimmy fell, a steamboat owner named Marcus Alexander and his first mate, Joe, were walking beside the Potomac River.

Up until April 1864, Joe had lived as a slave on a plantation in Northern Virginia. Marcus was from Maryland and had been a captain in the Union navy. They had arrived in Marcus' steamboat an hour ago, near the small town of Little Creek, Maryland. They were there to meet two passengers and transport them to Baltimore. Since the steamboat would not leave until morning, they were enjoying a walk along the river.

Joe was ahead of Marcus, and spied Jimmy lying on the ground. He stooped over Jimmy's body and yelled, "Marcus, come quick. This Reb needs help."

The next thing Jimmy knew, a man wearing a navy captain's hat was leaning over him with a canteen of water. "Say, Reb, you okay?" Lifting Jimmy's head, the man put the canteen to his mouth and said, "Here, take some water."

"Thanks." Jimmy began to gulp the cool water.

"Not too fast Reb, slowly does it."

Turning toward Joe, Marcus said, "Hey Joe, run back to the boat and bring me my haversack. This Reb needs food."

The young man ran and quickly returned. Reaching into the sack he handed Marcus a biscuit. Marcus broke off small pieces of the biscuit and began feeding Jimmy. He fed him half of the biscuit and gave him more water.

"Feel better?" he asked, "Can you sit up?" Jimmy let Marcus help him sit up and said, "I'm fair to meddling. Thanks for your help. I don't know what made me black out. I was all right when I left the prison camp."

"If you've been in that rat hole of a prison, that's enough to make anyone pass out, from what I've heard." He extended his hand to Jimmy and said, "Name's Marcus Alexander, what's yours?"

Standing up slowly, Jimmy took his hand. "I'm Jimmy Grimball. I left the camp before breakfast this morning. I drank a little water back down the road, but have had no food since last night, and that was only thin soup and crackers. No food can make a fellow weak."

"Here, eat the rest of the biscuit, and there are soft pears in my sack." Joe tossed a pear to Marcus, and he handed it to Jimmy,

He brightened up and said, "This is better than gold. I have not seen fresh fruit since November. It's like a fairy tale."

"Don't eat it all at once. Your stomach may not take it," Marcus reminded him. "Here's my knife, best cut small pieces."

"Thank you, sir, I think you're right," Jimmy said, sitting down on the ground. He began to slice and eat the pear slowly, one bite at a time. He savored each bite. It was the best-tasting pear he had ever eaten.

No longer dizzy, he felt more like himself. Marcus and Joe sat beside him quietly. They waited for him to speak. The sun was very hot, but luckily they were in the shade.

Jimmy finished eating the pear and said, "I cannot thank you enough. I did not realize how weak my body had become."

"Where are you headed? Marcus asked.

"Baltimore, if I can get there," Jimmy said.

"Is that home?" Marcus asked.

"No, home is Charleston, South Carolina," Jimmy said.

"Then, why Baltimore?" Joe asked.

"My father's younger brother lives there. He has a law firm in the city. I'm hoping he will help get me to Charleston. He's got the means to do so, and my family would repay him," Jimmy explained.

"Well, Jimmy, my lad, you are in luck," Marcus said, standing up. "See that steamboat over there? It is mine. Joe's my first mate, and I am the captain. Since April, we've been taking soldiers home, up and down the Potomac River and the Chesapeake Bay. We can take you to Baltimore. That's one of our last stops before turning around to come back here to Little Creek."

"How far is it to Baltimore? Jimmy asked, elated at his luck.

"About sixty miles," Marcus said.

"I don't have money enough to pay you to travel that far," Jimmy said with a frown.

"Forget it, Reb. It will be a thank you for your serving with the Confederacy. I'm a Reb at heart," Marcus exclaimed. "So, it's my pleasure."

"I want to pay you. In fact, I can give you gold coins now," Jimmy insisted.

"No, Jimmy, you may need them in Baltimore," Marcus said. "We are here to pick up a family who are going to Baltimore, anyway, to fetch their dead son's body. There is plenty of room for one more. Glad we found you."

Jimmy was, too. To him, they were more like angels than sailors. He truly believed this had been a divine intervention, that his prayers had been answered. He would soon be with family whom he believed cared about his fate.

Marcus told him, "The steamer won't leave till morning. You are welcome to stay on the boat tonight, unless you have somewhere else to go."

"No place to go. Thank you. You are too kind." Jimmy was humbled by Marcus' generosity.

Little did Jimmy know that Marcus, a disabled Union sailor, had fought in the battle of New Orleans [21] in 1862. By mistake, he'd been sent to a Confederate hospital and recovered there before being discharged from the Union Navy. The Confederate nurses had been instrumental in his recovery.

Marcus remembered how difficult it was to get back to Maryland from New Orleans. He wanted to help Jimmy, especially knowing the dire situation in prison camps. His brother had died in Belle Isle Prison, [22] in 1863.

Marcus thought about when he'd first returned home to Maryland. He'd needed a job to support himself. He read in a newspaper the need for steamboats on the Potomac River and Chesapeake Bay. With his sailing experience, he knew he could do the work. He purchased a steamboat in 1864 and began his business. Joe had joined him later. Joe was a freed slave from Virginia. At first he had come along for a ride, but then he had turned into a hard-working first mate. They made a great team.

At suppertime, Marcus made a small fire there on the beach, and placed a coffee pot over it. Out of his sack he took cold biscuits, some ham, and more pears. When the coffee boiled, he took two tin cups out of his sack.

"We will share the cups," he said, handing one to Jimmy. "Joe, you take the other. I'll wait till later drink my coffee."

Marcus handed Jimmy a ham biscuit and another pear. In a voice of authority, he said, "Don't eat too fast, and you might want to save that pear until morning. You may eat another biscuit if you like. We won't need them all for breakfast."

Jimmy could tell that Marcus had been an officer by his air of authority. It didn't bother him. He wanted to eat the ham biscuit. He had not seen nor smelled ham in over five months. Slowly, he took a bite of the biscuit. He savored it on his tongue for a few seconds, then swallowed it down. He took another bite. He knew that his stomach might not take to pork very well at this time, but he didn't care. It was too delicious not to eat.

And real coffee! Jimmy drank it eagerly. It was like drinking eggnog at Christmas. In the shadows of the firelight, he wiped tears from his eyes. He may not be home yet, but he knew there were still good people in the world.

# CHAPTER 28

# BATH IN THE RIVER

With supper over and night falling, Marcus headed for the boat and Jimmy followed. Marcus turned to him and casually said, "Jimmy, now that it is dusk, would you like to bathe in the river? Joe and I bathed there this morning. I can give you soap and a towel."

He did not mention that Jimmy badly needed a bath. His clothes smelled of dried vomit and urine.

Jimmy answered, "Thank you, I desperately want a good scrubbing. My clothes need washing, too."

"Do not worry about your clothes. I have extra clothing that will fit you," Marcus replied quickly. "When I began operating the boat, I purchased clothing to give to the soldiers that were going home."

Marcus went into the steamboat and returned with soap, towel, and a poke-bag which held a pair of pants, a shirt, a man's undergarment, socks, and shoes. The man's generosity greatly impressed Jimmy.

He hastened to the river at the back of the boat, stripped off his raggedy uniform, and threw it to the shore. He lathered soap over his whole body and sank into the river. The cold water felt so clean that he swam around a bit before finishing his bathing. The water made his skin feel soft again. He never realized that his skin was so encrusted. He also scrubbed his head, hair, and beard.

While in prison he'd had no razor. He'd shaved only five times in five months, using a buddy's razor. He surely needed a shave now. Even without seeing a mirror, he knew he must look like a hairy beast. Maybe Marcus had scissors. That would help.

Jimmy didn't want to get out of the water, but Marcus beckoned to him. "We need to get inside."

The towel, though old and thin, felt good as it caressed his body. In prison the few times he'd bathed, there were no towels. As he put on the clean clothes, he choked back tears of joy. He felt almost human again. He gathered his sack with his prayer book and Bible, and followed Marcus to the end of the dock, climbing through the open door of the steamship. His body ached from the day of running and his stomach groaned a bit, but it felt so good to be clean once more. He lay down on a seat near the door in case he needed to get up during the night. He said his usual nighttime prayer, and added thanks for his freedom from prison. A fog horn blew in the far distance as he fell asleep.

At five a.m., he woke with a start. At first, he couldn't remember where he was. Hearing voices on the dock, he recognized Marcus talking with a boarding passenger. Joe was still asleep in the midsection of the steamboat. Jimmy waited until the traveling couple were seated before hurrying off the boat to relieve himself.

The stillness of the morning hour was soothing compared to the total chaos he'd awakened to during the past five months. Looking up at the stars, he felt like shouting, "I'm free, everybody! I'm free!"

Marcus joined him as he stargazed. "How did you sleep?"

"Like a baby," Jimmy said. "The best night's rest since I left Petersburg."

"Ready for food?" Marcus asked as he poked at a small fire he had started. "Sit down, have some coffee. It is hot now. I'll have eggs and biscuits momentarily."

Jimmy poured himself a cup of coffee and sat down. Was this a dream? Real coffee, and food, too? His body ached all over, but he felt elated to see a new day dawning outside the prison camp walls.

# CHAPTER 29

# THE WATSONS

After breakfast, Jimmy returned to his seat inside the steamship. A grieving couple sat near the engine room door. Marcus said the family name was Watson. Their son was Private Thomas Watson, age 22, from Popes Creek, Maryland.

The man's arm was around his wife's shoulders. Occasionally, a soft sob came from the woman. This was a sad time for the Watsons. They were on their way to Baltimore to retrieve their son's body. He had died on April 6, 1865, at the battle of Saylor's Creek, (Sailor's Creek) in Farmfield, Virginia. [23]

The battle, part of the Appomattox Campaign, had been the last engagement between General Robert E. Lee and General Ulysses S. Grant before the surrender of Lee at the Appomattox Courthouse. The bloody battle was one of the worst defeats of the war for the Confederate Army. Both armies lost over four-thousand men, including Thomas Watson. It had taken the past three months to arrange for his body to be sent home. They were fortunate to have the opportunity to claim their son's body. Most soldiers had been buried on the battlefield.

As Marcus started the steam engine of the boat, Jimmy felt enormous sympathy for the grieving couple. But at the same time, he wanted to shout for joy. With the war finally over, he would soon be going home. As the boat moved forward, the stench of oil coal from the steam engine smelled to him like lilacs in bloom.

The journey would take most of today, but by the end of the day tomorrow, he would be in Baltimore and, hopefully, would be able to find Uncle Fred. He did not have his address, but surely, someone could tell him how to locate a well-known lawyer like Frederick Grimball.

Jimmy settled down in his seat, dreaming for the coming hours about what it would be like to finally see family again. At least he wasn't coming home in a wooden box like the Watson boy. Jimmy's prayers went out to the family. What if it had been him instead? It could easily have happened. Five months as a POW in a Union prison certainly hadn't lent itself to staying alive. He'd known that he must figure out how to survive, one way or another. He'd prayed long and hard, believing that God would help him, and now he was certain his faith had brought him through the ordeal alive.

Later that afternoon, outside a steady rain began to fall. The raindrops falling on the cabin made a rhythmic drumming sound. He liked it. It reminded him of raindrops on the red tin roof of the house on the South Bay in Charleston. As he listened to the sounds of the rain, he fell asleep again.

As the boat neared the Baltimore Harbor, he woke with a start. Seeing big ships moored in the harbor gave him goose bumps. It reminded him of the Charleston Harbor and home. Remembering where he was, he picked up his haversack. Marcus was in the engine room, and Joe was standing near the Watson couple speaking softly to them. Jimmy couldn't hear what they were saying, but presumed it was something about the docking of the steamship.

Joe turned to him and said, "Massa Jim, we'll be docking soon. Anything I can get for you before we do?"

"Can you get me scissors and a mirror? I need to cut some of this unruly hair before I disembark," Jimmy said.

"The captain keeps scissors and a mirror in the engine room. I'll get 'em for you," Joe replied, heading to the engine room door. He returned shortly with them.

"Thanks, Joe," Jimmy said, looking at himself in the mirror.

"Good heavens! I surely need a haircut and a shave. It's a wonder I didn't scare you and Marcus away when you found me. Do you have a razor I could borrow, too?"

Joe grinned and said, "I thought you might need one." He reached into his pocket and produced a folding razor. "I will get some water for you when we dock."

"Thanks for being so helpful. You are an accommodating skipper," Jimmy said with a smile, beginning to cut his beard.

"Pardon me, Massa Jim, but I used to cut hair on the plantation. I was hoping you let me help."

Handing the scissors to Joe, Jimmy said, "Great! Go to it, my friend. Cut the beard, too. And please, just call me Jimmy."

"Yes, sir, Jimmy, I'll do my best."

"So, are you a barber by trade?" Jimmy asked.

"Not really. My pa taught me to cut hair. He was the barber at the Three Trees Plantation near Alexandria, Virginia. He even cut the massa's hair," Joe said. "I took Pa's place when he went to his heavenly reward in fifty-nine. Ain't done much since the war, but I'll do a fine job for you, you'll see."

As Joe cut Jimmy's hair, Marcus guided the steamship into the port. After stopping the engine, he began to make preparations for loading the Watson boy's coffin onto the boat. He checked the side portal through which it would be brought, and adjusted the sawhorses and plywood plank that would hold it. Nearby, he placed several cables which would secure the coffin to the plank. This was a job he had done many times in the past year, and was not a job he enjoyed.

Upon completing the preparations, he walked to the front of the cabin where the Watsons sat. In a reverent voice, he said, "Everything is ready. I will disembark now and find out where we are to go. It shouldn't take long. However, y'all may want to get off, too, since it's been a long journey. I'm sure you need food and water. Just stay near this side of the port so I can find you."

"Thank you very much, Captain. My wife and I will get off at least to stretch our legs. We still have food in our basket for supper, but we could use some drinking water," Mr. Watson said, holding onto his grief-stricken wife.

Marcus turned to Joe and Jimmy. "I'll be off to the port's military office now. I will bring water and food when I return. Take care of things, Joe." Glancing at Jimmy, he smiled and asked Joe, "By the way, who's that strange Reb you got there? Surely looks better than the last one."

They laughed as Joe swept up Jimmy's fallen hair.

Jimmy did look better, and he felt better, too. He was finally a human being again, instead of a prisoner of war. Joe had trimmed some of his worst facial hair, but he badly needed a real shave. But with Marcus off the boat, Joe was now in command and could not leave to get water for his shave. Jimmy didn't dare go himself for fear folks might think he looked like a criminal. Jimmy suspected it would be awhile before Marcus got back to the boat. He'd just have to wait it out.

# CHAPTER 30

# NEW PROBLEMS

Water was needed. Not only for Jimmy's shave, but for drinking, too. When the sun was starting to go down, Joe fetched the large bottle used to store water in, and walked over to where the Watsons sat eating food from their basket.

"Mr. Watson, sir," Joe said. "Would it be possible for you to go and bring us back some drinking water? Marcus will bring water when he returns, but that will be a while yet."

"Don't leave me!" Mrs. Watson cried, standing up. "I cannot abide to be alone."

Mr. Watson patted her shoulder and said, "You won't be alone. Joe and the soldier will be here. We all need water. It won't take me long."

Joe said, "There is a large public fountain just inside the main gate of the port. I've gotten water there many times. We will take good care of Mrs. Watson while you are gone. Everything will be okay."

"No! No slave is taking care of me," Mrs. Watson screamed irately.

Jimmy became aware of the situation and hurried to the front of the steamship. He could hear the fear in Mrs. Watson's voice.

Gently, Jimmy said, "Maybe I can help, Mrs. Watson. Joe is from Northern Virginia and he is no longer a slave. He is the first mate on this boat and is here to help you and your family. He and Marcus saved me from dying of starvation just a day or two ago. I trust them with my life. But if you don't want to stay with us, you may go with Mr. Watson to get the water. You can stretch your legs at the same time. The choice is up to you."

Mr. Watson, still standing by his wife, said, "Thank you, we will decide shortly."

Jimmy walked over to Joe, who didn't quite understand the problem.

Bewildered, Joe said, "Thanks for stepping in. This is a difficult situation. Is she afraid of me?"

"Marcus told me a little of the Watsons' background last night. It seems they live in Pope Creek, on the Potomac," Jimmy explained. "The Watsons owned no slaves. But since Maryland was a slave state, it is hard for some folks to understand and accept the new laws. It will take them time to adjust."

Just then, Mr. Watson tapped Joe on the shoulder. "Mrs. Watson is coming with me. She will not let me leave her side. I am sorry for the scene. I will take the bottle and bring water when we return."

As the Watsons left the boat, Joe sighed. "I guess I've still got a lot to learn about white folks. I'm glad you talked to Mr. Watson. He is upset about her problem. Her fear could be from her son's death."

"You could be right, Joe. Death is scary to many people. But I hope they will soon get back with water. I need to shave and get out of here," he said. "It's almost dark."

Joe said, "Since it is so late, my advice would be to stay another night on the boat. Most places will soon be closed, and you will need a place to sleep."

"You are probably right, it is getting late. I am anxious to find Uncle Fred, but tomorrow will be better," Jimmy said, thinking he could use another meal before seeking his relative. He still had hunger pains. He was also getting antsy waiting on Mr. Watson to return with the water.

"My haircut looks nice, Joe. You are an excellent barber," he said.

"Glad you like it. I'm a little out of practice since the war," Joe replied. "You will look even better after the shave."

"If I ever get one," Jimmy said with a groan. "It is taking the Watsons a long time to fetch that water. But I do look a little more human with the haircut. After a shave and with the new clothes Marcus gave me, I will look splendid to go relative hunting."

Joe put the scissors and mirror in a small box, and asked, "How long has it been since you've seen your uncle's family?"

Jimmy thought a minute, then said, "It will be five years Christmas. In 1860, Uncle Fred, Aunt Jane, and Freddie came south for Christmas at the plantation. Their son Freddie and I are the same age. As children, we always had fun together. However, the last time he was at the plantation he acted like he was better than I am. He bragged about what he could do, and what he was going to do. He made fun of my southern drawl, and showed off in front of my parents."

"That wasn't very nice."

"No. Then Uncle George's family joined us on Christmas Day for dinner. Freddie made fun of my cousin Susanna's hair because it was braided in pigtails. He said in front of the whole family that no decent girl in Baltimore would go out with her hair fixed like that. It made Susanna cry. Aunt Jane just smiled, and Uncle Fred said nothing. I wanted to box Freddie's ears. Oh, yeah, and he now calls himself Fred, not Freddie."

"Sounds like a spoiled Yankee. Did he fight in the war?"

"Yes, he was in 9th Baltimore Calvary. Fought in a battle in Baltimore and later in Texas. He should be home by now, I think," Jimmy said. "Hopefully the war changed his attitude."

"If they are like that, why are you so anxious to find them?" Joe asked.

"I want to get to Charleston as soon as possible, and Uncle Fred will know the quickest way to get me there. Whether by land or sea, he will make it happen. He has the means to help me, and my family will repay him. I'm still too weak to go all that way on foot."

"Good reason," Joe agreed. "I hope it works out for you. By no means should you travel on foot in your shape. It's going to take a while to build up your strength again."

The side portal door opened and in came Marcus. "I found the place where the Watson boy's body is stored," he said, and then looked around. "But where are the Watsons?"

"They left to stretch their legs and to get water. They should be back by now," Joe said.

Frowning, Marcus said, "I hope they will soon get back. The morgue closes at eight and it is six o'clock now. We need to fetch the body tonight or it will throw us off schedule in the morning."

Marcus' frown turned to a big smile when he again saw Jimmy's haircut.

"Wow, nice haircut, Reb. Chopping it off, you must have lost at least a pound or two!"

Jimmy laughed. It felt good to hear something funny for a change. "Joe cut my hair. He is a great barber."

"My Joe?" Marcus questioned in surprise.

"Yep, your Joe."

"I learn something new about this man every day. He seems to have an endless list of skills. I'm lucky to have him as my first mate," Marcus said, patting Joe on the shoulder.

"Mrs. Watson doesn't think so. She thinks I am still a slave," Joe said in a hurt tone.

"I wouldn't worry about her," Jimmy injected, "She will just have to get used to the new laws of our country."

"What's that all about?" Marcus asked.

Just then, the side portal opened and Mr. Watson came onboard carrying the big bottle of water. Mrs. Watson walked behind him, looking at the floor.

"Joe will tell you later," Jimmy quickly murmured to Marcus.

"Sorry it took us so long. The port was very crowded. We waited in line to get water," Mr. Watson said.

Joe took the heavy water bottle from him and said, "Thank you." He turned to Jimmy, grinning. "Ready for that shave? I can do that, too."

While Joe poured some water into a bowl, Marcus spoke to the Watsons. "Your son's body is ready to load onto the boat. We need to hurry, as it must be out of the warehouse by eight. This is a man's job, so Mrs. Watson will need to stay here while you and I bring the coffin. Jimmy and Joe will remain here with her."

"No! I'm going, too," shrieked Mrs. Watson.

"Let her go with you," Joe said, not wanting to relive the earlier scene.

Marcus looked at Joe in wonderment. "I guess if it's okay with you, Mr. Watson, she can come along."

By nine p.m., the coffin was in the lower room off the deck, and the Watsons were back in their seats in front of the engine room. Mrs. Watson was very emotional and cried loudly. That was expected, with the body of her beloved son now on the boat.

In spite of it all, Marcus made a late supper. He'd purchased some fresh tomatoes at the dock store along with a dozen homemade biscuits. Adding tomatoes and biscuits to the ham leftover from last night, he fixed plates for Joe, Jimmy, and himself. He located another cup in the cabin room and poured everyone coffee. For dessert, he sliced two pears, covering them with syrup.

The meal tasted delicious to Jimmy. He took part of a biscuit and sopped it in the syrup. Having had no sugar in prison, he especially savored the syrup. It tasted so good.

He would leave in the morning, and he would really miss Joe and Marcus. They were two great men, and he would always be grateful to them.

As Marcus moved the steamship to another dock to get an early start the next day, Jimmy walked into the engine room. "Will I be able to disembark from here?" he asked.

"No problem. But I plan to leave at six, so it will still be dark out," Marcus replied.

"That's fine with me," Jimmy said. "I will miss you fellows. I can't thank you enough for saving my life and for getting me to Baltimore." Tears of gratitude rolled down his clean-shaven face. For the first time in over five months he tasted the salt from his tears. "If you ever get to South Carolina, come see me. You will always be welcome at the Grimball's home."

"We will miss you too, Jimmy. It's been great knowing you. I pray you will find your uncle and will soon be on your way south," Marcus said, putting a strong arm around Jimmy's shoulders. "Take care of yourself. You've been through a difficult time. Good luck in every way."

Jimmy turned away, crying like a baby. He walked over to Joe and embraced the former slave. No words were needed.

Leaving the engine room, he put his Bible and prayer book into his haversack with the biscuits and pears Marcus gave him at supper, then stretched out on a seat to sleep. He had survived prison life and soon he would be home. The thrill of knowing he was here in Baltimore and thoughts of finding Uncle Fred kept him awake most of the night. The sudden movement of the boat as the tide came in made him aware that it would soon be daylight. He heard Marcus go into the engine room and start the engine.

Jimmy reached into his bag for a biscuit to eat. He would save the fruit until later. As he finished eating the biscuit, Marcus appeared and handed him a cup of coffee.

"Time to go, my friend," Marcus said. "The right portal is open for you to disembark. God be with you."

He turned away as quickly as he had appeared. It was better that way. In the past forty-eight hours, Jimmy had bonded for life with Marcus and Joe.

Jimmy drank the coffee, placed the cup in the seat, picked up his sack, and walked out of the steamboat onto the docks of Baltimore, Maryland. The sun peeked over the horizon into the city.

It was a fine, sunny day to find family.

# CHAPTER 31

# THE BALTIMORE GRIMBALLS

Not far from the harbor in a prestigious section of Baltimore City, stood the home of Frederick and Jane Grimball. Frederick had purchased the house for his wife two years after they married. Jane, being from a Baltimore high society family, believed they must live in this neighborhood, otherwise the Grimballs would not be accepted socially.

After Jane and Frederick married, Fred, as the family called him, set up his law firm in the city. The law practice did well until the war began. So close to Washington, D. C., Fred's major cases were with the government and the railroads.

With Maryland being a border state, Fred found great discord over the war among the people. Eighty-five-thousand men joined the Union Army, and twenty-five-thousand joined the Confederate Army. His own son, Frederick Jr., joined the 9th Cavalry of Baltimore.

With the state in turmoil, Fred had closed his office in the city, and for the past three years, he had worked from his home. Much of his work was with the Baltimore & Ohio Railroad Company centrally located in Baltimore. His move home did not sit well with Jane, as his office limited her space for social entertaining.

With the sudden death of President Lincoln, Fred's business suffered a big loss in contracts from the railroads. For the month of April 1865, he received no income at all from his practice. There was only his inheritance from the plantation, to be used as a last resort.

Amidst all this confusion, Fred Jr. came home from the war. His parents were elated to have him home uninjured, but Freddie showed signs of unrest at being home. He fumed over things about the war, and constantly grumbled about the many freed slaves in Maryland. In almost every conversation, Freddie said something derogatory about the Confederate Army or the South.

Frederick gave little thought to what Freddie said about the Rebels. He had always made fun of his father's people in South Carolina, and their lives with slaves. Fred had taken these comments in stride...until lately, when the comments had begun to bother him.

Recently, Freddie had made a cutting remark to his father. "This city looks like a plantation," he'd said, referring to the freed slaves.

Fred countered, "The slaves are now free men, son, and many want to come north for work. You'll just have to get used to it. The government has spoken."

As if Freddie's statement hadn't been alarming enough, this morning he'd really showed his true colors. Seeing photos of freed slaves on the front page of the newspaper, he'd shouted loudly in a beastly voice, "Great blazing tarnation! Baltimore is worse than Heartland!"

Fred couldn't believe what he was hearing. The intended insult to Heartland was the last straw. "Who do you think you are?" Fred roared. "That's enough about Heartland. It is my heritage, and also yours. For some reason, you think you are better than Southerners. Well, you aren't! Your bread and butter has always been paid by the hard work of a Southerner—none other than your father. I am tired of your bad attitude. If you keep this up, your inheritance from Heartland will be cut off. Do understand me? My brothers still live in the South and have done well.

Something you should think about. We Southerners may have lost the war, but we haven't lost our integrity as human beings."

Freddie was speechless. He had never heard his father raise his voice.

Fred said, "I thought you actually seeing war would help you mature."

In shock, Freddie replied, "You can't talk to me like that. I am mature. Maybe I have seen too much war. I don't hate my heritage, but I don't care for the Southern way of life. Their army was a sorry sight to behold compared to the Union forces."

"There's your attitude again. No compassion, no empathy for others. I can't believe your mother and I have raised you to have these ideas."

"You didn't. The cavalry was full of South haters who think like I do."

"You are old enough to think for yourself, and if you can't, you are in big trouble," Fred said, disgusted. "You don't have to believe everything you hear others say."

"What's going on in here?" Jane asked as she entered Fred's office.

"It's your son. He thinks he is better than people in the South," Fred answered. "I am tired of his ill regard for Southern ways. He needs to grow up."

"Well, you have to admit that Southerners do have some strange ideas," Jane said with a cunning smile. "I should know, I've lived with one for twenty-three years."

"There you go, always taking up for Freddie. Military life didn't help him a bit, and it's time you quit treating him like a child," Fred chastised.

Jane, stunned by this statement, said, "What is the matter with you, Fred? I can't believe what you just said to me. You've always been the one to baby him. Just because he doesn't think like you, you are berating him? I am glad he is home from the war uninjured."

"That's okay, Mother," Freddie said haughtily. "He knows that much of what I say about his dear South is true."

Fred, outraged with them, spoke even louder. "You both better think twice about what you say about the South. If our finances continue as they have this month, you may find our family living at Heartland in South Carolina."

"You can't do that to us," Freddie cried. "I won't go!"

"Neither will I," Jane shrieked. "Fred, I want you to stop it now. Did you hear me? Stop it!"

Fred said, "If the economy gets any worse, we may have no other choice. I must bring in enough money to pay the taxes on this house and the taxes for Heartland. If not, moving South is the only thing we can do. My brother James will never be able to run the plantation again with his war injury, and if push comes to shove, it will be left up to this family to do so."

"Fred, stop talking like this. We aren't poor, you're just trying to scare us," Jane said.

Freddie stood up. "Come on, Mother, he's lost his mind. We don't have to listen to this kind of talk!"

Jane was in tears. She took Freddie's hand, walked out of the office, and slammed the door.

Fred sat quietly at his desk. He had scared himself by getting so upset. Anger was not a normal reaction for Frederick Grimball. While stressing over the future of his career, he had blown up. He hung his head in shame.

Freddie needed a scolding about his attitude, and the family may still have to move South, but he could have told them in a more gentlemanly way. An apology would be necessary for his rudeness.

# CHAPTER 32

# UNCLE FRED

Jimmy Grimball walked from the seaport of Baltimore toward the main city. As he walked, he thought of Uncle Fred's life in this place. Although he noticed scars from the war, the city looked as if it had survived fairly well.

Businesses were going on as usual. He crossed a street and saw the post office building. He hastened toward it. They would have Uncle Fred's address. Hurrying, his breath began to shorten, reminding him he wasn't able to rush. Slowing down, he went up the steps of the building. His heart beat faster as he anticipated finding Uncle Fred. Holding onto the marble banisters, he walked to the door and entered.

A clerk said, "May I help you?"

"Yes, sir. I am trying to find my uncle, Frederick Grimball, a lawyer in Baltimore."

The clerk smiled and said, "Sure, I know Fred Grimball. We've been friends for years. He's a good man."

Jimmy said excitedly, "Can you give me his address?"

"Be glad to. It is only three blocks from here. Does he know you are coming?" the man asked.

"No, I have been a prisoner of war and am on my way home. I am hoping he can help me get there," Jimmy said.

"He is an exceptional man. I am sure he will help," the clerk said. "His house is easy to find. Go straight down this street three blocks to Congress Street, turn left, and the house is the third house on the right. It's 803 Congress Street, a gray stone house."

"Thank you very much," Jimmy said, turned, and left the building excitedly.

While Jimmy made his way to Congress Street, Frederick sat at home wondering how he could apologize for his angry words. A simple apology would do for Freddie. No explanation would change his attitude. To Jane, though, he must be able to justify his reaction. Whenever she was upset, things became hectic around the house, and he did not want that happening at this time.

He heard a knock on the front door, but continued to ponder. Sam, their butler, would answer the door. He hoped it was not someone for business. He could not handle a case today.

Sam appeared at the door. "Sorry to bother you, Mr. Grimball, but there's a young man at the door to see you. He called you Uncle Fred."

"Thank you, Sam, I'll take it from here."

Frederick headed to the front door. George only had daughters. Was it James' son, Jimmy? Why was he in Baltimore? The last Fred had heard, Jimmy was in Virginia.

Frederick smoothed his hair, straightened his tie, and walked down hall to where Jimmy stood waiting. Frederick was instantly alarmed at seeing the skinny lad standing at his door. Could that really be our Jimmy?

"Jimmy, is that you?"

"Uncle Fred," the boy replied, turning to face him. "Yes, siree, it's me. Sorry I could not let you know I was coming. Things happened so fast, there was no way to contact you."

Frederick embraced Jimmy and shuddered at the thin, bony state of his body. "Come in, sit down. Tell me all about yourself. Where have you been? Your mother has been worried about you," he said gently.

Jimmy sat down on the settee next to Fred. He lowered his head, and in a whisper said, "I have been in Point Lookout Prison for five months."

Horrified, Fredrick said, "I didn't know. Your mother didn't tell me."

Jimmy shook his head. "I didn't tell her. I couldn't. I quit writing. I guess she probably thinks I am dead."

"Oh, Jimmy, my boy, we must let her know as soon as possible that you are with me. You know she always does think the worst, and with your dad's injury, you must not let her worry any longer."

"That's why I didn't tell her. I was afraid it would be more than she could bear," Jimmy said remorsefully.

"Worse than thinking you are dead?" Fred said with empathy. "The war years have been hard on all of us, but when it comes to family, it seems twice as hard. We must depend on the family at all times."

Saying these words reminded Fred of the recent scene in his own family. He needed to heed his own advice.

"Uncle Fred, I have come to see if you can help me get back to Charleston. Mother will repay any expenses you incur. I need someone to advise me. I am in no physical condition to try walking home," Jimmy said.

With concern, Fred said, "You know I will do what I can to get you to Charleston. No way would I allow a nephew of mine to walk that far, even if he were physically fit. The first thing is to get you to a doctor for a health checkup. The doctor will know if you are even able to travel. Do you have any health symptoms other than weight loss?"

"I have a cough, and get out of breath when I hurry. I think it is from lack of exercise. I am lucky not to have contracted any of the many diseases that were rampant in the prison. Multitudes of comrades were sick throughout the time we were at Point Lookout. Many died."

Fred suddenly realized that Jimmy could be hungry. He asked, "What about food? Have you had enough to eat since you were freed?"

Jimmy smiled and said, "A Navy captain rescued me from a fainting spell outside the prison. He gave me water and food for two days, and was the one who brought me to Baltimore on his steamboat. The rations were light, mostly pork, hardtack, corn meal, and sometimes beans. Yes, I think I am ready to eat something more."

Frederick stood and grabbed the servant's bell.

Sam appeared at the door of the parlor. "Yes, sir? What can I do for you?"

"This is my nephew, Jimmy, my brother James' son. He was recently freed from Point Lookout Prison and is in dire need of food. He has not had a complete meal in months. Please ask the cook to prepare some potatoes and add last night's green beans and chicken to the plate. A slice of her chocolate cake is a must. And ask Mrs. Grimball to come to the parlor."

"I am sorry, sir, but the missus went to her room and asked not to be disturbed. But Freddie is in the drawing room," Sam said.

"Thank you, Sam. Send him to me," Fred instructed.

Frederick turned back to Jimmy and said quietly, "Before Freddie gets here, I want to warn you that since the war, he is a South Hater. Please don't let it bother you. I am working on him. Hopefully, he won't take his hate out on you."

Jimmy said, "I'm not too surprised. Many opinions have hardened because of the war."

Fred went to the parlor door. "Excuse me for a minute. I will be right back." He hurried down the hall looking for Freddie. He met him coming from the drawing room.

"Freddie, I must talk to you. Your cousin Jimmy is here, in the parlor. He has been a prisoner at Point Lookout Prison for the last five months. I know you are upset with me, but please be nice to him. He has been through a terrible time."

"Of course, Father, I'll be nice to the Rebel. You can count on me," Freddie answered rudely.

"I mean it," Fred ordered. "Remember your inheritance."

Freddie huffed. "You wouldn't dare."

"Just try me," Fred responded, turning back to the parlor.

Freddie walked into the parlor behind his father. He greeted Jimmy saying gleefully, "Well look who's here, my Rebel cousin from South Carolina. Are you missing your slaves?"

Ignoring Freddie's bad manners, Jimmy offered his hand. "That's the least of my problems at this point. I'd have to be home to miss them."

Freddie hesitated to take his hand until his father said pointedly, "Give your cousin a big Baltimore welcome, son."

With that, Freddie reached and took Jim's hand. Grinning, he said, "Welcome to the northern side of Dixie."

"Glad to be here," Jimmy said in a pure Southern drawl. "My first Yankee welcome."

Fred was proud of his nephew's ready wit and Southern comportment. He could see that Freddie was disappointed he didn't get a rise out of Jimmy for his remarks.

Freddie's mood changed suddenly. He asked, "How long were you at Point Lookout? I hear it was a tough place."

"Tough is hardly the word I would use. I was there five months, and yes, it was tough. Thank God, I survived," Jimmy answered gracefully.

Jimmy's Southern way irritated Freddie. If his father had not been in the room, he would have blasted the entire Southern culture. But his father's warning kept him from saying more. Trying to appease, Freddie asked, "Why are you here in Baltimore?"

"Being that the prison was here in Maryland, I knew I had relatives who could possibly help me get home."

Fred said to his son, "I am honored your cousin came to me for help. That's what a family is all about, helping one another. If you were in trouble down South, Charlotte and James would help you in your time of need."

Freddie was sizzling. The South, the South! He felt malice even just hearing the word. But he kept quiet, hoping Jimmy would get help in a hurry and be headed home as soon as possible. It was hard enough to live with his father's Southern manner, let alone having a Southern cousin to rub it in.

Jimmy began to feel the tension between Freddie and his father. Had he come at a difficult time? What is going on in this house of Grimball?

# CHAPTER 33

# A HOME-COOKED MEAL

Just then, Sam appeared at the door and bowed to Mr. Grimball, saying, "Cook said the food is ready and is being served in the dining room."

"Come, Jimmy," Fred said. "Your meal is ready. You may want to wash up at the basin in the hallway. I'll meet you in the dining room. While you eat, Sam will fetch the doctor. His office is just on the next street."

Jimmy walked to the basin and poured water into the large bowl. With a small towel, he washed his hands and face. The smell of cooked food filled the air. He was hungry and ready for a home-cooked meal. He entered the dining room and sat down at the table.

A steaming hot plate of food was put in front of him. It was the most food he had seen on a plate since he joined the army. It looked like a complete banquet. He placed a napkin in his lap, bowed his head, and blessed the food. Tears ran down his face. Looking up he met the smirking face of Freddie standing in the doorway.

"You Southerners and your blasted religion. I didn't see much of your God on the battlefield," he muttered.

Jimmy picked up his fork and said, "Well, He was surely there, or I would not be here. You'd be grateful for food, too, if you had been at Point Lookout."

In a chastising voice, Freddie replied, "Believe what you will, but I don't buy it."

The plate of food smelled delicious. Jimmy didn't know what to eat first. He stirred the mashed potatoes smothered with gravy, exchanged the fork for a spoon, and dug in. The taste of gravy on mashed potatoes had been a dream of his in prison. Often, when forcing himself to eat the substance the prison called potatoes, he'd wished for Liza's gravy on top.

Next he ate a few green beans, which brought back the memory of sitting on the porch at Heartland stringing beans with his mother.

Freddie, still standing in the doorway of the dining room said sarcastically, "I thought you were hungry, Reb. It sure is taking you a long time to eat that plate of food. It must not be cooked like the Southern fixings."

"It's all wonderful. It's been so long since I've eaten a large plate of food, I must be careful not to eat too fast. Too much at one time could put my stomach in shock," Jimmy said wistfully.

He happily continued to eat, ignoring Freddie's presence. He did not wish to listen to Freddie's arrogances unless it was necessary. He ate the last bite of chicken and pushed his plate forward on the table.

"You did not clean your plate, cousin. Cook will not like that," Freddie said, sneering at Jimmy.

"I have eaten more food in the last fifteen minutes than I have eaten at one time in months. Tell cook what you will, but I know when I should stop," Jimmy said firmly. "I will tell her myself that the meal was sublime. I am not helpless." Wiping his mouth with a linen napkin, he caressed it to his cheek. Eating in a formal dining room again reminded him of Heartland and his family.

Pushing his chair away from the table, he stood up as Uncle Fred, accompanied by another gentleman, entered the room.

Smiling, Uncle Fred asked, "Did you enjoy the food?"

"It was heavenly, just delicious. I am sorry I left some on my plate. I didn't want to overeat and get sick. But everything was superb. I can't thank you enough," Jimmy said.

"You can eat more later on, if you like," Uncle Fred said, turning to the gentleman beside him. "Jimmy, I want you to meet Dr. Long, my personal physician. He is here to give you a thorough examination."

Dr. Long shook hands with Jimmy. "Glad to meet you," he said. "Shall we begin?"

"Take him into my office. You will have privacy there," Uncle Fred suggested.

Jimmy followed the doctor into the office. Behind closed doors, he removed his shirt and pants. He felt proud to be wearing the clothes Marcus had given him. He would have been embarrassed to still be wearing his ratty old fatigues.

"How do you actually feel?" the doctor asked. "Any pain?"

"No real pain. I feel weak and get out of breath easily. A few aches here and there. I have a cough, and occasionally, I have had bilious attacks. My stomach growls a lot because of hunger, but no constant pain."

"You are fortunate not to have more symptoms caused by the environment in the prison. Sounds as if you may have a lung problem. Let me check your heart and lungs."

Taking his stethoscope out of his bag, he listened to Jimmy's chest.

"Yes, you seem to have a touch of walking pneumonia, but your heart sounds extremely good. The shortness of breath and cough is coming from the pneumonia. Proper rest and light exercise should help you. Nothing strenuous, but a regular routine. I am giving you a plug of opium for the pneumonia. It may make you feel strange at first, but it will knock that infection out in a few days. You are also somewhat dehydrated, so drink lots of water."

"That I will. Pure, clean water. It's what I missed most in prison," Jimmy said.

Dr. Long checked the rest of Jimmy's body and was pleased that he appeared none the worse for his imprisonment. "Your skin is encrusted with dead skin. Rubbing your arms and body with lye soap and a hot bath every day will moisten your body. You are lucky to be able to walk and feed yourself after being exposed to so many diseases at Point Lookout."

"Thank you, sir," Jimmy said, putting on his shirt and pants.

There was a knock at the door and Uncle Fred and Freddie stepped into the room.

"How is my nephew?" Uncle Fred asked.

"He needs some tender loving care and nourishing food. I do not see any life-threatening health problems. A touch of pneumonia is all. I recommend that he get plenty of rest and no heavy exercise at this time."

Freddie slapped Jimmy on his back, saying, "You can't keep a Grimball down. You can go horseback riding with me. I will show you what I learned in the Union Cavalry. That will be the best exercise for a Rebel."

"No thanks, I think I will stay on the ground. I probably could not get on a horse, anyway, in my state." Being alone with Freddie was the last thing he wanted to be doing, now or ever.

The doctor closed his bag and said to Fred, "He is blessed to be in such good shape after having been a prisoner of war. His health is better than many soldiers coming off the battlefields. Continue to keep his food soft for the next two weeks, or so.

"Will do, Doc. Thanks for coming. Send me the bill," Fred said.

"Not necessary. My gift to your nephew for service rendered," the doctor said, turning to Jimmy. I am leaving a bottle of quinine for the bilious problem. It will also help with pain. I will be back in a week to check on you."

"I hope I'll be on my way home by then," Jimmy said cheerfully.

Uncle Fred said, "I will let you know if we can arrange to get Jimmy back to Charleston, but I have a feeling he'll be here longer than a week. Thanks for coming. Excuse me, Jimmy. I will walk the doctor out."

"Thanks to both of you," Jimmy said. "I feel better knowing things on my insides are not as bad as they might seem."

Uncle Fred and the doctor exited the room, leaving Jimmy alone with Freddie.

Before Jimmy could leave, Freddie spoke in a baby-talk voice, "So, the little Southern baby wants to go home, back to the cotton fields and to his Mamma."

Suddenly, something came over Jimmy and anger began to rise within him. Before he knew it, he bellowed, "Yes, I want to go home! And I am not a baby. But I am sick and tired of your insults and belittling remarks because I am from the South. You are just as much a Southerner as I am. Grimball blood flows in your veins, too. Your ancestors were Southern born and Southern bred. As I recall, your grandfather Foster is also from Northern Virginia, making you a true Southerner. We may have fought on different sides in the war, but I think I gave more to our country than you ever thought of doing. You are the baby, thinking only of yourself and how to hurt others. You should try being in a prison for a few months and learn how to appreciate being alive."

Freddie's jaw dropped in shock.

Jimmy lowered his voice but continued, "You are such a wimp. You will never make it as a Southerner or as a Northerner until you get over being so selfish. I do not know how long I will be here in your home, but I will not tolerate you putting me down every chance you get. Try being a real man for a change, instead of a spoiled brat."

Freddie stood speechless. This couldn't be coming from his weakling cousin, Jimmy. He was saying some of the same things his father had said this morning. Freddie did not even know how to respond.

In a normal voice, Jimmy said, "I do not want to be in the same room with you any more than you want to be with me. However, when we are together if you begin your beef, I will personally talk to your father. It's got to stop now. Do you understand?"

Freddie said in a frantic voice, "I am sorry. I did not mean to upset you. Please don't tell my father. He is already agitated with me."

Jimmy could not believe this weak Freddie was the same hurtful bully who'd first greeted him in the parlor earlier.

"I hear you," Jimmy said. "But if your attitude remains the same, I will."

"I promise, even though I hate the South. I hate my father's wrath more."

At that moment, Uncle Fred came into the room. "Jimmy, I have a telegram machine here in the office, so let us inform your mother that you are here and in good health. Anything else?"

"Thanks. Yes, tell her I will soon be home," Jimmy said. "But I don't want her to know everything just yet." He watched as his Uncle Fred sent the message.

*Am at Uncle Fred's in Baltimore. Coming home soon. I love you. Jimmy.*

# CHAPTER 34

# THE POKER GAME

Freddie was waiting outside the office when Jimmy came out. He was smiling a genuine smile, the first Jimmy had seen since arriving. "What do you feel like doing?" he asked.

Jimmy was so surprised he couldn't answer. Instead he asked, "What did you have in mind?"

"How about a game of cards?" Freddie suggested. "Maybe a game of poker. Do you play?"

"Played a little while in prison. Sure, I'll play you a hand. However, remember, it's been a while since I played," Jimmy said, hiding a smile. In reality, he'd cut his teeth playing cards.

"Want to play for money?" Freddie asked.

"I only have ten gold pieces left and I may need them to get home," Jimmy said. Too bad. He wished he could play this web-footed Yankee for big money.

"You can use two gold pieces and I can use two," Freddie suggested, thinking how he would beat the socks off this sand-hopper. "Whoever wins will be two dollars richer."

"Well, just this once," Jimmy said, pretending he was unsure about gambling.

Freddie went to the bookcase and brought back a deck of cards and a book of matches they could use as chips. He shuffled the cards, allowing Jimmy to cut them.

"Five cents a match," Jimmy suggested.

"No, let's make it ten cents," Freddie said.

"Okay, you in a hurry?" Jimmy asked.

"No, I'm counting the cards in the deck," Freddie said.

"What's the game?" Jimmy asked.

"I usually play five card stud. Is that okay with you?" Freddie asked.

"Sure, let's cut for the deal," Jimmy said.

He reached over, picked up part of the deck, and produced the queen of spades.

Freddie reached for a card and showed the four of clubs. "I win, I win," he said with a childlike chuckle. He picked up the deck and began to shuffle, then he offered a cut.

Jimmy reached out to touch the top of the deck. Then he began to deal. The match sticks used for chips passed back and forth for a while but soon it became apparent that Freddie was accumulating more of the match sticks.

After an hour of playing, all the match sticks were on Freddie's side of the table. Freddie was elated.

Knowing his own strategy, Jimmy just laughed and asked, "Just what measure of you should I take away from that?"

Becoming angry, Freddie snapped, "You can't take a darn thing from that. It is only two dollars. That means more to you than it does to me."

Jimmy asked, "So, you are saying that the stakes have to be high for one to see the measure of a man?"

"Well, yes, or it is at least important," Freddie replied.

"Just give me an example of what you think is important enough for one to see the true measure of a man," Jimmy asked.

"I mean, making a bet on something important like property, land, big money. You know, things that can give you prestige, or power in life," Freddie replied.

Jimmy felt like slapping Freddie as he showed his true egotism and selfishness once more. Instead, he said, "That would be impossible for me, as I have nothing of importance to gamble with."

"Oh, yes, you do, and so do I. Remember, when we turned eighteen we both inherited fifty acres of land on Heartland Plantation. I plan to sell my land, as you will never catch me living on a Southern plantation. If you put up your fifty acres, I'll have one hundred acres to sell. How about it, cousin?"

"Are you crazy? Our inheritance? Why would I put up my fifty acres against yours?"

"Because I am a better businessman and poker player than you will ever be," bragged Freddie.

By now, Jimmy was sizzling inside, and he had to do something about it. "Okay, it's a deal. My fifty acres against your fifty acres. One hand takes all," Jimmy said, almost exploding in wrath.

"Great," Freddie said. "Seven card stud, and I deal."

"Seven card stud is fine, but we cut for the deal."

Freddie hesitated, then agreed. He reached for a card, pulled a queen of diamonds, and was greatly relieved. Jimmy picked up and showed the king of clubs.

Jimmy gathered the cards and shuffled, then he placed the deck in the middle of the table. Freddie reached out and cut the deck. Jimmy put the deck together, then picked up two matches. He offered one to Freddie and took one for himself.

Placing his match in the center of the table and said, "My fifty acres."

Freddie placed his match on the table and said, "My fifty acres at Heartland."

Freddie dealt the cards to each of them face down, with one card face up. Freddie had a jack of clubs showing. He looked at his other dealt cards. He had an ace of spades and a jack of diamonds.

Jimmy had a six of hearts up, and a seven and an eight of hearts in his hand. He looked at Freddie and dealt the fourth card. He then dealt the jack of hearts and the ten of hearts.

Jimmy saw the tension melt from Freddie's face and shoulders. He must be feeling pretty good about his chances.

Freddie sighed, thinking he didn't need to worry. This lame-brained cousin couldn't beat him. However, there could be a flush or even straight flush draw on the table for Jimmy. Freddie didn't have a win yet.

The fifth card was a four of clubs for Freddie and a ten of clubs for Jimmy, who was showing a pair of tens against Freddie's jacks. The sixth card was an ace of hearts for Freddie and a nine of diamonds for Jimmy, which gave Jimmy a straight and a flush draw showing.

No problem for Freddie, as he now held a full house in his hand. This was surely a winning hand, even if he didn't hit his straight or his flush. He smiled a little, waiting for the next move.

The last card was dealt face down and each man checked his cards.

Freddie said in jest, "It is too bad we don't have anything else to bet."

Jimmy said, "Well, I do have four gold pieces," and put them on the table.

Freddie reached into his pocket and pulled out a five-dollar US bill and said, "I call!" He turned over his hand, revealing the full house.

Jimmy turned over his hand, revealing his river card and a nine of hearts, giving him a straight flush—six to the ten of hearts. It was the winning hand.

Seeing it, Freddie pushed back from the table. His loss hit him like a mule kick. His mouth dropped open and the breath was sucked out of him.

He jumped to his feet and blurted, "You cheated!"

"If we were not so close, I might feel insulted," Jimmy said. "Tell me how I possibly cheated. You watched me shuffle and cut the cards. You watched me like a hawk as I dealt. When was I supposed to have cheated?"

Freddie sat back down and said, "I'm sorry, I just didn't see this coming. I knew I had it won. It is a shock."

"Well think about it. Surely, you saw I had a flush draw. Anyway, I've been pretty lucky lately."

"I guess I haven't given you the applause that you deserved."

Freddie picked up the cards and the matches and replaced them on the bookshelf.

Jimmy said, "I'll need you to give me the deed for the land. I hope it won't be any trouble."

"You'll have it by tomorrow afternoon, but please don't tell my father about any of this," Freddie responded. "He has high hopes for me at Heartland even though he knows I hate it there."

"Silence it is," Jimmy promised, walking to the hall door. Turning back into the room, he held out a dollar bill and said, "Here's your change. It was a four dollar bet, and you put a five on the table."

Freddie took the bill and walked out into the hall without saying another word. He was still in shock. Losing was too much to take in. He hurried out the door and ran to the stables. Mounting his horse, he galloped faster than usual out of the stableyard, heading for the meadow behind the house. Riding always cleared his mind, and today he must forget that his cousin from the South had beaten him in a game of poker.

Jimmy laughed as he picked up the five dollar bill from the table. "I did warn him. I told him I didn't like to gamble."

# CHAPTER 35

# THE APOLOGY

When Fredrick saw Jimmy and Freddie playing cards in the dining room, he was quite surprised. Wishing not to disturb them, he decided to go upstairs and apologize to Jane for his morning actions. He didn't know what he was going to say, but he must make peace in the family, especially now that Jimmy was here.

Fred knocked on the bedroom door and said, "It's your husband. May I come in?"

"Yes, come in," Jane answered coolly.

He went into the bedroom and found Jane reclining on the bed.

"I am here to apologize to you about my terrible actions this morning concerning Freddie," he began. "I know I came on too harsh to you and Freddie. Freddie needed a good chastisement, but I am sorry for the way I spoke to you. Will you forgive me?"

Jane sat up and softly said, "I am glad you've come to your senses, and I accept your apology. However, if you ever talk to me like that again, you will find yourself sitting in this room alone. That being said, upon reflection and rethinking your comments concerning Freddie's attitude, I realized that his bitterness against his Southern heritage is unhealthy, and we both may have influenced his opinions. Fighting a war against his heritage certainly may have added to his judgment. He is a grown man, after all, though maybe a bit immature. But hopefully, as he grows older, his sentiments will mature with him."

Fredrick sat down on the bed beside her and gave her a hug, saying, "You are right, I sometimes make judgments without knowing why things are as they are. I will try to do better. But guess what? We have a houseguest, and I would like you to come downstairs with me before supper. My nephew Jimmy is here."

"Here? Why didn't you send for me before now?" she said, getting to her feet, "How long will he be here? I thought he was in the army."

"Calm down, there's more. Jimmy spent the last five months as a Union prisoner of war at the Point Lookout Prison. He's had a pretty brutal time there. He is here asking for help getting back to Charleston. You wouldn't recognize him due to his weight loss. I had Dr. Long here while you were resting. Jimmy has walking pneumonia and some other less serious problems. We must do what we can to get him well enough to make the trip home," Fred said.

"How is Freddie handling it?" she asked.

"First he showed his antagonism toward the South, until he heard that Jimmy had been a POW. The change was amazing. Just before I came up, they were playing a game of poker. It's like a miracle that things could change so quickly," Fred said.

"Maybe our boy is maturing faster than we think," she said, and went to the door. "I must go quickly and give Jimmy a positive northern welcome."

---

Jimmy didn't know what to do next. He wished he could take a nap, but he hated to ask Uncle Fred for a bed. He would go into the parlor and rest on the settee. As he walked out of the dining room, he met Aunt Jane coming down the stairs.

She smiled and said, "Jimmy, it is you? Fred just came to our chambers and told me you were here. I am sorry for all that you have been through. You are very welcome in our home. I hope your dinner was satisfying. Cook's food is usually the best."

"It was just that and more. It was the first complete hot meal I've had since I left Charleston," Jimmy replied. He couldn't believe that Aunt Jane was actually talking to him. She usually ignored his presence.

As she stepped from the stairs, she held out her arms to him. "Come, give me a hug."

Could this be the same prim and proper auntie that he had known before the war? He gratefully returned her gesture, as he felt the hug was genuine. She truly seemed glad he had come.

Releasing him from her embrace, she said, "Sounds as if you had a terrible time in the prison camp. So sorry you had that awful experience. The whole war was a disaster. How did Heartland survive, do you know?"

"It must have survived the war, or Uncle Fred would have heard by now. He has received news from Mother since I have. We did not get mail often in the prison camp," Jimmy said shyly.

"I'm sorry, I wasn't thinking. Forgive me, Jimmy," she said. "Your Uncle Fred said he would try to get you transportation to Charleston as soon as possible. However, he doesn't want you to travel alone. He'll work things out. For now, you may stay as long as you like. It is good to have relatives visit. Feel free to go to the guest room and rest, if you like. We'll call you for supper."

Jimmy said, "Thank you, I am glad to be here, too. Yes, I will rest now. See you at supper."

She smiled. "Have a good nap," she said, and disappeared into the drawing room.

Jimmy was glad to have time to himself. He was feeling rather weak, and finding it hard keeping a conversation going with Aunt Jane. She seemed genuinely glad to see him, but she was still a complete stranger. What had come over her to change her so?

# CHAPTER 36

# BAD NEWS

A knock on the guest room door woke Jimmy. He sat up quickly, not recognizing where he was until he heard Sam's voice say, "Master Jimmy, Mr. Grimball sent me to tell you supper will be served shortly."

Still half asleep, Jimmy managed to say, "Thank you. I'll be right down."

He sat up to get his bearings. Much had happened in the last twenty-four hours. Thanks to Marcus and Joe, he was now at Uncle Fred's home in Baltimore. He had eaten home-cooked food and taken a nap between clean white sheets. Now he was going to eat again. All without spending a single gold piece. Not to mention being fifty acres of land richer. What more could an ex-POW need?

Standing up, he straightened his clothes, smoothed his hair, and walked to the door. As he headed down the stairs he thought of one thing he did need. He needed a hot bath. After supper he would asked Uncle Fred about getting one, but now he was going to enjoy home cooking again. Twice in one day was like a miracle.

Sam met him at the foot of the stairs," Did you sleep well?" Sam asked.

"Yes, sir. Best sleep I've had in five months," Jimmy said as he headed into the dining room.

Sam walked behind Freddie and said, "Mr. Jimmy, you may sit here beside Master Freddie," and pulled the chair from the table for him.

Jimmy smiled and sat.

Freddie greeted him in a loud, obnoxious voice, "Are you ready to clean your plate this time?"

"I will try," Jimmy answered.

Uncle Fred sat down at the table and said, "Jimmy, eat what you can eat. You must not overeat. Cook understands. Don't let Freddie bully you." He gave Freddie a stern look.

"I am just teasing my cousin. He knows I'm just joshing him," Freddie replied.

Jimmy laughed to himself. *Right. Keep it up, and you'll be doing anything but teasing, dear cousin.*

Before Cook and Sam began to serve the food, Uncle Fred bowed his head and said a prayer of thanks, which included thanking God for Jimmy's safety.

Jimmy was quite humbled by his words.

Cook and Sam began bringing in food from the kitchen. Jimmy was served first. There was roast beef, rice, green beans, yams, and homemade rolls on trays. Just the smell of the food increased Jimmy's appetite. It was hard to decide what to eat. All the food looked so delicious.

As Jimmy took his time choosing his food, Freddie made another jab at him. "Are all people from the South as slow as you when it comes to making decisions?"

Jimmy hastily took yams, rice, roast beef, and two homemade rolls, then set back in his chair.

This time Aunt Jane reproved Freddie. "Leave Jimmy alone. He must eat the foods that are best for him at this time."

Uncle Fred gave Freddie a look of disappointment without saying a word. Freddie got the message and changed the subject.

As they continued to eat, there was a knock at the front door. Uncle Fred asked, "Who could be calling at this hour?"

Sam stepped from the dining room. "Please go on eating. I will get the door."

Sam came back carrying a dish with a yellow envelope upon it. "It's a telegram for you, Mr. Grimball," Sam said, handing the dish to Frederick.

"Maybe it is from Mother," Jimmy said. "She hasn't responded to the telegram I sent about being here."

Uncle Fred opened the envelope and sat quietly for a moment before speaking. By now, everyone knew it was bad news.

"Fred, please read it to us. If it is bad news, we need to know," Jane said.

"The message is from a constable on John's Island." Fred cleared his throat and read, "Dear Mr. Grimball, A fire at Heartland destroyed barn and smoke house. Big house saved. Owens badly burned. In hospital. No other injuries. Constable M. Rivers, John's Island, South Carolina."

Jimmy let out a sob. "Oh, no. Not the plantation."

"Jimmy, it's okay, the main house did not burn, just the barn and smokehouse," Uncle Fred repeated calmly, trying to comfort Jimmy as well as himself. "It is sad about Owens' injuries, but at least no lives were lost."

Jimmy felt flustered, and asked, "Was my mother there?"

Uncle Fred shook his head. "The constable did not say who was there. In the last letter I had from Charlotte, she was back in the city preparing for your father's homecoming. Chances are she was not at the plantation during the fire. I know this news is hard for you to hear, but it could have been much worse. Let's finish eating, and then we can discuss the telegram further after supper."

Hearing the sad news from home, Jimmy lost his appetite. He felt like crying, but could not let Freddie see him cry. That would give him an open opportunity to throw more stones. Sam and Cook continued to bring more trays of food to the dining table. Everyone ate in silence. Jimmy ate a small piece of beef roast, a yam, and two rolls. He found it hard to swallow, with his mind so worried about Heartland. After all, he had spent most of his life there and had so many wonderful memories of playing in the hayloft of the barn that was now no more.

Cook served apple pie for dessert. It looked so delicious and smelled heavenly, but Jimmy had to force himself to eat it.

Uncle Fred noticed his change and asked, "Jimmy, are you all right? Do you need to lie down?"

"No, sir. But I lost my appetite after hearing about the fire at Heartland. I am sorry I cannot finish my supper," he said sadly. "I'm wondering how Mother is taking the loss without Father being there."

"Your Mother is a strong woman and has been through a lot. I am sure she is in control, even in this terrible situation. I will send a telegram in the morning to get the latest news," Uncle Fred assured, comforting Jimmy with his words.

Freddie had sat quietly listening to his Father comfort Jimmy, but he couldn't be quiet any longer. He said smartly, "At least you no longer have to haul hay to the barn."

Jimmy ignored him, but Uncle Fred scolded Freddie. "That's enough, Freddie. Please leave the table. This is no time for jokes."

"But Father, I was trying to cheer Jimmy up," Freddie whined.

"Just leave, Freddie. Jimmy needs to be alone with his thoughts," Uncle Fred said impatiently. Turning back to Jimmy, he kindly asked, "Is there anything I can do for you?"

Jane left her chair and came to stand by Jimmy, continuing to comfort him. "Do you want to go to the guest room and rest awhile? When you feel like eating more, Sam and Cook will be glad to bring you a plate. Just pull the servant's cord."

Jimmy was embarrassed by the fuss Aunt Jane and Uncle Fred were making over him. "I am all right. Learning about the fire shook me up, but

I am sure Mother is at Heartland taking care of everything. The only thing I really need has nothing to do with the fire. I need a bath. Do you think Sam could manage to prepare one for me?"

Uncle Fred and Jane both laughed, and assured Jimmy that Sam would have bath water ready within the hour. Uncle Fred left the room to find Sam.

Jimmy said, "Aunt Jane, is it possible that you can provide me with some clean clothes? Some of Freddie's old clothes will be fine. Do you think he would mind?"

"Whether he minds or doesn't mind, you'll have clean clothes to put on. I am sorry I did not offer you a hot bath before now. It was an oversight on my part. Forgive me," Jane said.

"Nothing to forgive. I'm sure it's not every day a former prisoner of war knocks at your door," Jimmy said.

Aunt Jane directed him to the water closet near the kitchen. "I will bring you towels and lye soap with the clothes," she said.

"Please don't go to any trouble for me. I just need to wash. I have had only one bath since I got out of prison, and that was in the Potomac River," Jimmy said.

"No trouble at all. We are here to please," Aunt Jane replied, and turned to the stairs.

Jimmy walked into the water closet. In the middle of the floor stood a ship-shaped copper bathtub. Jimmy had never seen such a fine tub. A small wooden towel rack stood on the floor nearby. A soap dish made of copper hung from the side of the tub. As Jimmy stood admiring everything, Sam and Cook came into the room carrying large iron kettles filled with hot water. They poured the water into the tub.

"Be careful, Mr. Jimmy. This water is very hot," warned Sam. "The missis is bringing soap and towels."

"Thank you. I will be careful," Jimmy assured them.

Sam and Cook left when Aunt Jane entered carrying soap, towels, and an armful of clothing. She draped the clothing over the back of a chair near the door, hung two small towels on the wooden rack, and placed a bar of lye soap in the copper soap dish.

"Now, I will leave you to enjoy your bath. Sam will assist you if you need help," she said in a motherly tone.

Jimmy hooked the latch on the door and began taking off the clothes that Marcus had given him at his last bath. They had sufficed until now, but they were somewhat soiled and beginning to have an odor. After undressing, he carefully slid into the copper tub.

Oh, how good the hot water felt on his skin! Taking the soap and one of the small towels, he lathered his whole body, then sat back to let his body soak awhile. Rinsing the soap from his body, he took the towel and scrubbed his face, neck, and hair. While the water was still warm, he gave his feet a good scrubbing. The soles of his feet were not as encrusted as they had been when he came out of prison. The lye soap must do wonders.

He wanted to linger in the tub longer, but he should probably dry off and put on the clothes Aunt Jane had brought for him. Even though he dreaded what would come next, he knew that Uncle Fred wanted to discuss the happenings at Heartland before bedtime.

There was a knock on the door and Sam asked, "Do you need anything, Master Jimmy?"

"No, thank you," Jimmy replied. "I am just finishing up. I will be out as soon as I am dressed."

"No hurry," Sam said. "Take your time."

Jimmy dried his body and put on the clothes Aunt Jane had provided. They looked almost new. He wondered if they had belonged to Freddie. Jimmy hoped they were Uncle Fred's so Freddie wouldn't have another reason to poke fun at him. The clothes were a little big on his prison-slender body, but they would be satisfactory until he put on weight and could get some clothes of his own.

He unlatched the door just as Sam knocked. "Mr. Jimmy, I am here to give you a shave. I shave your uncle and Freddie every day. Do you mind?"

"Oh, no, that would be wonderful. I was wondering where I could find a razor," Jimmy said. "Clean body, clean clothes, and a shave. What more could a man want? Thank you, Sam."

Sam removed Jimmy's dirty clothes from the chair and Jimmy sat down. As Sam began shaving his face, Jimmy thought of Joe and Marcus and the memories of his first days of freedom. A tear of thankfulness ran down his cheek.

He was no longer a prisoner of war, and hopefully would soon be going home to Charleston.

"How was your bath?" Sam asked as he raked the razor down Jimmy's face.

"So wonderful that I can't even express it. You know, that was only the second bath I've had since prison, and the only hot one since before I joined the army. Lying back in that hot water was a real treat, a true luxury. How often can one have a hot bath? Even at home, I always took cold baths. And yet, Father would take hot baths."

"I suppose it depends on the conveniences that a family can afford. I prepare Master Grimball at least two hot baths per week, and the missus usually takes three."

"Maybe I can have another one before I start home," Jimmy said with a grin.

# CHAPTER 37

# HOME ON THE BATTERY

For the month of July, Charlotte and Elijah spent most of their time repairing ruined parts of the Grimball's home on South Bay. Elijah helped her for two weeks while the captain and his cousin sailed to Pennsylvania to visit relatives. Elijah bricked the entrance steps, replaced window boxes, repaired the fireplace in the drawing room, and replaced broken windows and shutters on the carriage house.

Charlotte was elated to see things coming together, thanks to Elijah's workmanship. Not knowing how well James' wounded leg would be when he got home, she encouraged Elijah to renew the house and grounds for his homecoming. But yesterday, Elijah's captain returned to Charleston, and today Elijah went to his job on the ship.

While Charlotte ate breakfast, she thought how good it was to have a day to herself. Since returning home, she had only left the house six times, and that was to attend church services at St. Michael's on Meeting Street. She would like to attend more, but without her own transportation, she attended only when George's in-laws, the Gilliards, gave her a ride in their buggy.

Mr. Gilliard's health did not permit him to attend every Sunday, and Charlotte really didn't mind. With St. Michael's steeple still painted black, it made her sad, and anxious about Jimmy. It gave the part of the city at the intersection of Meeting and Broad Streets a haunted feeling that was very depressing. Many of the buildings had sustained considerable damage when struck by shells during the bombardment of Charleston.

Charlotte went upstairs and put on one of her best dresses and her Sunday shoes. Picking up her purse and parasol, she walked out the front door onto South Bay.

The street looked the same as it did the day she'd returned home from the plantation. She often thought it could be disheartening, but not today. Today she would walk to the post office at Broad and East Bay Streets for the first time since the war.

As she turned onto South Bay, she saw excessive damage to the ocean wall. Much debris and rubble lay in the streets. She tried not to let it bother her. She must learn to live with the remnants of war. But so many houses and buildings were blackened by smoke and cannon residue, and it gave her a real shock.

"How could this happen?" she asked herself, yet knowing it was the result of the Northern aggressors.

She hurriedly passed the houses, trying not to become despondent. Today of all days, she did not want to feel sad. She was glad to see the cobblestone streets off East Bay were still intact. They made her remember a more glamorous time in Charleston.

Arriving at Broad Street, she crossed East Bay to the Exchange Building, where the Post Office was now located. Since 1714, the building had served the city in many ways - a provost, a post office, a custom house and headquarters for the Lighthouse Commission of South Carolina.

During the war, the building was damaged and the Post office was closed. The post office was moved to several different locations. One of the last locations had been on King Street near Radcliff Street. Just recently the Exchange Building was once again a Federal Post Office of Charleston. [24]

Charlotte could see where the building had been hit by Union shells, but it looked as if it could be restored to its former condition. She climbed the front steps. The entrance doors had been boarded up and the glass of several windows were missing. She walked through the ruffled hallway to the post office in the back half of the first floor. Only one window was open. She saw the familiar face of the head postmaster, Jesse Hart.

"Mrs. Grimball, how good to see you. How long have you been back in the city? Sally asked me just recently if you were still at Heartland."

"I returned to South Bay the last of May. Our house survived with very little damage, yet there has been much to do since coming home. This is my first trip into town."

"How are things at Heartland?" Jesse asked. "I hear there was a fire over that way two nights ago. Was it near your place?"

"Not that I know of. Sorry to say, I have had no word from Heartland since May. Everything should be fine, or George would have let me know. How is your family? What's the news from the island?" she asked.

"The family is fine. We were fortunate with no damage to the plantation. We have been busy trying to help Sally's sister. Her place was severely damaged by cannon fire. She and the children have been with us since March. Things will be better when her husband, Thomas, gets home from the war," Jesse replied. "How about your James and Jimmy? Are they home?"

"James' injury to his left leg has healed and he is on his way home," Charlotte said. "And as for Jimmy, he's still in Virginia, hopefully on his way home as I speak."

She didn't want to tell him she had not heard from her son in six months. She did not like to lie, but in this case, it made more sense than stirring up bad news.

"It will be wonderful when our families are together once more," Mr. Hart said, turning to the mailboxes behind him. "By the way, here is a letter for you. It first went to Heartland and someone forwarded it to your post box here. I saw it yesterday. It is postmarked McClellanville. Know anyone up there?"

She took the letter and quietly ripped it open, thinking it was from Jimmy. She didn't recognize the handwriting. Unfolding the paper, she read the letter.

*Dear Miss Charlotte,*

*I am in McClellanville, South Carolina, but I want to come home. I will work for free if Lilly and I can stay with you. We are doing good. Big Tom is not with us. Hope you are well. Love from Liza.*

Charlotte said aloud, "Yes, my child. Oh, yes!"

"Is it good news?" asked Mr. Hart.

Charlotte blushed, realizing her outburst. "It is good news. I am going to have house guests from McClellanville. It will be good for us all."

"Is it someone I know?" he asked.

"No, it is someone I knew years ago," she answered, turning to get away from the gossipy man.

Now she remembered why she always sent someone to get the mail. Mr. Hart was too nosey. It wasn't any of his business who was coming to South Bay.

While crossing the floor, she remembered her manners and called, "It was good to see you. Tell Sally hello. Have a nice day."

Before crossing East Bay Street to head home, she read Liza's letter again. She could hardly believe that Liza and Lilly were coming back to Charleston. She folded the letter and tucked it into her purse, wondering who wrote it for Liza. That person had nice handwriting.

As she walked back toward South Bay, Charlotte began to feel the effects of the Charleston summer. Gnats flew about her head and the humidity caused her to perspire heavily. She liked summers at Heartland better. The sea breezes helped keep the bugs away and cooled the hot sun. She laughed, remembering that once she had disliked even the thought of the plantation. But at this moment, she wished she could be there. Not for the weather, but to see how it had survived the past three months. She would have to write to Mr. Owens to see how things were. She had been so busy since coming home that she had neglected Heartland. With James coming home soon, she must find out the condition of the plantation.

As she passed the Gibbs' demolished place, she saw a buggy parked in front of 10 South Bay. Who could be calling on her this time of day? She did not recognize the buggy. It was more like a service vehicle than a family buggy. Approaching her home, she saw two official-looking men sitting on the porch. What was going on?

She hastened to the house and saw that the men wore law enforcement uniforms. She froze for a second and wondered why they were here. Something must be wrong.

Before she could say a word, one of the men stood and greeted her. "Good afternoon, Mrs. Grimball. I am Constable Rivers, and this is Deputy Jones." He pointed to an empty chair on the piazza and said, "Why don't you sit down? We come with disturbing news."

She quickly sat down. Before she could ask, the officer continued.

"Two nights ago, there was a fire at Heartland. No one knows how it started, but the barn and the smokehouse are gone. The wind blew sparks to the roof of the second floor balcony, setting a small fire there on the roof, but Mr. Owens and Big John were able to put it out."

"Oh, dear. Was there much damage to the big house?" Charlotte asked, horrorstricken.

"There was a very small area of the balcony roof that burned. Nothing that can't be repaired. But Mr. Owens was badly burned while saving the house. Both arms are severely scarred. He is in the city hospital. They say he will survive, but it may take a long time for the burns to heal. Our concern is that there is no one in charge of Heartland at this time."

She felt faint at the terrible news. What would she do now?

"We sent word to George Grimball," the constable said, "He is coming tomorrow. A telegram was also sent to your brother-in-law in Maryland. He may not be able to be here, but being a legal owner, he must be notified. We thought you needed to know what is happening. We are here and prepared to transport you to the island this evening, if you wish. I talked to Owens' wife, and she will have a bedroom ready for you. Her daughter, Isabella, is coming from Georgetown to be with her while Owens is hospitalized. She will be of help to both of you."

"Is Mrs. Owens all right?" asked Charlotte, shaking badly.

"Yes, she got out of the house when the blaze started and her husband went to the attic to deal with the roof fire. Mr. Owens reached to put it out, but a burning piece fell, landing on his arms. It could have been worse but, just in time, Big John reached the roof by ladder and poured a bucket of water on Owens' arms."

By this time Charlotte was in tears. "The poor man. I must leave immediately. I am glad Isabella is coming, but I need to see Heartland for myself. Let me pack a few things and write a note for my border."

"It is now three o'clock, and we must get to the river for the five o'clock crossing. Go quickly. We will wait," the constable said.

She hastened up the stairs to her bedroom. Her mind was racing. *A fire at Heartland, fire on the roof, Owens burned.* Thank goodness the house hadn't burned to the ground.

She grabbed her tapestry bag and stuffed her nightgown and a few undergarments into it. From the bureau, she took two dresses and an apron, placing them in the top of the bag. Looking down at her feet, she realized she would need her work shoes. They were at the foot of the stairs. She would get them on her way down.

Out of breath, she sat down on the bed and told herself to stay calm. Things were under control and getting upset would not help the situation.

From the night table, she took a pen and paper and wrote a note to Elijah. She hoped he could read it.

> *Elijah, there has been a fire at Heartland. Officers are here to take me to the plantation. Owens is in the hospital badly burned. The house survived. I do not know when I will return. Please take care of things. I will pay you for your help. There are plenty of vegetables in the cellar, and potatoes in the pantry. Fix what you need to eat.*
>
> *Sincerely,*
>
> *Charlotte L. Grimball*

# CHAPTER 38

# THE FIRE

Charlotte hurried down the stairs, grabbed her work shoes at the bottom, and headed into the kitchen. She placed Elijah's note on the table where he would find it. Standing in the kitchen she searched her mind, trying to remember if there was something more she needed to take to Heartland. Thinking she had everything, she swiftly walked to the piazza where the constable and the deputy waited.

"I am ready, sir. I hope I have packed sufficiently," she said, handing her bag to the deputy.

"Thank you for being so prompt. We will make the five o'clock ferry in plenty of time," the constable said, giving Charlotte a helping hand into the buggy.

As they left the city and headed toward the islands, she settled into the buggy and sat thinking more about the fire at the plantation. The fear of fire had kept her from leaving Heartland when Charleston was evacuated. She did not want the place unattended. War or no war, fire was still an enemy, if unseen. Hopefully, the officials had reported the whole situation. To lose Heartland would be the last straw. She shut her eyes to keep from crying.

Upon opening her eyes again, she noticed the devastation along the way. Four months since the war had ended, and things looked the same as they had in May. Fences still down, boat and ship parts scattered along the marsh, and several of the grand homes on the Ashley River still stood without occupants.

Several Yankee soldiers stood along the Battery where the cannons were located. Only three ships were in the harbor and, for the first time, she noticed Elijah's captain's ship near Atlantic Wharf.

Questions ran through her head. What if Elijah couldn't read? How would he know why she'd left? Would he know the note was for him? She was sure he'd recognize his name, at least. He could get the captain to read it, if necessary. She shouldn't worry so.

The constable drove the buggy down Ashley Avenue, turned toward the Ashley River, and stopped at the pontoon bridge located near the city hospital. Other than a ferry, the bridge was the only way a buggy could cross the river when traveling to James Island.

Charlotte disliked crossing this bridge. It was a floating structure that allowed buggies and wagons to cross the river. But she feared the structure would break and she would land in the water. She always closed her eyes as she crossed.

The constable had travelled this way so often that the trip seemed quicker than usual.

She opened her eyes and laughed as she said, "Thank you, Constable Rivers. Maybe I'll get used to this crossing someday."

"Don't worry about it. Some folk refuse to use the bridge. The only way they will go to the city is by ferry," the constable said. "To me, this is quicker."

"I suppose you are right, but I like the ferry best," she replied.

"You'll get to do both on this trip. We will soon be at Fleming's ferry landing," he said. "It's less than five miles from here."

"Good," said Charlotte. "James always laughed at my fear of the floating bridge, but I'll feel safer on the ferry."

"My sister will not travel across it, at all," the constable said. "She misses out on many trips because of her fears."

Charlotte and the constable continued chatting, and in no time, the Fleming ferry landing was in front of the buggy. No one was waiting to take the ferry to James Island, giving plenty of room for their horse and buggy.

The ferry landing was near the McLeod Plantation, a well-known estate on James Island. She cast a glance at the plantation. To her horror, she hardly recognized the place. Once it had been such a beautiful place, but now it was hard to imagine that before the war it was a splendid, thriving plantation.

The plantation covered seven hundred acres of fields and woods on James Island. It had belonged to William Wallace McLeod, who bought it in 1851. He built a house on the property, a showplace on the island, and a place for wonderful social events until the war. She and James had attended several lavish parties there.

McLeod moved his family to Greenwood, South Carolina, to live out the war, leaving a slave named Steve Forrest in charge of the place. William had joined the Charleston Light Dragoons, but died on his way home from the war 1865. [25]

During the war, the plantation house was used by both the Confederate Army and the Yankee troops. At one time, the Union Army took over the house, using it as headquarters for a Union brigade. It also served as a Confederate unit headquarters, a field hospital, and a commissary.

Charlotte wondered if Mrs. McLeod had returned from Greenwood. The place was in terrible condition.

Curious, she asked the constable, "What is happening at the McLeod Plantation?"

"I hear it is being used as the headquarters for the Freedmen's Bureau, but I am not sure. However, it's going to take much work to restore it to its original beauty," he replied.

She sighed. "And help is in short supply. We will restore Heartland's damage from the fire, but I am wondering if it will ever look or feel the same."

"We are all feeling the need for reconstruction. It will take the state years to come into its own physically and politically," the constable agreed. "We are going to see many hard years before we land on our feet."

She wished she had never started this conversation with the constable. He made the future sound so dreary. She wished James would hurry home. He was so understanding of her needs and anxieties. Four years of making all the decisions and carrying the burdens of war had not been easy, and now she had to think about the future of Heartland. She suddenly felt all alone in a confused world. Tears began to run down her cheeks.

"Are you all right, Mrs. Grimball?" the constable asked, handing her his handkerchief.

"Thank you. I am just a little worried about Heartland," she admitted.

"I understand. Hopefully, we will find things tolerable."

The boat attendant wasn't someone she knew, so Constable River quickly introduced them. "This is Harold Simons, a new attendant here at the landing. He is helping old Mister Seabrook for a few months. Seabrook fell from a ladder, breaking an arm while repairing the gate to the ferry boat. He's doing well, but it will be a while before he can handle the landing."

"Glad to meet you, Mrs. Grimball. I know your boy, Jimmy. We were at military school together. I didn't go into the army because of my lung disease. This job was the only thing I could find to do on the island. How is Jimmy?" Harold asked. "Is he home from the war?"

"No, he is still in Virginia, the last I heard," Charlotte said, and changed the subject. "But I had a telegram this past week that my husband is on his way home. I really need him here to help me know what to do at Heartland."

"I am sorry about the fire. At least the big house is still intact. I am sure the folks on the island will be glad to help until Mr. Grimball gets home,"

Harold said. "Mr. Owens' daughter came yesterday to be with her mother while he is recovering. She brought her horse, which should be helpful to the plantation."

The boat slowed and then stopped. Charlotte realized they had arrived at John's Island landing. Her heart began to flutter, thinking about the conditions she might find at Heartland.

Constable Rivers guided the horse and buggy to dry land. The deputy took the reins and steered the horse to the nearby road.

The sun was beginning to set as they arrived at the gates of Heartland. Charlotte twisted her gloves in a nervous gesture as the constable turned the buggy onto the tree-lined carriage lane. The beautiful live oak trees with their hanging moss usually gave her a thrill to see, but tonight she wasn't concerned about the trees. Instead, she strained her eyes looking to see the big house. Sighting the tall white columns of the porch, she relaxed, seeing proof the house had survived the fire.

The buggy came to a stop at the steps leading to the porch. On the wrap-around porch, Jennie Owens sat with a young lady that Charlotte didn't recognize. This must be the Owens' daughter who came yesterday to be with her mother.

Anxious to get out of the buggy, Charlotte pushed on the door, but before she got it open, Big John was opening it for her.

"Welcome home, Miss Cha'lotte, I's so glad yuh come. T''ings have bin bad around hea the last few days," Big John said, taking her luggage and helping her from the buggy.

"Thank you," she said sincerely. "I am so glad you were here to help during the fire. We could have lost everything. And poor Owens, I am so sorry."

At that moment, she felt like hugging Big John. He had actually saved her home. Things would have been much worse if he had not been on the plantation the night of the fire. Big John was free, but to hug him would not have been proper. A Southern lady didn't hug a man unless she was married to him or he was a family member.

Jennie Owens came down the steps to meet Charlotte. Tears ran down her face as she greeted her. "I am so glad you are here. I need you, and the plantation needs you. With Owens in the hospital, I feel helpless. Thank you for coming so quickly."

Charlotte steadied Jennie and said, "I would have come sooner, but I was not told of the fire until this afternoon. Have you heard how Owens is doing?"

"One of the neighbors went over to see him this morning. He said his burns were beginning to heal, but that he was still in much pain," Jennie said, clearly upset.

They walked up the steps to the porch. The young lady rose from a chair and walked toward them.

Jennie said, "Mrs. Charlotte, this is my daughter, Isabella. She is here to be with me while her father is ill. I hope that is agreeable with you."

Charlotte reached out and took Isabella's hands, "My dear Isabella, it is good to see you again. The last time you came here, you were just a little girl! Of course it is fine for you to be here. You are family. Make yourself at home."

CHAPTER 39

# GOOD NEWS AT LAST

Big John came out to the porch and said, "Miss Charlotte, Sarah sent me to invite you to the dining room. Supper will be served shortly."

"Thank you, John. We are on our way. I would like to wash up before I eat."

Jennie said, "There's a basin in the downstairs hall with water and soap. We will go on to the dining room. Take your time. I will help Sarah finish up in the kitchen."

As she walked through the parlor, Charlotte looked around the room. Everything looked the same as it had in May. The only thing she had really missed in Charleston was the piano. She walked over to it and rubbed her fingers over the shiny mahogany wood. James had bought it as her wedding present. She laughed as she thought about the day they brought it to Heartland. It had taken George's largest wagon, four slaves, and both brothers to bring it from the city. James had said it would have to stay at Heartland because he would never move that heavy thing again.

On top of the piano was a yellow envelope, which looked to Charlotte like a telegram. She picked it up and saw her name on it. Forgetting about washing up for supper, she hurried to the dining room. Everyone was seated and waiting for her.

"Jennie, is this telegram for me? I found it on the piano. When did it arrive?" she asked nervously.

Jennie stood and said, "Oh, I am so sorry. It came the day of the fire. I put it on the piano to keep it safe until someone could deliver it to you. With all the excitement and Owens' injuries, I forgot it completely. Please forgive me. Sit down and open it. I hope it is good news. We've had enough trauma of late."

Charlotte sat down at the table and, with trembling hands, tore open the envelope and read the message aloud. "Am at Uncle Fred's house in Baltimore. Will be coming home soon. I love you, Jimmy."

She began to weep, and through the sobs, she cried, "He is alive! Thank you, God, he's alive!"

Jennie ran to where she sat and hugged her, crying along with her. By now, there wasn't a dry eye at the table.

Sarah got up from the table and began taking the food back to the kitchen. The warming oven was still hot and would keep the food warm for a while. Food was the last thing Charlotte wanted to think about at the moment. Jimmy was alive, and supper could wait!

Jimmy was in Baltimore with his Uncle Fred. This was good news to everyone, but especially to his mother. The people at Heartland had said little about her not hearing from Jimmy for so long. Everyone had presumed him dead.

"I was about to give up on his ever coming home," she said, tears of joy running down her cheeks. "He doesn't say where he has been, but he is now safe with Frederick's family in Baltimore. We can be sure Fred will see that he is taken care of, and will get him home as soon as possible. Strange, he was in Northern Virginia when he last wrote. I wonder how he got to Baltimore? Oh, well. I am just thankful he is all right and out of danger."

"Amen," said everyone at the table together.

She lifted her water glass and said, "Jennie, let's not postpone supper any longer. Let's eat and be merry to celebrate that my Jimmy is alive and will be home soon."

Everyone cheered as the hot food was brought back to the table. Charlotte bowed her head and said grace. "Thank You, Lord, for this food, and thank You for answering my prayers that my Jimmy be alive and well. Amen."

She could feel a burden lifting from her shoulders as she began to eat. She was so glad that Jimmy and James were both coming home. It made the loss by fire not near as frightening. She would have her men home to love and help make life a little easier.

---

Isabella Owens sat at the supper table as Charlotte read the telegram from Jimmy. It was good to be back at Heartland where she had spent the first eight years of her life. Her father, Lewis Owens, was the plantation over-seer. Isabella, being the family's only child, had often spent long periods of time alone in the one-story house designed for the overseer's family. Her only playmates had been the slave children.

She remembered Jimmy well, but his being the master's son and five years older, she was not allowed to play with him. She'd always looked forward to the times when Uncle George's family came to visit. His two daughters, Becky and Susanna, were nearer her age, and they always came to her house to play. In the summertime, the girls were at Heartland more often, and sometimes spent weeks there. Those were the times Isabella had enjoyed the most. They spent much time playing in the waters of the creek that ran into the rice paddies. Master James had taught all three girls how to swim in that same creek.

Isabella also remembered Jimmy's cousin Freddie's few visits. He had been so good-looking, even at age twelve. She would watch him ride, and longed to ride horses with him. Sometimes the stable manager would let her feed the horses. When she was eight, Master James had taught Isabella to ride a horse. She'd taken to riding like a fish takes to water.

That year, she begged for horse of her own. Owens said she was too young, and a horse cost too much. When she was old enough to go to school, her parents had decided to send her to live with her grandparents in Georgetown, South Carolina. There she could attend school regularly, and learn social graces from her grandmother.

She remembered being sad when she left Heartland, but found life with her grandparents a better place for a little girl to have friends to be with every day. She'd liked going to school. She'd loved learning, and did well in all of her studies. She excelled in all subjects and won many honors at the end of each school year. Her grandmother was so proud to have such an accomplished granddaughter that she gave her piano and voice lessons. At age twelve, she sang in the church choir.

Everyone told her she was not only talented, but also beautiful. By the time she was thirteen, she'd been considered a stunning young lady, and all the young men had tipped their hats when they saw her with her grandmother.

With the rumors of war, and with Isabella growing up so fast, her grandmother had decided to send her to Woodberry Hall in Atlanta, a private school for girls. She did not want to leave her life in Georgetown, but with the encouragement of her parents and grandparents, she went off to boarding school in the fall of 1860.

The school was highly recommended for its social curriculum of making fine ladies out of little girls. Isabella accepted the challenge and took to the social graces readily. She excelled as a scholar, a dancer, and was considered the best horseback rider in her class.

That Christmas, her grandparents gave her the gift she had wanted for a long time. They gave her a horse of her choice. However, as the war began the enrollment of the school dropped, and by the beginning of the 1862 school year, Woodberry Hall had closed its doors. Isabella went back home to her grandparents. In Georgetown, she found delight in teaching piano to young children, and in her spare time, she rode her beloved horse, Tilly.

When she received word that her father had been burned in a fire at Heartland, she quickly came to John's Island and made plans to stay as long as she was needed. She knew she would be of help when her father came home to recuperate.

Being in the big dining room at Heartland tonight brought back childhood memories. She remembered how she'd loved the smells of the food cooking in the kitchen, and climbing the tall staircase. She also remembered watching Jimmy and others ride horses, and her first desire to have a horse of her own.

After supper, Miss Charlotte took her to her parent's suite of rooms in the big house. Jennie was there to help arrange her clothes and other belongings. They would remain here until her father's burns were better before moving back to the overseer's house. Isabella was very tired after the long trip from Georgetown and went to bed early.

———

Miss Charlotte told Isabella goodnight and went to her own bedroom. She too, decided to get ready for bed. With the shock of learning of the fire at Heartland and the hasty trip from Charleston this afternoon, she was ready to rest.

For the next three days, she busied herself helping Big John and his sons clear off the burnt wood and materials from the burned barn site. Most of the charred wood could be used in the fireplaces of the house and kitchen. Clearing the property was hard and dirty work, but Big John insisted that it must be done as soon as possible. A new barn must be built before winter.

A few days later, George came with his mule-pulled wagon loaded with lumber that would be used to rebuild the barn. He left it stacked on the spot where the smokehouse once stood, and told Big John he could not stay but would see him in a few days.

Two days later, at six o'clock in the next morning, Charlotte was awakened by noises from the corral. She rolled over. With no barn, why was she hearing hooves stomping? Was she dreaming? Sliding out of bed, she looked out the window to see several mule-driven wagons coming up the carriage lane. She recognized one as George's wagon.

Good heavens. She counted seven more wagons and two buggies. All the wagons carried lumber and ladders. The drivers seemed happy to see one another as they gathered where the old barn had once stood.

"It's a barn raising!" [26] Charlotte cried happily. "How wonderful!"

She should dress quickly and go down to the kitchen. The women would be bringing food for the workers before noon. She was sure Big John and George were in charge, and one of them should have told her! It was amazing that so many of the folks who were having hard times themselves were giving their time and materials to help Heartland. God bless them!

By noon, the whole plantation was buzzing with excitement. Everyone was busy working together in order to get as much work finished as possible on the barn before sundown. Charlotte and Isabella joined the women and kept the workers supplied with water.

Charlotte rang the plantation bell at noon, and the workers stopped to eat the food brought by the local families. It was a sight to behold. She marveled at the fellowship she felt among the crowd, reminded of a verse of Scripture. *Love thy neighbor as thyself.*

By suppertime, the walls of the new barn were completed and the floor of the loft had been laid. The rafters for the roof were attached, but it would take another day or two to build the stables inside. Some of that could be done by the men at Heartland.

By sundown, the workers had cleaned up the building site and were leaving. Everyone carried home a feeling of a job well done.

# CHAPTER 40

# ALMOST HOME

James was glad it was not as hot today as it had been yesterday. There was a little breeze, and several plantation houses were on this road if he needed water for himself or Lucky. There were many oak trees where he could rest in shade. About high noon, he came to another cypress swamp, and Lucky watered up. James found a log in the shade and sat to eat the food Esther had packed for him. He enjoyed the bacon biscuits and half of the piece of chocolate cake. He sat nodding until the horse began to get restless. Taking one last drink of water from his canteen, he mounted Lucky.

By midafternoon, he came to an intersection in the road. A sign pointing to the right read Bee's Ferry Road. That would take him across the Ashley River, then to Chaplin's Landing and onto John's Island. By tomorrow night, he would be at Heartland, holding his beautiful wife, Charlotte.

He gave Lucky a swift kick. "Sorry fellow," he said. "Do your thing and get me home, it's been a long, long way!"

Only twelve miles to Heartland, but soon the sun was setting. Lucky couldn't go very far in the dark, and the ferry landing was now closed. The railroad station was the only place he knew to stay until morning. Old man Harper might still work there. It would be good to see a familiar face.

Giving Lucky a pat, he said, "Hey, fellow, we'll head to the railroad station, then you can rest."

He slapped the reins to a slow gallop. The railroad station was less than two miles from the entrance of the island. They would make it just at dark. Good timing.

Getting to the railroad tracks, he turned and followed the path that led to the station. The place was dark with no sign of life. He wondered if the train from Savannah was still running, especially after Sherman's march.

He stopped in front of the darkened station and dismounted. He would stay here even if it was not open. He could bunk on the platform. He was too near home to be particular. He turned the knob of the door. It was locked, and too dark to see anything through the window.

"Well, Lucky, the platform is my bed. I am sorry I have no water for you, but you were watered about an hour ago. It should take you through the night," James said, hoping his horse could understand.

He lay down on the platform, using his haversack for a pillow, and soon fell asleep.

As the sun rose in the east, he opened his eyes, wondering why he was sleeping on a hard floor. Recognizing the station and its surroundings, he quickly got to his feet.

"I'm home! I'm on John's Island, almost to Heartland!" he shouted.

Lucky stirred as James picked up his haversack and hastened to mount. He turned the horse back to the main road on the island, and gave him a quick kick. "Giddy up, boy, we are almost home."

Away went Lucky, who did not stop until they arrived at the Limehouse Ferry Landing at the Stono River. James dismounted and led the horse to water. Lucky drank until full, and then James led him onto the ferry boat. He was the first passenger of the morning.

"Good morning, sir," greeted a young captain. "Welcome to John's Island. I am Gerald Limehouse, Gus's grandson. He'll be here by noon."

"I am James Grimball from Heartland plantation, coming home from war," James replied.

"Welcome home. I heard about the fire at Heartland. Hope all is well," Gerald said.

"A fire? Goodness, I know nothing about that. I haven't heard from my wife in months. Was it a bad fire?"

"Sorry to have mentioned it. Mr. Owens was injured, but the house was saved. That's all I know about it," Gerald said.

"Well, I will soon be there and see for myself," James said.

The ferry reached the landing before he could get any more information. He thanked the young Limehouse lad and mounted Lucky. Giving the command to gallop, he directed his mount toward River Road. He rode fast, passing the Fenwick property, and on toward the eastern end of the island. To his right he began seeing the beautiful live oak trees that lined the carriage lane that led home to Heartland.

He eased on the reins to slow Lucky and turned into the lane that would lead him home and to Charlotte, the love of his life. Suddenly, tears began running down his face. It had been four long years without seeing her beautiful face. Four long years without holding her close. He felt like a teenager going on a first date. Wiping his tears away, he began looking for the two-story white house with a wrap-around porch, the place he had dreamed about for the past four years. Having heard about the fire worried him. He hoped the blaze hadn't turned his house into ruins like the Bowman's home.

He finally caught sight of the plantation house and galloped the last few yards.

"Home!" he cried, stopping at the front steps. He dismounted Lucky and ran up the steps, only to find the front door locked. Everything was so quiet. Where was everyone?

He knocked on the door. Soon he heard footsteps.

A male voice asked, "Who goes dere?"

"Master James Grimball," James said loudly.

The door was quickly unlocked and Big John rushed through, hugging James like a bear.

"Yuh's home! Praise de Lawd! Does Miss Charlotte know yuh's coming?"

"Well, she knew I was on the way home. Where is she? Is she here?" James asked anxiously.

"Yes, suh, she probably still asleep in de guest bedroom on the balcony," Big John said. "We's all tired out from yesterday's barn raisin' and waz late getting to bed. Come on in, Massa James. Is you tired and hongry? I'll git Sarah up tah cook fuh you."

"Don't worry about food now. I want to see my Charlotte! Don't worry, I know the way," James said as he headed to the stairs. Then he stopped and looked back at Big John. "Is my Jimmy here?"

"No, suh, he be in Baltimore with his uncle Fred," Big John said.

"Thank you. I'll go to Charlotte now," James said, turning back to the stairs.

Big John stood in the open door, thinking. Miss Charlotte gonna be so happy.

CHAPTER 41

# HEARTLAND AT LAST

James took two steps at a time getting to the door of the balcony hall. Just inside was a washstand with a basin, water pitcher, and towels. He wanted to see Charlotte, but knew he needed to wash his face, hands, and his feet. He poured water into basin and, using one of the hand towels, he hurriedly washed. He stripped off his shirt and washed the sweat from his upper body. Sitting down on the chair next to the wash stand, he took off his boots and pants, and using another towel, he gave himself a hand-bath the best he could.

Shaking the dust from his clothes, he put his pants and shirt back on his somewhat cleaner body. He left his boots near the washstand and tip-toed down to the door of the guest room and knocked softly. His body was shaking all over, but his wounded leg had no pain.

The first knock brought no response, so he knocked louder.

"Who's there?" Charlotte's sweet voice asked.

"Sweetheart, it's James. May I come in?"

You could have heard Charlotte's reply all the way to Charleston as she jumped out of bed, crying, "Oh, my dearest, come in! Come in!"

He turned the door knob as Charlotte turned the key. She ran into his arms before he even took a step. Through joyful tears, they kissed over and over. The sunrise gave enough light for them to see each other's faces. Nothing was said as they moved closer to the bed. He could smell the sweetness of her hair and feel the warmness of her arms.

With a sudden sweep of her body, he lifted her and gently placed her on the bed.

He held her tightly and whispered as he kissed her again and again. "I am home, my beloved. Home for good. It's been a long, long time."

A few hours later, James and Charlotte were awakened by the sound of the plantation bell ringing the emergency signal.

She turned quickly from his arms and said, "Don't worry. Big John is only ringing the bell to let everyone know the master is home. With Owens living in the big house, your brother George and family spent the night in Owens' house. With no horses to ride, the bell is the best way of sending news. In a few minutes, everyone will be here at the big house. We should get up. Sorry, my darling."

He sat up in bed and said, "I should be dressed before everyone gets here. Are any of my old clothes still here? Maybe in the old wardrobe?"

She frowned and said, "After the war, Big John moved the cedar wardrobe to the attic. I will dress and go see. Do you think they will still fit?"

"They may be a little large. I loss several pounds when I was first wounded. But they will be cleaner than what I've been traveling in," he said, sitting on the side of the bed.

She put on a clean housedress and hurried out to the attic stairs. She easily found the cedar wardrobe, which contained three shirts and two pair pants. She couldn't remember if they belonged to Jimmy or James. She hurried back and gave the clothes to James. "Here. Try these."

He kissed her softly on the lips, and said, "Thank you, my love."

He put on the clothes and found they all fit him, although the pants were a little large in the waist. His army belt took care of that. "They may be old, but they feel great. How do they look, my dear?" he asked.

"They look grand, dear, but you smell a little like cedar."

They laughed, hugging each other. Then he presented his arm and they walked out of the room as happy as a newly wedded couple.

On the back stairs that led to the kitchen, she asked, "How is your leg? You are not limping."

"No limp, I am thankful. But at times a sharp pain will come and go, mostly when it is going to rain. The doctors say I am fortunate to have come through this type injury so well."

She squeezed his arm. "I prayed a lot for your leg to heal. I am sure that helped."

"Thank you, my love. I did a lot of praying myself," he admitted, caressing her closely.

As they walked into the kitchen, they were greeted by cheers, hugs, and warm welcomes. Big John, Sarah, Jennie, Isabella, George, Caroline, Becky, and Susanna filled the room with merriment. Pug and Ham sat on the banisters. They were a little afraid of Master James. He'd always had great expectations for the boys, even as children. They didn't know what he would expect of them after the war.

Jennie said, "Master James, are you hungry? I have pancakes and biscuits in the warming oven."

He let go of Charlotte's arm. "I would love some of both, and I hope some of your strawberry jam, too. Care to join me, Charlotte?"

"I'll have the same, and coffee for both of us," she replied as they sat down at the kitchen table.

Oh, yes. Master James was home, and all was right with the world.

# CHAPTER 42

# TROUBLE FOR LIZA AND LILLY

Liza and Lilly said their goodbyes to Mr. Willard and walked the path to Sewee Beach.

Lilly noticed the beach and ran toward it, crying, "Water, water!"

"It is not for drinking, but we can play in it," Liza said, grabbing her hand before she reached the surf. "Just wait and we'll go in."

She spread a blanket on the sand, and on it placed her bag of belongings and the food basket Miss Willard had prepared. She took Lilly's hand and they ran into the water. The water felt cool on the warm summer day. Liza removed Lilly's apron dress, and together they played in the waters of the Atlantic Ocean. It was great fun. The ocean was all new to Lilly, and Liza's memories of the rushing tides made her feel like a child again. Dinnertime had passed when Liza realized they must find a place to stay for the night. Remembering Mr. Willard's words, she knew they couldn't sleep on the beach.

Taking Lilly's hand, she said, "Dearie, we must get out of the water now. We will go in again later, down the road."

Lilly pulled away and said, laughing, "This is the most fun I ever had."

"I know, dear, but it is getting late and we haven't eaten. Miss Willard made us a big basket of food," Liza said.

Lilly followed her to the blanket on the sand. They were both hungry, and playing in the water had increased their appetites. Liza dried her with an old towel and reached for the food basket. Even before she opened it, she could smell the fried chicken Miss Willard had cooked for Lilly. My, how that child loved fried chicken.

Liza held up a drumstick and said, "Look what we have to eat."

"Yippee," Lilly shouted. "May I have my chicken now?"

"Wait until I get everything out of the basket," Liza replied, and reached for more food. There was cheese, carrots, apples, boiled eggs, onions, a chocolate cake, and a loaf of homemade bread.

Lilly ate two pieces of fried chicken. It was delicious. After eating a piece of cake, she lay down on the blanket and fell fast asleep while Liza put everything back into the basket. Liza felt the warm sun shining on her face. There was nothing like a nap after playing in the surf and eating good food. She decided to join Lilly for a short nap.

Where would she and Lilly spend the night? She had barely drifted off to sleep when she suddenly woke to the sound of a horse's neigh. She lay still, waiting to hear it again. There was a rustle near her head, and she saw a hand reach for the bag that held her belongings and for the food basket.

Without thinking, she jumped up, knocking the bag and basket from the man's hand, and shouted, "What do you think you are doing?"

A shabbily dressed man stepped back and said, "Now, now, little missy, don't get upset. I am hungry, just need a little food."

"Hungry nothing, you are a thief," shrieked Liza, reaching for Lilly, who was now awake and crying.

Comforting her frightened child, Liza held Lilly tightly and stepped off the blanket, away from the man.

The man continued to stand on the blanket, and reached for a pistol in his belt. "You listen to me. If I want it, I will take it. You and your child, too."

"Put the gun down, you varmint. I am not afraid of you," Liza said loudly. "You best not touch my young'un or I'll kill you."

Pointing the pistol at Lilly, he laughed. "And just how do you plan to do that? I've got the gun. You freed slaves think you own the world, but you don't. Just watch me."

He picked up the food basket, "All mine now!"

Putting his pistol back in his belt, the thief opened the food basket and smiled. "Fried chicken. My, my, you sure are eating fine. I ain't had fried chicken since before the war. This is a feast for me."

Liza put Lilly down behind her, telling her to take six giant steps then stop and wait. Crying, Lilly obeyed her mom and took six giant steps, counting as she walked.

Liza reached down and grabbed the blanket with both hands, and pulled it with all her strength. The scalawag fell backward and his pistol flew from his belt. It landed at Liza's feet, along with the contents of the food basket. Nervously, Liza picked up the pistol and pointed it at the unwanted visitor.

He was having difficulty getting to his feet.

Pointing the gun at the thief, she shouted, "Now who's in charge?" Holding the pistol with shaky hands she said, "Stay down or I'll shoot."

A voice from behind her said, "If she doesn't shoot you, I will." It was the voice of a colored Union soldier on a horse, his rifle pointed at the thief's head.

Liza felt relieved to see this gentleman soldier, who had come out of nowhere. She stepped back, still holding the gun. "He all yours," she said, shaking with fear.

She handed the gun to the soldier. Her next thought was for Lilly. Calling her name, she ran to meet her. They watched to see what the soldier would do with the thief.

Holding his rifle in one hand, the soldier reached for the rope on his horse. With the rifle still pointed at the thief, he said, "Get up you rascal." Grabbing the man's arms, he tied them behind his back.

"But I was just hungry," the frightened thief replied. "I meant no harm to the woman."

"And yet you held a gun on the woman and the child. I don't call that hunger," the soldier said as he tied the man's legs together and put a bandana over his mouth. "That should shut you up until I decide what to do with you."

Liza and Lilly stood quietly until the soldier pushed the thief back to the ground and looked at Liza. "Didn't mean to break up your battle, but I thought you could us a little help. Glad you two are safe."

Liza and Lilly walked to where the soldier stood near his horse. "I can't thank you enough, mister. You saved our lives. What are you going to do with him?" she asked.

The soldier walked to a grazing horse a few feet away. "I am going to let him ride his own horse."

The soldier took hold of the reins of the horse, pulled the thief up from the ground, and threw him over the horse's back. Using a small whip, he hit the horse's rear end. The horse flew like a house on fire, and soon tossed the thief off into some sandy mud.

Lilly laughed and asked, "Is he dead?"

"I think not," the soldier said. "But he'll be sore for a day or two. I will ride down the beach and check on him shortly, but first I need to know what a young woman and her child are doing all alone here with no house is sight? The war may be over, but there are many carpetbaggers, scalawags, and thieves roaming the state. You could be in worse danger than what just happened."

"I know. And thank you again."

The soldier extended his hand. "My name is Henry Moore from Boston, Massachusetts, formerly a soldier in the 54th colored regiment. I am on my way to Charleston."

"I'm Liza Grimball, and this is my daughter, Lilly. We are on our way to Charleston, too," Liza replied.

"You are walking to Charleston?" Henry asked, curious.

"Hope to get there by Christmas," Liza said, only half joking.

"That's a long walk. Would a horse help?" he asked.

Puzzled, Liza asked, "Then how would you get to Charleston?"

"I meant the thief's horse," Henry said. "When I check on him, I'll bring his horse back if I can find it. I'll drop the thief off at the next town. Where he's going, he won't need a horse. You and Lilly can ride his horse to Charleston."

"Wonderful," Liza said. "Thank you!"

She turned to Lilly and explained they might have a horse to ride to Charleston.

Lilly clapped her hands. With her eyes sparkling, she asked, "Can I pet the horse?"

"Yes, child, you can pet the horse," Liza happily answered.

While Henry rode off to check on the rogue. Liza made a fire on the beach and managed to retrieve some of the food that had been in the food basket. She stuck sticks in the fried chicken and held the pieces over the fire to burn off the dirt. The boiled eggs had cracked, but were ready to eat. She washed the dirt from the ham in the water. She found the cake and bread still wrapped in paper.

She had supper prepared when she heard horses coming up the beach. Henry was riding his own horse and the thief, still tied, was thrown over his horse's back. Henry stopped at the fire and slid to the ground, grinning. Pulling the thief from his horse, he said, "Ma'am, here is your transportation to Charleston," and handed her the reins of the thief's horse.

Liza smiled and took the reins. "Thanks. But please do something with the thief."

Henry laughed loudly. "That I will do, miss. I'm tying him to a tree. He'll not bother you again."

He took the reins and walked the horse to a group of palmetto trees near the road and tied him to a tall one. The thief was plenty mad. Because of the bandana in his mouth, they could not understand what he was saying, which was probably just as well. They were probably not words for the ears of a five-year old.

Henry joined Liza and Lilly on the blanket. Lilly, who was usually shy to strangers, looked up at Henry and asked, "Is he hurt?"

"No, little one. He's a little roughed up. He is just mad because he is tied up. He can't hurt anyone or steal anything now."

Liza was pleased to hear the man speaking to Lilly in such a kind voice. He was nothing like Big Tom. Henry's voice sounded more like Mr. Willard's, with the softness of a tone speaking from the heart.

As the shadows became longer, Henry said, "Miss Liza, you and Lilly can't sleep on the beach tonight. I suggest you make camp on the other side of the grove of palms, away from the road. I plan to guard our prisoner on this side of the grove."

"Thank you, Henry. We will follow your suggestion. But first, will you take a biscuit and ham to the thief? I hate to see him go hungry," Liza timidly said.

"That is very thoughtful of you," Henry said. "Yes, I will feed him. He's making much noise on an empty stomach. Maybe food will calm him down."

Liza fixed two ham biscuits and placed them on a cloth napkin. She added a piece of cake alongside the biscuits.

Lilly watched her mother hand the meal to Henry, and said, "Don't let him bite you, Mr. Moore."

Liza and Henry laughed. Henry said, "If he bites me, I'll just bite him back."

All three were laughing now. Henry rose and walked to the prisoner. He knelt down and removed the bandana from the man's mouth.

"Cut me loose!" the thief screamed, "I'll have you arrested, you Yankee!"

Henry said in his gentle voice, "Open your mouth, I will feed you supper."

The prisoner used a few choice words and cursed Henry. "Cut me loose. I can feed myself."

"Can't do that, mister, just eat the pieces I put in your mouth. If you can't do that, you'll go to bed without supper," Henry replied.

The prisoner silently admitting defeat began to chew the food given to him. He must have, indeed, been hungry.

While Henry fed the man, Liza put the leftovers into the food basket. Gathering up the blanket, she handed it to Lilly. "Be my big girl and carry the blanket for me. It's almost your bedtime, and we must walk to the palm trees and find a place to sleep."

"I am a big girl, and see? I can carry the blanket," Lilly said, picking up the blanket while letting part of it drag on the ground.

Liza smiled and said, "You are doing well."

She picked up the sack of belongings and the food basket, and they found a place between two trees. She took the blanket from Lilly and placed it on the ground, praising the girl for a being a big help. She placed her sack near a palm tree and the food basket at arm's length.

Sitting down, she pulled Lilly into her lap. Lilly said her prayers, and Liza began singing a Gullah lullaby.

*"Hush little baby, don't say a word, Momma gonna buy you a mockingbird. If that mockingbird don't sing, Momma gonna buy you a diamond ring. If that diamond ring turns brass, Momma gonna buy you..."*

Lilly was soon asleep, and so was Liza.

On the other side of the trees, Henry was guarding the scalawag. He smiled as he heard Liza singing. Liza sure was a spunky woman, and a good mother, too. She was smart and good-looking. What more could a man want?

# CHAPTER 43

# CALL ME MAC

The thief woke early. He tried to escape the ropes that bound him. Unable to do so, he began to holler through the bandana, waking Henry.

Henry reached for his rifle and pointed it at his prisoner. "Be quiet. You are loud enough to wake the dead. Quiet down and I will remove the bandana from your mouth and give you some water to drink."

The thief stopped the hollering and was happy to have the bandana removed.

Henry opened a canteen and held it to the thief's mouth. He was very thirsty. He even said thank you to Henry, the first kind thing he had said since his capture.

"Let me loose, sir. I am sorry for what I did yesterday, but hunger will make one do strange things. I am really a good person. Please, untie me. I will do you no more harm," the thief pleaded.

"I don't believe you," Henry replied. "Once a thief, always a thief, is what my grandfather used to say. I have found that to be the truth in most cases. How about that US brand in your horse's ear? I am sure that horse was a gift to you! Oh, well. No more bellowing for now, and I will make breakfast shortly. I don't want you to be hungry again. By the way, my name is Henry. What's yours?"

"Call me Mac," the grouchy thief said, and then demanded, "I need some coffee."

Henry began to make a fire. Mac settled down, and Henry put the coffee pot over the fire to boil. He took a frying pan out of his saddlebag, along with a glass container holding four eggs. From his haversack, he brought out a small loaf of bread.

He broke two eggs into the frying pan and scrambled them with a fork. When they were done, he raked half the eggs onto a tin plate and added a piece of bread. He walked over to Mac and untied his hands. "Now eat. It is all I have."

Mac grabbed the plate and gobbled the food down. This time, he was really hungry. Henry poured coffee into two tin cups and handed one to Mac. For the first time since being taken prisoner, he smiled and quietly drank the coffee.

Meanwhile, across the grove of palm trees, Liza was awakened by the voices coming from Henry's camp. Lilly was still fast asleep. Liza lay there listening to Henry talking to Mac. Such a kind man. He would make a great papa for Lilly. Liza hoped he would stay around when they got to Charleston. It would be her task to win his heart.

She heard him say, "We've got to get going. Sorry Mac, but I must tie you up again."

"Please, sir, not again. I'll behave, I promise," Mac pleaded.

"We start out with your hands being tied, and without the bandana. If you show you can travel without making trouble, I will loosen them later."

As he tightened the ropes on Mac's wrists and legs, Mac began to howl.

"Keep quiet or I will use the bandana. I am going to leave you just long enough to see if Liza and Lilly are awake. I will be close if you try to escape," Henry said, picking up his rifle.

Mac sat quietly while Henry walked through the grove of trees and greeted Liza, who was awake and ready to leave.

"Did you rest well?" he asked, whispering so as not to wake Lilly.

"Surely did. I dreamed we finally got to Charleston," Liza said. "Lilly is still asleep. She was really tired last night. Too much excitement for a child her age. I'll wake her now."

Leaning over the sleeping child, she began to sing, "This little light of mine, I'm gonna let it shine. This little light of mine, I gonna let it shine…"

As Liza sang, Lilly opened her eyes. She smiled and began singing with her mother. Spying Henry, she jumped up and asked, "Do you know my song?"

"I used to sing it when I was your age. It is a good song," he said. "We can sing it while riding the horses today. Come over to my camp and I will make breakfast for you before we leave. I must get back to check on Mac."

"Thanks, we will be there shortly," Liza said with delight. The more she saw of that man, the more she wanted to be with him.

Liza nursed Lilly for a short time, then she combed Lilly's hair and straightened their clothing. Picking up Lilly and their bag of belongings, she hurried to Henry's camp.

Henry had saddled the horses and made ham biscuits for their breakfast.

Mac said, "Good morning, Miss Liza and Little Lilly. It's a beautiful day for traveling."

Lilly looked at Liza in surprise that he was being nice, then grabbed her mother's skirt and hid behind it.

Liza realized she was afraid and patted Lilly's head, whispering, "Yes, he is trying to be nice."

Henry put out the fire and loaded his frying pans and utensils into the saddlebags on his horse. He instructed Liza and Lilly to mount the other horse, the one the thief had stolen from the army, which Henry had given them to ride for the journey to Charleston.

Then he told Mac to stand up, that he would be walking beside Henry's horse.

At that, Mac began to yell and use words that were not meant for a five-year-old's ears.

Henry quickly reached in his pocket for the bandana and thrust it into the prisoner's mouth. This made Mac madder than ever, and his howling got worse.

"Stop it now, or I will leave you stranded here on the beach. My plan was to let you walk awhile and then ride behind me if you behaved yourself. But with the way you are acting, I think I will just leave you tied up here and report you to the law at the next trading post. That may be the best thing to do."

Liza was shocked beyond words. Would this kind man truly leave the thief stranded on the beach alone without food or water?

Without thinking, she blurted out, "That would be cruel!"

"Yes, it may seem that way to you, but from what I have seen of this prisoner, he is going to be a hindrance to our travel. And as you know firsthand, he can be dangerous. You and your child may still be at risk as long as he is with us," Henry said. "What do you think we should do with him?"

Liza had never had to make an important decision like this. She had no solution to offer. "I am sure you know best. Do what you have to do," she told him.

Her heart felt heavy to think of Mac being left on the beach alone, but she trusted that Henry would do what was best in the situation.

"I'm sure there will be someone riding past here before dark. He will be all right. I will untie his hands and he can remove the bandana and untie his own feet. Be ready to ride as soon as his hands are untied. He is going to be angry.

Liza guided their horse away from the trees to wait for Henry.

Lilly was confused and asked, "What's going to happen to the bad man?"

"We will leave him here. Someone will be by soon to help him get where he has to go," Liza said. It was the only thing she could think to tell a five-year old so she would understand.

It took only a minute or two for Henry to untie Mac's wrists and mount his horse. As Mac began screaming, Liza and Henry were long gone down the beach, headed for Charleston.

After riding for a while, they came to a watering hole. Henry dismounted and helped Liza down from the saddle, leaving Lilly on the horse. He found a well from which to fill their canteens, and he asked several men standing around where he could find a lawman.

"There is a lawman stationed at the general store at Awendaw, down the road a piece. You can' miss it," one of the men volunteered.

"Thank you, sir," Henry said.

While Liza filled her canteen, Lilly still sat quietly on the horse. This was her first horseback ride, and she was curious about the saddlebags that hung from the saddle. She untied the right saddlebag and reached inside. She felt a small sack and pulled it up to examine.

"Mommy! Mommy come quick. I found something."

Liza put the cap on the canteen and headed back to the horse and Lilly. "Child, what do you want? I'm bringing you water. Mr. Moore will fix food as soon as he gets back."

"But Mommy, I found something," Lilly exclaimed, holding up a small cloth sack.

Liza hastened back to her. "What did you find?

Lilly handed the small sack to her mother.

"Where did you find this?" she asked.

"It was in the saddlebag. Open it, Mommy. It is heavy."

"It must belong to the thief. We will wait and let Mr. Moore see what is in the bag," Liza said, taking it. "It is heavy. It is probably bullets for his gun. It could be dangerous."

"What could be dangerous?" Henry asked, walking up behind her.

She turned to face him, "Lilly found this sack in the thief's saddlebag. It is heavy and I was thinking there may be bullets inside." She handed the bag to Henry.

They watched closely as Henry loosened the drawstring and opened the velvet sack. Reaching his long fingers inside, he brought out a string of pearls.

In stunned silence, they watched Henry reached back in and bring out a gold bracelet and a cameo broach. Last came a golden ring with a three-diamond setting.

Lilly squealed, "Jewelry! Pretty, like Mrs. Willard's."

Liza was in awe as Henry let the pearls drape over her arm. "They are beautiful, but they are not Mrs. Willard's. I used to clean her jewelry. She had a pearl necklace and a cameo, but her ring had only one diamond. She did not have a gold bracelet," Liza said. "How can we find who they belong to?"

"We probably never will, unless we ask Mac. We have ridden too far to go back to where we left him. I will ask the law officer if this jewelry has been reported missing," Henry said. "It is worth a lot of money."

"Mac was apparently a jewel thief as well as a horse thief," she said.

"I am glad we didn't bring him along. There is no telling what trouble he would have gotten us into before we turned him over to the authorities," Henry replied.

"You made the right decision, Henry," she said. "You've encountered more types of people than I have. I am learning."

"Liza, you have a kind heart. My heart has gotten a little rusty in doing good since the war," he said. "I am learning, too. We make a good team."

She hoped he meant it. This was the man she wanted in her life for always. She must try hard to please him.

# CHAPTER 44

# WANTED

Liza and Henry rode in silence for the next few miles. For the first part of the ride, Lilly amused herself with a cup of sand and a few shells she'd found on the beach. But now the sun was extremely hot and Lilly began to fuss, wanting water and wanting to stop for a while.

Liza hushed her as much as she could. She didn't want Henry to get upset with Lilly's whining and leave them behind. He was too important to her. He was a man she felt safe with, a man she wanted to spend the rest of her life with. She wasn't going to take a chance of Lilly spoiling her plans. She began singing some old slave songs. Lilly joined in, and soon Henry sang along when he knew the words.

She sang, "He got the whole world in His hands. He's got the whole wide world in His hands."

Lilly like to sing that song, especially the second verse. "He got the little bitty baby in His hands. He got the little bitty baby in His hands. He's got the whole world in His hands," Lilly sang loudly. "I like to sing!"

"So, do I," Henry said just as he saw a sign nailed to a post that read General Store.

"At last," Liza said. "I was beginning to think there wasn't a general store."

"Me, too," he said. "It will be good to stop and rest for a while. I'll find the law officer while you and Lilly rest in the shade. Then we will see if we can find something to eat before we make tracks again."

Liza helped Lilly get off of the horse. "I'm hungry," Lilly said.

"The only things still in my food basket are some of Mrs. Will's biscuits and the jar of honey," Liza said.

"Give me a biscuit, please, but no honey," Lilly said. "I like her biscuits. Can she make us more when we get home?" Lilly asked as Liza reached for the biscuit.

Liza had not taken the time to figure how she would explain to Lilly that they would not be going back to the Willards. She'd have to think about the best way.

She answered, "I am sure she would. She likes to make biscuits."

They found a shady spot to wait for Henry. He had gone into the store to find the law officer. Soon the two men came out of the store and headed toward the horses. Henry opened the saddlebag on Liza's horse and took out the jewelry.

"What are they doing?" Lilly asked.

"Mr. Henry is telling the lawman about Mac and how he tried to hurt us, and about the jewelry you found."

"Is the lawman going back to get Mac?" Lilly asked.

"I'm sure he will if he needs to," Liza said.

"I hope the man can find Mac. He is bad, but he must be hungry by now," Lilly said.

Liza was so touched by her little one's concern about Mac that she gave Lilly a big hug. "I am sure he will take care of Mac. Don't worry your sweet head about it. That's what lawmen are for." Liza felt glad that her child cared so much about a stranger's welfare, even though he had mistreated them on the beach.

After Lilly finished eating the biscuit, Liza handed her the canteen. She drank for a long time, then handed it back.

Liza drank and said, "The canteen is almost empty. When Henry gets back we will need to fill it up before we start to ride."

At that moment Henry and the lawman came walking up to them.

Henry said, "This is Constable Cooper. He knows all about our Mac. Seems he's been robbing houses and stealing things around this part of the state, and was released from jail only two weeks ago. We should be thankful he didn't do us more harm."

"That's right," Cooper said. "He can be quite dangerous. He killed a man during a robbery but lied his way out of it. Ma'am, you and your child were mighty lucky on the beach. He's known to have done terrible things to women and children. As for the jewelry, there has been no loss reported. You may keep it, as we have no safe place to store it."

"Thank you," Liza said, looking at Henry. "I am thankful for Mr. Henry. He is the one who saved us from harm. He came just in time."

Henry bowed his head, saying nothing, but he was thinking what a wonderful woman and child he'd saved.

The lawman wished them good luck and returned to the store. Liza and Henry stood quietly smiling at each other.

Lilly said, "Mr. Henry, do you have anything to eat besides biscuits?"

"Sure, I do. I have some dried beef, hardboiled eggs, and several apples. Would you like something from my food basket?"

"I have eaten a biscuit, and I would like an apple, please, sir," Lilly said.

Henry laughed and said, "Yes, little one, at your service. I think your mother should also eat before we travel again."

"Yes, sir, Liza said, "and you, too, must eat."

The three of them laughed together, then Henry opened his food basket and began setting out food.

After eating an egg, some dried beef, and another biscuit, Liza asked him, "Is your food bag empty? I was wondering if we should buy food for tonight and tomorrow while we are here at a store."

"I was thinking the same thing. My food is almost gone and we will need something for this evening and tomorrow. Do you have any suggestions?" he asked.

"Some cheese would be nice. It can be eaten even if it gets hot, when it is wrapped in the right kind of paper. We will need bread and possibly a jar of jelly," Liza suggested. "And some fresh fruit."

"Sounds great. I am also going to buy some hardtack. It is not very good, but if we run out of food, it will keep us alive until we find more. The lawman said that the next town is Mt. Pleasant. It is a big enough town to have more food, if needed," Henry said as he stood and loaded up his saddle bags. He turned to Liza. "You can get the horses watered and fill the canteens while I go to buy more food. We need to travel as far as Mount Pleasant."

Once they were on the road again, Lilly went to sleep. This gave Liza and Henry time to spend the next few hours chatting as they rode along. There was something she really wanted to ask him, so she worked up her courage.

"Henry, we are getting close to Charleston, and I was wondering what your plans are when we get there?" she asked. "Do you have a friend there? Where do you plan to stay?"

He hesitated. "I do not have a plan. I am traveling there on faith. I have enough money to rent a place for a while, but other than that, my plans are open. You see, I was raised by my grandfather, who was a gentlemen farmer. He owned a large farm near Plymouth, and I was his heir. While I was away at war, grandfather died and left the farm to me. But I don't want to be a farmer, so my uncle is living on the farm until I decide what to do with it."

"So, what kind of work can you do in Charleston?" she asked, completely stunned by Henry's past.

He smiled and said, "I am sure I can get some sort of work. If nothing else, I can help rebuild places that were destroyed by the war. I like working with my hands. Grandfather sent me to college to study agriculture. I liked the study of farm animals, especially horses, but I do not want to be a vegetable farmer. I hope traveling will show me what I should do for a career." He paused. "That's enough about me. What about you and Lilly?"

Liza was so flabbergasted by Henry's background as a college-educated freeman, it took her a few minutes to speak. "I wanted to come home to help Miss Charlotte," she said. "I have no idea what she will want me to do. With the slave system gone, I am sure she will have a need for me more than ever. She is like a mother to me."

"She sounds like a great person. I hope I will get to meet her," Henry said.

"Sure, you will. I have an idea. Why don't you go to Heartland with us and stay until you have a chance to investigate the situation in the city of Charleston?"

"I thought about that, but was afraid your Miss Charlotte might object," he said quietly. "I wouldn't want to impose on the family."

Liza could hardly contain herself. Yet she felt herself unworthy of him since learning how educated he was. Even so, she wanted Miss Charlotte to meet this fine man, and this would give Liza more time to be with him.

"I've never been to a plantation. Do you really think Miss Charlotte won't mind? he asked.

"Oh, no. She'll be glad to have you to visit. It is such a beautiful place. That's one reason I wanted to come home."

Just then, Lilly woke up. "I'm hungry," she said. "Let's eat.

Liza and Henry laughed.

"When are you not ready to eat, little one?" he said, and pulled the reins on his horse. "This time you must wait for food. We have to look for the ferry boat landing that will take us to Charleston. That is Mount Pleasant just ahead."

Lilly asked, "Will I get wet in the boat again?"

Liza couldn't believe that Lilly remembered what happened in Tom's boat when she was only three years old. "No, this is a big boat that takes people and horses across the water. We'll be safe."

# CHAPTER 45

# JUST A BOAT AWAY

Henry saw a sign that read Hibben Ferry Landing, with an arrow pointing to the right.

"Ladies, we are almost to Charleston. We must get to the ferry now."

Liza was excited to know they would soon cross the Cooper River and once again be in Charleston, not far from Heartland. Dismounting her horse, she took Lilly in her arms while Henry took care of the horses.

Together they walked onto the ferry. Henry paid for their tickets while Liza found a bench to sit. Lilly was strangely quiet, with a questioning look on her face. Several other people came onboard, then a buggy with four horses drove onto the ferry boat, stopping beside Henry and the horses. The couple in the buggy were dressed formally, as if going to a party.

Lilly sat up and looked at the woman. "Pretty jewelry like Mrs. Willards."

Liza was afraid Lilly would start asking about the Willards. To distract her, she said, "Look, Lilly, our boat is moving. That means we will soon be in Charleston. No more traveling for a while. Won't that be great?"

The crossing took longer than Liza had expected. She didn't know that after leaving Shem Creek there were several small islands that the boat must go around before heading to the main peninsula of Charleston.

Lilly sat quietly holding onto Liza's hand the whole time. As the ferry turned into the landing on Concord Street near the city market, she smiled and said, "We didn't get wet this time."

"No, dear one. This is a much bigger and safer boat than Tom's. It has brought us home to Charleston," Liza said, hugging Lilly.

As soon as the boat anchored, she picked up Lilly in her arms and walked to where Henry stood with the horses. Happy tears rolled down her face. She wanted to hug him, but instead she said, "We are home at last, thanks to you. And we made it before Christmas!"

Henry laughed as he led the horses down the gangway, with Liza and Lilly walking behind.

Liza was shocked to see so many freed slaves loitering around the market place. The stench of spoiled meat and fish coming from the meat market made her gag. They walked to Meeting Street in silence. Not only did she feel sick from the smells, but she felt heartsick as she saw the damage to many buildings in the city. Having lived at the Willards during much of the war, Liza had missed many miseries of the siege.

Lilly lifted her arms to be picked up, and asked, "Why are the houses broken, Mommy?"

Liza picked her up and said, "Because of the war."

"What is war?" Lilly asked.

Henry heard the question and quickly said, "I think we can ride the horses now." He gently took Lilly in his arms and placed her in the saddle.

Liza mounted, and sat close behind Lilly, who had a fearful look on her face. Henry rode quietly beside them. He was recalling his time in battles that actually destroyed property. It made him sad to think about, especially seeing the ruins of this beautiful city.

Liza finally spoke. "Let's ride toward the Battery. The Grimball's city house is near there. We can stop there and eat, and still have time to get the ferry to John's Island by sundown. There are many trees in Miss Charlotte's backyard, where we can sit and eat."

"Good idea," Henry said. A good shade tree is always a great place for a picnic."

"Yippee! I like picnics!" Lilly squealed.

Liza gave Henry directions to the Charleston Battery, and to South Bay. "There is a public well at the Battery to water the horses and fill our canteens."

Henry and Liza rode without talking. They both were overwhelmed by the devastation along the streets and the extreme damage to houses and churches. Liza wanted to cry, but held it back for Lilly's sake. She didn't want to answer any questions about war. She was anxious to see if Miss Charlotte's house was still standing.

# CHAPTER 46

# BACK TO SOUTH BAY

Liza was horrified when she saw the Gibbs' house and began to cry soft-ly. "The next house is the Grimball's. Is it still there?"

Henry rode ahead and said, "Yes, my dear, the house is still there, and it is beautiful."

Trotting faster, they arrived at the front walk. Liza slid off of her horse, holding on to Lilly, and ran to the piazza. She put Lilly down and shouted, "Thank you, Lord. Thank you!"

Henry picked up Lilly, who was confused. "Is Momma all right?" she asked.

"Yes, she is just happy to be home. She is fine. We all are fine," he said joyfully. "Stay on the porch with your Mother, while I take the horses around back and hitch them. I'll be back shortly."

The house looked like new to Liza. If there had been damage, it had been repaired. The only thing she wondered about was the one broken chair on the porch. It was Charlotte's favorite chair for lounging. How did it get broken?

"Lilly, do you remember this big house?" Liza asked.

"It looks like Mr. Will's house, but no swing," Lilly replied. "Not as many steps to climb."

"Yes, it does make me think of the Willard's, but this is where we lived when you were a baby. That room at the end of the porch was our room."

Liza walked across the porch. She turned the door knob and to her surprise, it opened.

Inside, she was surprised that the usual beautiful, floral hand-embroidered bedspread no longer covered the bed. It had been replaced by a handsome masculine quilt. There was a pair of men's boots sitting neatly by a different chair. The rocking chair where she rocked Lilly had been removed from the room.

As Henry joined her, she stood wondering who was now living in her room.

"Nice bedroom," Henry commented.

"This used to be Lilly's and my bedroom, but it doesn't look the same. Evidently, it is now a man's room. I wonder whose? I just hope there will still be room for us."

"That's one reason I didn't asked to come home with you. Things do change," Henry said.

"We shouldn't worry. There are many rooms in this house, and two extra over the kitchen where the household slaves stayed, including Big Momma."

Lilly pulled on Liza's dress. "I'm hungry. Let's have the picnic," she said.

Henry took her hand. "Come on, Lilly, let us walk to the back yard to find a good place for the picnic. Your mother can come when she's through looking at the house."

Liza was glad to have a few minutes alone. Everything looked the same except her bedroom. Knowing it was no longer hers made her feel a little sad.

She stepped from the porch and walked to the back of the house. Henry and Lilly were putting food on a grassy spot near the cellar doors. She went to join them.

Lilly said, "Look Mommy, Mr. Henry brought some cheese and grapes. I like grapes."

"Wonderful! It all looks good. I am hungrier than I thought," Liza said.

"It has been a long time since breakfast, so let's eat," Henry said.

Liza was still on cloud nine being back in Charleston, and was especially glad to be in the yard of the Grimball's house. The three of them had planned to continue on to the plantation before dark, but it had taken them longer to get from Mount Pleasant by ferry boat than they had anticipated.

They ate without talking. Lilly was the first to finish. Getting up, she ran over to the fig trees. "Look, Mommy, figs like Mr. Willard's." She picked a fig and began eating it.

Liza stood and walked over to her. "Yes, they are figs like at the Willard's, but you shouldn't eat someone else figs without permission."

"But Mr. Willard let me eat them," Lilly said, picking a second one.

These figs do not belong to Mr. Willard. They belong to Mr. Grimball. I don't think he would mind your eating his figs, but you must learn it is not polite to take things without permission. Do you understand? Not without asking the owners."

"She can eat as many as she wants," a masculine voice said in a Gullah dialect.

Liza turned to see a man coming toward her.

"She is welcome to as many she wants to eat. Miss Charlotte is not in the city and she cooked up a batch before leaving town."

"Thank you," Liza said. "Do you live here now?"

"I's Elijah, I stay here while Miss Charlotte is at de plantation. I use to work on de plantation."

"Elijah, I'm Liza, Big Momma's daughter. I cooked for Miss Charlotte before I left. Do you remember?" Liza asked excitedly.

With a look of recognition, he replied, "Of course, I know you! But you waz just a child yourself when you left with Big Tom. Where be Tom?"

"I left him near McClellanville. He was headed north to get rich, but the trip was too hard on Lilly and me. I stayed with a nice family there until the war was over, and then we started home. I finally made it."

Henry put the picnic things back into the food basket and stood up. He walked over to Liza and said, "So, you two know each other?"

"Yes, Henry, this is Elijah. He is taking care of the house while Miss Charlotte is at the plantation."

Henry shook Elijah's hand. "I am Henry Moore from Boston, Massachusetts."

"Glad to meet you," Elijah said in his heavy Gullah accent. "I's live in the bedroom on de porch, use to be Liza's room. I's bin here over two years, now."

Lilly ran to Henry. Picking her up, he walked to the pump at the back door and washed the remains of the fig juice from her hands. Lilly said, "Pretty house, big pretty house. Can we stay here?"

"Where is you planning to stay tonight?" Elijah asked.

"I really don't know," Liza answered. "I thought we'd be at Heartland by tonight, but it is too late to catch the ferry."

"You can stay here," Elijah said. "I know Miss Charlotte wouldn't mind. De beds are made up, since Massa George's family slept here on der way to Heartland a few days ago."

"What do you think, Henry?" Liza asked.

"It's a good idea," he answered.

Since we have just eaten, cooking will be no problem. We'll just sleep," Liza added.

"True," Henry agreed. "Just tell me where to sleep. I am really tired. It's been a long day."

Elijah said, "Liza, you can decide where y'all sleep. I be getting lanterns ready for de bedrooms."

# CHAPTER 47

# COMPANY FOR ELIJAH

"Henry, you can take the downstairs guest room to the left of the front door. Lilly and I will take the extra room on the second floor," Liza said, pointing the way to each room as she gave directions. "There are washstands on each floor and chamber pots under each bed, and there is an outhouse behind the carriage house. Henry, you can get the horses settled in the stable in the back of the carriage house. There is plenty of room for two horses."

Elijah went to the front hall shelf and got lanterns for each bedrooms, and returned to the kitchen. He said goodnight to all and went to his room on the porch.

Henry fed and stabled the horses, and then found the downstairs guest bedroom.

Liza and Lilly walked up the cascading staircase to the second floor. She had forgotten how as a child she'd loved climbing these stairs. It had seemed much easier then.

Lilly was running ahead to be the first at the top. When she got to the top step, she sat down and waited for Liza.

"My, you are getting too fast for me," Liza said with a big sigh. "This lantern slowed me down."

Lilly followed her to a bedroom door, and held it open as she walked in carrying the lighted lantern. Liza placed the lantern on the dresser. Looking at the big bed, she was very pleased to see the beautiful embroidered bedspread that had once been in her room was now on this guest bed.

"Look, Lilly. Your grandmother, Big Momma, made this bedspread before you were born. Miss Charlotte is still using it," Liza said, her eyes misting up.

"Pretty," Lilly said sleepily, climbed into the big bed, and quickly went to sleep.

Liza pulled a sheet over her sleeping child. The embroidered bedspread was truly a masterpiece, an heirloom from Big Momma. Someday Lilly would appreciate the bedspread as much as Liza did.

Liza dressed for bed, blew out the lantern, and crawled into the bed beside Lilly. In her usual nightly prayer, she gave thanks to God for being back in Charleston. Wiping tears from her eyes, she went to sleep.

She woke at sunrise. She first thought she was dreaming, being in such a fancy bed. She sat up. Seeing the bedspread, she knew this was no dream. She was finally home in Charleston. Hearing the neighing of horses from the backyard, she walked to the window and saw Henry watering the horses at the well.

"What time could it be?" she murmured. Had Henry gotten up early or had she slept late? Sitting down on the bed, she fingered Big Momma's spread. It brought back so many memories of her years with the Grimballs.

Lilly opened her eyes. "Where are we?" she asked. "Are we in the big house? Can we live here?"

Liza reached for her. "We must go to the plantation to find Miss Charlotte today. Maybe we can live here someday, but not for now. Henry is already outside with the horses, and someone is in the kitchen cooking something that smells good. Let's get dressed and go see what's going on downstairs."

When they were dressed and their hair combed, they walked downstairs to the kitchen.

Elijah was cooking pancakes. "Is you hungry?"

"I am. I like pancakes," Lilly happily answered, sitting down at the kitchen table.

Liza took a seat beside Lilly. "Elijah, this is so nice of you. We could have waited and eaten later. Did Henry already eat?"

"Yes'um, he be eatin earlier so he could water the horses. He's a nice man, even if he be a Yankee," Elijah said, putting the last pan of pancakes and the syrup on the table.

"We like him. He helped us get to Charleston. If we had not met Henry, we probably wouldn't have been here until Christmas," Liza said.

"Liza," Elijah said, "I leave now and go to work. Would you mind washin' de dishes?"

"Be glad to," she said. "Thank you for cooking. Have a good day. I will tell Miss Charlotte this place looks great. She will be proud of you."

"You be careful gwing on the ferry. I guess I will be seeing you, now dat you is home," Elijah said as he headed out the door.

She and Lilly finished eating and Liza was drinking her coffee when Henry came in from the yard.

"I am glad you both are up," he said. "I think we should try to make the ten o'clock ferry to John's Island."

"Is it that late?" she asked.

"No, it is just nine. We have plenty of time, but I thought we could get to the landing a little early," he suggested.

She finished the dishes and said, "We can go now. All I need is to get our baggage from upstairs and lock the back door."

"I'll get your baggage. You and Lilly go on out. Do you have the key?" he asked.

"No, but I remember where it is hidden. I will meet you at the horses," she said. Taking Lilly by the hand, they walked down the steps and out the back door.

Liza walked to the terrace. Beside the first step was a large rock. She picked up the rock and found the hidden key. "I told you I remembered where it was. It has been there since I was six years old. Big Momma hid it there." Liza laughed and said to Lilly, "Go stand by the horse. I must lock the back door, then we will be ready to ride."

Henry came out of the house with their belongings just as Liza got to the door.

"I was about to lock you inside," she said. "I wouldn't want to do that. We'd miss you too much."

Henry laughed. "I'd miss you, too, but I would like the house." He stood watching as she locked the door and returned the key to its hiding place.

Lilly was standing by their horse when Liza came from the house. "Mommy, why doesn't our horse have a name?" she asked.

"I hadn't thought about it," Liza said. "I suppose you can name her."

"I will call her Sugar. Sometimes Mr. Henry gives her sugar for a special treat."

"The horses are ready to go," Henry said, lifting Lilly into the saddle.

"Our horse is named Sugar. I just named her," Lilly proudly said. "Does your horse have a name?"

"Well, yes. His name is Zebulon. Zeb for short." Henry said.

Liza mounted Sugar. "Let's see how fast Sugar and Zeb can get us to the ferry landing. I want to find Miss Charlotte!"

# CHAPTER 48

# ON TO HEARTLAND

Liza, Henry, and Lilly rode quickly to the ferry landing that would take them to James Island. This time they stayed on the horses as the boat moved toward the Elliott Cut's Inlet and the Fleming Ferry Landing.

Lilly asked, "Is the plantation house big at Heartland?"

"Yes, very, very big, but different. It has high steps and a wrap-around porch."

"What's a wrap-around porch?" Lilly asked.

"It's a porch that goes almost all the way around the house. Heartland also has a smaller porch off the second floor that is called a balcony. The plantation has several small cabins beside the big house, where my people once lived. They are probably all empty now," Liza said, finding it difficult to explain a plantation setting to her five-year-old who has never known slavery.

At the landing they rode their horses off of one ferry and onto the other ferryboat that would take them to John's Island.

Liza felt excitement at seeing the John's Island Landing.

When the boat pulled into the landing, Lilly asked, "Why are we stopping?"

"We are on Johns Island. It's just four more miles to Heartland and Miss Charlotte!" Liza was so elated she could hardly talk. Tears ran down her cheeks.

Henry took Sugar's reins and led them off the boat. "Well, my dear, you are really home now. The oak trees with the Spanish moss are magnificent. I cannot wait to see the plantation." He added, "You know the way. Ride on ahead and I will follow."

Liza pointed Sugar toward the path that led to River Road, which would lead them to Heartland. She rode faster. Henry gained speed to keep up with her. Finally, she turned onto the familiar tree-lined carriage lane that lead to Heartland Plantation. She slowed Sugar as she saw the white columns of the plantation house.

She wiped her tears and said, "Henry, it is so beautiful. See why I wanted you to come home with me?"

"It is a big, big house," Lilly said.

They rode up to the house, and Liza stopped at the front steps. Without a word, she just wiped her eyes and continued to sit on the horse.

Lilly said, "Lots of steps. Can we go in?"

Henry dismounted and hitched Zeb to a nearby hitching post. He walked over to Liza. "Are you all right?"

"Yes, the place looks wonderful. But there is something missing... Take Lilly. I want to sit here a while longer," she said.

"Mr. Henry, get me down. I want to go in the big house," Lilly said.

Henry lifted her from the horse and they walked to the high steps. "Let's sit down here and wait for your mother before we go inside to find Miss Charlotte," Henry said.

Liza continued to sit and ponder what was missing. Then with a few new tears, she realized what she did not see. There were no slaves in the yard, nor in the corral. No slaves in the alley, nor at the well. No colored children playing in the lane. Everything was so quiet. That was it, she missed her people, the slaves of the plantation.

Just then, Master James came from the back of the house, leading a horse to the corral. He saw Liza sitting there on her horse and asked, "Can I help you? I am Master Grimball of the plantation."

She quickly dismounted and walked to where he stood. She was grinning big as she said, "Master James, it is me, Liza, your former house slave and cook."

"Liza, of course," he called, walking to greet her. "Is there something wrong?"

"No, sir," she said. "I am just a little shocked at seeing so few people here. I knew my people were freed, but I didn't think about them all being gone."

"I know. I've only been home for a week, and the quietness of the plantation has been a shock to me, too. It is strange not seeing and hearing the slaves, especially their singing. But Big John, Sarah, and the boys are still here. I have no idea where the others went."

"I can't wait to see them," Liza said.

"How did you get back to Heartland?" he asked. "Charlotte mentioned that you and Lilly were in McClellanville. Believe it or not, I ran into Big Tom in Richmond, Virginia. He's working with a clean-up crew there."

Henry was watching the welcoming scene, still holding Lilly by the hand.

"Who is that talking to Mommy?" she asked.

"Let's go and see," he said, and they walked down the steps to where Liza stood with the man.

Liza smiled and turned to Henry. "Master James, I want you to meet our new friend, Henry Moore from Boston. He is the one who got us home."

James reached out and shook Henry's hand. "James Grimball here. I'm glad to meet you. Thanks for bringing them home."

Lilly reached out her small hand to Master James and sweetly said, "I am Lilly, glad to meet you."

Everyone laughed as James picked up the child and said, "I know who you are. I've known you since you were a baby. You have grown up and are no longer so little. I'm so glad to see you again. Have you seen Miss Charlotte yet?"

"I've been looking for her. Where is she?" Lilly asked eagerly.

"She is probably in the kitchen. Our son, Jimmy, is coming home this week, and she is busy planning meals for him. Now that your mommy is here, maybe she can help with the cooking," James told Lilly.

"Oh, yes," Liza said, taking Lilly from him. "Let's go find her."

James turned to Henry, "Why don't you bring the horses to the corral and water them while Liza and Lilly find Miss Charlotte."

"That's a good idea, thanks," Henry responded. "I'll follow you."

James picked up Lucky's reins, and Henry led Sugar and Zebulon toward the corral.

Liza straightened her clothes and smoothed her hair, ready to find Miss Charlotte.

Lilly pulled on Liza's dress. "Let's go in the big house. It is hot out here."

Liza took her hand and began climbing the many steps of the plantation house. "Yes, it is hot here, but we are home, home at Heartland. Let us go inside and find Miss Charlotte!"

Entering the front door, Liza could smell the wonderful aromas of plantation foods. Miss Charlotte was surely in the kitchen. Liza led Lilly through the parlor, the dining room, and into the kitchen. Miss Charlotte was leaning over the fireplace, stirring a pot of beans.

Liza walked quietly to the stove and, without a word, she threw her arms around Miss Charlotte's neck and shouted, "Surprise!"

Charlotte turned around and took Liza into her arms, hugging her as a daughter. Lilly stood behind them until Charlotte spied the child and enveloped her into the hug.

"I got your letter and have been expecting you. And just look at you, Lilly! My, you are a big girl. I hear Big Tom is in Virginia. I prayed for your safety every day. I am so glad you are home," Miss Charlotte said, not realizing half what she was saying in her excitement. "Are you hungry?"

"No, ma'am, we've had breakfast. We spent last night at South Bay and this morning Elijah cooked breakfast for us. I was so happy to see that the house survived the war. It looks grand," Liza said.

"How did you get to Charleston so quickly?" Charlotte asked. "Didn't you and Lilly walk?"

"No, we rode on a horse," Liza said, blushing, "A gentleman helped us, Henry Moore from Boston. He was a soldier in the Union Cavalry and was coming to Charleston for a visit. He got us a horse and traveled with us. He is outside now with Master James. I like him, and I hope he could be my man. I don't think I am good enough for him, but he seems to like Lilly and me. He treats us both very kindly. I can't wait for you to meet him."

"Sounds like Liza's in love," laughed Charlotte. "I am glad he is not like Big Tom. I never thought he was a good papa."

Suddenly, Miss Charlotte paused and looked at Liza in surprise. "You are no longer speaking Gullah!"

"You are right. The lady we stayed with after leaving Big Tom was a schoolteacher. She taught Lilly and me to speak proper English, and also to read and write. I wrote the letter I sent to you myself."

"How splendid! I did notice the nice handwriting. Being able to read and write will open many doors for you in the future. I am so happy for you."

Miss Charlotte moved the pot of beans away from the high heat, wiped her hands, and said, "Let's sit down. I want to hear all about your gentleman friend."

Lilly sat at the kitchen table, and Miss Charlotte reached to a top shelf of a cabinet and brought down a rag doll. "Lilly, come play with this doll. It was yours when you were here before. I kept it, hoping you would come back someday, and here you are."

Lilly took the doll and hugged it gently. "I love it," she said.

"What else do you say?" Liza asked.

"Thank you, Miss Charlotte. She is a pretty doll," Lilly said.

As Lilly began to play with the doll, Miss Charlotte turned to Liza and said, "So. Tell me all about Mr. Henry."

Liza settled into a chair. "He is from Boston, Massachusetts, and his grandfather raised him on a big farm. For two years, he attended college and studied agriculture. In 1862, he left college to join the Union Cavalry. He fought here in Charleston, in the battle of Fort Wagner and on Morris Island. His grandfather passed away while he was in the cavalry. The big farm now belongs to him. But he says he doesn't want to be a farmer, so he is traveling for a while to make up his mind about what he really wants to do for a career. He is so smart, I am afraid he won't stay around here very long," she said worriedly.

"He sounds wonderful, and don't be sad. Enjoy being with him. You never can tell what love will do," Charlotte said, giving Liza a little hug. "You certainly have grown up and become very smart yourself, young lady. Be patient. He did come here by choice, didn't he?"

"Why, yes, I hadn't thought of that. Thank you Miss Charlotte, I knew you would give me the right advice, as always," Liza said with a smile.

Just then, Isabella came into the kitchen on her way to the corral to get her horse. "Miss Charlotte, I am on my way to the City Hospital to visit my father. He is doing so well that I think he should come home as soon as possible. A nurse said yesterday that Father can go home if we have a place for him to recover."

"Oh, that is wonderful," Charlotte said. "You and your mother could move back into the overseer's house, and Liza can help me in the big house. Do you think your mother would mind moving? If not, maybe she could bring him here to continue his recovery. Go on and see your Father and I will speak to your Mother. We will decide the details later."

"Okay." Isabella gave Liza a curious look.

Charlotte exclaimed, "Pardon my manners! Liza, this is Isabella Owens, Mr. Owens's daughter. She has been staying with us since the fire, and rides her horse every day to the hospital to check on her father's progress. Isabella, this is Liza, a former beloved house servant who has come home, and this is her daughter, Lilly, my adopted grandchild for now."

Lilly was confused by what Miss Charlotte was saying, but smiled and said to Isabella, "You are a pretty lady. Glad to meet you."

Isabella responded, "And you are a pretty little girl. Glad to meet you, too. This is nice, but I must leave now so I can get back before dark. Thank you, Miss Charlotte."

"Bye, now. Be careful. See you at supper," Miss Charlotte said.

"Good bye!" Lilly crawled under the table to play with her doll.

"What is wrong with Owens?" Liza asked after Isabella left by the back door.

"Oh, my dear, a little while ago Heartland had a fire. We lost the barn and the smokehouse. Some sparks flew to the balcony roof, starting a small fire there. Mr. Owens ran up the balcony stairs to try to put it out. As he reached the fire, a piece of the burning roof fell and landed on his arms. Thankfully, Big John reached the roof with a bucket of water and dashed it on Owens' arms. It put the fire out and saved him from more injuries. He has been in the City Hospital ever since. Isabella came to help him and be with her mother."

"I noticed the new barn," Liza said, "but I didn't think anything about it, except it looks nice. Will Owens still be able to take care of this place?"

"That is what we do not know. I hope so. This has been his home for so long, he has nowhere else to go, especially if he can't use his arms," Charlotte said sadly.

"I am so sorry. If he can't be caretaker, who will be?" Liza asked.

"James may have to do it," Charlotte said wearily. "Without slaves, there will no rice crop. James and his brothers will decide what is to be done with the land."

"How is Master James' injury? Wasn't it his leg?" Liza asked.

"Yes," Charlotte said. "He says it doesn't hurt anymore, but he hasn't done any hard work since he returned home. It still may give him trouble later. I am hoping we can get some crops or business going here at Heartland so we can go back and stay at South Bay. With Jimmy at home, he could go back to college and live at home."

"I'm sorry about the fire," Liza said. "And I'm sorry about Owens. But at least the house was saved."

"I wasn't here, but they say it was a very scary day," Charlotte replied solemnly.

Just then, James and Henry walked into the kitchen.

Liza jumped up, taking Henry's hand. "Henry, this is my Miss Charlotte."

"So glad to finally meet you," Henry said with a smile. "I've heard so much about you, I feel I already know you."

"Welcome to Heartland. I hear you helped to bring Liza and Lilly home. We are so thankful they didn't have to go all that way alone. It would have been dangerous. Make yourself at home here. We are glad you came our way," Charlotte said happily.

"Thank you, Miss Charlotte. This is the first plantation I have ever visited. It is such a special place. I love the oak trees. They give me a feeling of closeness. I am glad to be here," Henry said, his voice eloquent.

Miss Charlotte was, indeed, impressed with Henry. Liza had picked a smart one this time. Charlotte hoped he would stay.

James asked, "Is George around?"

Charlotte said, "I'm not sure. He took Caroline and the girls home yesterday, and said he'd be back before Frederick arrives. He may be at Owens' house. He'll be up for supper, if he has gotten back."

# CHAPTER 49

# READY TO TRAVEL

Frederick arrived at his Congress Street home in Baltimore at supper time. The walk from town had taken a longer than he'd anticipated. He washed up and headed to the dining room, meeting Jane in the hall.

"Did you get your business completed in town?" she asked.

"Yes, dear. I will tell you all about it during supper. Walter sent his greeting. He seems to be doing well. Clarence wasn't there today. His wife is sickly and he is currently working from home, unless there is a trial. Sometimes I do miss my office in the city."

Fred sat down at his usual place at the dining table, and Jane joined him.

"Where are the boys?" he asked.

"Freddie went riding after dinner. He should be back by now," she said. "Jimmy was sitting in the porch swing reading earlier. I'll ask Sam."

Just then, Sam came in to see if the family was ready to eat. He was surprised to see only the master and his wife at the table.

"Have you seen the boys?" Fred asked him.

"Not in the last hour. Jimmy was in the swing on the porch, and I suppose Freddie is still out riding. Shall I check on them? Sam asked.

They heard the slam of the screen door in the kitchen, and in rushed Jimmy, almost out of breath.

"I am sorry to be late for supper. I was reading and accidentally dozed off. Where is Freddie?" Jimmy asked as he took his place at the table.

"He is still riding, as far as we know," Jane replied.

Sam came in again, and seeing Jimmy seated at the table, asked, "Shall we serve supper?"

"Yes, go ahead and serve the food. No telling where Freddie is if he's on his horse. He seems to forget all measure of time when he is riding. His rides seem to be getting longer and longer," Fred said. "I am wondering if he's seeing some young lady we haven't met."

"Could be," Jane said. "If so, she must be from our side of town."

Jimmy sat quietly. He was always glad when Freddie was not in the same room. He tried his best to get along with his cousin, but it was hard to take his behavior much the time. If he were not so obnoxious, Jimmy might enjoy being around him. He was glad when Sam and Cook began to serve the food. He was hungry.

A few minutes into eating, Uncle Fred put down his knife and fork. He cleared his throat and said, "Jimmy, I was hoping Freddie would be here to hear the plans I have made to get you to Charleston. But since he is not, I want you to know that in my pocket I have tickets for the trip to Charleston. We will leave Baltimore on the first of August by way of a steamship owned by Captain Marcus Alexander. We will have a one night layover in Norfolk, Virginia, then on to Charleston. You should be home by the fifteenth of August."

"Hurray!" Jimmy shouted. "Thank you, Uncle Fred! And you are coming with me?"

"Jane and I will both accompany you, along with Freddie. That is, if I can tear him away from his horse long enough."

Tears of joy ran down Jimmy's face. He was overjoyed to be going home soon. However, he did not cherish the thought of being on a boat with Freddie for that long.

Uncle Fred turned to Aunt Jane and said, "I hope these plans will suit you, my dear."

"They took me by surprise, but I will adjust my calendar. We do need to get Jimmy home, and it will be good to visit family. I hope we find things in good condition since the war," she said in a concerned voice.

Uncle Fred said, "Two former navy officers will be traveling with us. They will continue on to Savannah, Georgia. There they will pick up a steamboat they have purchased and steer it back to Baltimore. It will join the fleet of steamboats sailing out of Baltimore's port. It should be an interesting group of passengers."

"Sounds so," Jane said. "August is a hot time for traveling the waterways, but it will be good to see James and George and their families again after these five years."

"My brothers and I need to check on the fire insurance and decide what to do with the seven hundred acres of land at Heartland. Without slave labor, rice plantations will become a thing of the past. We will have to come up with another way to use the land. Our families' incomes from Heartland will depends on what the land will be used for in the future. It is somewhat frightening to think of no more income coming from the plantation. The war years have been difficult, and things don't look to be getting better anytime soon."

"You are scaring me, Uncle Fred. I hadn't thought of that consequence of the war," Jimmy said worriedly.

Uncle Fred began to eat again, and the room went silent.

Freddie came running in from the kitchen door, saying loudly, "I'm sorry, I'm sorry. I got lost in my own memories."

He quickly sat down at the table next to Jimmy. The silence continued as Freddie heaped his plate with food.

In a business like voice, Uncle Fred said, "Freddie, the family is going to Charleston on the first of August. Make your plans now to be gone for the whole month of August, or longer. We are taking Jimmy home, and I will meet with my brothers to decide what to do with the seven hundred acres at Heartland and settle on an alternate plan to earn an income from the land. You may take your horse. We are traveling by steamboat, and there is plenty of open space for you to ride at Heartland."

Freddie was speechless. His father had spoken and there was no room for argument.

"But I don't want to go," he stammered.

Uncle Fred, looking very serious, repeated, "The family is going South on the first of August. You can't stay here by yourself for a month. I am giving Sam and Cook time off with pay."

Jimmy leaned over to Freddie and whispered, "Now, your father will learn about the missing fifty acres. It's too late to cry."

Freddie's face turned as white as a ghost as he thought of the wrath of Frederick Grimball.

"We can play another game, and I will win back the land. I can do it," Freddie sputtered.

"When pigs fly." Jimmy chuckled. "I told you I am not much for gambling."

Freddie gobbled down his food and left the table without permission.

"What's the matter with him?" asked Uncle Fred.

"Maybe he's anxious to get started," Jimmy said, laughing softly.

# CHAPTER 50

# THE STEAMBOAT

In Baltimore, the Grimball household was very busy getting ready for the long trip to Charleston. Jane and Cook pulled the traveling trunk from the attic, taking out the winter clothes stored there and packing summer clothes for the family.

Uncle Fred took Jimmy shopping for clothes of his own. He was still wearing Uncle Fred's clothes, but needed at least a change to wear while traveling. In fact, he needed a whole new wardrobe after his stay in prison, but he would wait until he got to Charleston to buy everything he needed. Uncle Fred bought Jimmy and Freddie new shoes and Freddie some new riding pants and boots.

Freddie was still unhappy about having to go South. He was glad that his horse was going with them. The only thing he looked forward to was riding Barabbas on the open land and sandy beach of the plantation.

The day of departure came quickly. Sam arranged for a mule wagon to take the luggage to the port of Baltimore early that morning. He would drive the family's buggy to take them to the steamship.

At the port, Captain Marcus and First Mate Joe were ready to travel. The new cook, Abner, was also onboard. He had cooked for the

Confederate Navy. He was a large, jovial man and an extremely good cook. Being from Alabama, he was glad there would be other Southerners on the trip.

The steamboat was scheduled to leave at eleven o'clock. The Grimballs arrived at the port a little after ten. Aunt Jane and Uncle Fred stepped from the buggy, followed by Jimmy and Freddie. The two navy officers soon joined the group. Freddie's horse had been loaded the night before.

The navy officers introduced themselves and asked to be called by their surnames, McKinley and Roberts. Captain Marcus and Joe welcomed the passengers, giving Jimmy special buddy hugs. The three friends were really happy to see each other again.

Freddie was glad to find that he would sleep in a separate cabin from Jimmy. Jimmy was not only happy to have a separate cabin, but was glad to have a cabin to sleep in, at all, remembering the long nights in the cushioned chair where he'd slept coming to Baltimore. It had been comfortable enough for a short trip, but not for two weeks.

Captain Marcus and Joe went to the engine room to get the steam up while the passengers settled themselves for the long trip.

Everyone had been asked to assemble in the lounge as they left Baltimore. Uncle Fred and Aunt Jane sat together, as did the two navy men. Jimmy was seated far away from Freddie, and he planned to keep it that way.

Exactly at eleven o'clock, the steamboat left the harbor, headed down the Chesapeake Bay to the Potomac River, and on toward the Norfolk, Virginia. In Norfolk, they had a night's layover to reload coal for the engine.

Every day onboard was almost the same. Breakfast was served between six-thirty and seven-thirty a.m. A bucket of water was brought to each cabin after supper to be used for the passengers' needs. One towel and one wash cloth were provided for the week.

There was very little to do for entertainment. Some of the passengers played card games or read. The lounge cabinet held several board games, including checkers and a couple of jigsaw puzzles. Several nights, the navy officers played poker. Oh, how Freddie wanted to play, but not with his father watching.

By the fifth day, Freddie was ready to jump ship. He fumed about the smoke from the engines. He fretted about the weather. He fussed with Abner for cooking Southern foods. Everyone was ready to throw him overboard. Aunt Jane and Uncle Fred were so embarrassed by his behavior, they ignored him as much as possible.

On the sixth day, the steamer arrived at the port of Norfolk, Virginia, in the middle of the afternoon.

After docking, Marcus left to check on getting more coal and to take care of the docking business. Jane and Fred disembarked to take short walk before supper. Jimmy took his usual nap in his cabin. McKinley and Roberts went into a port shop to buy tobacco and cigars, and try to find a newspaper. Joe stayed in the engine room to take care of the boat if anything was needed.

Freddie went to the stable as he always did, to check on Barabbas. But today, he took the horse's reins and led him down the gang plank and onto the pier. He mounted Barabbas and disappeared into the crowd of the port city.

By suppertime, all passengers with the exception of Freddie were in their places at the mess table, waiting for supper to be served.

Marcus was upset to see Freddie missing from his place. "His horse is missing, too," Joe said. "I didn't see him leave, but I did notice the empty stable while you were out. I could not locate him on deck."

Uncle Fred and Aunt Jane couldn't believe that Freddie had actually escaped without anyone noticing.

Marcus said, "It's good that the boat is staying the night. Surely, he will return on his own by dark. Otherwise I will have to report him being missing to the police."

Jimmy felt sorry for his uncle and aunt, and told Marcus, "I am beginning to think Freddie is suffering from shell-shock. Several soldiers in prison with me were said to be shell-shocked. They did crazy things for no reason, just like Freddie. Some of them came around after a few weeks, but others went home with the problem. For his family's sake, I hope Freddie isn't suffering from that disorder. It can last a long time."

Abner served supper, and still no Freddie. Aunt Jane was a basket case and couldn't speak without crying. Uncle Fred thought he might have to take her to the port doctor, but she refused, saying she would be all right when Freddie got back to the ship. After supper, Jimmy went to his cabin. He couldn't help the situation, so he figured he would go to bed.

McKinley and Roberts sat with Fred and Jane. Abner made fresh coffee for everyone. Joe sat with Marcus in the engine room, wondering what could be done before morning.

Jane finally went to sleep with her head on Fred's shoulder. At three-thirty in the morning, a shore patrolman came to the boat asking to see the captain. Marcus came from the engine room and followed the lawman ashore.

"Do you have a young passenger by the name of Grimball? He says he has been in the Union Calvary," the patrolman said.

"Yes, sir, we do. What has he done now?" Marcus asked.

"He got into a poker game near the landing pier. The game ended in a fight. Young Grimball is locked up in the port jail until the fine of five dollars is paid," the lawman said.

"Give me a few minutes. His parents are on the ship. I will send his father to you," Marcus said. He hurried back onto the boat and relayed the message to Fred.

Jane awoke hearing Marcus talking to Fred. "What's going on? Did they find Freddie?" she asked.

Fred hesitated, then said, "Yes, dear. Freddie is fine, but he is in the port's jail. He got into a fight over a poker game. I must go bail him out. You stay here with Jimmy. A port jail is no place for a lady."

"Joe, please go and wake Jimmy. Tell him he is needed here to stay with his Aunt Jane. Hurry!" Marcus urged.

Joe ran the length of the boat to Jimmy's cabin. "Jimmy! Jimmy, wake up," he called. "Freddie is in jail. Your uncle needs you to stay with your Aunt Jane while he goes to bail him out."

Jimmy jumped from his cabin bed and followed Joe to the portside where everyone sat. Uncle Fred explained what had happened.

"Sure, I will stay with Aunt Jane. Go quickly. I wonder what they did with his horse?" Jimmy said with concern.

"I didn't ask, but I hope he didn't lose it in the poker game," Uncle Fred said as he turned and hastened toward the lawman.

Aunt Jane began to cry and Jimmy truly didn't know what to do. Trying to comfort his aunt, he said, "Don't cry. Freddie will be all right. He's a tough one. Try to stay calm. Things sometimes sound worse than they really are."

Jane calmed down and sat silently waiting for husband and son to return. Hearing the sound of horses on the dock, Marcus rose from his seat and got to the gangway just as Uncle Fred and Freddie rode Barabbas onto the boat. No one spoke.

Uncle Fred dismounted and pulled Freddie off of his horse. "Go to bed. We'll discuss this in the morning. I'll put Barabbas in the stable."

Jane ran toward them, crying, "Are you hurt, do you need a doctor?"

Freddie shrugged and passed her without looking. Uncle Fred took her in his arms. He murmured softly as she clung to him and they walked to their cabin.

Marcus said to the others, "The show's over, we can all go to bed now. Sleep well. Breakfast at six-thirty!"

Joe and Jimmy walked together to the cabins. "Was he drunk?" Jimmy asked.

"I couldn't tell," Joe answered, "but he sure has a shiner around his right eye."

"Wonder how the other fellow looks." Jimmy chuckled.

When Joe got to his cabin, Jimmy said, "Good night, see you at breakfast."

Climbing into bed, Jimmy felt ashamed of the whole situation. And yet he couldn't help feeling that Freddie had gotten what he deserved. Not that he would ever say that aloud.

Six-thirty came too soon. Jimmy met Uncle Fred in the mess hall. He was alone.

"How is Aunt Jane this morning?" Jimmy asked.

"She didn't feel like facing everyone this morning," his uncle said. "I don't look forward to it, either, but I am here. I appreciate you being here for me. I would like to keep this incident as a family secret when we get to Charleston. I'll tell you the details later."

"Sure, you can count on me. I am glad no one was badly hurt. It could have slowed our travel time. We are about halfway now. Maybe Freddie will do better after this incident," Jimmy said.

Uncle Fred said, "Let's hope so." He patted Jimmy on the back. "Come on, let's eat, I'm hungry!"

Marcus came in and got a cup of coffee. He asked Fred, "Is everything all right this morning?"

"I suppose so. Freddie is still in his cabin. Thank you for your help earlier. I hope he learned a lesson," Fred said with humility in his voice. "His mother and I are trying to understand his actions. I'm sure it has something to do with memories of the war."

"Let's hope it will soon pass," Marcus replied, and headed back to the engine room.

"Hey, Marcus, do you have a telegraph?" Fred called out.

"Sure do."

"I'd like to send a telegram to Heartland to let Charlotte know we are coming to John's Island within the next ten days."

"No problem. Come to the engine room. My office is the glassed-in section," Marcus said.

"I'll follow you," Fred said, then followed Marcus to the office.

"What is the message?" Marcus asked as he got the telegraph ready.

Fred dictated, "James, the family and Jimmy will reach John's Island on the fifteenth. Seabrook Steamboat Landing. Frederick."

"That's it?"

"Yes. Thanks, I didn't want to pile in on the family without them knowing we're coming," Fred said, handing Marcus a gold piece. Then he headed back to the cabin to check on Jane. She may want some coffee. He should probably look in on Freddie, but he'd really rather not this early. He'd check in on him later.

Meanwhile, Freddie lay on his bed, thinking about last night's poker game. His black eye still hurt him enough to remember the fight. He was sure he'd won the game, but the Southern roughneck had cheated and then called Freddie the cheater. That was more than Freddie could take, and he'd begun the fight. Two other men jumped in to help the guy against Freddie, and then things got really rough. That was when someone went for the constable.

Freddie had been arrested for disturbing the peace and hauled off to that sorry jail. The jail had been tiny and unclean, just what he'd expect in the South. Freddie was hungry, but he was not ready to see his father again. His father had been nice enough at the jail earlier, but today Freddie was sure he would feel and hear his father's full wrath, especially when he found out that Freddie had lost all his spending money in the poker game.

Freddie also had to go and check on Barabbas. The horse needed water and food. After washing his face and combing his hair, he slipped quietly out of his cabin and ran down to the stable. Barabbas neighed loudly upon seeing him.

"Yes, it is me. I have come to feed you," he said, patting the horse lovingly. It was a side of Freddie that not many had seen. After feeding and watering Barabbas, he sat down on a stool and talked to his horse as if he were a person. He apologized for his behavior ashore. It might seem strange to anyone that heard him talking, but they would know he loved his horse. His horse had been an important part of Freddie's life throughout the war, his partner in the cavalry.

At noon everyone came to dinner, even Freddie. Everyone was pleasant to one another. Nothing was mentioned about the early morning escapade. Aunt Jane sat by Freddie and was, indeed, happy that he was present.

Captain Marcus announced that the boat would leave promptly the next morning and asked everyone to please be inside the boat at that time. No one was allowed on the deck until they were in the Atlantic Ocean, heading for Charleston.

Everything went smoothly, and for the rest of the journey, Freddie stayed either in his cabin or in the stable with Barabbas. He came to all meals but ate silently. Aunt Jane worried about him, but Uncle Fred said to leave him be. "He will come around when he needs us."

Everyone was ready to get to Charleston. The weather was very warm, and a tropical storm battled the Gulf Stream, causing some rough waters. Aunt Jane felt seasick on two mornings. On August fourteenth, Marcus told the passengers that they had passed the Wilmington Lighthouse during the night. They would soon pass Georgetown harbor, and Charleston would be the next harbor they would come to.

Everyone was excited, even Freddie. For the first time since Norfolk, he talked with his parents at dinnertime. He sounded like his old self, and said he was looking forward to riding Barabbas on the plantation.

Fred said, "If nobody is at the dock, you and I may have to ride to Heartland to get someone to come for your mother and our luggage. Marcus will stay docked until we are all off the steamship. If it is the same dock as before, it is less than two miles from home."

"I am sure Barabbas will like being on the ground again. I know I will," Freddie said.

"Won't we all," Jane said. "Just be prepared for the hot weather Charleston has this time of year."

"That I have never missed," Fred said. "Let's hope for a sea breeze."

The passengers spent most of that day gathering their belongings and packing their bags. It had been a really good trip, all in all. Fred had been impressed by the leadership of Captain Marcus and First Mate Joe. They were good examples for McKinley and Roberts. Fred took time to express his appreciation for their kindness and cooperation on the trip.

The next morning at breakfast, Marcus told everyone that the steamboat had passed Georgetown Harbor at five o'clock that morning. They should get to John's Island by mid-afternoon if the weather stayed sunny.

# CHAPTER 51

# READY FOR JIMMY!

Charlotte was so excited about Jimmy's homecoming, for the next two days she stayed in the kitchen cooking his favorite foods. With Liza being home, Charlotte put her to work baking a cake and making cookies.

James and Henry hit it off right away. Henry was intrigued by the whole plantation system and the beauty of the land. This morning James invited him to ride with him to locate the Seabrook boat landing. He wanted to know exactly where the landing was. He would also tell the person in charge to expect the steamboat tomorrow, Friday.

Big John had prepared the buggy last week and parked it in the barn. James would hitch Lucky and Big John's horse to it to fetch the family.

John's horse had once been a Union Army horse. After the war she'd wandered onto the plantation without a saddle. John had been using her for a workhorse. She was strong and beautiful, and well trained. Big John had named her New Girl. With the barn unfinished, New Girl was stabled in the small barn near the Owens' house. It was good to have a horse again. Heartland's horses had been taken by the Yankees over two years ago. Between Isabella's horse, James' horse, Henry and Liza's horses, and

New Girl, James would now be able to hitch the buggy for travel. Horses were needed on an active plantation.

James and Henry left the plantation and headed east on the island. James took the back paths instead of the roads. He noticed that some of the old paths had been used by the Yankees for camps right in Heartland's back yard. He was again thankful that his plantation had been spared.

Not far into their ride, they came to the burned-out village of Legareville. [27] It had been burned by the Confederate Stono Scouts to prevent it from being used by the Union troops who had retreated to the nearby Kiawah Island during a battle on John's Island. James had friends who'd owned summer homes in the small village. It saddened him to see the charred and burned homes.

He was glad to get back to the road that would lead them to Seabrook Island and the boat landing. The horses were able to ford the causeway onto the island, and he hoped the family buggy would make it through the next day. Following the dirt road to the ocean side of the island, he easily found the dock. He and James dismounted and walked to the landing.

The dock looked small. Henry asked, "How big is the steamship?"

"I have no idea, but I hope this is the place they plan to put in," James said.

From the house next door, a man came toward them. "May I help you?"

James put out his hand to the stranger. "I am James Grimball from Heartland Plantation, and this is my friend, Henry Moore. We are here to check on the steamboat landing. Is this the right place?"

"I am Lawton Hay, the manager of the landing. You are at the right place. How can I help you?"

"My brother and his family are on their way to the island and are scheduled to arrive at the Seabrook Landing tomorrow afternoon. I wanted to make sure this was the right landing so we can meet them."

"Right you are. We are a small landing and have just begun having steamboats use our facilities. I had a telegram from Captain Alexander and he is scheduled to be here tomorrow about midafternoon with the Grimball family."

"Great. I will bring our family buggy to pick them up. What time should I be here?"

"Any time after one o'clock. My son will be here to help them disembark. I hope the trip has been pleasant. There have been some storms out on the ocean. I hope the boat missed them," Mr. Hay said with concern.

"I hope so, too. Thank you, we will be back tomorrow afternoon," James said, mounting Lucky for the ride back to Heartland.

As he mounted, Henry asked, "Do you have many bad storms here? In Boston, we often get storms that they say are remnants of storms from the South."

"From June to November are considered the most likely months for hurricane and tropical storms around Charleston. The last one I remember was in 1860. However, not being home for four years, I really don't know. People were probably concerned more about the war than the weather. How is the weather in Boston?"

"Very cold in the winter, with snowstorms and cold winds. I know it is hot here in the summer, but I do like the Southern winters. The cold up in Boston often yields poor crops at harvest time," Henry said.

"You were a farmer?" James asked.

"I was raised by my grandfather, who was a gentlemen farmer. I liked working with the animals, but am not too fond of planting and harvesting crops. Grandfather died two years ago, so the farm is now mine. My uncle is running things until I decide what I want to do with it. Grandfather sent me to agricultural college for two years. If I go back to school, I will study horses. I've always liked horses, and being in the cavalry gave me a desire to learn more about them."

"That would be a great thing to study. We always need horses. South Carolina 'doesn't have enough of them since Sherman came through. He took all the horses he could find, from Atlanta to Savannah and back to

Charlotte. The only one on Heartland Plantation is a stray that showed up in May. Thankfully, we were also able to buy two mules."

"That's good," Henry said. "But I don't know much about mules. My uncle always had horses."

"Mules are good for heavy work, but not much for riding," James said, then they headed home.

They arrived back to Heartland at dinnertime. Charlotte met them at the back door. "Did you find the right place? When will Jimmy get here?"

James hugged her. "Now, dear, he'll be here tomorrow, so you need not worry anymore. Let's eat, I'm hungry, and I am sure Henry would like dinner, too."

They washed up and went into the dining room.

Lilly was still sitting at the table. "Mr. Henry, where have you been? I looked all over the yard for you this morning. I missed you," she said.

"I've missed you, too, he said, walking to Lilly's chair. "After I have dinner, maybe you and I can take a walk. How about that?"

Lilly squealed, "Goody, goody! I will like that. Hurry and eat."

"I'll do that for you," Henry laughed and sat at the table.

Liza heard Lilly's squeal and came into the room. "What's going on?"

Henry smiled at her. "It is just like you said. Heartland is a wonderful place to be. I can see why you wanted to come home."

"Liza blushed and said, "And you haven't seen the half of it yet. How was your ride?"

"Just great. Lilly wants me to hurry and eat so we can go walking. Would you like to come with us?"

"I'll bring you and Master James your dinner, and if I get through my work by the time you finish, I will go with you," Liza said, grinning as she headed back to the kitchen.

Henry ate dinner while Lilly ran to the kitchen to make sure her mother was going walking with them. Being the only small child at Heartland, she demanded much attention from Henry and Liza. At times Liza became a little worried that Henry would grow tired of Lilly. But today, he was the one who had suggested they go walking. Maybe she was worrying for nothing. At least, she hoped so.

Liza finished her kitchen duties just as Henry came to the door, bringing his empty plate with him. "Do you want more food?" she asked.

"Oh, no. Everything was delicious. I just brought the dishes to be washed before we go on our walk," he said.

She reached for the dishes and quickly washed them and put them in the cupboard.

Charlotte smiled at them and said, "Liza, go now. I'll wash the rest when James is through eating. It's a beautiful day for a walk."

As Liza and Henry followed Lilly out the back door, Charlotte went into the dining room to talk with James.

He greeted her with a smile and gave her a kiss on the cheek. "Everything was delicious. It is so good to eat your cooking again, dearest."

"It is good to cook for you again. I really missed that. It is also easier to cook if you have someone to share the meal with," she said, putting her arms around his neck as she stood behind his chair. "I have a problem I need to talk to you about."

"Sure, my dear. What's going on?" he sweetly asked.

"I hate to bring it up with Jimmy coming home and with Fred's family visiting," she said seriously as a tear rolled down her cheek.

"What is wrong?" James asked, standing and taking Charlotte in his arms. "Tell me!"

"I had Big John kill our last two chickens. That means we will have no eggs while your family is here, and no chickens to eat. I have enough flour and several jars of milk in the well house, but I am afraid we may not have enough food for all our guests. George took Caroline and the girls back to the city on Wednesday, but he will return here sometime tomorrow. I should have asked him to go to the market. What can we do?"

"Why didn't you tell me this before today?" James asked.

"I just couldn't make myself believe it had come to this," she said as more tears fell.

He took her into his arms and let her cry. "I am sure I can get several chickens from Mr. Jenkins' farm, and he always has eggs. I'll ride over there right now to see what he has. I have gold enough to pay, so don't you worry your sweet head about food. We also have the jars of canned vegetables in the cellar. John and Sarah can help you bring up the canned green beans and sauerkraut. There are still several bags of yams, and we have plenty of rice. There are tomatoes and peppers in the garden. We'll be fine." He kissed his wife, saying, "Don't worry, I will go now. You go to our room and rest while I am gone."

She whispered, "Thank you, my love. I knew you would know what to do. Be careful."

She returned to the kitchen and washed his plate and cup. She felt so much better now that her darling James was home, the one she could always depend on.

# CHAPTER 52

# HOME FROM PRISON

On Friday morning, Charlotte was up at six o'clock, having slept very little. All night she'd been thinking about Jimmy coming home after four years in the army. For six months, she had not known if he was dead or alive. She still wondered why he hadn't written during that time, but she would find out soon.

She started a fire in the fireplace and hung the coffee pot to boil. As she reached into the cupboard to get a cup, Liza came down the back stairs.

"Good morning Miss Charlotte. Today is going to be especially great for your family with Jimmy's homecoming. Now you will have both your men home again. Is there anything special I can do to help?" she asked.

"Why yes, Liza. James went to Jenkins' farm yesterday and bought several dozen eggs. See the basket there on the table? Would you go to the cellar and get several glass jars? We can put the eggs in jars and hang them in the wellhouse so they will keep longer."

"That's a great idea. Is there anything else you need from down there?" Liza asked as she turned to the cellar steps.

"That's all for now, thank you," Charlotte replied.

Using the leftover rice from last night's supper, Charlotte added two eggs to the rice and a little sugar. She poured the mixture into a pan and put it in the oven. Rice pudding made a wonderful breakfast with fresh fruit. Big John had brought in some ripe pears last night.

Everyone was soon up and ready for breakfast. It wasn't a feast, but she needed to make the food stretch as far as it could go. One of her greatest fears was hunger.

The rice pudding was a big hit. Jennie even asked for the recipe. Charlotte chuckled and said, "It really is difficult to make."

Jennie had baked her usual pan of biscuits and after the rice pudding and pears she had served them with butter and blueberry jam.

In the words of Lilly, it was all, "Yum, yum, good."

Still sitting at the table, Charlotte said to James, "I am going with you to meet Jimmy."

"You can't dear. The buggy only holds four, and with their baggage, there will be no room for another person. We will be home within an hour of their arrival. You've waited this long. An hour more will pass quickly," James said. "John will drive the buggy and I will follow on my horse to help with their baggage."

Charlotte was disappointed. She had not thought about the lack of buggy space. "I am sorry. I just want to see my son."

"That is understandable. We'll hurry home just for you." James said reassuringly.

After dinner, Big John hitched New Girl to the buggy and followed James and Lucky down the carriage lane to River Road, and onto the path that led to Seabrook Island. It was exactly one o'clock when they arrived at the causeway to the island. James rode Lucky close by the side of the buggy in case any issues should arise with the crossing. Thankfully, they made it over the causeway without problem. But he was still worried about crossing the water with all the passengers and baggage on the return trip.

James and Big John stood on the dock for several minutes. Then Mr. Hay and his son came to greet them.

"We should be seeing the steam from the boat anytime now. I do hope they are on schedule," Mr. Hay said. "A fishing boat is expected at three-thirty."

In the distance, the foghorn of the steamboat sounded.

"It is here," Big John shouted. "I heard the foghorn."

"I heard it, too," James said. "It should be in sight shortly."

Mr. Hay and his son walked to the edge of the dock. "Yes, indeed, it is coming around that savannah and headed this way," he said, stepping back on the platform.

The next thing they saw was the front of the boat coming alongside of the dock. Everyone stood still as the boat anchored and Captain Marcus opened the gate to the deck. He waved at all on shore as he put the gangplanks down for the passengers to disembark.

James saw Fred and Jane walk to the gangway, followed by Jimmy. James wondered if Freddie was with them or not. Then out came Freddie, leading his horse. That was Freddie for you, James thought.

He hurried to welcome Jimmy. They had not seen each other in four years.

He grabbed his son with both arms, hugging him and lifting him off the ground. Neither spoke as the tears fell and they just held one another.

Finally, James said, "Welcome home, son. You are looking good, except you need to put some meat on those bones. Good thing your mother is already preparing to do that."

Fred turned to James and gave him a big hug, too. "How's my little brother? Sure am glad to see you walking. How is your wounded leg?"

"Fine. It has really done well since I've been home. Maybe that was what it needed all along," James said.

Jane took James' hand and said, "It is good to see you. How is Charlotte?"

"Charlotte is well. She wanted to be here to greet you, but the buggy couldn't hold five people. She will be so glad to see all of you. Come, let's be on our way."

Fred said, "I must talk to the captain before we leave. I will be back shortly."

Fred wanted to thank Marcus for the trip. "I am not sure when or how we are going home, but thank you and your staff for a great trip. Sorry about the earlier problem. Glad it didn't last the whole trip. God speed to you and Joe. Till we meet again." He shook Marcus and Joe's hands and quickly left the boat.

At the dock, James was assisting Jane into the buggy. Mr. Hay and his son were lifting the trunk and other baggage to the top of the buggy.

Fred called to Freddie, "Follow the buggy or ride beside Uncle James. It is not very far to Heartland."

Uncle Fred climbed into the back seat next to Jane. Jimmy sat in the front next to Big John. John clicked his teeth, and away went New Girl, headed for home.

Back at Heartland, Charlotte was waiting on the porch. Happy tears rolled down her face as she thought of seeing her Jimmy again. In her morning prayers, she had given thanks for Jimmy's homecoming.

James and Freddie's horses trotted into the yard, stopping at the steps. By the time the buggy got to the steps, Charlotte had made it to the ground. She ran and waved until the buggy stopped.

Jimmy opened the carriage door before the horse had completely stopped. He jumped out, right into his mother's arms. They laughed and they cried. James shed tears right along with them and joined them in a threesome hug.

Fred and Jane took their time getting out of the buggy with Big John's help. Freddie and Barabbas were still riding. They were all happy to be on solid earth again.

Charlotte finally turned from Jimmy, saying to Jane and Fred, "Forgive me for not welcoming you to Heartland, but I know you understand about our boys. You both look wonderful. How was the trip? I know you must be hungry, Sarah has dinner waiting. Make yourself comfortable. This is your home."

"Yes, it is home," Fred said. "But it seems so different. It's too quiet."

James nodded and said, "It took me a while to adjust to the echo of the place. It's the sounds of the slaves that's missing. I especially miss the sounds of the blacksmith's hammer. Big Tom and Sarah have stayed on, and Liza has come back, too. I hope we can figure out a job for her. She is a hard worker."

They all walked up to the porch, and then went inside to the dining room. As they were taking their seats, George came into the room. Fred went to greet his brother.

"I am sorry I wasn't here when you arrived." George said. "I've been here since the barn raising, and had to leave yesterday to take Caroline and the girls home. School starts next week. I also needed to check on the saw mill since I've been away. Thankfully everything is going great. My assistant is doing a good job delivering orders on time. I am doing business on faith because money is scarce, but people must rebuild in order to get back to a normal life."

"I am glad you are here now," Fred said. "Come sit with Jane and me. Most everyone is at the table."

George sat down by Fred, and Jane sat by Charlotte. James and Jimmy sat on the other side of Charlotte.

Jane said to George, "I am sorry I missed seeing Caroline and the girls. I am sure they are no longer little girls but grown-up ladies."

"Yes, they are fourteen and sixteen. So, now I have to worry about their social life," George said.

"I know what you mean," Jane said. "Sometimes I wonder if children ever grow up socially."

When everyone except Freddie was seated, James stood to say grace. Before he prayed, he welcomed the family. "It is wonderful to be together again after five hard years. We are thankful to our Heavenly Father for allowing this day to happen. We are truly blessed to have all our family members home without serious injuries."

Everyone murmured their agreement.

He paused, then in a breaking voice said, "Our Heavenly Father, thank you for family. Thank you for bringing us together again. Bless us and bless this food that has been prepared for us. In Thy holy name we pray. Amen!"

Charlotte and Jane wiped tears from their eyes as James sat down. While the food was being served, Charlotte asked, "Where is Freddie? I thought he was coming with you."

"Heaven only knows. When he is on his horse, he forgets about time and schedules. I'm sorry," Jane apologized.

"That's fine. I just wasn't aware he brought his horse," Charlotte said. "I was too preoccupied with Jimmy's arrival and I missed seeing him. But Heartland is a good place to ride a horse."

Jane said, "Well, it was really the only way he would come along and be happy. He has been strange since returning from the war. He has nothing good to say about the South. Don't be surprised by anything negative he might say or do while we are here. I regret having to warn you, but it is true. Frederick is very upset with him. Let's hope he stays on good behavior during our visit."

"I understand that war does change a man who's been in battle. I see a difference in James. He is much more serious in his thinking and in wanting things completed right away," Charlotte said. "War can leave scars for life, good and bad. I am glad this one is over and our soldiers are back home where they belong."

"You are right. I am happy to have Freddie home, even with his terrible moods," Jane said.

# CHAPTER 53

# A POW?

Charlotte and Jane ate the food before them between their pleasant chatter. The fried chicken and the cornbread dressing with gravy were delicious.

Jane took a second helping of the fried okra and said, "This is one Southern dish we don't often get in Baltimore. I remember eating it often when I visited Grandmother Foster as a child."

"By the way," Charlotte said, "I want to thank you and Fred for taking care of Jimmy while he was in Baltimore. It was a blessing that family was there for him."

"We were glad to have him. He'd been through such a terrible time in prison, we were glad he came to us."

"Prison?" Charlotte wailed, shocked. "My Jimmy was in prison?"

Jimmy heard what Aunt Jane said and mouthed the words, "Not now!"

But it was too late. Charlotte lamented, "He didn't tell me. I didn't know. I thought he must have been badly wounded." She started to cry uncontrollably, and her body began to shake.

James rose from the table and quickly took her in his arms. "What is it my love? What is it?"

Jimmy went to her side, crying, as well. "I am so sorry. I couldn't tell you. It was too horrible to tell and I didn't want you to imagine the worst."

Now Jane was in tears. "Oh, dear. I didn't know you didn't tell your parents," she said, distressed. "I didn't mean to upset everyone."

James was bewildered and asked Jimmy, "Tell us what?"

Jimmy was able to get control of his emotions, and said, "Father, I was in a Union prison camp for five months. That's why I was in Maryland. When I got out of prison, I took a steamboat to Baltimore and found Uncle Fred to get help. That was all I could think to do. I'd barely survived."

Fred said to James, "I should have told Jane that Jimmy had not mentioned his imprisonment to you yet. But now that you both know, we must all pull ourselves together," he said with a voice of authority. "Perhaps we should all go to our rooms and rest. We are tired from the journey. We can discuss this as a family in the morning, after you and Charlotte have had time to be alone with Jimmy."

Charlotte stopped weeping, hugged Jimmy, and said, "I am the one who should apologize, but I went into complete shock hearing the news. I think Fred's idea is a good one. I need to lie down. Please finish your meals, and then Jennie will direct y'all to your individual rooms. Have a good rest, everyone. Goodnight family. I love you, and am glad you are all here at Heartland."

James helped Charlotte from her chair and Jimmy took her other arm. Together the three walked upstairs in silence.

———

At the corral, Freddie was feeding and watering Barabbas. He stood brushing him while the horse ate. Suddenly, a horse and rider trotted swiftly from the carriage lane into the corral. Wondering who else rode horses here, Freddie watched as the rider took off a straw hat. To his surprise, it was a woman. A beautiful young woman with shiny black curly hair.

As she dismounted, she saw Freddie. "Hello there. You must be Jimmy. Welcome to Heartland."

She hitched her horse to a post and walked toward Freddie.

"Wrong. I am Freddie Grimball, Jimmy's cousin. Who are you?" he asked.

"Of course. Jimmy is the blond-haired son, and Freddie's hair is black. Sorry, my mistake," she said, joshing with him.

Staring at this beautiful girl with goggle eyes, he asked. "How do you know me? I am not from here."

"I used to live here, and you used to come and visit. I always wanted to ride horses with you, but they always said I was too young," she said with a laugh.

Freddie was floored. Who was this magnificent, provocative creature? A master horsewoman, and a beauty to behold. Moving closer to her, his heart began to beat faster. He hadn't felt this way since before the war.

"Are you one of Uncle George's daughters?" he asked.

"No kin, just once a neighbor," she said, still toying with him.

"Ah, come on now, tell me who you are!" he said with frustration.

He was now close enough to touch her, and the temptation entered his mind. But he didn't even know her name.

"Enough is enough." he said. "I am going inside for supper as soon as I put Barabbas in the stable. Come with me, but don't keep me guessing. I am not a patient man."

As he turned to get his horse, Isabella decided she had done enough teasing for one day. She didn't want to overdo it. Freddie had at least noticed her, and that had been the general idea.

"My name is Isabella Owens, daughter of Mr. Owens, the overseer here. Don't you remember the seven-year-old little girl who used to follow you and Jimmy around years ago?"

"Isabella? But you were so little! It is hard to believe you are the same person all grown up. Well, we didn't always treat you fairly, so I don't blame your teasing me. Let's get our horses to the barn and go in for supper. I haven't had food since breakfast," Freddie said.

Together they took their horses to the barn and prepared them for the night. Then they walked to the big house, talking about horses. Freddie felt the first sense of elation since being in the South. He was pleased that someone understood that a horse could be a real friend in trying times.

They went into the dining room. Isabella's mother, Jennie, was clearing the table. "Oh, Mother, are we too late for supper? This is Freddie, Jimmy's cousin. He was out riding, and I have just returned from seeing Father. We both would like something to eat, if possible."

"Of course, dear. There are plenty of leftovers. Supper was cut short. I will go to the kitchen and fix you both a plate. Sit down at the table. It won't take long."

Isabella sat down and Freddie sat beside her. He was happy to be allowed the pleasure of her company a little longer, with or without food.

# CHAPTER 54

# A DIFFERENT FREDDIE

Isabella batted her eyelashes at Freddie and asked, "How long is your family staying at Heartland?"

"I really don't know. At first I didn't want to come, but I changed my mind when Father said I could bring Barabbas," Freddie said cheerfully. "I do hope we can ride together soon. You are certainly a great rider. There were men in the cavalry who didn't ride as well as you. And you are a—"

"Don't you dare say anything about my being a woman," Isabella injected intensely. "I am proud to hold that title."

"I think its fine. You are the first lady equestrian I have known," Freddie said seriously. "I just hope I can keep up with you."

That was a real compliment coming from Freddie Grimball, especially to a Southern lady.

Liza and Henry walked into the dining room on their way upstairs and were surprised to see Freddie and Isabella sitting at the table. Recognizing Freddie by his dark hair Liza said, "Hello, you must be Freddie, Master Fred's son, right? You and Isabella are no longer the children I used to chase out of the cookie jar years ago. It is good to see you both." Turning to Henry, she said, "This is my friend Henry Moore from Boston. This is his first visit to a plantation."

Henry shook Freddie's hand and nodded to Isabella. "I noticed you riding your horse yesterday. You handle yourself extremely well in the saddle. Been riding long?"

"Since I was twelve. I love it," Isabella replied. "Do you do much riding?"

"Well, if you call being in the United States Cavalry riding, I suppose I have done a good bit for the past four years."

Freddie found himself wanting Henry to go away. Isabella was giving him too much attention, but he was intrigued by this Yankee Bostonian and said, "You were in the U.S. Cavalry? So was I, discharged in May. What brings you South?"

"I fought in Charleston and liked the city, so I decided to return to check it out. I find Charleston an interesting place, with the exception of the humid weather."

With mixed emotions about a colored Yankee being in the South, Freddie said, "You will have to go riding with me while I am here."

"Great. I'd love to," Henry said, then, turning to Liza, asked her, "Do you ride?"

Somewhat embarrassed, Liza said, "Not well. I never had the chance to learn properly."

"We will have to do something about that. You rode well on Sugar on the way home."

Just then, Jennie came from the kitchen bringing Freddie and Isabella's supper. She apologized for taking so long. "Everything was cold, so I warmed the food for you. Enjoy!"

Liza said, "It is good to see you both. Go ahead and eat while it is hot. Henry must check on the horses while I check on my daughter. She is on the porch playing with the baby kittens. It is her bedtime. Good night. See you tomorrow."

Henry said, "Nice to meet both of you. Have a good night's rest."

Liza took Henry's hand as they walked to the porch to find Lilly. To their surprise, Lilly was curled up in the porch swing, fast asleep.

Henry picked her up. "I'll take her to your room, and then check on the horses."

Jennie lingered in the dining room to ask Isabella how her father was feeling.

"He is doing so well the nurse is talking about him coming home. Master James said we can move back to the overseer's place anytime. With Liza here, she can do your chores until Father is up and better."

"That is great. We can go to the overseer's house in the morning and do the cleaning it needs and get a bed ready for your father. I know he is tired of being in the hospital," Jennie said. Then she turned to Freddie. "Pardon my manners. I didn't mean to ignore you, but I did need to ask Isabella about her father's condition. It is good to have you and your family back at Heartland. It's been a long time since the family has been together. I hope you enjoy your visit."

Freddie grinned thinking, *I will enjoy being with your daughter.*

"Thanks for the supper," he said aloud.

Isabella stood up from the table. "I look forward to riding with you, but now I must say good night." She walked to the door, paused and, turning back, she blew him a kiss and waved.

Freddie couldn't believe his eyes. She'd blown him a kiss! Would his heart ever slow again? Wow, she was some woman. He needed to go to his room, but all he could do was to stare at the door and relive the moment.

# CHAPTER 55

# JIMMY'S STORY

Jimmy followed his parents into their room on the balcony porch and sat down on the bed. James and Charlotte sat on a small love-seat together. No one spoke for a long while.

James finally cleared his throat and asked, "Jimmy, when did you become a prisoner?"

Jimmy said, "It was October 29, 1864, after the Battle of Boydton, near Petersburg.[28] It was a Confederate victory, and as my regiment celebrated, a Yankee soldier pointed a bayonet at me while another grabbed my rifle and pushed me from the crowd. My cry for help could not be heard over the merriment. If I'd run, I would have been shot. Another soldier was taken the same way. We were led to a steamboat dock and spent the first night sleeping on the ground. The next morning, with nothing to eat, we traveled overnight to the Union Army's Point Lookout Prison in Maryland, near the Chesapeake Bay. I was there until April 10, 1865."

James said, "Son, you don't have to tell us the whole story now, only what you want to tell us."

Charlotte asked sadly, "Why didn't you write?"

Jimmy hung his head. "First of all, I had no paper or pencils, and conditions were so horrible I just didn't want you to know what I was going through. I couldn't write anything good about the place, so I didn't write at all. I'm sorry to have made you worry so."

Charlotte tried not to weep, but she couldn't stop the tears.

James said, "Mother, I think Jimmy has talked enough for one evening. Let's all go to bed. He's had a long trip getting here. What do you think, Jimmy?"

"I think you are right, Father. A good night's sleep will help us all." Jimmy said, getting up from the bed. "I love you both. It is great to be home. Thanks for everything." He hugged his parents and left the room quickly.

"I messed up big time," Charlotte said between sobs. "I don't want him to talk about the prison unless he wants to. He seemed a little hesitant. I think we should let him be, and if he wants to tell us about prison life, he will."

"I think so, too," James agreed. "Many of the soldiers who escaped prison camps came to the field hospital. Very few ever talked about their lives in prison. All we knew was that they had been prisoners. You are right. After tonight, we will not ask questions about his imprisonment unless he brings up the subject."

"It will be hard for me to hold my tongue, but I know it is best," she agreed. "Let's go to bed. I am exhausted. Things may be less stressful in the morning." Leaning over to James, she gave him a kiss on the cheek. "I love you, James. Thanks for being here for me."

James returned the kiss. "And thank you for being here for me. We need each other to get through this situation. He's our only son."

Everyone was on time for breakfast the next morning, even Freddie. He excitedly hastened to the empty chair beside Isabella. "Did you sleep well?"

"Yes, thank you. How about yourself?" she asked, giving Freddie a flit of her eyelashes.

"What are you doing this morning?" he asked.

"Mother and I are going to the overseer's house to get things ready for Father to come home. If we get everything done, I will ride to the hospital to see that all the paperwork for his discharge is completed." Isabella smiled. "What are your plans?

Just then, Isabella's mother came in from the kitchen and interrupted them. "I talked to Master James this morning. He said that he and Big John plan to go and fetch your father in the morning. It will be easier for them to transport him home in the buggy. You and I are to have everything ready for his arrival. Miss Charlotte made arrangements for Liza to take over my kitchen duties for now."

"Perfect," Isabella said.

Jennie turned and went back into the kitchen.

Freddie sat patiently while Isabella talked to her mother, then said, "Maybe we can ride together soon."

"I will see you at supper," she said, giving him a coy smile as she left the table. "Save a chair for me."

This time she didn't look back.

# CHAPTER 56

# THE FENWICK PAPERS

After the scene at the table last night, Jimmy was in no hurry to get up early. He lay in the bed, thinking of his time in prison. What should he tell his parents about his experience? He didn't want to think about it. He knew he should have written, but if he had, his mother would just have worried more. It was a bad scene either way you looked at it.

All he wanted to do was to forget the horrible situation and go on with his life. He knew one thing, he would not go back to military school. With his father's war experience, Jimmy didn't think he would insist he continue. He could go to the College of Charleston...but what should he study? He'd studied the Bible while in prison, and thought about going to a theology seminary. Mother would like that. At this point, he had no idea what he was going to do with his life. Though, he did know that he wanted to live in town, not on this plantation.

Hearing the grandfather clock strike nine, he knew he must get up before someone came to see if he was alive.

Downstairs, George and James sat in the library discussing the fire insurance. Yesterday, George had gone by the insurance company in the city to check on the fire insurance on the barn. Yes, the policy was current and the claim would be paid. However, there was confusion and some difficulty about when it would be paid. The money had been under Union control for the past four years, and was being replaced slowly by the Northern partners. Heartland's account was on a waiting list, and no one knew when the money would arrive.

"This is distressing news. We need to complete the barn as soon as possible," James said with a frown. "It's all right to house the horses outside for now, but they will need stables by winter. The small stable at the Owens place can hold only two horses. We will need at least six in the new barn."

After breakfast, Fred walked down the lane that led to the idle rice fields. He wasn't ready to talk business about Heartland. In fact, the whole situation scared him. He felt he needed to walk awhile before discussing financial business. Suddenly, he realized how far he had walked, and found himself where the rice fields had been. The place looked lonely without plants growing. He stood for a few minutes remembering all the many years he had watched the slaves harvesting rice this time of year. The words of the slave songs resounded in his ears. The laughter of the children playing in the creek rippled through the air.

"Ole times, they're not forgotten."

He sat down on the stump of an oak tree and pondered. Heartland Plantation was a different place, a lonelier place, and the slaves were missed. They had very much been the life of plantation. Things would never be the same. He kicked a few stones along the path for old time's sake, and turned back toward the big house.

He climbed the front steps, counting them as he'd often done as a child. Fourteen steps, still there, one thing that had not changed. At the top, he found Henry sitting in one of the big rocking chairs on the porch.

"This is some life," Henry said as he greeted Fred. "Rocking in a big ol' rocking chair on a beautiful day in late summer. It is a great view from here, but I miss the changing colors of the leaves. Do oaks change colors?"

"I am afraid not. They stay green all winter. That's a beauty of them. Other trees around here do change autumn colors, but sometimes it is

Thanksgiving before the colors come," Fred said. "We have very colorful trees in Baltimore this time of the year."

"So does Boston. That is something I will miss in the South," Henry said.

"Why are you sitting all alone here on the porch?" Fred asked.

"Your brothers are talking business in the library, and the ladies are still in the kitchen," Henry replied. "I've been riding with Freddie. He is an excellent horseman, really loves the sport. Do you ride with him?"

"Used to, but haven't since he came home. I should, but since the war ended, I've spent most of my time trying to keep my law practice above water. Hopefully with the railroad companies getting things back together, I'll soon have some new contracts. If not, and with no income from Heartland, times may get very hard for my family. That is one reason I came to Charleston to find out what we can do with the land here. I should go and meet with James and George. Maybe they have come up with some ideas. You went to agricultural college. Come on in with me, maybe you can give us some suggestions."

Fred walked inside and Henry followed. They found James and George in the library. Jimmy and Freddie were seated in the back of the room, but were not together. Their fathers seemed to be in a heavy discussion about the lack of money.

As Fred took a seat, Henry said, "Your brother invited me to join you, but I do not wish to interfere in your family business. Say so, and I will be glad to leave."

James said, "You are indeed welcome. Maybe someone outside the family can give us helpful advice. Family ties often make it difficult when important decisions are to be made."

"Thank you. I will sit and listen for now," Henry said, seating himself at the end of the table.

As Fred picked up his briefcase and opened it, a folder of papers fell onto the floor. He said, "These old documents were stored with my legal papers from the plantation. I don't know where they came from. They must have been some of father's old papers. They contain a map of the Fenwick race-track and information about the stud farm that he owned on John's Island in the seventeen-hundreds. Interesting reading, but hardly relevant today."

James and George shrugged. "No clue what they are."

"May I see those papers?" Henry asked. "I learned something about early horse racing in the South while at college. I'd like to read them."

"Be our guest," the brothers said in unison, and Fred handed the papers to Henry.

Henry silently began to read.

> *The John's Island Stud Farm was one of the first horse farms in America. John Fenwick helped found the South Carolina Jockey Club in 1758 and built a three-and-a-half-mile race track for thorough-breds on the Fenwick plantation, Johns Island, South Carolina.* [29]

As Henry read those lines, the gears in his mind began to turn. Was there still a horse farm or racetrack on the island now? South Carolina needed horses. James and his brothers had the land. Freddie, Isabella and Henry all had experience with horses, and Henry had money to invest. This would be too good to be true. Did he dare mention all this to the Grimball brothers?

He needed to think it over and talk to Liza to see what she thought of the idea.

Folding the paper back with the others, he quietly left the library and walked to the dining room where Liza was wiping the table. "You are just the person I need to talk to," he said.

"Glad to see you, too." Liza said. "Let me finish cleaning this table and I'll be through until the supper bell rings. What is so urgent?"

"Master Fred gave me some interesting papers I wish to share with you. But they can wait. Where is Lilly?"

"At breakfast, Lilly started talking about riding horses, which brought to mind Jimmy's old rocking horse. Miss Charlotte took her up to the attic to see if they could find it. I think it may have been thrown out years ago, but Charlotte insisted. Seems like everyone talking about horses lately," Liza said with a laugh.

"Yes, it seems that way. I also want to talk about horses. Come, let's sit on the back porch. I have something to show you."

Henry headed for the porch. Liza dried her hands on a towel and followed.

He pulled her onto the swing and put the papers in her hands. "I want you to look at these papers Master Fred gave me to read," Henry said.

All Liza saw was a hand-drawn picture of an oval shape with a starting and finishing point and some stables outlined. A caption was written under it, "Johns Island's Racetrack." Below the picture were numbers that seemed to represent the size of the track and stables.

"What is this?" Liza asked, puzzled, "I've never heard of this place."

"No, my dear, it doesn't exist anymore. Back in the seventeen-hundreds, the Fenwick family of Johns' Island had one of the first horse farms and racetracks in America. From all I've learned, it was a great success. Since the war ended, South Carolina has been in dire need of horses. Heartland Plantation desperately needs a new way to produce income for the Grimballs. I could put up some money to help get the business started. I think the idea could work well here."

Liza's mouth dropped open in surprise. She didn't know what to say.

"We could breed horses, sell horses, and race horses. Master James could be in charge, and it could be a big business in the future," Henry said with excitement and extra enthusiasm. "Freddie might like to be a part of the business, too. He certainly would be an excellent trainer."

"Whoa," Liza said. "You are getting ahead of yourself now. It all sounds great, but these men don't know you. And frankly, you can't expect them to be overly excited about a colored Yankee Bostonian's get-rich-quick idea. I love you and believe in you, but you must go slowly in introducing an idea like that to the Grimballs."

Henry expression fell as if Liza had shot him. He sat quietly for a short time. Liza was afraid he would surely leave her now, but she knew what she was saying to be the truth.

Finally, he took her hands and smiled. "You are right. One reason I love you is because you're so smart, and have so much common sense. I will talk to Master James about the idea, but I'll let him talk to his brothers. I do think it could work."

"It's a splendid idea, and I am sure it would grow into a big business in time," Liza said calmly, but her heart was anything but calm.

Heavens! Henry had said he loved her! And she had confessed her love for him, too!

She was beside herself with happiness.

She reached for his hand, but he took her into his arms, kissing her over and over. Nothing was said until they heard the door to the dining room open and footsteps coming toward the porch.

"Gotta go." Henry hurriedly left by the back stairs.

"Liza," Isabella called. "Is it too late for dinner?"

"Not at all. I am here." Liza answered, coming in from the porch. "Is Freddie with you? He missed dinner," she said.

"No, I haven't seen him today," Isabella replied. "I worked at the house with Mother until noon, then rode to the hospital and arranged for Master James to bring my father home tomorrow. I didn't see Freddie's horse in the stable. He probably got himself lost on the island."

Liza suddenly heard Lilly and Miss Charlotte coming down the stairs from the attic. There were several thumps and a bumps as they dragged the old rocking horse down with them.

"Look Mommy! Miss Charlotte found a horse for me! See?" Lilly said, letting the horse land at the foot of the stairs. Lilly climbed up and began rocking back and forth.

"Well, aren't you something?" Liza said. "Mr. Henry will be proud of you."

"Where is Mr. Henry? I want to show him," Lilly said, and began rocking again.

"He just left. You can show him your horse later," Liza said.

In the kitchen, Isabella told Miss Charlotte, "Tell Master James that everything is arranged for Father's release from the hospital. He must be out by one o'clock tomorrow."

"I am glad that he can come home. Is he able to use his arms at all?" Charlotte asked.

"Oh, yes. However, he can't lift things yet. His muscles are not as strong as they once were, but in time, they should get stronger," Isabella said. "The doctors also said his bones are much more fragile after such a severe burn, so he needs to be careful not to break an arm."

"How awful. Well, I think I will go on to my room for a while before we eat," Miss Charlotte said. "Liza, after Isabella finishes eating, would you mind closing up the kitchen? Sarah will be in charge of supper."

"But Master Freddie hasn't eaten yet." Liza added, "Should I wait for him?"

"Oh, dear, I hope he is all right. Where could he be?" Charlotte murmured.

"He's riding his horse like me." Lilly said, continuing to ride the wooden horse.

Isabella laughed and said, "I bet he is. Since I am staying with Mother tonight at the house, I will check the stable to see if his horse is there. Thanks for the dinner, Liza."

"Oh!" said Charlotte. "I just remembered. Today Freddie and Jimmy were meeting with their fathers and Uncle George to discuss Heartland's financial problems. The boys each own fifty acres. They may all still be in the library."

Liza took Isabella's dishes into the kitchen and washed them, then she called to Lilly, "Get off the horse, it is your nap time."

Miss Charlotte turned to Lilly. "Come, dear, you heard your mother. You can walk up the stairs with me. Say goodbye to your horse."

Lilly reluctantly got off the horse, gave it a kiss, took Miss Charlotte's hand, and walked to the stairs. "I will call my horse Rocky."

"That is a good name for the horse. Especially this one," Charlotte said gleefully. "Such a sweet child."

"See you later, Isabella," Liza said, trying to hurry her on her way.

Liza didn't want to stay in the kitchen. She would leave Freddie's dinner in the warming oven. If he was still in the library, he could get it himself. At the moment, her love life was more important than Freddie's food. She wanted to find Henry.

Liza left the kitchen in haste. On the balcony porch, she found Henry sitting in a rocker talking to Lilly and Miss Charlotte. Lilly was telling him all about her horse, Rocky. Henry was as patient as always, even though he really wanted to run his idea for Heartland past Miss Charlotte, who he'd found to have a good, level head.

Seeing Liza coming to the porch, he told Lilly, "Here comes your mother. I think it is your nap time. I will see your horse later."

Turning to Miss Charlotte, he said, "Mrs. Grimball, I really would like to speak with you for few minutes. It's about plans for Heartland."

"Let me take Lilly to her room for Liza, then we can talk," Charlotte said.

Liza rushed to his chair, beaming. "We need to talk," she said.

"Yes, we need to talk, but first I want to talk to Miss Charlotte. I'd like to share my suggestion with her," Henry said seriously. "You and I will talk later. I am not putting you off, please understand. This is very important for our future."

Tears welled in Liza's eyes. "I do understand, but your words on the back porch were so sudden, I need to understand your true motive for saying them. I've waited so long."

He leaned forward and kissed her just as Miss Charlotte came across the porch.

"Well, it does look like we have something to talk about, you two love birds," Charlotte said with a lilt of laughter.

Liza blushed and said, "You may call us love birds, but that's not what Henry wants to talk about. He has an excellent suggestion to share with Master James concerning Heartland. Talk to him while I go and put Lilly down for her nap." She kissed him on the forehead and hastened to her room.

"Please sit," Henry said, as he took the papers from the faded folder. "Miss Charlotte, what do you know about the Fenwick plantation here on the island?"

Taken by surprise, Charlotte said, "It is the oldest plantation house left on the island. It was once a horse farm, and I think it had a racetrack. I remember hearing my grandfather refer to it from time to time. The Fenwicks are somehow related to the Grimball's way back. Why do you ask?" Charlotte asked, very curious.

Holding the documents in his hand, he said, "Fred gave me these to read. They were written in the last century. They tell the story of the success of the Fenwick horse farm and racetrack. They contain a map of the racetrack and details of its measurements. I believe Heartland has enough land for a horse farm, and probably for a small racetrack, too. Since the war, South Carolina has a great need for horses. We already have four thoroughbred horses between us. I would be willing to invest a sum of money to get it started. What do you think about the idea?"

Her eyes widened. "That is a lot to think about. It sounds like a big enterprise. We do have the land and a few horses. How can I be of help?" she asked.

He continued without hesitation, "I'd like you to talk to James about this idea, and maybe he can present it to his brothers. I know you haven't known me long, but I am sincere about the investment. I was able to save most of my army pay, and had always plan to invest it in something worthwhile. Take these papers to James and give him the idea. Whatever the plans for Heartland end up being, I would like to invest."

Charlotte was impressed with the plan, and with Henry. She would, indeed, talk to James. The idea sounded great to her, but she wasn't exactly a businesswoman.

Taking the documents from Henry, she stood. "This has been very enlightening. Thank you, Mr. Moore, for your interest. Your idea is amazing. I will say adieu now, and will see you at supper."

"Thank you, Miss Charlotte," Henry quietly said.

Henry sat for several minutes thinking excitedly about the possibility of the horse farm. But that would have to wait. For now, he must get back to his own life. He stood and walked rapidly to Liza's room. Knocking softly, he said, "Liza, are you there?"

She quickly opened the door. "I thought you might come. I hoped you would."

He took her into his arms. "I am sorry I left you, but our future is at stake. I do want us to stay together here at Heartland."

"We'll find a way," she said, and sank into his arms.

She could scarcely believe this was happening. This wonderful man loved her? She had never known love like this. Even the touch of his fingers gave her a thrill, and his lips were like fire whenever they touched her. If this was true love, she wanted it to last forever.

At that moment, Lilly turned over in bed and murmured, "Mr. Henry, are you going to be my papa?"

Liza and Henry laughed.

"Little peepers have big ears," Henry said. "With that, I must say goodbye for now, my sweet. Lilly needs her nap. I think I will go riding to clear my thoughts about our future. See you at supper. You too, Lilly."

# CHAPTER 57

# THE FAMILY MEETING

Freddie and Jimmy had been the first two family members to arrive in the library that morning, followed by Fred, George, and James. However, Freddie didn't stay long.

Fred, acting as the attorney for Heartland Plantation, opened the meeting by discussing the fire insurance information. He went over the expense reports, and each brother gave an account of how much they had received from the proceeds at Heartland during the past five years.

Typically, Freddie would have found the report very dull. However, today he couldn't focus, thinking now he was surely about to be found out about the loss of his fifty acres.

When Fred was done with his financial reports, he said," Now with that part of the business out of the way, we need to check that the acreage is in fact divided equally."

Having already located the three brothers' six hundred acres on the maps he'd brought and matched them with their own records, he turned to Freddie. "Son, what about you? Where's your deed?"

"I don't have it," Freddie replied sheepishly.

"What do you mean, you don't have it? Did you leave it in your room?" Fred asked.

"I don't have the deed anymore," Freddie said.

"I can't believe you would leave it in Baltimore. How many times did I tell you to pack it with your things before you left? But all you could think about was that horse of yours. Well, I guess I could telegraph Walter to mail it to us," Fred said.

Freddie jumped up and shouted, "No, I don't have it anymore! I lost it! I wagered it as a bet in a poker game and I lost it. Okay?"

Everyone in the room went silent, afraid to speak.

Fred finally realized what he had just heard, and his face turned a shade of red. "I'm sorry, did I hear you wrong? Did you say you lost your inheritance...in a poker game? This isn't the time for jokes, Freddie."

Seeing Freddie's expression of misery, Fred understood he wasn't joking. He exploded, "You idiot! I know you hate the South, and I have tried to deal with you and your negative attitude, but this...this is just idiotic! I can't believe I've raised a moron for a son!"

Everyone continued to sit in silence as Fred ranted on and on, seemingly forever.

Finally he ended it by declaring, "You know what boy? Get out. Just get out! I don't know what to do with you. Right now I don't even want to look at you."

Freddie got up and quickly headed for the door.

His Father managed to throw one more insult on his way out. "You don't have a prayer, son!"

George and James exchanged glances. Fred grabbed his briefcase, stuffed his papers into it, and shouted, "This meeting is adjourned!"

The afternoon passed quickly. The supper bell rang at six o'clock sharp, with no sign of Freddie.

After checking for him in the barn, Isabella mounted Tilly. Where could he be? She quickly settled Tilly and went to the front porch. In a whisper, she called, "Freddie? Freddie, where are you?"

"I am here," he answered from behind the fence of the rose garden. "I've been waiting for you. I need to talk, and I don't want to see my parents."

Walking over to the fence, she asked, "Are you all right?"

"Yes. I wanted to catch you before you went inside," Freddie said, and came to meet her. "I am all right, but my Father is furious with me. Back in Baltimore, I gambled and lost my inheritance, fifty acres of Heartland, in a poker game. But the thing is, I lost it to Jimmy, so it's not so bad. Before Jimmy could come to my defense, though, Father blasted me to kingdom come and told me to get out. I ran to Barabbas, and have been riding since."

"You must be hungry and tired," Isabella said calmly. "Come on in the house. I am sure Mother has something left from dinner. You can stay here tonight. There is a bed in the room off the kitchen."

She opened the front door. Her mother was asleep in a chair with a dust mop in her hand. Isabella shushed Freddie as he tiptoed in after her. With a finger to her mouth, she led the way to the kitchen. He fell into a chair. Poor fellow, she thought, as she found four hoe cakes in the warming oven and put them on a plate for his supper.

"This is all that is left over, but it's better than nothing." She put the coffee pot over the small fire to heat. In the pie safe there were two sweet potato pies, her father's favorite. She cut a piece for Freddie. Her mother would understand.

Putting the pie beside his plate, she sat next to him. "I am so sorry. Is there anything I can do for you?"

"Just stay with me. I don't know what to do to fix this," Freddie said pitifully. "I need to talk to Jimmy. He won the fifty acres from me, but it was my idea to bet them. Father will blame me for it all."

"Why didn't Jimmy speak up this morning?" Isabella asked.

"Father didn't give him a chance, and I left. I don't know what happened after that. I would hope Jimmy explained, but I haven't been very nice to him since he came to Baltimore. I've been so down on the South since the war, this may be a chance for payback from Jimmy," Freddie said despondently.

"I don't believe Jimmy would stoop so low," Isabella said. "He seems like a nice person. He will come around and do the right thing."

"Even if he does, I don't know if I can ever forgive Father for the chastisement he gave me this morning. The enemy never called me such names, even in the height of war," Freddie said, looking defrocked.

"We will find Jimmy and find out what happened after you left the library. James, George, and your father are going to the hospital to bring my father home. With them all gone, we can get things straightened out with Jimmy."

"You are so kind to me, even knowing I am a Yankee. I have not given Southerners a chance. You are the most beautiful thing that has ever come my way, and you are from the South."

He leaned over and kissed her. "You are the only thing keeping me here after what happened. I almost left to go home earlier today."

"Don't go," she said. "I want you to be a part of my world forever. I have had a crush on you since I was a little girl watching you ride your horse. Please don't leave. Give yourself time to think this through."

"You are right. I will get some sleep now. Tomorrow, with your help, I will face my problem with Father. Goodnight, my beautiful Isabella." He kissed her again and walked to the small bedroom off the kitchen. As he closed the door, he threw her another kiss.

Isabella was pleased to know that Freddie cared for her, but she was afraid of what he might do if he was completely rejected by his father. She reached into the pie safe and cut a piece of sweet potato pie for herself.

Things were happening way too fast.

# CHAPTER 58

# FRED'S GUILT

Up at the big house, Jane and Fred were still awake. Jane had cried most of the afternoon after hearing what happened in the library. Fred had truly lost it when he found out Freddie had bet his inheritance in a card game. Jane had done her best to comfort him and calm him down. Fred's health may have been endangered. Men suffered from strokes and heart attacks from such stressful situations.

James came up to the room with a bottle of spirits that the family kept for medicinal purposes. He measured out a dose for Jane to give him. In a few minutes, Fred fell asleep.

"Thank you James. I didn't know what to do. I have never seen him this way. He's been worried about Freddie, and also worried about our finances. This was just the last straw. Freddie is still not home. Where can he be?"

"Go to bed, Jane. Sleep while Fred sleeps. Freddie can take care of himself. He will not go too far. Things will look different in the morning, you'll see. I will go to my room, but if you need me in the night, just call. I will come. Get some sleep, now!"

When James walked into the balcony room, Charlotte was in bed, still reading the old papers about Fenwick Hall. She could see this happening at Heartland. Especially with Henry's investment added to the brothers' account. Could they trust this colored Yankee with their land?

Before, they had always trusted their colored slaves to work the land properly. They had trusted them to take care of the children, and to cook the food they ate. Why not trust a man who can help redeem the plantation? What did it matter if he was colored?

As James came in the door, she sat up and asked, "Is everything all right? I haven't talk to you all day."

He sat down on the bed and said, "It's been one of the hardest days of my life."

"What happened?" she asked in surprise. "Tell me what is going on."

James let his head fall back on his pillow. He began with Fred's deplorable action toward Freddie, and ended with his giving Fred a dose of spirits to calm him down and prevent a stroke.

"My dearest, you must be distraught. How is Jane, and where is Freddie?" she asked.

"Jane is hanging on, but she is terrified for Freddie. He and his horse have been gone since before noon. Frederick really did show himself today. I was afraid he would have a heart attack, it was unreal. I am beginning to think Fred is overstressed from worry. He said he has received no income from his law practice since the war ended. That's almost six months. With Freddie's problems added, it may be too much for him to handle," James said worriedly.

"I can see why your day was awful. I suppose you haven't come up with a plan for Heartland, either, have you?" she said.

"Not by a long shot. We are all worried about the future. If we only had a little more money to work with..." he lamented.

She decided to take the leap.

"I may be able to help. Liza's friend, Henry, came up to talk to me about an idea he has for the future of Heartland," she said, handing him the Fenwick papers.

"Why do you have grandfather's old papers? They date back a hundred years," James said with a frown.

Charlotte held up a hand. "Just hear me out. When Fenwick had land, he started a horse farm, and when he had horses, he built a race track. Heartland has land. South Carolina needs horses. We have a fine horseman visiting who wants to invest a sum of his money into a business in order to stay in the South. So...that new business could be Heartland."

"Did Henry really say that?" James asked in wonder.

"Indeed, he did. He told me he was able to save most of his army pay, and now he wants to invest it and stay in the South."

"Do you trust him?" James asked.

"Yes, I do. He looks into your eyes when he talks. I believe he is sincere. He is a kind gentleman. He adores Liza and Lilly."

"It sounds too good to be true," James said, and leaned in to kiss Charlotte.

"Talk to him tomorrow. It might be the answer we are looking for."

"Goodnight, my sweet Charlotte. You have made my day end with new hope for tomorrow."

# CHAPTER 59

# OWENS COMES HOME

James was up early knowing he and George must be in the city before noon to bring Mr. Owens home from the hospital. Charlotte was still asleep. Yesterday had been such a hard day for them both, he let her sleep.

Before going downstairs, he walked to Fred and Jane's room. He tapped lightly on the door. There was no answer. He waited and tapped a second time. Still no response. He figured that was good news and proceeded to the kitchen. Liza was making coffee.

"Good morning, Master James. Breakfast is about ready. What else can I get for you? Sarah made her honey biscuits, and there is strawberry jam."

"I'll have a couple of biscuits with jam. Have you seen George this morning?" he asked.

"He said to tell you to meet him at the barn. Big John already has the buggy ready," she reported. "No hurry."

She poured coffee and waited for him to eat the biscuits and jam before asking, "Is Master Fred going with you?"

"No, not that I know of. He wasn't feeling well last night, so it's best for him to stay and rest." James wiped his mouth and said, "Thank you, Liza. I must not keep George waiting. Have a good day. See you later."

It was a beautiful morning. An early autumn breeze swept through the trees as James passed the creek near the barn. He was glad to finally have some cooler weather. It had been a very hot summer. Big John stood by the buggy, ready for the trip to the city.

George was already seated in the back. "I brought along two pillows that Owens might rest his arms on the trip home. The last time I visited, his arms were on pillows. By the way, how is Fred this morning?" George asked.

"I really don't know. I knocked on the door twice with no response. I really think he lost it yesterday in the library. I feel sorry for Freddie. Frederick was very unkind to him, regardless of what he had done. I hope Freddie will be able to forgive his father. It was a bad scene," James ventured.

Big John got into the buggy, ready to set off for Charleston. "It is a nice morning to be travelling. It shouldn't take us too long to get to the hospital. Is there anyplace else you want to go while in the city?" John asked.

James said, "I need to check Heartland's mail while we are near the Exchange Building. It shouldn't take long. Maybe we should stop there before going to the hospital so as not to disturb Owens once we pick him up."

"Yes, sur, Master James. We will go der first," Big John replied.

The post office was no problem to get to after leaving the ferry landing. John stopped the buggy at the front steps of the building and James climbed out.

"Be back shortly." He entered the Exchange Building [30] and walked to the post office in the back hall.

Postmaster Jesse Hart greeted James. "It is good to see you home and doing well. How can I help you?"

"I am here to check Heartland's mail. I've been so busy since I came home, haven't been to town," James said, opening his post office box and finding two letters. "Good that I thought of checking the mail this morning."

Jesse Hart, nosy as usually, wanted to know if he had received any news in the mail.

James responded that he had not read his mail, but it was good to see him. "My whole family is at Heartland this week and all are well. I am on the way to the hospital to bring Owens home. How is your family?" James asked, anxious to leave.

"Fine. They are—"

Turning back to Jesse, James interrupted, "Do you know where the Gibbs are living since their house was destroyed? Charlotte wanted me to find out."

"Their mail has been forwarded to their summer home in Flat Rock, North Carolina," Jesse replied. "I haven't heard if they are planning to rebuild."

"Thank you. Charlotte will be glad to know they are safe," James said.

He hurried back to the waiting buggy. Big John turned and drove up Broad Street, headed to the City Hospital near the Ashley River.

James looked down at his mail. The return address on one letter was Timothy Bowman, Route 2, Bowman, South Carolina. The second letter's return address was Daniel Jeffcoat, RFD # 3 Orangeburg, South Carolina.

"Any mail for me?" asked George. "I seldom get any at the sawmill."

"Afraid not. Only two letters for me. One is from the young soldier I rode with on the train home. The second is from a soldier I never met. His house was destroyed by the Yankees and I met his surviving slave boy. Together we put grave markers on his parents' graves," James said, hoping both soldiers were doing well despite the hardships. "We are too near the hospital to open the letters now. I will wait until we return to Heartland. I hope they both bring good news."

Big John turned the buggy into the hospital's lane and stopped at the door that read DISCHARGE. James and George stepped from the buggy and went inside.

Mr. Owens was sitting in a wheelchair, ready to go home. George and James thanked the nurses and, without much ado, wheeled the chair out the door with a happy Owens talking non-stop. George picked up Owens in his strong arms and put him into the back seat of the buggy, placing the pillows where needed.

"Whoa. It is nice to be out in the sunshine," Owens said. "Whose fine horses are pulling the buggy?"

"They are ours," James said. "The one on the right is Lucky, the horse I rode home from Columbia. He was found alone near the train tracks in North Carolina. The railroad had no place to keep him, so they gave him to me. He's a splendid horse, a thoroughbred. The horse on the left is New Girl. She wondered onto our land back in May, a stray army horse. US is tattooed in her ear. Big John has taken her over to care for and use in his work."

"Great, two horses! We sure needed them at Heartland. By the way, where is Master Fred? I thought he was visiting from Baltimore," Owens inquired.

"Oh, he is here, but wasn't feeling too well this morning. We let him sleep," James said. "Tell us, how do your arms feel?"

Owens smiled and said, "The bad pain has gone away. They hurt some at night, but the pain is much less than at first. I am just thankful I am alive and still have my arms and hands. There were many amputees in the ward."

"I understand," James said, "The doctors wanted to amputate my leg after I was wounded, but after much persuasion, they let it heal on its own. Thank God.

Back at the caretaker's house, Freddie, hearing voices from the kitchen, sat up on the bed wondering where he was. Coming completely awake, he remembered yesterday and his being with Isabella last night. He stood up and went to the basin and washed his face. Looking into a mirror on the wall, he shuddered. Did he really look that haggard? He ran his fingers through his hair, giving it some control, and quickly straightened the bed covers and walked to the kitchen door. He knocked softly.

Isabella's voice said, "Come in, breakfast is about ready."

"Everything smells so good," he said. "I am starving."

"Good morning to you, too. How about some hot biscuits with straw-berry jam?"

"Sounds wonderful," he said, taking a chair at the table. "Do you have coffee?" he asked.

"Sure. I should have offered you coffee first of all. When I finish frying this sausage, the bread will be ready. The jam is on the table. Make your-self at home," she said.

Freddie sounded better this morning, and he even smiled at her as she handed him the coffee.

"When do you expect your father home?" he asked.

"Master George and Master James left right after breakfast. They should be back by early afternoon unless they go somewhere else in the city."

Jennie came into the kitchen and added, "I don't think your father went with them. I was feeding the cats and didn't see him in the buggy when they passed by."

"I wouldn't show my face, either," muttered Freddie. "I must find Jimmy this morning." Turning to Isabella, he asked, "Do you have time to go to the big house to help me locate him? It can be a big place when looking for someone."

She turned and asked if her mother would need help before dinner.

"I don't think so. We cleaned everything yesterday. I will cook up a pot of vegetable soup and some cornbread for dinner to have ready when the brothers get here with your father. Go on with Freddie. I will be fine. While you are at the big house, check on your father, Freddie. Yesterday Charlotte said he wasn't feeling well," Jennie said.

His father should feel sick, Freddie thought, finishing his breakfast. "Ready, Isabella?" he said. "I will get the horses and bring them to the front porch. They will be ready whenever you can leave." Then Freddie thanked them for breakfast and the place to sleep, and left for the stable.

Isabella freshened her hair and picked up her straw hat. "I'll check back with you around noon" she told her mother, bouncing out of the front door.

Jennie grinned. Her daughter was fascinated by the young man. He would be leaving soon, but Jennie was glad she was enjoying herself, for a change. She had given up her social life to be with them since the fire.

Back in town, Big John drove the buggy out of the hospital's lot and asked, "Are we ready to go to the ferry landing?"

James said, "Since we are so close to the Battery, let's ride past South Bay. I haven't seen my house there since I've been home. Charlotte says it is fine, but I would like to see for myself."

"It looks good, but I don't blame you for wanting to see it," George replied.

"I haven't seen it in years," Owens said. "I am glad it survived. Looking around the town, many were not so lucky."

"Miss Charlotte said that Elijah, one of the former slaves, is taking care of the place and sleeps there at night," Big John said.

"That's correct," James said. "He works days on a Yankee ship that is anchored in the harbor. He was always a helpful young man."

"He is lucky to have a job," George said. "I've hired several freed slaves at the saw mill, but there are still so many without work."

"True," said James. "Money is scarce with the end of the Confederate dollar. Not everyone can afford to hire workers."

"I's know, Master James, and t'ank you," Big John said appreciatively.

"I am so glad you wanted to stay with us. You and your family are a real asset at Heartland."

Big John stopped the buggy at 10 South Bay and James stepped out. He was amazed at how good the house appeared. It looked almost as it had twenty-five years ago when it was new.

"I will take a quick walk around the outside. I won't go inside today, but I am proud to see it looking so great. We have been blessed," James said happily.

"I am glad to see it survived the war," Owens agreed.

As James walked around the house, he suddenly remembered that he and Charlotte would have their twenty-fifth wedding anniversary the next month. Maybe they could celebrate it before Frederick's family returned to Baltimore. He'd talk to Charlotte about that.

Not wanting to leave Owens and the others in the hot buggy for long, he hurried back to the front of the house, satisfied that his home was safe and secure. He was ready to go back to Heartland.

At the plantation, Isabella and Freddie rode their horses up to the big house and tied them to the hitching post near the barn.

"I will go into the house and see if I can find Jimmy," she told him. "Why don't you walk around back and the barn and see if anyone knows his whereabouts. I'll meet you back here in an hour."

"Thanks. I don't want to run into my Father before I find Jimmy," Freddie said with a sigh of relief.

She ran up the steps and into the house, and stopped at the dining room door. Fred, Jane, Jimmy, and Charlotte were still at the breakfast table, engaged in a deep conversation about Heartland's future.

"Good morning, Isabella. Would you like some breakfast?" Charlotte asked.

"No, thank you, I've already eaten. I just came by to see if Jimmy felt like going horseback riding. The exercise would be good for him. How about it, Jimmy?" Isabella asked with a pleading smile.

"I have been thinking about riding. I used to love riding at Heartland. What do you think, Uncle Fred? Do you think the doctor would say yes?" Jimmy asked.

Fred was taken back by the question. "Why, I'd say he would approve riding as being good exercise," Fred answered.

"I think the sunshine would be good for you, son, Charlotte agreed. "You are a little pale. Thank you, Isabella, for thinking of Jimmy."

Jimmy rose from the table and went with Isabella. "See ya'll later!"

He was thrilled to get away from Uncle Fred. He despised what his uncle had done to Freddie. His cousin may not be his best friend, but never in his life had he experienced a browbeating so demeaning. Thinking about yesterday's meeting made Jimmy sick to his stomach. He hoped Isabella knew where Freddie had gone.

Jimmy followed her down to the barn.

Freddie was waiting there. "Say, you are a hard man to find," Freddie said.

"I'd say you are the one hard to find. Where have you been? Your parents are worried about you, and so am I," Jimmy said. "I am sorry about what happened yesterday. I would have spoken up if you had stayed. I didn't know what to do when you left so quickly. I still don't know the best way to handle the problem. Even if I clear the matter up, what your father did was wretched."

"I don't have the answer, either. I don't know if I can forgive Father for his words. But he should be told that you now own those acres. I know I did wrong in persuading you to wager the land, but at the time, I was sure I would win. But either way, it still would be a problem," Freddie said sorrowfully.

Isabella stood quietly, letting the cousins talk. Then she said to Freddie, "I think the best thing to do is to tell Master James and Master George the truth, and let them talk to your father. That should soften the conflict between the two of you. He should realize that all is not lost to Heartland."

"How did a pretty lady like you get so smart?" Freddie asked seriously. "The truth is always the best way to go. It doesn't hurt quite as much. Big John will be bringing my father home from the hospital around noon, and James and George will be with him. After we get Father settled, it will be a good time to talk to them. We can only hope for the best."

"That is a great plan," Jimmy said. "We've got to do it."

"You are right," Freddie said. "At least Father will not be there."

Isabella said, "With that settled, let's go riding. I saddled Sugar for you, Jimmy. She is a gentle horse. You will like riding her."

As the three mounted their horses, Freddie smiled at Jimmy and said, "I am glad to see you are still able to ride. I know you missed it."

"Right you are cousin, let's go!" Jimmy shouted, leaving the barn in a hurry.

# CHAPTER 60

# NEW PLANS FOR HEARTLAND?

Big John made good time getting to the ferry landing from South Bay. James was greatly disturbed by the damage he saw to the houses and churches below Broad Street. He thought of Richmond and Charleston. Both beautiful cities, both received much damage and destruction from the Union Army. He was thankful to still had two houses fit for living. He silently breathed a prayer of thanksgiving as the buggy entered the ferry boat. His family had been truly blessed.

As the buggy made it to Johns Island, James thought about Henry's plan for Heartland. It was an excellent idea, and with Henry's money, it could work. He mentioned the plan to George earlier but with Big John there, didn't have time for discussion. This afternoon, after Owens gets settled, he would find Fred and the three of them could discuss the idea before supper.

James hoped Fred would be in a better mood than he was last night. He should not object to the plans. After all, we have no other plan for the land, and that means we will have no income unless we come up with a means to execute an income.

It was mid-afternoon when the buggy rolled off Johns Island's ferry, four miles from Heartland. James was lost in thought and did not notice Owens was asleep. When he did notice Owens, he thought, "Poor fellow, I surely hope he's going to be able to work again. Taking care of horses is no easy job."

"Hey George," James called, "have you given Henry's plan any thought?"

"I think it might work. It is the only plan thus far that makes sense. I'm all for it," George replied.

"That makes two of us, one more brother to go," James said hopefully.

As Big John turned into the carriage lane, Owens awoke from sleep. "Sorry I went to sleep. I usually take a nap this time of day. It is good to be home to Heartland."

John stopped the horses in the yard of the overseer's house. George again picked Owens up and carried him into the house. Jennie was as excited as Owens was to have him home. They talked at the same time. George put Owens into the bed that was set up in the living room. Jennie took the pillows and placed them gently under Owens' bandaged arms. She reached and kissed him on the forehead and said kindly, "Welcome home my husband, I am glad you are better."

Jennie turned to James and George, "I know you missed dinner. I have a big pot of vegetable soup and cornbread and potato pie. Please eat."

They were hungry and it would have been impolite to say no. Big John had already driven off in the buggy leaving the brothers to enjoy home-made soup, cornbread and sweet potato pie with sweet tea to drink.

As Jennie refilled James' glass with more tea, the front door opened and in walked Jimmy, Freddie, and Isabella.

"Just in time to eat. Come sit. I have soup and cornbread. It should hold you until supper," Jennie said. "How was your ride?"

"It was wonderful. It did me good. I had forgotten how much I enjoyed horseback riding," Jimmy said, with fervor. "I feel so free when I am riding. Thanks for the invitation."

"Freddie, how are you today? Sorry about the episode on yesterday. Have you talked to your father?" James asked.

"No, but I need to talk to you and Uncle George," Freddie said seriously. "As you heard yesterday, I lost my fifty acres at Heartland in a poker game, but what Father didn't let me say was that I lost them to Jimmy Grimball while he was in Baltimore. I was the one who persuaded Jimmy to put up his acres as I thought I would surely win the poker game. I know it was wrong in even thinking about what I did, but all is not lost, the land is still in the family. I was trying to show that I was smarter than a Southerner."

Jimmy interrupted Freddie, "I was as wrong as Freddie. I knew it was wrong to gamble the land, but I wanted to show Freddie that I was the better poker player. A little cousin rivalry, I reckoned. I am truly sorry. I will give the deed to your father, if is all right with Freddie. In that way, the acres will still be in the Grimball name. What do you say, Freddie?"

A surprised Freddie blinked. How generous this was of Jimmy. Knowing it was the best way to handle the situation, he answered, "I approve." But deep down, he wished he would have come out innocent.

James was stunned to hear that Jimmy had been in the poker game, but he tried to understand Freddie's attitude toward the South and the rivalry of the cousins. He said in his business voice, "Jimmy, thank you for your honesty. I accept your apology. However, the whole family must discuss your offer to return the acreage to Heartland. Thank you, Freddie. I'm sorry you went through that chastisement yesterday. The whole situation will be discussed with your father and we hope that Frederick will understand and forgive the situation. Thanks for coming clean to the family. May this be a lesson to us all. Honesty is always the best policy."

"Anyone for sweet potato pie?" Isabella asked, getting up from the table to get the pies.

"Bring them on," Freddie said. "They're the best." Everyone seemed to relax, and laughter returned to the room.

After eating the delicious pie, James stood and said, "Thank you, Jennie. The dinner was wonderful, but I must get to the big house and talk to Frederick before supper. If you need help with Owens, please send for me."

"I will go with James," George said, following his brother to the living room. "Thanks for everything. We will say goodbye to Owens as we leave."

However, they left without speaking to Owens, as he was fast asleep.

"Thank you for dinner, Mrs. Owens," Jimmy said, turning to Freddie. "Things went well with Father, don't you think?"

"For you," Freddie said, disgruntled. "I still have to face my father. Your generosity was a little overly done, don't you think?"

"It was the only thing to do. I don't plan to stay on the plantation for the rest of my life," Jimmy said. "Didn't you want your deed back?"

"No, not really. I guess I didn't want it all to be in Southern hands. It is hard to accept an entire Southern lifestyle overnight," Freddie said. "But I am trying. I hope my father will accept our explanation."

"He will have to. There is no other way to explain the situation. And he's already done all the damage he can do to you," Jimmy added.

"That's right," Isabella said. "He should be feeling guilty. Let's all show up at supper. Master James will have talked to him by then. Are you with me?"

"I know I must face him sooner or later, but it isn't going to be easy," Freddie said worriedly. "I'll be there."

"Me, too," Jimmy said. "I will see you then."

# CHAPTER 61

# AUNT JANE

Jane was sitting on the porch pretending to read. She was miserable and wanted to go home. Frederick's actions yesterday had upset her terribly, and even today he wouldn't stop belittling their son. Sure, Freddie made a terrible mistake, but he wasn't the monster Fred was making him out to be. She wanted to see Freddie to let him know that she did not agree with his father's opinion. She was afraid of losing Freddie. His being away at war had been bad enough. She wanted him home. She wanted to cry, but would not in public. Maybe she should talk to Charlotte. She might know where Fred stayed last night.

Just then, James and George came up the front steps. "Good afternoon, Jane," James said merrily.

And with that, Jane burst into tears.

"Are you all right, Jane?" James asked in alarm.

"I am so upset with Frederick. He won't stop blasting Freddie. I know Freddie did wrong, but Fred is like a crazy man and won't let go of it. Could you talk to him? I can't take much more of his behavior."

"Yes, I will talk to him. I have come from seeing Freddie and Jimmy, and things are not as bad as they seemed yesterday. Do you know where Fred is now?"

"He's in our room. I had to get away from him," Jane said, drying her eyes.

Turning to George, James said, "Come with me to talk to Fred. This can't go on. If he hears the whole story, maybe he'll cool off."

"Of course."

"By the way, Jane," James said. "Do you know when Fred is planning to go home to Baltimore? Charlotte and my twenty-fifth anniversary is September fourth, and I would like to celebrate it while you are here. Today is August twenty-fourth, and I was thinking the weekend of the twenty-ninth would be a good time. I need to know your schedule before I ask Liza to bake a cake."

"I really do not know. I think we will leave by September first if he can get reservations. I am glad we came, but I am ready to go home," Jane admitted.

Leaving the porch, James followed George up the balcony stairs and knocked on Fred's bedroom door. "Who's there?" Fred called out.

"It is George and me," James answered. "We need to talk to you."

"The door is open, come in," Fred said. "I was hoping you both would come. I have some great news. How is Owens? I am sorry I missed going with you to the hospital. Jane didn't wake me up in time. How was the trip to the city?"

James and George went into the room. James was shocked. Fred was dressed in his Sunday best, sitting in a chair, writing a letter.

"Well brother, you look lot healthier than you did the last time I saw you. Are you feeling better?" James asked.

"It's good seeing you look so well," George said. "Sorry you didn't get to go with us today. Everything went fine. Owens is back home with Jennie and Isabella to take care of him. He seems to be his old self again, although his burns are still bandaged. He says they are doing well. Only time will tell."

"Sit down," Fred said. "We need to talk."

"Right you are, we do need to talk," James said as he and George sat down on the bed.

James felt he had to be sure Fred was really all right. "Have you talked to Freddie since our meeting in the library?" he asked.

Fred hung his head and said, "No, I have not seen him, but I must find him and apologize for my reaction about the land. I really showed myself. I can't believe I said all that to my only son. I am sure he is upset with me, and I only hope he can forgive me for being such a polecat."

"More like a donkey's behind," George said, laughing.

Watch your mouth, brother. You are at Heartland," James joshed, then said to Fred, "We think you should hear the whole story from Freddie. You may find that you lost your temper too soon. We still have the land."

"We still have the land? What do you mean?" Fred asked, bewildered.

"Talk to Freddie, you owe him that. His story should take care of the whole mess, except for his feelings," James added.

"Where is he?" Fred asked. "I need to see him as soon as possible."

"He stayed at Owens' place last night. He didn't want to see you. He will be at supper tonight. You can see him then," George said.

"We also wanted to talk to you about plans for Heartland. Liza's friend, Henry, has come up with a suggestion for the use of Heartland's acres."

Fred said, "Yes, I know all about the horse farm and the racetrack. I had a visitor this afternoon. Miss Charlotte came to see me when she saw Jane alone on the porch pretending to be reading but really crying. Charlotte gave me a good talking to, but then she told me all about the Yankee's plan. I think the plan is very good, and I think we should do it."

"Hooray!" said James and George. "And that makes three!"

"I am already working on the organization of the farm. As the estate lawyer, much of the planning is up to me. That is what I was working on when you came in. Since my family will be leaving for Baltimore on the first of September, we have much to do this week," Fred said.

"We will get to work tomorrow. I'll tell Henry about our decision to-night," James said excitedly. "Are you definitely going home the first of September?"

"Yes, if I can get reservations on a steamship. I telegraphed Captain Marcus two days ago about reservations from Charleston to Baltimore. He is to let me know when we can get a boat home. Sam sent me a letter saying I have had requests from two different railroad companies, both wanting my law services for their new contracts. I was getting nervous about my law business, but things are looking up. If we can get things settled here at Heartland, I can go home a much happier man."

"Things seem to be coming together at last," James said. "I feel good about the horse farm, and I am impressed by Henry's business sense. He is a well-educated man. He says he wants to hire a tutor to school Lilly and possibly John's sons. That's another asset for the plantation."

"The way I see it," said Fred, "I should draw up legal papers to present to the county with tentative plans for Heartland, giving the three of us as owners, and adding Henry Moore as financial advisor and partner with us. How does that sound?"

"Sounds good to me, but I am no lawyer," George replied.

"You know best," James said. "We trust you to do it the legal way."

"This is getting exciting. A horse farm at Heartland!" George exclaimed.

"The first thing we need to do is to complete the inside of the barn. We can use wood from the slave cottages to build the stables," James suggested. "Maybe leave two of the cabins to be used for housing, if it's ever needed. I'll get busy. See you at supper. I am happy that we all agree on this project."

CHAPTER 62

# CLEARING THE AIR

James flopped down on the bed. He reached in his pocket and took out the two letters that came for him earlier. He reread the return address on the first one. Timothy Bowman, Route 2, Bowman, South Carolina. His mind went back to the burned plantation he'd encountered on his way home from Orangeburg, and thought of Noah, the young slave boy who had survived the fire and was waiting there until the son of the plantation got home from the war. This letter must be from that son who made it home. James carefully opened the letter and read it silently.

> *Greetings from Timothy Bowman. Jr.,*
>
> *Having returned from the war and finding the homestead and my parents gone, I was pleased to find Noah still here protecting the land. I read your letter and I wish to thank you for your help in identifying the graves on the plantation and for the kindness you showed to Noah while you were here. I do not know what I will do in the future as I cannot stay here without a dwelling place. Noah and I are staying with a relative in the small town of Bowman. He is carving every day, thanks to your encouragement. We go into town*

on Saturdays. He is making enough to pay his way. Now I just need to decide how to proceed myself.

 Again, I say thank you for your help. May God bless and keep you safe.

*Sincerely,*

*Timothy Bowman, Jr.*

*Bowman, South Carolina.*

James put the letter back into the envelope and opened the second one. It was from the young soldier that rode on the train with him all the way from Richmond, Daniel Jeffcoat.

*Greetings to my friend James Grimball,*

 *I thank God for every memory of you. Here's hoping you found everything well at Heartland. Father and I have been very busy since I arrived home. It is hard to get materials to sell in the store. The neighbors have helped us by bringing their own vegetables to sell. We have planted a winter garden to help out. I have some good news! Emily and I are to be married at Thanksgiving. We will travel to Charleston for a short honeymoon. Abigail will come with us to help drive the buggy. We would like to visit you and your family, if possible. I hope Jimmy is now home. I would like Abigail to meet him.*

 *Please write if it is possible for us to visit you the day after Thanksgiving.*

*Sincerely,*

*Daniel L. Jeffcoat*

*Orangeburg, South Carolina*

James stood up and put the letters in the dresser drawer. He would share them with Charlotte later. He needed to talk to Liza about his plans for the anniversary party. With Fred leaving next week, they would celebrate on the weekend. He combed his hair and straightened his clothes, then left to find Liza. He would go to the kitchen and see if this was her day to prepare supper.

As he walked into the kitchen, Lilly said, "Master James, I want you to meet my horse, Rocky."

"Glad to meet you, Rocky. You are a good-looking horse and have a fast rider," James said, thrilling Lilly. "Is your mother here?"

"She is in the dining room. She will be right back," Lilly said.

"How fast can Rocky go?"

Lilly began rocking very fast on the wooden horse as Liza came into the kitchen. Without seeing Master James, she said, "Whoa, Lilly, slow down. Rocky is going too fast."

James said, "It's my fault. I asked her how fast Rocky could go."

"Sorry, Master James, I didn't see you there. Rocky can go too fast," Liza exclaimed, laughing. "But he is good at keeping his rider busy."

"I came to see you, Liza. September fourth will be Charlotte and my twenty-fifth wedding anniversary. I want to celebrate it while Fred is here. Do you think you could take time to bake a cake that would serve all of us? There will be at least eighteen, or more if I can get word to Elijah."

"Sure, I can do it. It will be fun. I remember when you two got married. I was about Lilly's age. Big Momma was so proud of the cake she baked and decorated," Liza said smiling. "What else will we need to cook?"

"Cake and lemonade are all we need, and maybe some mint candies and nuts. I'll send Big John to the market for supplies. We can make coffee for those who don't want lemonade," James said. "There may be a bottle of homemade strawberry wine in the cellar, but Charlotte would say no to the alcohol. I do not want to make her unhappy. It's been a great twenty-five years together."

"I am so excited," Liza said, though secretly wishing it were her own wedding. "Supper is ready. Master James, could you ring the supper bell while I get the food from the oven?"

"Would love to, it's been a long time since I rang it," he said, heading out the back door to the bell post and taking hold of the rope. He'd miss hearing this bell when they went home to the city. But the bell was the least of his worries. He was just happy they'd made it these many years, especially with his being wounded in the war. God is good.

Hearing the bell toll, folks headed to the dining room. Isabella had a hard time getting Freddie to come. He didn't want to see his father, but she persuaded him he couldn't put it off any longer. She would go with him and would bring supper back for her parents while he talked to his father.

In the dining room, Jane saw Freddie before he saw her, and she ran over to hug him. "Darling, are you all right?" she gushed to Freddie.

"Yes, I am fine. I just needed to be away from Father. After all, I am twenty-one, you know," he replied.

Isabella realized that Freddie was embarrassed and hurriedly found them seats away from Jane. However, his father came over and took the chair next to Freddie, saying, "Son, I need to talk to you."

"I think you've talked enough. After supper I will tell you what really happened in the poker game, but not while we are eating. Go and sit with Mother for now."

Fred was taken aback by the way Freddie spoke to him. He knew he'd said some harsh things to Freddie in the library, but he didn't think they were that horrid. "Fine. I'll see you after supper. I will sit with your mother to eat," Fred said, somewhat flustered.

"Freddie, if bitterness is going to be your way to get through this," Isabella chided, "it will only linger, my dear. Why not try kindness? It will go a much longer way."

"I am sorry, Isabella, but you didn't hear what he called me and the way he spoke to me. I have a hard time looking at his face," Freddie said, agitated.

Right then, James stood to speak. "Before we say grace this evening, I want to say that George and I brought Owens home from the hospital today. He and Jennie are back in their home. His burns are healing well. Go by to see him if you'd like. I'm sure he will appreciate visitors." James prayed and supper was served.

Isabella ate without talking. She would take her parents supper, but she wanted to be back here for Freddie if he needed her. Excusing herself from the table, she said, "I am taking supper to Mother and Father, I'll be back as soon as I can."

"Do hurry. I need you," Freddie said with a tiny grin.

Everyone left the dining room with the exception of James, Freddie, Jane, and Fred.

James walked to Freddie and asked quietly, "Would you like me to stay?"

"Yes, sir, I think it will help Father be more acceptable of the truth," Freddie answered. "But I do not want Mother to stay."

Jane walked up and asked, "Where should I sit?"

"Mother, I do not want you to stay for this business talk. Go be with Aunt Charlotte. I saw her go into the kitchen," Freddie said.

"But I need to hear what you did at the poker game," she said.

"Jane, please," Fred said, "leave us men alone. Freddie will be talking business. I will tell you all about it later."

"Very well. But do be kind to him. He is our only son," she warned. "Freddie, I will be in the kitchen if you need me."

"Where is George?" Fred asked. "He wasn't at supper."

"The last I talked to him, he was going to his room to take a nap. He probably overslept," James said. "Shall we wait for him?"

"Where is he staying since he left Owens house?" Fred asked.

"Here. In the guest room on the first floor," James said. "Jimmy, will you go up and see if he is awake? He should be at this meeting. We'll wait until you get back."

Everyone sat quietly at the table. Freddie looked at the floor. He could not look at his father. He thought, of all times to oversleep. But then maybe Isabella would get back by the time George and Jimmy came down.

The dining room door opened and in hurried George followed by Jimmy. "Yes, he overslept," Jimmy said, laughing.

"Sorry, brothers. I am here now. You may begin, Freddie."

"I am here to tell my side of losing the fifty acres in a poker game. It was after Jimmy came to Baltimore. Thinking of something to do to entertain him, I asked if he played cards. When he said yes, I decided I would outshine him as poker player. We each bet two dollars on the first game. Jimmy won. I didn't like that a Southerner beat me, so I suggested that we bet something of value, like our fifty acres at Heartland. Jimmy didn't want to do it at first, but with my persuading, he agreed to accept the offer. Jimmy won again. I couldn't renege on the bet, so I gave him the land deed. I knew what I did was wrong, but I thought since the land was still in the family, we need not worry. Mark it up to immaturity," Freddie said evenly. He stopped talking and looked at his father.

Fred didn't know how to respond, and turned to Jimmy. "Why didn't you back up his story in the library?" he asked.

"I would have, but you were too busy fuming at Freddie, and then he left in such a hurry, I couldn't get a word in edgewise. I am sorry I didn't speak up at that time. I will give Freddie's acres back to Heartland, along with my own fifty acres, to stop this confusion and hurt," Jimmy said seriously.

Fred could not believe what he was hearing. Jimmy was the winner of the poker game. The land was still owned by the Grimball family. He felt dumbstruck. He also realized how harsh he was on Freddie, without giving him time to defend himself. No wonder he'd left the library. He hid his face in his hands. Would Freddie ever forgive him?

He could think of nothing to say. He felt like running away himself.

James spoke up. "Our sons made a grave mistake, but I hope they learned from the experience. As family members and still owners of all seven hundred acres of Heartland, I suggest that we accept his apology and move on."

"I second it," George agreed. "How about you, Fred?"

Fred murmured, "I agree. And I am sorry how I reacted, especially to my own son." He reached for Freddie and hugged him, saying over and over, "Forgive me, Freddie. I am truly sorry."

Everyone sat quietly, feeling the pain of father and son. The door to the dining room opened and everyone looked up as Isabella walked swiftly across the room to the table where Freddie sat.

"I am sorry it took me so long. Father wanted to get out of bed and sit in his favorite chair. I knew Mother couldn't manage by herself, so I helped lift him from the bed to his chair. He is heavier than he looks," Isabella lamented.

Freddie stood up, looking a little harried from the situation. "Are you all through with me?" he asked the group. "May I be excused?"

"Yes, to both questions," James said. "Thank you for clearing up the matter of the land. You may go now. We can talk later if we have more questions."

Freddie walked to Isabella's side and reached for her hand. "Is there enough sunlight left for a short horse ride?"

"There is about an hour of sunshine left, long enough," Isabella agreed.

Hand in hand they walked out of the dining room.

"That went very well," James said. "We will have to make the change in ownership legal."

"What do you mean legal? The land is still Freddie's, isn't it?" Fred questioned.

"No, it now belongs to us, the brothers. Jimmy gave it back to us. He won it fair and square. One must honor his wishes."

"But the way it happened, it doesn't have to be honored, does it?" Fred asked.

"Yes, Fred, it does. You of all people should know that. They were not children when it was done. They knew right from wrong, and it was a fair game which Freddie lost. Understand?"

"Forget my questions. You are right. It is hard for me to understand how Freddie could have done this," Fred said with a groan.

"Same about Jimmy. I never thought he would accept a bet like that. I guess we don't know our sons as well as we thought we did," James said.

"At least they came clean," George said cheerfully. "You both have done a great job in raising them. They are no longer children, but men who have minds of their own. You've done your part, let's pray they have learned a lesson from this situation. Don't beat yourselves up for this one misstep. I am proud to call both of you brother. Let's try to put this behind us and look forward to the new plans for Heartland."

"I still don't know how Freddie feels about the chastisement I gave him," Fred said, thinking only of himself.

James ignored Fred's comment and said, "We've talked enough for one evening. I say we leave our new business to another time. I am going to bed. Goodnight." Without another word, he left the dining room and headed to the balcony stairs.

Jimmy and George followed.

Fred sat at the table, alone in his bewilderment of where he stood in the midst of this family of Grimballs. Would he ever understand Freddie?

## CHAPTER 63

# ANNIVERSARY AND WEDDING PLANS

When James reached his room, he found Henry waiting for him. "Master James, sir, may I have a few minutes of your time before you retire?"

"Sure, come on in. Charlotte is still in the kitchen. I think she and Liza are busily making plans for the anniversary party," James said. "Please sit. How can I help you, my friend?"

"Planning a party for your anniversary is a wonderful idea. I hope someday I can celebrate such a long and happy marriage. You know I want to marry Liza soon. I think it would be a good idea to be married before I begin working for Heartland."

"Do you think so?"

"Yes. With the end of slavery, I suspect there may be problems in your hiring a colored Yankee as an equestrian for Heartland. If I am married to a local woman, it may help to smooth the way. I dearly love Liza and Lilly, and we want to be a family as soon as possible. I wanted to ask you and Miss Charlotte if Liza and I could get married at your anniversary party. After the celebration, of course. Everyone will already be here, and we would be honored to have the same date as our anniversary day," Henry said with anticipation.

"That is a splendid idea, Henry. I must run this by Charlotte, but knowing how she loves Liza and that child, I am sure she will agree. Your thinking about the future of Heartland is impressive. I will be proud to have you working here," James said. "I will talk to Charlotte tonight and let you know our decision at breakfast."

"Thank you, Master James," Henry said. "See you then."

In the kitchen, Charlotte and Liza finished the dishes, chatting about the plans for the anniversary party.

"What will I wear?" Charlotte asked. "My clothes are all so old, and I don't have time to sew a new dress."

"You do own a few dresses that still look nice. I had several pretty dresses that Mrs. Willard made for me, but I couldn't bring them." Liza said sadly.

"You know, when I took Lilly to the attic I saw James' mother's cedar chest. I didn't take time to open it because Lilly was asking so many questions about all the old stuff up there. In the morning, we can go up and see if any of Mother Grimball's clothes are still there. She was a fancy dresser and often sent to England for new outfits. She was a petite lady, about your size, Liza. Maybe we can find a nice dress," Charlotte said and beamed.

"Oh, yes! It will be fun anyway," Liza said cheerfully. "I did bring a church dress that Mrs. Willard made for Lilly. I think she can still wear it. Mrs. Willard was a great seamstress. The hem may need to be let out, but I can handle that. I am so happy."

"Happy about what?" Henry asked, standing in the kitchen door.

"About the anniversary party. It is going to be a great time." Liza beamed and walked to him, taking his hands and pretending to dance.

"Should I practice the waltz?" he asked, taking her in his arms and dancing around the kitchen.

"You two are too cute. So young and in love. It should be your wedding along with our party," Mrs. Charlotte said lovingly.

Henry almost let out the secret plans he'd asked Master James about minutes before. It could wait until morning, but he felt sure the answer would be affirmative.

He whirled Liza around once more and kissed her. "It won't be long until our wedding, I promise."

Fred woke early the next morning. He needed to check the telegraph machine and see if Marcus had replied about reservations. It was good to be at Heartland, but he was anxious to get home and check on his law practice. He certainly would not miss the Charleston weather.

Jane rolled over, still half asleep, and asked, "Is Freddie all right? I didn't see him after your family meeting last night."

"He went off with Isabella. I am afraid they are more serious than we thought. I do hope he doesn't plan to stay here longer than we do," Fred grumbled.

"I don't think we need to worry about that," Jane said. "He hates the South too much."

"Love of a woman can do strange things to a fellow. That's why I moved to Maryland," Fred said with a laugh.

"Aren't you glad you did?" Jane asked.

"I like the weather better there," he said, "and most of the people. But you must admit the folks here are pretty nice to be around, even the former slaves."

"Yes, I have been greatly surprised," Jane admitted. "Sarah, John's wife, has been extremely nice and helpful to me. I thought she wouldn't care for Northerners, although we helped set the slaves free. I feel sorry for her boys, Pug and Ham. There is not much for teenaged boys to do on a former plantation. They should be getting some schooling."

"I really like Henry and Liza. Henry is very intelligent. He plans to hire a tutor for Lilly and will include Sarah's boys."

"This visit to Heartland has been an eye-opener for me. Heartland is a big place undergoing many changes. I hope the new plan for the land is successful. George seems to be the only one of your brothers with a steady income, and he refused to go to college," Jane said.

"I am going to breakfast and then to the plantation's office to check the telegraph. I need to do more research for the layout of the horse farm. If you need me before dinner, I will be in the library," Fred said, sounding like his old self again.

In the kitchen of the Owens' house, Isabella was making breakfast. In the bed in the small parlor, Owens was awake and roaring to be put in his chair. His body had no pain and he was tired of being bedridden. The doctor's orders were that he stay in bed with his arms on pillows for healing. Jennie was afraid that getting him out of bed too often put too much pressure on his arms. It was getting to be a problem.

"Owens, you know it is hard for Isabella and me to lift you from the bed. You will have to wait until one of the men come by to get to your chair," Jennie told him. "Your arms are still too tender to put your weight on them. You must be patient or we will have to hire someone to take care of you."

"I know," groaned Owens, "but staying in bed is getting old. I need to be working to help Master James and the brothers with the plans for the horse farm. It is a great idea for Heartland and for Johns Island."

Isabella listened to her parents as she scrambled eggs. She heard Freddie moving around in the porch room, where he'd stayed again last night. "Breakfast is served," she called in a loud voice, bringing Jennie and Freddie to the table.

Jennie said, "I am glad your father is home, but he thinks he can do the same things he did before the fire. I am so afraid that he is putting too much pressure on his arms. They are not yet strong enough for all his moving around."

Freddie took a cup of coffee and said, "I am sure he is tired of staying in bed. He has always been so active, it must be hard to be still."

"That is true," Isabella agreed. "I have never known a time that he was unable to work outside. At harvest time, he would always carry the largest baskets of rice to the boat."

Jennie poured Owens a second cup of coffee and took it out to him.

"Freddie, what do you think of the new plan for Heartland?" Isabella asked.

"It sounds great to me, a true adventure. Horses and more horses. I'd like to be here to see it grow into a big business," Freddie admitted.

"Why can't you stay? What are your plans in Baltimore?" she asked. "I don't want you to leave."

"Father would throw a hissy fit if I stayed after all I have said against the South," Freddie said with a scowl.

"I want you to stay for my sake. I've told you I want you to always be a part of my life. How can we be together if you are so far away? How do you feel about me?"

"I love you Isabella, but I fear my father's wrath," he said. "I'm afraid he would disown me. I can never please him, and whatever I do is not good enough."

"That's more the reason you should stay here and prove to him that you can make it on your own. I will be here to help you. If you get unhappy, you and Barabbas can always ride on home."

"I have thought about staying. It is a temptation. I am sure Uncle James would give me a job. I would love working with horses."

"We could get married," Isabella said.

"I am not ready for that, and neither are you," he admitted. "We both need to grow up a little more. I should know. I've made too many wrong decisions since I came home from the war. I love you, but am not ready for that responsibility. I hope you understand what I mean, my dear."

"Yes, Freddie. Your mother also thinks you are immature. I would marry you to keep you here, but you are right. I know I need to wait until I am at least eighteen to take a husband. I just hope it will be you," she said. "But I do wish you would think about staying and working with your uncles. You are such a great horseman, you could help the business grow."

"Thanks, my pretty one. I am still thinking about it. It is a temptation to stay."

"Give it some more thought," she said. "The big house will have extra rooms since we moved back to the overseer's cottage."

"I will talk to Father and find out if his feelings are still as negative as they were, then I will make my final decision. If I stay, it will upset Mother more than Father. She still treats me like a five-year-old. It is embarrassing, especially in public," Freddie mused.

"After I finish the dishes, would you like to ride to the beach for a picnic? I made sandwiches for us before breakfast," Isabella said, clearing the table.

"That will be fun. I've wanted to go back to the shore before leaving," he said. "I can put your father into his chair while you finish in here."

"That is thoughtful of you. It will be a great help to Mother," Isabella said, smiling.

Back at the big house, Henry hurried down to breakfast to see what James had to say about the wedding plans. James was already seated with Miss Charlotte having coffee. Seeing Henry hurrying toward him, James smiled.

Breathless from rushing, Henry said, "I didn't sleep well wondering what your answer will be."

"You have no reason to be worried. Charlotte and I are honored to share our wedding date with you. Do you need a minister?" James asked.

"I talked to Big John and he knows a colored minister, pastor of the House of Praise on Wadmalaw Island. When he goes to the market, John will ask him to officiate at the ceremony. If he is not available, I will ask Master Fred, since he is a notary public. But now I must tell Liza the good news."

Henry was so excited he didn't take time to eat breakfast but hurried into the kitchen to find Liza. She was in the pantry getting a bag of sugar when he rushed in and fell down to his knees, saying sweetly, "Liza, will you marry me?"

Liza was stunned. "Right now?" she answered, thinking he was joking.

"No, on Saturday at Miss Charlotte's party," Henry said. "She and Master James think it is a good time for our wedding on their special day. Will you marry me?"

"Of course I will!" Liza said, dropping the bag of sugar as he took her in his arms.

Fumbling in his pocket, Henry pulled out two rings. He took Liza's left hand and placed a diamond ring on her finger. "This was my mother's engagement ring. Now it is your engagement ring, signifying my love to you forever."

By now Liza realized that Henry meant business. They were really getting married this week! Tears of joy ran down her face as Henry kissed her over and over.

Sarah called, "Liza, are you getting the sugar?"

"Yes, ma'am, the best kind." Liza giggled as she answered, then she and Henry walked out of the pantry.

"We are getting married on Saturday," Liza called, flaunting her ring.

Henry picked up Lilly who was at the table and said, "Lilly, my sweet, I am finally going to be your papa."

"Yippee!" Lilly cried. "Now I can have a real horse?"

Liza and Henry laughed as he lifted Lilly to his shoulders. The three entered the dining room to tell the family their news. Everyone clapped, sharing joy with them.

Liza was ecstatic. It wasn't hard for her to picture being Mrs. Henry Moore. It was a dream come true. From the day he appeared on the beach, saving her from Mac the thief, she'd hoped that she would someday marry that Yankee soldier.

After breakfast, Henry told Liza he was riding into the city to get the marriage license and asked if she had a birth record.

"If I do, it is filed in the plantation office, and Master James can get it. All I know is I was born a slave on June 1, 1834, and freed in May of 1865. I do not know Big Momma's surname nor my father's name. Ask Master James if there is a record of my birth."

Henry found James at the breakfast table and asked about the birth records and surnames. "I am sure there are some birth records in the plantation office. As for surnames, there were few. Let me finish my breakfast and I'll walk you over there."

"Thanks, I didn't know there would be difficulty getting that information," Henry said. "I just want to get married."

"I am sure we can find enough information to get a license," James assured him. He finished his coffee and they headed to the plantation office near the carriage lane.

# CHAPTER 64

# AN IMPORTED WEDDING DRESS

"**M**iss Charlotte, you might as well take Liza with you. I am happy for her and little Lilly, but I can't get any work out of her this morning. The wedding is all she's got on her mind," Sarah said.

"Good. I really need to take Liza up to the attic and see if we can find her a dress to wear for her wedding. Some of James' mother's clothes were stored in the old cedar chest, and if they are still there, I am sure there will be something lovely for Liza," Charlotte said.

"I's just thinking, I do some ironing for Miss Isabella, and she wears some fancy clothes. If you don't find anything in de attic, maybe she will let Liza wear one of her fine dresses," Sarah suggested.

"Thank you, Sarah, that's a good idea. We will go to the attic first." Charlotte said happily.

"Liza, are you ready to go with me to the attic? We need to get you something to wear for your wedding as soon as possible," Charlotte said.

"May I go with you?" Lilly begged.

"If you will listen to your mother," Charlotte warned. "It is hard to walk in some places. We have to be careful. Remember when we searched for Rocky?"

"I will be careful," Lilly promised.

Liza picked Lilly up in her arms and followed Miss Charlotte up the stairs to the attic. Putting Lilly down on the landing, she said, "Wow, you are getting to be such a big girl, I will let you walk the rest of the way."

Lilly took her mother's hand as they climbed the attic stairs together, following Miss Charlotte.

"The last time I saw the cedar chest it was over behind the wardrobe. It should be still there. You two stay here at the top of the stairs until I find it. It is a little dark up here."

Charlotte squeezed between a rice bed headboard and a marble-topped dresser, and spied the cedar wardrobe and chest. "Come this way, Liza, but be careful. It's tight in some places. I can see the cedar chest. Hopefully I can get to it," she said.

She stooped to pass a tall brass floor lamp and found the cedar chest in front of her.

"I found it," she yelled. "I will wait until you get here to open it."

Liza held on to Lilly as they stooped under the lamp and found Miss Charlotte.

"It is scary up here," Lilly said. "Lots of stuff."

"But we found the chest," Liza said. "I hope we find clothes inside."

Miss Charlotte wiped a cobweb from the chest and opened it. To their wonderment, the chest was filled with ladies clothing, satins, taffetas, linens, and cottons, with frills and bows.

Charlotte and Liza stood speechless.

Lilly whispered, "Pretty party clothes."

"James always said his mother wore beautiful clothes. She died a year before we married," Charlotte said. "I only saw her at holidays and at church, a beautiful lady. I wish we had more light up here, so we could see the clothes better." Charlotte picked up a taffeta dress from the chest. "This one is lovely. It would make a nice dress for a wedding."

Liza took a dress from the chest and held it up to her body. "This would fit me. It's ivory colored silk with lace around the neck and sleeves.

Why don't we take an armful of dresses down to the second floor to see them better?"

"Good thinking," Charlotte said. "Pick several dresses from the chest and I'll do the same. Lilly, you follow close behind your mother."

Charlotte led Liza and Lilly down the stairs to the second floor's porch. There they could see the real beauty of the clothes. Liza was completely overwhelmed. She had never seen so many choices of clothing to pick from.

Charlotte was having the same feeling. "They are all so gorgeous, it is hard to decide. Pick out the ones you like best and I will, too, and we'll go to my room to try them on."

Leaving the unchosen dresses on the bannisters, Liza and Lilly followed Charlotte to the balcony room. Liza put on the ivory-colored silk dress with a big skirt. It fit perfectly and enhanced Liza's beautiful black, curly hair. The second dress was of baby blue taffeta. It fit well, but the skirt was a little heavy for a wedding dress. Charlotte handed Liza a homespun cotton dress, dark blue with a white collar and white cuffed sleeves. It wasn't dressy enough for a wedding. Charlotte handed her the last choice, a silk satin embroidered floral gown with a simple shape and an off-the-shoulder "V" neckline, cap sleeves, and a bell-shaped skirt covered with embroidered flowers.

"It fits perfectly, right length and shoulder width," Liza said, glowing.

"Mommy looks like the princess doll in Miss Willard's book," Lilly said, clapping her hands.

"She looks beautiful," Miss Charlotte agreed. "What do think, Liza?"

"Isn't it too dressy?" Liza asked.

"Not if you like it. James and his brothers will be proud for you to wear their mother's dress to be married. You look so pretty. Let's not let Henry see it until the wedding day," Charlotte said, beaming. "You may also keep the other two. They are in good condition and it is better for you to have them for them to sit useless in the old chest."

Liza was amazed. She had never had such elegant clothing. She knew they would please Henry. He always talked about buying her store-bought clothes.

"Thank you, Miss Charlotte, I am so glad I came home to Heartland, and especially to be married!"

"I am overjoyed to be able to be a part of your wedding. Now that we have your dress, we need to see about Lilly's. I will be glad to hem it for you if it needs it," Charlotte said. "Take your dresses to your room. I'll take the others back to the attic. Later we can get the rest of the clothes from the chest. You'll have new clothes all year long."

"Come Lilly, we must take these to our room. See you at dinner, Miss Charlotte. This is like a dream. Thank you for everything," she said, weeping tears of happiness.

"Mommy, why are you crying? Are you sad?" Lilly asked.

"No, my dear, these are happy tears. I am going to marry Master Henry on Saturday."

"And I can call him my papa," Lilly said with a grin.

---

James and Henry walked across the backyard of the house going to the office. They saw George and Big John with Pug and Ham removing boards from the side of a slave cottage.

"George doesn't let grass grow under his feet. He's already hired help to begin getting wood for the stables," James said admiringly. "He will be leaving in the morning to go into the city to get his family for the anniversary party on Saturday. I am so happy that you and Liza will share our special day together. You two can move to the first floor of the big house. With Owens back home, Isabella and Jennie have vacated their rooms there."

"Do you think John and Sarah will mind?" Henry asked.

"No, I already talked to them and they say they are happy where they are on the second floor and prefer using the back stairs to the kitchen," James replied. "Their sons are happy there and do not want to move downstairs."

"Will it be all right if we buy some new furniture for Lilly?" Henry asked.

"Do what you like, but don't sell the piano. That was my wedding gift to Charlotte. We had a hard time getting it to Heartland and I promised we'd keep it forever," James said with a laugh.

Getting to the plantation office, James unlocked the door and led the way for Henry.

"This is a nice size building. Just right for an office for the horse farm, don't you think?" Henry said.

"I was thinking the same thing," James replied. "It needs to be cleaned out. Since we will not be selling rice, there are many things we can sell or throw away. We can get Big John to help us with clearing the place. He'll know what we can still use on the horse farm."

James walked to the telegraph machine to check the messages. There was a message for Fred from Captain Marcus.

*Boat arrives September second from Savannah. High noon. Three tickets. Marcus.*

"That will give us three days after the party to finish up the legal papers for the farm. He's already gotten much of the paperwork done," James said.

He walked over to a desk and pulled out the top drawer. "This is where we kept the slave records. They are filed by the year. Liza was born in 1834. Let me see, 1833, 1834... Here it is.

*June of 1834. Baby girl born to Moselle Grimball, June 1, 1834, Father unknown. Name: Liza Mae Grimball, Heartland Plantation, Johns Island, South Carolina. Signature: James Grimball. 6/4/34.*

James handed it to Henry. "You and Liza may keep this in your family file. She may need it later in life."

"Thank you, Master James. Now I can ride into town for our license," Henry said with a big smile.

"While you are in town, could you go by the South Bay house and invite Elijah to the party on Saturday? If he is not at home, leave him a note. If he can't read it, his captain will read it for him. I hate not to invite him. He was such a big help to Charlotte while I was away," James said. "Do you mind?"

"It will be my pleasure, sir," Henry responded readily. "I will go to the corral and get Zeb right now. Do you mind walking back to the house alone?"

"Not at all. I may stay here awhile longer. This is the first time I have been to the office since I got home," James said. "Be careful riding to town. I will see you at supper."

Henry left the office and headed to the corral. James certainly was a good man. Henry was looking forward to working with him.

James sat down at the desk in the office and began to write a list of things they would need if it became an office for the farm. He felt good about the new plans for Heartland, but was a little uneasy about having enough workers for the project. He could count on Henry and Big John for heavy work, but Owens was still not able to ride a horse, let alone train one. Jimmy would be here, but James was not sure how much he wanted to be involved. Jimmy wanted to go back to school. George had his own business to take care of. He could spare only a day or two per week. James was sure they could hire a couple of freed slaves, but he hated to ask Henry for more money to pay them. He was being so generous already.

# CHAPTER 65

# NO SOUTHERN GIRL FOR MY SON

As James sat pondering the fate of the plantation, Fred left the house to check the telegraph in the office. He was getting anxious to get back to Baltimore. He had stayed at Heartland longer than first planned. However, much had been accomplished toward the future of Heartland with his being here.

Fred was surprised to find the plantation office door unlocked, and even more surprised to see James sitting at the desk.

James handed a telegram to Fred. "Looks like you are on your way to Baltimore. It's been great to be together again. I wish we lived closer. When the trains get back in good running order, we will come to Baltimore for a visit."

"That would be great."

"What are Freddie's plans when he gets home?" James asked.

"Heavens only knows. Riding that horse, I suppose. This trip seems to have helped his attitude toward the South, especially with his new lady friend."

"Isabella is one lovely and educated lady. He could do much worse," James said.

"Jane would never have it! No Southern gal for her son," Fred scorned.

"Famous last words," James said with a chuckle. "I wish Jimmy had a lady friend. He seems to be a loner since he got home. At least he's riding again, thanks to Isabella. If she wasn't so googled over Freddie, I'd be proud for Jimmy to look her way," James said cheerfully.

"Maybe that will happen when we leave for home," Fred said.

"It must be close to dinnertime, so we best head back to the house," James said, getting up from the desk. As he locked the door after them, he asked, "How is the legal paperwork coming along, Fred? We need to get everything signed before you leave Charleston."

"I've worked on them this morning and plan to do some more research this afternoon. They will be finished by Friday," Fred answered.

"Great. It is good to have a lawyer for a brother," James said, patting Fred on the back.

After dinner, Big John hitched New Girl and Sugar to the buggy and went across the island to locate the Reverend Samuel Jenkins, pastor of the House of Praise Church on Wadmalaw Island Road. He would come back via the market and get the mint candy and lemons for Miss Charlotte.

Meanwhile, Sarah and Liza were in the kitchen baking cake layers. Sarah decided that Henry and Liza needed their own wedding cake. While Liza baked the anniversary cake, Sarah baked a wedding cake.

Miss Charlotte hemmed Lilly's church dress before she washed and starched it. The dress was a lovely shade of pink and would be beautiful for the wedding.

Charlotte decided to wear her blue crepe church dress for the occasion. While the sewing basket was handy, she replaced the old lace with some newer lace to refresh the dress for the party. The dress always brought out her blue eyes.

Big John came home from the market with lemons and candy mints and a bag of nuts. He had talked to the Reverend Jenkins, who had accepted the invitation to assist at the wedding on Saturday. While unhitching the horses from the buggy, John discovered that Sugar was acting strangely. He must talk to Master James right away. A sick horse was bad news on a plantation. He put Sugar in the corral and went to find James.

James was helping Pug and Ham stack lumber from the slave cabins where they had stripped the wood. He was pleased to see that the lumber was still in good condition and could be used to build the stables.

Seeing Big John hurrying toward him, he stopped what he was doing and met him. "Is something wrong?"

"Yes, sir. Sugar be acting strange. She didn't want to pull de buggy when we were driving. I's t'ink she be feeling poorly. We no need a sick hawes here," John said.

"Where is she?" James asked.

"In the corral," John replied.

"Let's go there now. We may need to put her inside for the night," James suggested.

Hurrying to the corral, James and Big John found Sugar eating grass. James checked her and she seemed to be in good condition. Then he remembered what his grandfather used to say about a mare. Watch how she shakes her body. If she shakes her whole body she is fine, but if she shakes only her head and neck, she is in foal. He watched Sugar for a few minutes and said to Big John, "I think Sugar is in foal, and if she is, this will be our first delivery for the horse farm. It is hard to tell how far along she could be, but it takes eleven months for horses. We should be in full business by then."

"Dat's a long waiting to foal," Big John said in wonderment.

"Take her to Owens' barn tonight. Freddie's horse uses one stable, but there is no horse in the second stable. Henry can check her out tomorrow. He knows more about horses than I do," James said.

As Big John led Sugar toward the overseer's barn, James headed to the big house. He was glad to see Jimmy on the lawn helping Pug and Ham putting up sawhorses to make a table for the anniversary party. Jimmy's health seemed to be back to normal. The daily horseback riding was probably giving him the exercise he'd needed. He was much more active now than when he first came home.

From the porch James heard Charlotte calling his name. "James, come to our room. I need you to try on a suit to wear for our celebration."

"I'm on my way," he answered, climbing the house steps two at a time.

Charlotte was waiting on the porch. "I went back to the attic and located one of your old suits. It is in good condition, but you must try it on. I think it will be fine for you to wear for the party. See if it still fits before I press it," she instructed.

The suit fit well, just a wee bit large in the waist, which Charlotte took care of with her needle and thread.

"I will need a tie to wear," James said.

"I brought several from the attic. Look in the right dresser drawer and pick the one you like," she said. "I must go to the laundry room to press your suit. Sarah has kept the fire going all day for us to use. I pressed my dress earlier and as soon as I get your suit pressed, we will be ready for Saturday. I will see you at supper."

She picked up the suit and vest, kissed him on the cheek, and left the room.

---

The morning of the twenty-eighth of August was a busy one at Heartland. Everyone was up early and busily completing tasks for the anniversary celebration and for Liza and Henry's wedding. Liza and Sarah were putting the last touches on the cakes. They were beautifully decorated. Liza tried to decorate the wedding cake as she remembered the first cake years ago. Sarah put roses made of icing around the top layer of Liza and Henry's cake. Liza and Sarah were proud of the outcome of both cakes.

Isabella came to the big house bringing an armful of flowers from her mother's garden. She was there to make flower arrangements for the house and the yard. Using fall mums, asters, violas, and marigolds, she arranged four large vases for the party, adding the lovely purple stems of the sweetgrass to give height and more color to the arrangements. For the archway that was put up for the wedding, she used small mums intertwined with sweet potato vines.

Big John brought in colorful gourds along with decorative collard greens and several pumpkins. The pumpkins and gourds were displayed on the hearths of the fireplaces. The centerpiece for the dining table was an arrangement of fall mums and colorful peppers.

By dinnertime, the house looked lovely. Charlotte was hoping everything would stay fresh overnight and that the cakes would not melt. The weather was much cooler today, which gave her confidence.

After eating dinner, Isabella began making bouquets of flowers for Charlotte and Liza. She took a small basket and decorated it with climbing roses for Lilly to use as the flower girl. Then using small roses, she created boutonnieres for James, Henry, and Jimmy.

Freddie came to eat dinner with Isabella and was very impressed with her talent of flower arrangements. "Why didn't you tell me you were an artist with flowers?" he asked.

"To me it comes natural. I have no reason to brag. I learned most of it from mother. She is usually the one who arranges the flowers at Heartland, but with Father's condition, I volunteered for the job," she answered sweetly. "I am sorry that Mother is missing all the excitement today. I am enjoying it now because I will miss everything tomorrow. I will stay with Father so Mother can be at the celebrations."

"I have a better solution for tomorrow," Freddie said. "I will stay with your father so you and your mother can enjoy yourselves together. You are closer to these people than I am, and I don't mind looking after your father. He is a kind man."

"Mother probably won't agree. But I think it is a wonderful idea. Mother really wants to be there. It is so sweet of you to offer. I'll tell her at supper. Thanks for coming up for dinner. I was missing you," Isabella said, and began cleaning up the unused flowers. "I am about finished here. If you can wait, I'll ride back to the house with you," she said, smiling at Freddie.

"I am honored to wait for Heartland's best florist. Meet me at the barn when you are finished." Freddie leaned over and kissed her, then hastened out the back.

She grinned. The man never ceased to amaze her. He'd actually offered to stay with Father so she and Mother could attend the celebration. Some folks said he was immature, but what did they know?

After dinner, James, Henry, Fred, and Jimmy rode to the river to take a bath. With so many ladies waiting for the tub and hot water, it was easier and quicker that way.

Charlotte asked Sarah if she would take over the rest of plans for the evening and the celebrations. That pleased Sarah, and her first assignment was to talk to Lilly and explain that after the wedding she would be staying with Sarah and Big John. She would sleep in Sarah's bed Saturday night, and possibly Sunday night.

"Why?" Lilly asked. "Why can't I sleep with Mommy and Papa Henry?"

"A bride and groom like to be alone the first night after they are married," Sarah explained.

"Why?" Lilly asked.

"They want to be by themselves," Sarah said.

"Why?" Lilly asked.

"That's what grown-up folks do on their wedding night," Sarah said.

"Good, I will sleep with you. Can I help cook pancakes for breakfast?" Lilly asked contentedly.

At supper, Sarah laughed while telling Liza about her conversation with Lilly.

Liza thanked Sarah and said, "This will be the first time in her life that we have not slept in the same room. I hope she doesn't give you any trouble."

"I think everything will be fine. I am looking forward to taking care of her. My boys are too grown up to have fun with. Don't worry about her," Sarah said with assurance.

Sarah sent Ham and Pug out to the front yard with a few chairs that would be used for the wedding. They would take more after the celebration dinner on Saturday.

Charlotte and Liza helped clean up the kitchen, then retired to the parlor.

Liza said, "I need to see Henry before bedtime. On our way home to Charleston, Lilly found some nice jewelry in the thief's saddlebag. I would like to wear the pearls if Henry can locate them. He should know where we put them. Have you seen him since supper?"

"The last time I saw him, he was on the back porch polishing his boots," Charlotte replied.

"I will go and check, but if you see him before I do, tell him why I want to see him," Liza said.

She hurried through the kitchen to the back porch where she found Henry still shining his boots. They were so shiny Liza could see her face in them.

"Don't wear your boots out shining them. You must be nervous about something," she said and threw her arms around his neck. "Getting married shouldn't be that worrisome."

"I know, my dear. I am just so excited, I have to keep busy. How about you? Are you holding up?" he asked, hugging her tightly.

"Trying to stay busy. It scares me that I can be so happy. I am afraid I will wake up and it was all a dream," she confessed.

"It is no dream. Tomorrow by this time you will be Mrs. Henry Moore," he said, kissing her over and over. "By the way, why were you looking for me?"

"Do you remember where we put the thief's jewels?" she asked. "I would like to wear the pearls for the wedding."

"That's a great idea. I hid them in my haversack, in my room. When we go up for bedtime, I will get them for you, sweet," he said. "By the way, where is Lilly?"

"She is with Sarah. Sarah is to keep Lilly Saturday and Sunday so we can have some privacy after the wedding."

Holding Liza tighter he said, "You've thought of everything, sweetheart. I had wondered how it would work out with the three of us."

She began laughing, "That would have been some situation with all the questions she would have asked."

Henry joined her in a roar of laughter. "Goodnight, my sweet. I must take my boots upstairs. See you at bedtime when I bring the pearls," he said, kissing her again. Taking his boots, he disappeared up the back staircase.

Liza sat quietly trying to take it all in. Tomorrow she was marrying her true love. How could one person be so happy? Henry was such a special man. He saved her and Lilly from the thief on the beach and brought them safely to Charleston. With his financial help, he is saving Heartland from destitution, and now he is marrying a former slave woman. She was not only happy but she was so thankful for God's goodness. Sitting in the shadows of the sunset, she bowed her head and prayed as Big Momma had taught her, thanking God for all her blessings and asking Him to bless the new family that would be ordained tomorrow.

As she said, "Amen," big tears rolled down her cheeks, tears of joy and happiness as she thought of her future as Henry Moore's wife.

She wiped her eyes with her apron and headed up the stairs. She heard someone call her name. Looking back, she saw Jimmy coming from the kitchen.

He had a hand behind his back and was grinning from ear to ear. "I made you and Henry a wedding present." He handed her a broom decorated with fruits and flowers. "I always like to see the bride and groom jump the broom at a wedding, and I had Isabella decorate this one. I hope you aren't offended by it," Jimmy said humbly.

"Oh, Master Jimmy, no offense. I love it. I was wishing that we could jump the broom at our wedding. I always enjoyed that part of the plantation weddings. Thank you so much. I can't wait to show it to Henry. He's probably never heard of the custom," she said joyfully.

"I am glad you like it. Mother thought you would. I wish you much happiness in your marriage. I will see you in the morning. Good night," Jimmy said.

Liza held the broom handle tightly and thought of Jimmy as a little boy here at Heartland, always a gentle child and happy to please. This was indeed a special wedding gift, no longer a gift to a slave from a master's child, but a gift from one friend to another.

When she reached her room on the balcony, Sarah and Lilly were waiting for her.

Lilly grinned and began talking very fast. "Mommy, I get to sleep with Miss Sarah for two nights, and she is making me a rag doll, and we are going to ride a real horse on Sunday."

"Slow down my little one. You are talking too fast. Sounds as if you have a special weekend planned," Liza said, and Lilly continued to tell what new things she and Sarah were planning to do over the weekend.

"I only wish I could go with you," Liza said with a smile.

"It is my present for you marrying Mr. Henry. Next time it will be for our new family."

Liza hugged Lilly, "Have fun and be on your best behavior. I love you! Now, it is your bedtime. You must get a good night's sleep. Tomorrow is a special day for us all."

Liza helped Lilly get dressed for bed and heard her prayers.

"Bless Mommy and Mister Henry as he becomes my papa. Amen!" She hugged her mother and climbed into bed.

As Liza put cover over Lilly, someone knocked on the bedroom door.

"Come in," she said.

It was Henry with the pearls. "I found the jewelry. These are beautiful pearls. They will look stunning for the wedding," he said, and put them around Liza's neck and kissed her.

"Thank you, dear. They certainly are fine pearls. They will look outstanding with my dress," she said, deliriously happy. She picked up the broom. "Look. Jimmy brought us a wedding present."

"A decorated broom?" Henry questioned. "It is too pretty to use."

Liza laughed. "It's for our wedding. At most plantation weddings, the bride and groom jump the broom. It is a traditional ceremony that serves as an open declaration of settling down in a marriage relationship. It is done before witnesses as a public ceremonial announcement that a couple are choosing to be as close in marriage as possible."

"That sounds beautiful, darling. I will look forward to jumping the broom together. It's a very meaningful gift, and very thoughtful of Jimmy."

"Jimmy is to be Master James' best man, and Miss Charlotte will stand up for me," Liza said. "I hope I can sleep tonight. I feel all jittery inside."

"We both should go to bed and try to get some rest. Tomorrow is to be a busy and momentous day. Good night, my love, sleep well. I love you!" he said, kissing her lovingly as he left.

She turned and went into her bedroom. She felt that her heart would burst with love for Henry. So exhausted from all the excitement of the day, she fell on the bed, too tired to put on night clothes, and in minutes she slept with a smile on her face.

# CHAPTER 66

# CELEBRATION DAY

On Saturday morning, everyone was up early. Breakfast was hurried through, with only biscuits, jelly, and coffee. It was a magnificent autumn day. A splendid day for an outside wedding, and cool enough to keep the gnats and mosquitos away.

Down at the overseer's house, Jennie hurriedly cooked breakfast as she was to be at the big house as early as possible. Since Freddie was to sit with Owens for the day, she cooked extra food to leave for dinner. Isabella was in the bedroom gathering the things she would need for the celebration without having to return home.

Freddie was already in the kitchen eating breakfast and getting instructions on what he should do while staying with Owens. He would ride with Isabella to the big house to help take her dress for the wedding. Isabella would play piano at the anniversary celebration and at the wedding. Last night, James and Jimmy had rolled the piano to the front porch for her.

Jennie took breakfast to Owens and she found him already complaining that she was going to the celebration and wedding.

"Freddie will be here, and he certainly can take care of you if you behave yourself," she scolded. "Don't try to get out of bed and keep your arms on the pillows. No more complaining."

Isabella came to the parlor. "Is Freddie up yet? I am ready to go. I'll eat something later."

From the kitchen Freddie heard her and said, "I'm finishing breakfast. Barabbas is already saddled and waiting. I won't be long."

Jennie came back into the kitchen and told Freddie, "You two go to the big house. I will be ready to leave when you get back. I hope Owens won't give you any trouble today. He can be stubborn at times. I appreciate your willingness to stay with him. It's going to be a special day for us all."

Freddie took Isabella's dress bag and they headed out to where Barabbas was waiting. Isabella mounted first and reached for the bag as Freddie mounted in front of her. She held tight to both Freddie and the dress bag as they rode down the lane toward the Heartland Mansion.

"I wish we were the ones getting married," she said sweetly.

"When we are ready, it will happen," Freddie said seriously. "Time will tell."

At the big house, Jimmy was setting up a table on the lawn for the wedding cake. Pug and Ham were arranging chairs for the ceremony. They would bring more chairs from the dining room after the anniversary celebration.

Freddie hitched his horse near the back porch and took the clothes bag from Isabella. "Where are you going to dress?"

"In the guest room on the first floor. Just hang my dress on the back of the door. I'll bring my other things in shortly. Wait for me there," she said.

She walked through the kitchen and found Sarah washing the breakfast dishes. "I am sorry you are the only one helping with the work this morning. Mother will be here shortly. Freddie is going to stay with Father for the day. Isn't that nice of him?" Isabella said, glowing.

"I am glad your mother can come. I will need her at dinner time. Everything is in the ovens," Sarah said. "It is going to be a real celebration."

"I can help serve if you need me," Isabella said. "But now I must get my things to the guest room. See you later."

She found Freddie sitting on the bed in the guest room.

"Everyone is busy as bees around here. I am glad I don't have to put on Sunday best for today," he said, laughing. "I know you will be the prettiest lady there," he added as he pulled her into his lap and kissed her madly.

"And you say you don't want to get married anytime soon? Many more kisses like that we'll have to join today's wedding," Isabella said in surprise. "You need to go back to the house and bring Mother. Sarah needs help in the kitchen. Go now, before we get into trouble. Hope Father behaves himself for you." She walked to the door and took down the clothes bag. "I need to get dressed, my dear."

"I don't want to leave you, but I will go if you insist," Freddie said with a grin. "Have fun," he said, kissing her on the cheek before leaving.

At high noon Pug rang the dinner bell, and everyone walked to the front lawn and stood before the porch steps while Isabella played music on Charlotte's piano. A breeze from the water and the shade from the oak trees made it comfortable to stand for this part of the celebration. Among the attendees was the Reverend Samuel Jenkins from the House of Praise, and his wife, Othello.

When the piano music stopped, the front doors of the mansion opened and out walked James and Charlotte, arm in arm, smiling and waving at the crowd. They looked wonderful in their Sunday best. Charlotte held the flowers Isabella had chosen for her and the rose boutonniere was perfect on James' suit.

James let go of Charlotte's arm and held up his hand to get everyone's attention. He said, "Welcome to Heartland and to the celebration of the missus and my twenty-fifth wedding anniversary. Twenty-five years ago this week, Miss Charlotte Legare became Mrs. James Grimball, to have and to hold from that day forward. Today we celebrate those many years of joy and happiness together as husband and wife. Through good times and hard times we have kept the vows we made before God and the congregation on September 4, 1840. God gave us a wonderful son and a great life together in Charleston and here at Heartland."

Before James could go on, Isabella began playing the piano as secretly arranged.

Jimmy walked to the piano and sang, "Because you come to me with naught save love and hold my hand and lift mine eyes above, a wider world of hope and joy I see, because you come to me. Because God made thee mine I cherish thee, through light and darkness through all time to be, and pray His love may make our love divine. Because God made thee mine."

Charlotte was surprised and thrilled. She had almost forgotten the wonderful sound of Jimmy's baritone voice. James was as astonished as Charlotte, and both wiped tears from their eyes.

As Jimmy ended the song, he walked over and hugged his parents. "I love you. Happy anniversary."

Finally getting his voice back, James said, "That was not in our plans. But thank you son, the song said it all."

James reached into his pocket and brought out a gold locket he had purchased while in the field hospital, a gift for Charlotte. He unhooked the chain and gently put it around his wife's neck. As he clasped the chain, he turned and kissed her. "I will love you forever."

Everyone clapped for the lovely couple. Many ladies shed a tear.

James held up a hand again. "Before we go into the dining room for our meal, I wish to introduce you to the Reverend Samuel Jenkins and his lovely wife, from the House of Praise Church on Wadmalaw Road. Reverend Jenkins will officiate at Liza and Henry's wedding this afternoon at three o'clock. But first I would ask the reverend to say grace for the food we are about to receive."

Reverend Jenkins walked to the porch and spoke with a heavy Gullah accent. "My wife and I are very glad to be with you for dis celebration, and we look forward to de other event of de day. Now, let we pray. T'ank you

Lawd fuh us food dis day and every day. Bless dis here man and woman and keep dem together far always. In thy holy name we pray. Amen!"

James thanked him and said, "One last thing before we eat. I want to introduce the bride and groom who are to be married this afternoon." He nodded, and the double doors to the dining room opened, and out walked Lilly, Liza, and Henry. Everyone applauded. Lilly bowed like a princess in her Sunday dress.

"The bride and groom will follow us into the dining room," James announced. Taking Charlotte's arm, they walked past Liza and Henry into the dining room. Then came Lilly, Liza, and Henry.

Jimmy then invited everyone to join the couples for the celebration dinner.

Liza and Henry sat at the head table along with Charlotte and James. Lilly sat between Charlotte and her mother. Liza seemed unhappy. "What's wrong?" Charlotte asked.

"Isn't it bad luck for Henry to see me in my wedding dress before the ceremony?" Liza asked.

"That's an old superstition. James came to my house and we rode in the buggy to the church on our wedding day. I see no reason for you to worry. Things are good, and this is a beautiful dinner. Have you ever seen so much food on this table? Not even at Christmas. The girls have outdone themselves."

# CHAPTER 67

# IS THIS OUR LILLY?

Sarah, Jennie, and Caroline began serving the food while Big John and Elijah served the lemonade and coffee. They looked very nice in their Sunday best.

Henry said, "Aren't you going to eat, my dear?"

"I am too nervous to eat. How about you?" Liza asked.

"I am afraid to eat, my stomach already has butterflies," he admitted.

Lilly heard his remark and asked, "How did butterflies get into your stomach?"

"Honey, that's just an old expression which means your stomach is nervous," Liza explained. "Eat your dinner so we can have cake and candy."

"I want to eat cake now," Lilly said loudly. "That's all I want to eat."

"The cake is still in the kitchen. You can't have it yet." Liza tried to reason with her daughter, and wondered what had come over her. "Lilly, do you want to sit in the corner during the party?"

"No, but I want cake now!" Lilly said even louder.

Henry realized this was becoming a problem and said, "Lilly, listen to you mother. The cake will be brought out for dessert, but if you have not eaten your food, you will not get dessert. Do you understand?"

"So, if you and Mommy don't eat, you can't have cake either, right?" Lilly said in a sassy voice.

By now Liza was very upset with Lilly. Seeing Sarah serving gravy, she motioned her over.

"Is something wrong?" Sarah asked.

Liza whispered into her ear and Sarah nodded. Quietly she picked Lilly up from her chair and headed toward the kitchen while Lilly kicked her feet and screamed, "I want my mommy, I want my mommy!"

Liza hung her head in embarrassment, and tears ran down her face.

"What is it, dearest? What's happened? I have never seen Lilly act like that. Is something wrong?" Henry asked.

"No, not really. But yes, Lilly has just realized that things will be different after today. She will no longer be my only love. I will be sharing my love with you. She should be all right after the wedding, and if not, we will deal with it. I am so sorry for the disturbance. I hope Sarah can calm her down," Liza said.

Just then, Jennie and Elijah rolled the cake table to the center of the room. Isabella began playing the piano and everyone began singing. "Happy anniversary to you…Charlotte and James, happy anniversary to you!"

Charlotte and James cut the first slice. Jennie and Elijah began to serve everyone pieces of the delicious cake. Big John refilled lemonade and coffee cups. The merriment continued for everyone except for Liza. She tried to eat the cake, but all she could think of was her unhappy Lilly.

It was almost two o'clock when the guests began to say their congratulations and farewells to Charlotte and James. Liza and Henry were glad to be able to leave the room for a while before the wedding. James stood and thanked everyone for coming and that the wedding would take place on the front lawn at three.

Liza rushed into the kitchen, only to find Lilly sitting at the table, eating a big piece of the anniversary cake. "See Mommy, I did get some cake, but Miss Sarah made me eat a ham biscuit before I could have it. She acts like a mommy, too."

"She is a mommy. Pug and Ham are her two boys. They were once small like you. Big John is their papa."

"I will have a papa after today, right Mr. Henry?" Lilly asked, looking up at Henry who was standing quietly behind Liza.

"Yes, my little one, and I will have a daughter," he said with pride. Turning to Liza, he said sweetly, "We will be the Moore family of Heartland."

"Thank you, Sarah. We are going to sit on the back porch where it is cooler. We will come for Lilly before the wedding begins," Liza said, feeling much better about the situation.

She excused herself before going to the porch and went to the retiring room where she washed her face and hands. She straightened the neckline of her dress and placed the pearls the proper way.

"Please God, let Lilly get through the wedding without trauma," Liza prayed. "Let Big Momma help us."

Going to the porch she met Henry.

"I decided I needed to freshen up, too. The afternoon sun is getting a little warmer. You still want to get married?" he asked jovially.

"The quicker the better. This dress is too warm," she said happily. "I will go and get Lilly, and meet you on the front lawn."

Pug and Ham brought more chairs from the dining room for the guests. Only a few neighbors had stayed for the wedding. Jimmy, Fred, Jane, Big John, Sarah, Elijah and Jennie were the household guests. Freddie and Owens were the only Heartland's people that were not in attendance. Isabella was the pianist for the wedding.

At three o'clock sharp, Isabella began playing the wedding march. Reverend Jenkins and James walked with Henry to the archway and waited. Lilly appeared between the row of chairs dropping rose petals on the path as Charlotte walked behind her as the matron of honor. Everyone stood up to watch the bride meet Henry at the archway.

Liza looked lovely. Isabella had added more makeup for the wedding that emphasized Liza's brown eyes and sweet face. Mother Grimball's lovely dress looked as if it had been designed for Liza. The flower wreath on her head gave her a youthful look. She smiled every step of the way. She was, indeed, a beautiful bride.

She handed her flowers to Charlotte and took Henry's hand. The Reverend Jenkins began the service.

"Welcome to you dat are here to witness de ceremony of Liza Grimball and Henry Moore in holy wedlock. Des two hab chosen each other to be partner's fuh life, to love and cherish as long as dey shall live. Liza Mae Grimball, do you take dis man to be your lawful wedded husband, to hab and to hold, to honor and obey, in sickness and in health until dead shall separate you?"

In a nervous voice, Liza said, "Yes, sir!"

Turning to Henry, the Reverend asked, "Do you Henry William Moore, take dis ooman to be your lawful wife, to hab and to hold from dis day forward, to love and obey as long as you both do lib?"

Henry squeezed Liza's hand and said, "I do, sir."

Reverend Jenkins cupped a hand over Liza and Henry's hands and said, "In the name of de Almighty God, I pronounce you husband and wife. What God joins together, let no man put asunder. You may place a ring on her finger and repeat after me. With dis ring, I thee wed. In de name of the Father, de Son, and de Holy Spirit. Amen!"

After Henry repeated the vow, the reverend said, "The bride and groom will now jump the broom."

Jimmy brought the decorated broom to the archway and put it on the ground. Liza and Henry began to jump over the broom head, one at a time and then together. The jumping of the broom was a custom familiar to Liza, as it was often used at plantation weddings by the slaves. Henry had never seen the traditional ceremony, but enjoyed having it as part of their service.

There was much laughter by the bride and groom. Liza took Lilly by the hands and jumped the broom. Henry joined in for a family jump.

The Reverend Jenkins and his wife jumped the broom, and Charlotte and James finished up the ceremony. Almost out of breath, Reverend Jenkins said to Henry and Liza, "I now pronounce you husband and wife. Amen and amen."

Henry picked Liza up in his arms and kissed her.

Lilly pulled at his pants leg saying, "Papa! Papa Henry, you are now my Papa for true!"

While the jumping of the broom was going on, Elijah and Big John brought the wedding cake and lemonade from the kitchen for the reception. Liza and Henry hurried over to the table to cut the cake. After the first piece was cut, Liza cut a very large piece and put it on a plate to give to Lilly before she started a fuss like she did earlier. Lilly took the cake and sat at the table with Sarah, enjoying every bite.

# CHAPTER 68

# A DOCTOR IN THE HOUSE

Down at the Owens' house, Freddie was tearing a bed sheet into strips to use for a bandage. A few minutes before, Owens had tried to get out of bed and fell to the floor, breaking his left arm. Freddie picked him up and placed him back on the bed and started to set Owens' arm. He had set so many arms in the cavalry, he knew just what to do. Thank goodness the bones did not come through the skin, and he could feel that only one bone was completely broken. He continued tearing the sheet into strips. First, he would hold the bones together and wrap them in place so they would stay put while he looked for a piece of wood to use for a splint.

He spoke seriously to Owens. "I know you are in pain, but you must stay as still as possible. I have put the bone back together, but I must go find something to make a splint. There is no one here to watch you and I will leave you alone for a very few minutes. I will be back as soon as I can."

Owens gritted his teeth to his pain and said, "I will stay still. Hurry back."

Freddie ran out the kitchen door to the wood pile. Quickly he searched for the makings of a splint. He found two pieces of wood that looked flat enough, and hurried back to Owens, who seemed not to have moved at all.

"Is there any liquor in the house?" Freddie asked.

"Jennie keeps a bottle in the pantry for medicinal purposes. It is on the top shelf to the right."

Freddie ran to the pantry and found the bottle. Opening it, he grabbed a spoon from the food tray and gave Owens four big spoons of the liquor. He washed and dried the sticks of wood and scrubbed his hands and returned to the bed. Owens was beginning to sound sleepy.

"How's the pain?" he asked kindly.

"About the same," Owens said. "I am all right, do what you have to do."

Freddie unwrapped the bandage and placed a piece of wood under the arm. He rewrapped the arm with strips of cloth from the sheet. He secured the bandage with another width of cloth, tucking it gently into the first bandage.

"Does that feel better?" he asked.

"Yes, a little," Owens said, somewhat confused. He didn't hold liquor very well.

That was good, thought Freddie. Sleep would do him good. But he still needed a sling to hold the arm in place.

Using the remaining cloth from the sheet, Freddie folded it into a square, then folded it into a sling, which he tied around Owens' neck. He gently placed the arm into it. By now, Owens was feeling better, and soon went to sleep.

Even though Freddie had set many broken arms while in the medical corps of the Cavalry, this one had been extra tiresome. Probably because he hadn't had the regular equipment, and had to improvise in order to set the bones. But he knew the arm would be fine, if Owens would take care of himself.

After cleaning up around the bed, he washed his hands, and sat down in a rocking chair. He relaxed and soon fell fast asleep.

Up at the big house, the wedding reception was over and Jennie, Caroline, and Sarah were washing glasses and plates. Jane walked into the kitchen and asked if she could do anything to help.

"No thank you, we are just about finished here," Jennie said.

"How is Owens?" Jane asked. "Fred thought we might walk down to see him this afternoon if I'm not needed here. Is it a good time to visit?"

"I am sure Owens would enjoy seeing you. He is so tired of staying in bed. Your Freddie is often there. He has been such a good help with him. They get along well, and of course, Isabella likes having him around," Jennie said in a pleased voice.

"Fine, I will get Fred and we will walk to your place. The celebrations were wonderful and the food was delicious. I am glad we could be here. Thanks for everything."

Fred was out on the lawn talking to George and Jimmy when Jane came out.

"Fred, I talked to Jennie and she thinks now is a good time for us to visit Owens."

"I should visit him, myself," George said. "I think he is doing all right since he came home. Would you mind if I tagged along?"

"Of course not, George. The more the merrier," Fred said, and the three of them headed toward the overseer's house.

"It's a longer walk than I realized," Jane said with a groan. "These shoes were not meant for walking on a sandy lane."

"Shall I carry you on my back?" Fred asked, teasing.

"No, silly. I'll live," she replied. "It is just past that next tree. I will make it."

There was no sign of life when they got to Owens' porch. Fred wondered if there was anyone at home. He hoped Freddie did not leave Owens alone.

Then he heard a noise from inside. Fred called out, "Freddie, are you there?"

Suddenly, the screen door opened and Freddie greeted them sleepily. "Come in. I must have fallen asleep. Is something wrong?"

"No, we just came to visit Owens. Is he awake?" George asked.

The three went into the living room and was surprised that Owens was asleep.

"I guess he is asleep. Come on in, he will be sorry to have missed you. He does like visitors," Freddie said.

Even though Freddie had cleaned up the bed, the liquor bottle was still on the table.

"How is he doing?" Fred asked with a frown.

"We won't know until tomorrow," Freddie replied.

"What do you mean, tomorrow?" George asked, noticing the sling. "Why is his left arm in a sling? Did something happen to it?"

"I am afraid so," Freddie said sheepishly. "He tried to get out of bed and fell, breaking a bone in his left arm. I did the best I could do in setting it since no one was here to get him to a doctor."

Fred and George jumped up and went to the bed. "What do you know about setting bones?" Fred bellowed. "We need to send for a doctor."

Jane was horrified and asked, "How did you know what to do?"

"Oh, settle down. While I was in the cavalry, I worked in the medical corps. I set at least one broken arm every day for four years. Arms are much easier to set than legs. I didn't have the best conditions here, but it looks good to me."

Fred gasped in shock. "You were in the medical corps? Why didn't you tell us?"

"You never asked what I did in the war. I even amputated arms and legs of many soldiers that were crushed beyond repair. I still have nightmares about some of the surgeries."

Jane walked over to Freddie and reached for him. "Sweetheart, I am so sorry you went through such horrible things while you were a soldier. We didn't realize that you didn't just ride your horse for four years. Forgive me for not understanding your needs when you came home. I am proud you took care of Owens so well."

"It was the only thing I could do, being here alone. I just hope Jennie and Isabella will be satisfied with the job I did," Freddie said nervously.

"I am thankful you were here," George said. "With all that was going on at Heartland today, it could have turned out very differently. Thank you for a job well done. Sure wish you were going to stay here at Heartland. The horse farm is going to need someone who knows about bones and medicine."

"I've set a few horse's legs, but they are much harder to take care of than people," Freddie said. "If I ever go back to school, I will study medical science."

Jane said, "It is almost sunset and I don't want to be walking in the dark in these shoes. I think we have to leave now."

"You are right, dear, it is getting late. We must get back to the big house before dark. I will tell Jennie what happened, so she won't be too upset about Owens' condition. One of us can ride for Dr. Le Roach in the morning, if necessary," Fred said.

George asked, "Freddie, are you all right? Do you need me to stay with you until Isabella gets home?"

"Thank you, Uncle George. I think Owens will sleep until then, and if not, I'll give him another dose of Jennie's liquor," Freddie said with a wink.

"I am proud of you, Freddie. You are a true Grimball!" George said.

Jane gave Freddie a hug, and Fred patted his son on the back.

"Good work, Son. Rest well, and I'll check on you in the morning."

Then Fred and Jane went out the front door.

Up at the big house, the dishes were washed and put away. Jennie was wiping off the dining table and Isabella was cutting slices from the wedding cake to take to her father and Freddie.

"Mother, it is getting late. We should be leaving for home before it gets dark. I don't like to walk the lane in the dark. You never can tell when a snake might be going your way," said Isabella.

"I know. I think we can leave things as they are until morning. One of us can come up early to start breakfast. I don't expect Liza or Miss Charlotte will be early risers in the morning, and the others can just wait for breakfast. Leave your fancy dress here, and I'll get Freddie to bring it home when he goes riding," Jennie said.

Isabella put the cake into a poke bag and joined her mother as she walked out onto the back porch. Going down the steps, they met George, Jane, and Fred coming up.

"Leaving?" asked George.

"Yes, it's been a long day. I hate that I left Freddie so long with Owens. Hope everything went well there," Jennie replied.

"We just came from seeing Owens," George said. "He was asleep." Jane and Fred stood quietly as George said, "Jennie and Isabella, come on back to the porch. I need to talk to you a minute before you go home."

"Is there something wrong with Owens?" Jennie asked anxiously.

Isabella asked, "Is Freddie all right?"

"Everyone's okay, but they've had a busy afternoon," George said. "Around noon, Owens wanted to get out of bed and decided to get out without Freddie's help. He fell to the floor and landed on his left arm, breaking a bone."

"Oh, no!" Jennie screamed. "Is he all right?"

"Yes, thanks to Freddie. Freddie was able to set the arm and wrap it well, and even placed it in a sling," George said. "We didn't know that Freddie was in the medical corps while in the cavalry and often set broken bones. Your father was sound asleep when we were there. His arm looked fine to us. We will contact Dr. Le Roach in the morning, but Freddie did a great job. I am proud of him."

"Thank goodness he knew what to do," Isabella said worriedly.

"Go on home. Freddie is very tired and needs sleep. I think one of you should sleep in the room with Owens. If you need help, Isabella, ride up and get me. I am staying in the second guest room on the main floor. If he wakes in great pain, give him a good dose of your mother's remedy. It's on the table," George said and chuckled as Jennie's face turned red.

"I told him to behave himself. He is some stubborn man," Jennie muttered. "We must hasten home, Isabella."

"Yes, Mother."

"Thank you, George," Jennie called back in a fearful voice as they both hurried down the back steps.

"It is getting dark, do be careful," Jane called after them. "You may need a lantern."

But Jennie and Isabella were running too fast and did not hear her.

Both breathless, they climbed the steps to the porch. As Jennie caught her breath, Isabella called, "Freddie, are you there?"

The door opened and he came to greet them. "Gosh, you shouldn't be walking the lane in the dark," he said. "Come in. It has been a long, long day. Your father is asleep. I was in the kitchen fixing some supper."

Jennie hastened past him to Owens' bedside and examined the arm in the sling.

Isabella said, "We saw George and he told us about your good deed for the day. A medical man! You didn't tell me. I am proud of the swift action you took when Father fell. Quick thinking on your part, since you were alone. Thank you, dear."

She walked to her mother's side to see the arm for herself. "Looks professionally wrapped. Well done, Dr. Grimball," Isabella teased.

Freddie checked Owens' pulse and said, "He is still in deep sleep. He has been asleep several hours. His breathing is good, and he seems not to be in heavy pain. I will sleep here on the settee and keep watch through the night."

"No," Jennie said. "I will sleep here, you need your rest. I am sure this was very tiring for you. Get some sleep. If he wakes up and needs help, I will call for you."

"Thank you, Miss Jennie," Freddie said. "I am a little weary, but you two had a hard day, too. Do call me if you need help." He said goodnight and started to his room.

Isabella followed and asked, "What did your parents say about your medical expertise?"

"They were completely surprised that I would possibly try setting a broken bone, but after I explained about my job in the cavalry, Mother and Father complimented my work. Father even said he was proud of me. At last I did something to earn his approval," Freddie said with a smile.

Isabella threw her arms around him. "I am proud of you, as well."

He kissed her several times, and said, "I now feel that I have somewhat proven myself to Father. I just hope he means it. I am ready to sleep. See you in the morning, my love," he said. "I pray that your father's arm will heal well."

Kissing her one last time, he left the kitchen and headed to his room, a tired but pleased former medical soldier.

# CHAPTER 69

# DR. LE ROACH

George woke early on Sunday morning. He knew he must check on Owens and see if he needed to go for Dr. Le Roach. Later, he would take the family home as the girls had school on Monday.

Caroline had already gone to the kitchen. With Charlotte sleeping late and Liza honeymooning, someone must start the coffee for breakfast. Sarah would usually start it, but she was caring for Lilly for the weekend.

As George put on his boots, there was a knock on the door. "Come in."

It was Fred. "I came to go with you to see how Owens fared for the night. I hope he made it through without too much pain. I still think we should go for the doctor. I believe Freddie did a good job, but for his sake, it will be good to know if he set it properly," Fred said, looking a little worried.

"You surprise me, Fred," George scolded. "Is it so hard for you to give Freddie the benefit of the doubt? He has finally proven that he's a man. Leave it alone, brother. Sounds as if he had a hard time in the army. Give him credit for knowing what to do under the circumstances."

"It was such a surprise to Jane and myself. It's going to take time for me to see him as a grown man," Fred said humbly. "But you are right, I am glad he took care of Owens and made the decision that he did. Let's go."

They went down the back stairs to the kitchen and found Caroline making coffee and toast.

"The coffee is ready and one pan of toast is waiting for butter. Pour your coffee while I butter the toast. I know you are in a hurry. I hope you find everything in good order at Owens' place."

They poured their coffee and reached for toast.

"Thanks, my dear, I will take another piece to eat on the way. You, too, Fred. Let's be going." George said, opening the back door and leading Fred down the back stairs. "Let's take the short path through the corral. It is the quickest way."

Arriving at the overseer's house, they both rushed to the front door, calling, "Jennie, are you awake?"

She came from the kitchen and greeted both of them. "Come on in. We've had a good night and are eating breakfast waiting for Owens to wake up. He woke up about one o'clock with a little pain, but said he felt good about his arm. I gave him more of my medicine, and he has slept since. The arm had a little swelling, but Freddie said that was to be expected."

"Sounds as if everything is under control," Fred said. "How is Freddie this morning?"

"Come, see for yourself. He and Isabella are eating breakfast in the kitchen," she said, motioning them in.

In the kitchen, Freddie and Isabella sat eating.

Freddie greeted his father warmly, "I hear I missed a nice celebration yesterday. Glad everything went well. Where will Liza and Henry live now that they are married?"

"I haven't heard anyone say," Fred said. "They will probably take a couple of rooms in the big house. Especially now that Owens is back here with Isabella and Jennie."

George said, "Freddie, would you like to ride with me to get Doctor Le Roach?"

"Do you think Owens' arm needs resetting?" Freddie asked. "The arm looks great this morning and he is in very little pain."

"Oh, no, I am not questioning your skills. But your mother wanted the local doctor to follow up on the accident," George said. "Since you'll be leaving soon."

"Sure, let's go. I'll get Barabbas saddled. Meet you at the barn."

"I'll saddle New Girl and see you shortly. Want to come with us, Fred?" George asked.

"I'll wait for you here with Jennie and Isabella. Owens might wake up and I can visit with him."

George hastened to saddle New Girl and met Freddie at the barn. Freddie was glad his father had not come. He wanted to talk to Uncle George alone.

They rode in silence down the carriage lane for several minutes, then Freddie asked, "Is the doctor's place very far away?"

"No, it is on River Road at Fenwick Corners. His office is a small building in his front yard. If he isn't there, we can usually find him at home," George said.

"Uncle George, you said something yesterday that I need to ask you about. You said that the horse farm would need to hire someone who knows about bones and medicine. Do you think I could fill the position?"

Somewhat surprised, George asked, "Would you really stay in the South to work with us? I thought you hated it down here."

"I did before I came on this visit. I have come to enjoy the slower pace of Southern life, and the people are so friendly, even to a Yankee. And of course I am more than fond of Isabella. The only thing I find disagreeable is the hot weather. I suppose I could get used to that," he said, laughing.

"Do your parents know that you are thinking this way?" George asked.

"No. And I know Mother will be dead set against it. She doesn't approve of my possibly marrying a Southern lady."

"I can't tell you what to do, but you would absolutely have a job here with the horse business, and there is plenty of room in the big house for you to live."

"I have only five days to make my decision. You may tell James, but please don't say anything to Mother or Father," Freddie pleaded. "Not until I can talk to them."

"The doctor's office is that building on the right. We will talk more, later. Your secret is safe with me," George said, slowing his horse and stopping in front of a small white building.

After tying their horses to a hitching post, they walked up to it and George knocked loudly. The door opened almost in his face.

"George Grimball! Why, I haven't seen you in ages. What brings you back to the island? Someone sick?" the doctor asked, giving George a friendly hug. "Is this good-looking young man your son?"

"Afraid not. This is Frederick's son, Freddie from Baltimore. He and the family are here for a visit. It's good to see you again after all these years. How is your family?"

"The children are all married, and the missus and I are fair to middling around the old home place. I am still delivering babies, more than ever since the slaves left the island. Those midwives stayed pretty busy before emancipation," the doc replied. "I was sorry to hear about the fire at Heartland. I never heard if anyone was hurt or not."

"That is one of the reasons we are here. Our overseer, Mr. Owens, was burned on both arms in the fire and was in the city hospital for over a month. He just came home last week and was doing well until yesterday when he fell from his bed and broke his left arm. Freddie, here, set the arm, but we would like you to check it out. Freddie was a medic in the cavalry for four years and set many arms, but he'll be leaving soon, so it's best a local doctor take a look. Do you have the time to ride to Heartland and check on Owens?" George asked.

"I will be glad to go with you, but I am almost certain the set is well done. Those army medics are given a lot of training before they are selected for the corps. I will get my horse and meet you out front," the doctor replied.

There was very little conversation among the three as they swiftly rode to Heartland. It was almost noon when they arrived at the carriage lane. They rode past the big house and on to the Owens' place.

Freddie dismounted Barabbas and hurried across the porch calling for Isabella. "We brought Dr. Le Roach. He is with Uncle George. They are old friends, apparently. Is your father awake?"

She came from the kitchen and greeted Freddie. "Yes, Father has been awake for over an hour. He seems like his old self, but says his arm pains a little."

Jennie went to the front door and greeted George and Doc. "Come on in. Owens thinks his arm was well taken care of, it's best to be sure." She gave Dr. Le Roach a handshake. "It is good to see you again. How long has it been since you've been to Heartland?"

"Not since Ham broke his toe and was afraid I was going to cut it off," Doc said with a laugh.

"He's sixteen now and his family is still here. Heavens, that has been at least ten years," she said.

"Is that you, Doc?" Owens called from his bed across the room.

Doc walked to his bedside. "What's this I hear about you falling out of bed? You are too old for that," he said. "Let me take a look at that break. Sorry about the burns. I will take a look at them, too, while I am here."

George brought a clean rag and a pan of water to the bedside table. "Thought you might need these."

"Thank you. Yes, to wash my hands," Doc said, using the water in the pan. "Now, let me see that broken arm."

Lifting the arm from the sling he exclaimed, "It is a perfect set. Couldn't do any better myself. The lad's got it down to an art. He should come work for me."

Uncle George called Freddie in from the kitchen.

"Yes, sir? Is there something wrong with the bone?"

The doctor gave him a big smile and said, "Son, that set is perfect. You can come to work for me anytime. Most hospitals could use a medic like you. You're a natural."

Isabella, standing behind Freddie, hugged his neck. "I am so proud of you."

Freddie blushed and turned to the doctor. "Thank you, sir. That means a lot. I've been thinking about my future plans."

"I am sure your mother and father will be proud to hear about your fine skill. I will pass the word," Uncle George said with Grimball pride.

The doctor finished checking Owens and said, "Mr. Owens, your burns are healing well, but they are still tender from the fire. No more getting out of bed without help or you will have more breaks to heal. Understand?"

"Yes, sir. Jennie's been telling me the same thing but I wouldn't listen. However, now I will follow instructions. No more climbing out of bed without help," Owens assured.

"I have a wooden wheelchair in my office that I can let you borrow for the time being, if someone can get it to you," Doc offered.

Isabella heard that and she quickly said, "We'll get it here somehow, thank you."

"If no other way, I will bring my mule and wagon on my next trip. A wheelchair is just what he needs to be able to get around," Uncle George said.

The doctor changed Owens' bandages and got ready to leave. Jennie thanked him for coming and wanted to know how much she owed him for his service.

"Nothing this time. Chalk it up as a visit with old friends and good neighbors. Unless you need extra doctoring, I think you have your own Doctor Freddie right at hand. Good luck!"

# CHAPTER 70

# DECISIONS, DECISIONS!

At the big house, Sarah and Lilly came down the back stairs. Lilly was on her best behavior and had mentioned her mother's name only twice since she got up. She wanted to know just where Liza and Henry were, and if they still wanted to be alone.

"I think they will be at supper tonight. They are trying to find a place big enough for the three of you to live," Sarah explained.

"Will it be here in the big house?" Lilly asked.

"Probably so," Sarah answered. "It may be on the first floor. The rooms there are larger than some of the other rooms."

Entering the kitchen, Lilly asked if she could cook pancakes for breakfast.

"That sounds delicious. Since we slept later than usual, pancakes will keep us from being hungry before dinner."

Sarah took a big bowl from the cupboard and measured flour for the batter. She added two eggs and milk. Giving Lilly a big spoon to stir the batter, she heated a frying pan. They took turns pouring the batter into the frying pan. Sarah flipped several pancakes, lifting them and placing them on a plate. Soon, eight pancakes were ready to eat.

"We did it," Lilly cried. "I like to cook with you, Miss Sarah."

"You were a big help," Sarah said proudly. "Now we can eat them."

Lilly took her place at the table and said her own blessing. She reached with her fork, putting two pancakes on her plate.

"May I have the syrup?" she asked politely.

Sarah handed the syrup jar to Lilly and said, "You are getting to be such a big girl, Lilly, and you have very nice manners."

"I will be six years old on November twentieth. I was almost born on Turkey Day. If I was born on Thanksgiving, the whole world would celebrate my birthday," Lilly boasted.

"This year you will have Papa Henry to help make it special," Sarah said. "That will make it a birthday to remember."

"Yippee! That will be fun for us all," Lilly said, quickly finishing eating. "You said we would ride a real horse today. Let's go now."

"Master Jimmy is to take you riding on New Girl. We are to go to the corral and meet him at eleven o'clock. We still have a few minutes, so let's go to the back porch and see the kitty cats. I think there may be several baby ones," Sarah said, trying to keep Lilly from asking for Liza. So far Lilly had done well, especially having never before spent a night away from her mother.

Lilly found the new kittens right away. "Can I name them?" she asked.

"Sure you can," Sarah said.

"This one has white paws. I will call it Mittens. The other one is all white. Let's name it Snowball," Lilly said, hugging both of them before placing them back in the box with their mother.

After several minutes, Sarah said, "Now we must go meet Jimmy. He will be waiting at the corral gate."

In the corral, Jimmy saddled New Girl and waited for Lilly and Sarah. Just then, Freddie came down the lane on Barabbas.

"Hi cousin. Glad to see you are out riding this beautiful day," Freddie said. "How are things going with you? My family is leaving next week to go home. Believe it or not, I have enjoyed this visit. The South is not so bad, after all. The only thing I find real fault with is the weather. Do you ever get used to it?"

"Not really. You just adjust to it," Jimmy replied, adding teasingly, "I thought you might be staying, with Isabella here, and all."

"It is a temptation. I am truly fond of her," Freddie said. "Maryland is a long way from here. I'd take her home with me if she weren't needed to take care of her father. But Jennie can't take care of him and do her work, too. If Mother wouldn't throw such a fit, I'd stay at Heartland and work for Uncle James on the horse farm. What are your plans?"

"My plans are undecided at this time. I know I do not wish to work with the new business. I love horseback riding, but training them is not my cup of tea. After Christmas, I will move back to our city house and will probably go to the College of Charleston," Jimmy said.

"Good luck to you! It really has been good for me to see life as it is in the South. I realized that it can be a good place to live, with a slower-paced life. I think I might come to enjoy it," Freddie said.

"Is this the same cousin that came to Heartland from Baltimore?" Jimmy asked, joshing.

"It is a somewhat happier and more contented cousin," Freddie said in a kinder voice than Jimmy had ever heard in Baltimore. Jimmy could possibly even like to be around him now.

From the barn, Sarah and Lilly came to the corral. "Jimmy, are you ready to ride?" Sarah called.

"Be right with you," he said. "Freddie, I am glad you came, and I wish you the best of everything as you return home. I will always be appreciative for your family getting me home after prison. Godspeed!"

Freddie clicked his teeth, and Barabbas took to the wind with a smiling rider in the saddle.

After dinner, George gathered his family to start for home. The girls were ready to go to the city as there were no young folk at Heartland their age, with the exception Pug and Ham. It was difficult to understand why they were not allowed to visit with them now. They had played together for years while the boys were slaves, but now, after the war, it wasn't considered proper.

Elijah would ride back to the city with them. He wanted to tell Miss Charlotte and Master James thanks for the invitation to the party, but did not know where to find them. They had not come to dinner.

George stopped the buggy at the Owens' to wish them well.

"Take care of him, Jennie. You've got good help here, with Freddie and Isabella. Tell James I will try to get back by Friday and stay until Frederick leaves. He should have plans written up by then."

He smiled at Freddie and gave him a wink, wondering if he would stay or go back North. Thinking about how upset Frederick could get, George was worried about either decision made.

Lilly and Sarah were back from the horseback ride in time to start supper—leftovers from Saturday's anniversary dinner. Sarah took the leftover rice and made rice pudding using Charlotte's easy recipe. With the leftover yams, she baked a potato pudding with raisins and nuts on top. There was plenty of turkey and ham for everyone to enjoy.

Lilly entertained herself by riding her rocking horse.

Pug and Ham rang the supper bell today at five o'clock. Since breakfast and dinner had been sparse, Sarah served supper an hour early. Charlotte and James were the first to arrive at the table.

Lilly squealed seeing them, and ran to Charlotte, talking as fast as she could. "I made pancakes, and we went riding, and have you seen—"

"Whoa," Charlotte said. "Slow down, you are talking too fast. Come sit with us and tell me about your weekend." Taking Lilly by the hand, she sat down at the table with her.

"Miss Sarah was a good mommy. She let me help cook pancakes this morning, and Mr. Jimmy took me horseback riding this afternoon, and I slept in Sarah's big bed last night. We ate more cake at dinner. I had fun."

Charlotte said, "I am glad," when she managed to get a word in edgewise.

Lilly opened her mouth to keep talking, but suddenly stopped. She looked up at Miss Charlotte and asked, "Have you seen my Mommy and Papa Henry? I miss them." Tears began to run down her cheeks.

Charlotte picked her up and put her on her lap, and let her cry. "A good cry makes us feel better sometimes," she said, "but I think your mommy and Henry have been in the attic this afternoon looking for a new bed for you to sleep in when you move to the first floor of the big house."

"When will I move?" Lilly asked.

"Maybe tonight? So eat your supper so you'll be ready if you do move to your new room tonight."

"Yes, please pass the ham and potatoes," Lilly said, crawling back to her own chair.

The dining room doors opened and in came Liza and Henry. Lilly dropped her fork, jumped down, and ran to meet them. Liza picked her up, giving her a big hug.

Henry reached down to hug them both. "We are finally a family. Let's have our first meal together."

He put Lilly on her chair, and they joined Charlotte and James and others at the table, who all gave them a rousing applause, welcoming them into Heartland's family.

# CHAPTER 71

# A PAPA FOR LILLY

Lilly smiled at Liza and said, "I missed you and Papa. Do you like being Miss Henry Moore?"

"Yes, darling, and your name will soon be Lilly Moore," Liza said. "Henry will be your real papa by law."

"What does by law mean?" Lilly asked.

Henry answered, "No one else can be your real papa now except me, just like Liza will always be your Mommy."

"When will we move in together?" Lilly asked.

"Tonight we will sleep in our new rooms on the first floor of the big house. You will have a new bed. Since you are such a big girl now, the bed is for only you. Neither your mother nor I can sleep on it. It is especially for you," Henry said.

Lilly's eyes got bigger as she asked, "Can my rag doll sleep with me?"

Liza laughed. "All your dolls and animals can sleep in the new bed to be near you. I can sit on it and play with you on the new bed, but when you sleep, only your dolls and animals are allowed to be with you."

"I am a big girl for true. I will be six years old in three months," Lilly boasted. "I want to see my new bed and room right now."

"We will go as soon as we finish eating supper," Liza said.

"I have finished eating. See? My plate is clean," Lilly said.

Henry finished a piece of wedding cake and tried to distract Lilly by asking her if she'd had fun with Miss Sarah. It didn't help.

Liza thought about what they had told Lilly about sleeping alone in a new bed. Would she be afraid of a different bed? Or was it that she would not be sleeping with her mommy?

Henry got quiet, remembering what happened on Sunday. He wanted to be a good papa, but he really didn't know how. Liza would have to teach him.

Miss Charlotte felt the tension and said, "Why don't James and I go with you and see the new rooms and beds?"

"That's a good idea. I think most of us have finished eating. Let's go now. We can eat cake later," Liza said. She stood up and took Henry and Lilly by a hand.

"Miss Charlotte and Master James, you lead. You know the way better than I do."

James and Henry each took Lilly's hands as they followed Liza and Charlotte through the parlor and the hallway to the rooms on the first floor.

Opening the door, Lilly was excited to see a large bed and a fireplace and pretty pictures on the wall. "Is that my new bed?" she asked, then frowned. "It is too big for me."

"No, my little one, that's your Papa and Mommy's bed. Follow me into your room."

Liza opened the door and Lilly saw a smaller room and a smaller bed with a pink bedspread. On the bedspread were pretty pink embroidered pillows, and in the middle sat the most beautiful doll Lilly had ever seen. She was dressed in a pink ruffled dress.

"Whose doll is that?" Lilly asked. "Can I play with it?"

"It comes with the room. I think it is for a big girl named Lilly. It is from her new Papa Henry."

"Wee! A new doll from Papa!" Lilly whooped and reached for the doll. "I will name her Miss Pinky. She is all pink like my bed."

Liza was pleased that Lilly was so happy and gave her a big hug. "How do you like your new bed?"

"A new bed and a new doll. I like them both," Lilly said, climbing onto the bed. "I like the pillows, too. One for me and one for Miss Pinky. Can I go to bed now?"

"Of course. Put on your nightgown and say your prayers, and you can go to sleep in your new bed with your new doll."

Lilly hurriedly put on her gown and Liza listened to her prayers.

"Dear God, thank you for my new room and bed. Bless Mommy and my new Papa Henry. Amen." She climbed back onto the bed with Miss Pinky's on one pink pillow and her own head on the other pillow.

Liza kissed her on the cheek and said, "Goodnight, my sweet."

Henry walked to the other side of the bed and said, "Don't leave me out. I want a goodnight kiss."

Lilly raised her head and Henry kissed her lightly on the cheek.

"Good night, sweet girl. I love you and I am glad to be your papa," he said sweetly.

Liza just happened to notice a few tears roll down her husband's face. She knew for sure that she loved this Yankee very much.

# CHAPTER 72

# NEW PLANS FOR HEARTLAND

With only a few days left for Fred to work on the plans for the horse farm, the brothers were up very early. Fred drew up the legal papers that needed to be filed with the county, and James measured the length of the barn and calculated the measurements for the new stables. Big John and his sons were still removing the wood from the slave cabins. There was plenty of siding to make sturdy fencing for the new stables. Big John wanted to get one stable built soon for Sugar to have a larger place since she was in foal.

Freddie joined his father and uncles in learning about the new business. If he did decide to stay, he would at least be knowledgeable about it. He believed the business would do well on John's Island. He only wished his family lived closer to Heartland. He did need a job, and working with horses was right up his alley.

Isabella was still asking him to stay, but she knew he wasn't sold on the weather in South Carolina. She loved him, but she realized if he did return to Maryland, it would significantly lower her chances of becoming Mrs. Frederick Grimball II. These last ten days with Freddie had been the happiest days of her life.

On Monday, James announced at breakfast that he would like everyone who lived at Heartland to meet him in the library at eleven o'clock, including Fred's family. The latest plans for the horse farm were to be discussed. Exactly on the hour, the library was filled with the Grimball families and the employees of Heartland. Isabella was there on behalf of Mr. Owens, who still was unable to get from his house to Heartland by horse. Fred read the legal documents that he had submitted to Charleston County the day before.

The county clerk had filed them for the next meeting to be approved. It listed the Grimball brothers as owners of a new business to be called Heartland Horse Farm. Legal Attorney Frederick Grimball of Baltimore, Maryland; James Grimball, President; George Grimball, Vice President; Financial Advisor, Henry Moore of John's Island South Carolina. The farm would board, train, and breed horses. A fee would be charged for all services, which would be directly paid to Heartland Horse Farm. Credit would be extended in a case of emergency. Other employees were to be hired when needed. Repairs on the barn and new stables would begin on September 15, 1865, under the supervision of John Grimball.

"Do you have any questions?" James asked.

There were several whispers across the room, but no questions.

"Thank you for coming to hear the plans for the future of Heartland," James said, and everyone applauded.

Fred stood and said, "Our family will be leaving Heartland tomorrow by steamboat. This has been a great trip and a wonderful visit. I will keep in touch with the business by mail and telegraph as our plans progress. The actual business will not open until January 1, 1866. To all relatives and friends, may God bless us all."

"Godspeed as you travel home," George said.

On the way to the dining room, Jane caught up with Freddie. "The plans for Heartland sound wonderful. I am sorry you can't be a part of this new endeavor. You are such a good horseman," she said.

"It is a great challenge for everyone. I could be a big part of this business if we stayed in the South," Freddie said. "We could even move back to Heartland."

"No, no, my son. That will never happen," she said with a groan. "I will never live in the South again."

"Never say never, Mother," Freddie said seriously.

# CHAPTER 73

# PARTING IS SWEET SORROW

Freddie heard Isabella call his name as he walked into the dining room. "Mother, I will see you later. I will be with Isabella."

"Of course dear. But be sure you have your baggage out front by eight in the morning. We don't want to be late for the boat. Enjoy your last day with Isabella," Jane said. It was good that Freddie would soon be home and away from this Southern lady. They were getting too involved to suit Jane.

Having heard the new plans for Heartland, everyone had a new feeling of gratitude and hope for the plantation.

James and Charlotte were delighted for the total acceptance of the plans by the family and staff members. Jennie sent word to James that she and Owens were one hundred percent in favor of the new plans. James hoped that Owens would soon be able to work again, though he was not sure what job the overseer would be able do after his accident and burns.

After the noon meal, Fred and Jane began packing for their trip home. Fred thought it had been a profitable visit businesswise, as well as a great family visit. Their last visit had been before the war began. Many things had changed. Boys had become men and childish things were put away. Some dreams had become reality, and many dreams had disappeared.

Much of the South was suffering from the loss of enslaved laborers to continue its standard of living.

Hopefully, through the new business plans, Heartland would rise again and adapt to the new way of life.

Big John would prepare the buggy to take Fred's family to the boat dock. They would leave Heartland at eleven o'clock to make sure they were at the landing by twelve. James would follow the buggy on Lucky, riding beside Freddie on Barabbas. It was not known if Isabella would go to the landing or not. Jane and Fred called an early bedtime to be sure of a good night's rest before beginning the long trip home.

Freddie and Isabella, however, wanted to spend as much time together as possible. In the moonlight they walked down to where the rice fields had been.

"Do you remember when the rice grew here?" she asked. "I always liked to hear the slaves singing as they worked." She sang, "Ain't gonna rain no more, no more, no more. I's going home to my Lord." She gave a sad smile. "That was one I love to sing with them. As a child, I didn't know what it meant, but tonight it is a song of someone going away, and I am thinking I need to change the words to: I ain't going cry no more, no more. He's just going North to live."

Without speaking, Freddie took her in his arms and held her tightly and said, "I really don't want to go home and leave you here for someone else to love. You mean everything to me. And yes, I do want to marry you as soon as I find a way to support you. However, it's a long way home and a long way back. I am so confused about what I should do."

"I have cried and cried about your leaving. If Father didn't need me, I would go with you. I could be a nanny for children or teach piano in Baltimore," she said, tearing up again. "I didn't know parting was going to be so hard."

"If it were not so late, we'd ride to Reverend Jenkins and be married tonight," Freddie said, kissing her again as tears from his own eyes met the tears from hers.

They stood there holding each other, sobbing like children.

He loosened his arm from her waist and said, "This isn't helping matters. The longer I hold you, the more I want you as my wife. We should go back to your family's house. I have a boat to catch at noon tomorrow."

Arm in arm, they walked slowly back to the house. On the porch they lingered, kissing over and over until Jennie heard them and called, "Come on into the kitchen. I have hot chocolate for you."

"Thank you, Mother. We will be right in," Isabella answered, and giving Freddie another kiss, she opened the front door and went into the kitchen.

Jennie left them alone to drink their chocolate. She was wise enough to know that this was not the time for a family conversation. Making her bed on the settee, she heard the door to Freddie's room close and heartsick sobs from her unhappy daughter come from the kitchen. Jennie wanted to go to her and take the hurt away. But only time could heal that kind of hurt. Shedding a few tears of her own, she finally fell asleep.

Morning came early and Freddie had his packed baggage ready for transport as his mother had instructed. He had slept only about an hour during the night. He'd asked himself over and over, should he go home or should he stay? Would he ever love again, or would a girl as lovely and fine as Isabella ever love him again?

As the sun begin to rise, he put on his traveling clothes and carried his baggage to the front porch. He went to the stable and saddled Barabbas. Having no destination in mind, Barabbas took off like the wind.

Isabella woke at six-thirty, groggy from crying. She dressed quickly, went to the kitchen, and knocked on Freddie's door. There was no answer. She opened it just enough to see if he was in bed. He was not there and his bed was made.

She ran out the back door to the stable. Barabbas was missing, too. She knew that he often went riding when stressed. He'd be back for breakfast. She turned back and saw he had already put his baggage out for Big John to load in the buggy.

Going back to the kitchen, she put the coffee pot on the stove and stirred the banked fire. "Maybe it is good that he has already left. I couldn't take another goodbye," she said despondently, with a choke in her voice.

In the big house, Jane and Fred were eating the breakfast that Liza had prepared. Their baggage and other belongings were sitting on the front porch ready to be put into the buggy.

"I am sorry Freddie has to leave Isabella," Liza said. "From what I've seen, they are very fond of each other. They have spent almost every day together since you got here."

"Well, I am glad to be getting them away from each other. I do not want him to marry that Southern girl, the daughter of a plantation caretaker," Jane said firmly.

Liza was shocked. "Why Miss Jane, Isabella is one of the most educated and polished ladies I have ever met. She has a heart of gold and treats everyone the same, whether white or colored. He surely could do much worse."

"That's your opinion," Jane said haughtily.

"Jane, you are being very unkind this morning," Fred said. "If he loves her, I will not stand in their way. After all, you seemed to have forgotten that your own grandparents were born in Virginia. Both from Southern parents."

"Shush, I am not a Southerner."

"Let's not go there today. We have to get our things to the buggy by eleven. We will discuss our heritage later," Fred said sharply. "As Liza said, he could do a lot worse in choosing a wife."

Jane jumped up and left the table in a huff. "I'll see you at the buggy," she said.

Liza was stunned but said nothing. Fred got up to leave. Shaking his head, he said, "Thanks for breakfast. Don't worry about Jane, she'll get over it."

As Isabella finished her coffee, the side door to the kitchen opened and Freddie ran in, huffing and puffing. "Let's go. Get Tilly. We must get to the boat before it leaves the island. Don't worry, I am staying, my darling. I am staying for you! I must tell my parents before they leave."

Isabella jumped up from the chair and was halfway to the stable before Freddie could catch up. By eleven, Big John had loaded the buggy, and Fred and Jane were sitting on the back seat waiting to leave. Jane was tearful. Freddie had not returned since morning.

Fred said, "He'll be at the boat. I am sure he will be at the landing waiting for us. And if he isn't, we will leave without him. He is over twenty-one and can take care of himself."

"You don't really believe that, Frederick Grimball. He is our only son, and I am not ready for him to be away from home again. Four years in the cavalry was hard enough," Jane cried.

She continued to pout and weep as Big John drove the buggy carefully to the boat dock near Seabrook Island. He slowed the horses as he drove through the causeway to the dock. It was easier this time. The sand was much drier.

C H A P T E R  7 4

# THE CHOICE

As Big John stopped the buggy at the boat landing, Jane jumped out quickly and looked around. It was already eleven-fifteen, and still no Freddie. Fred followed her as she hurried to the office at the nearby house to speak to the dock manager.

"Good morning. We are the Grimballs, here for the steamboat. Has our son arrived yet?" she asked politely.

"No, you are our first passengers for the boat. Just be seated there in the waiting room. I am sure he will join you soon."

James rode up on Lucky and stopped at the landing's office. He tied Lucky to the hitching post, wondering where Freddie's horse was. George said the boy had been trying to decide whether to go home or stay here in the South. If he was staying, he surely would have told his parents by now.

James found only Fred and Jane in the waiting room. "Where is Freddie?" he asked.

"He hasn't come. We don't know where he can be," Jane cried. "It is almost time for the boat to load.

"The manager hasn't seen him," Fred said.

Just then, Big John came in. "I see two horses with riders coming up the beach. Could it be Freddie?" he asked.

"It would be only one horse," James said. "Unless...?"

"Unless what?" Fred asked.

"George said that Freddie was thinking about staying here to work on the new horse farm," James said uncertainly.

"He wouldn't do that to me," Jane sobbed. "I told you that girl was not good enough for him. Do something, Fred. We have to stop this."

"What can I do? He is old enough to make up his own mind, and you don't know if he's staying or not," Fred said, trying to console her.

The office clock struck noon, and the manager stood. "The steamship is due at noon, and it's usually on time. I will check the water. I can tell if a boat is near by its movement."

As he left, James and Fred followed him outside. Walking to the dock, Fred asked James, "Why didn't you tell me what George said about Freddie's plans?"

"He swore me to secrecy. And you know George," James replied.

As James and Fred stepped onto the landing, a boat horn bellowed across the island.

The manager called, "Here she comes. It will leave the Island at one o'clock."

Jane came running from the waiting room. "Is Freddie here?" she asked nervously.

"Not yet, but I see two horsemen riding fast this way," James said and pointed.

She recognized Freddie and Barabbas, and hurried toward them. "Freddie, dear, are you all right?" she called.

"I am better than all right. I didn't mean to upset you by being late, but I didn't make my decision until just now," Freddie shouted, stopping near his mother.

Isabella stopped behind him and waited in silence.

"Son, what's going on?" Fred asked. "We were worried that something had happened."

"It has. I have decided to stay in the South and work for the new farm at Heartland, and also do some work for Doctor Le Roach," Freddie said.

Jane screamed, "No! No, you can't do that to me. You must come home." She turned to Isabella and shouted, "You are the one making him stay!"

Isabella was shocked at the outburst. "Don't blame me. I didn't know he was staying until an hour ago. I am glad, but until this morning, I thought he was going back North, and my heart was broken."

"Mother, please settle down. I know what I am doing. This past month had been a wonderful learning situation for me. I love the slower pace I have felt here at Heartland. I've never felt as easy in Maryland. I want to stay and help get the horse farm started. If I ever get disenchanted, Barabbas and I will ride home, back to Baltimore. I promise."

"But it is such a long way home," Jane said through her tears.

"Yes, it's a long way home, but I think Barabbas can make it," Freddie said happily.

The dock manager said, "You have fifteen minutes to get aboard the steamboat."

"We can't leave him here," Jane sobbed. "It's not home."

"It was my home for twenty-two years," Fred said. "And it was a great home. What do you say, James?"

"It's still a great home," James agreed. "And we are happy to share it with Freddie. We are glad you came and I promise to take good care of your son. God speed on your journey home."

Captain Marcus opened the lower deck and came over to speak to the passengers. He was surprised, but pleased, to find a different Freddie with a different attitude toward life.

Fred was a bit unhappy with Freddie's plan, but mostly for Jane's sake. Freddie already had work on John's Island, and in Maryland it would be harder for him to get a job to work with horses.

Isabella rode Tilly toward the water. "You say your goodbyes. I'll wait for you on the beach."

He dismounted Barabbas to hug his mother and father. Jane tried to smile, although her heart was breaking. She'd had to get used to her son being away in the army, and she would get used to it again.

Freddie got back on his horse and watched his parents board the steamboat. In his heart, he knew he was making the right decision.

After the boat left the dock, he rode his horse up beside Tilly and reached for Isabella's hand. "Shall we go home, my dearest?"

She squeezed his hand, and answered, "Yes, my darling. Back to Heartland, back to a Southern life."

# GLOSSARY

Gullah is a Creole language used in the Southern states by the enslaved Africans on the plantations, especially near the coasts of North Carolina, South Carolina, Georgia, and Florida. Since it is not a written language, and when translated, it is often written differently, considering the location of the descendants that still speak the language. It can be difficult to read for many readers. In the novel *A Long Way Home*, the author has taken the liberty to use substandard English, southern colloquium, mixed with the Gullah dialect for the enslaved's speech in the story. There is no gender in the language, and no *th* sound.

dem-them
kep- keep
ribbuh- river
de- the
waz- was
dey- they
gwing- going
wuh- what
dar- there
git- get
weh- where
t'ank- thank
day clean- dawn

fus- first

dan- than

chillum- children

en- in

fuh- for

crack'e teeth- speak

t'ing- thing

cher- here

hab- has, have, had

git- get

hep- help

e- he

budduh- brother

yuh- you

poch- porch

leabe- leave

um- mam

poly- poorly

lef- left

ooman- woman

po- poor

den- then

t'ing- thing

kin- can

t'ree- three

I's- I am

nuf- enough

tek- take

ain't- am not

aa'my- army

set- setting

# SELECTED BIBLIOGRAPHY

Archambault, Alan, *Johnny Reb*, Bellerphon Books, Santa Barbara, 2000.

Bostick, Douglas W., *A Brief History of James Island*, Charleston: History Press, 2008.

Bradfort, Ned, *Battles and Leaders of the Civil War.* New York, 1989.

Brown, Alphonso, *A Gullah Guide to Charleston.* Charleston, The History Press: 2008.

Burton, Milby E., The Siege of Charleston, 1861-1865, Columbia, University of South Carolina Press: 1970.

Campbell, Emory S., *Gullah Cultural Legacies*, USA, Gullah Heritage Consulting Services Publications: 2005.

Carroll, Andrew, *War Letters*, USA, Simon & Schuster: 2001.

Clary, Margie W., *A Gullah Alphabet*, Orangeburg, Written In Stone Press: 2008

Crane, Stephen, *The Red Badge of Courage*, Marboro, Marboro Books: 1992.

Curtis, Alice Turner, *A Little Maid of South Carolina*, Philadelphia: The Penn Publishing Company: 1929.

Edgar, Walter, *South Carolina A History, Columbia:* University of South Carolina, 1998.

Garrison, Webb, *True Tales of the Civil War,* Nashville, Rutledge House Publishers: 1988.

Gerty, Virginia M. Gullah Fuh Oonuh, Orangeburg, Sandlapper Publishers: 2006.

Hagy, James W. *To Take Charleston, the Civil War on Folly Island*, West
    Virginia, Pictorial Publishing Company: 1993.

Haynie, Connie Walpole, *Images of America, John's Island*, Charleston,
    Arcadia Publishing: 2007.

Jakes, John, *Savannah*, New York, Dutton Publishers: 2004.

Moore, Kay, *Lived at the Time of the Civil War*, New York, Scholastic Press:
    1994.

Moore Michele, The Cigar *Factory*, Columbia, University of South
    Carolina Press: 2016.

Nofi, Albert A., *A Civil War Treasury*, Edison, Castle Book Press: 2006.

Opala, Joseph A., *The Gullah*, Sullivan Island, Fort Sumter National
    Monument
Publication: 1999.

Ray, Delia, *Behind the Blue & Gray*, USA, Puffin Books: 1991.

Reader Digest Associates, *Civil War Battle Grounds*, Minnesota, Zenith
    Press: 2013.

Reeder, Carolyn, *Shades of Gray*, New York, McMillians Publishing: 1989.

South Carolina Encyclopedia *The Railroad Age*, Library of Congress: 2015.

Stokes, Karen, *Legion of Devils*, Columbia, Shotwell Publishing: 2017.

Ward. Geoffrey C., The Civil War, an Illustrated History. New York, Albert
Knopf Publishing: 1994.

Wilcox, Arthur & Warren Ripley, *The Civil War at Charleston*, Charleston,
Post and Courier Press: 2006.

Wiley, Bell I., *The Common Soldier of the Civil War*, Harrisonburg, Eastern
corn Press: 1989

# OTHER RESOURCES

Internet: https: www. Wikipedia:

Websites:

www. nps.gov/chch

www. nps. gov/Vicksburg

www, nps. gov/ Ft Sumter

www, nps. gov/ Petersburg

www. nps. gov/ Civil War

www. npas. gov/Richmond

www: History net

www: Britannica.com/events

www: American Civil War.com/net

www: History.net/com

www: Civil War History.com/net

ABOUT THE AUTHOR

# MARGIE WILLIS CLARY

Margie Willis Clary was born in the Piedmont section of South Carolina.. After graduating from Furman University with a Bachelor Degree in Education, she taught in Greenville County until moving with her family to Charleston in 1965. She received a Masters in Education from the Citadel and taught on James Island until her retirement in 1988. Since retirement, Clary has worked as an adjunct professor at the Citadel and at Charleston Southern University. She worked as professional storyteller,1990-2010 and traveled the state working in schools as an artist-in-residence with the South Carolina Arts Commission. In 1990 she published a volume of poetry, *A Poem Is a Memory*. Her first book for children entitled *A Sweet, Sweet Basket*, was published in 1995 by Sandlapper Publishing and listed among Smithsonian Magazine's "Notable Books for Children" in November 1995. Since that time she has published four other children's book, *Searching the Lights; A Gullah Alphabet; Make it Three (Story of the H.L. Hunley Submarine);* and *Spirits & Legends;* along with *The Beacons of South Carolina; and Lighthouses of South Carolina (McDermott)*.

*A Long Way Home* is her first novel.

A South Carolina native, Margie Clary has called the Charleston area home for more than fifty years. She and her husband live on James Island. They have two children and three grandchildren. She is active in her local church and continues to use her talents, teaching and storytelling for all ages.

# ENDNOTES

1   <u>Blockade of Charleston</u>: The Union blockade in the American Civil War was a naval strategy by the United States to prevent the Confederacy from trading. The blockade was proclaimed by President Abraham Lincoln in April 1861, and required the monitoring of 3,500 miles (5,600 km) of Atlantic and Gulf coastline, including 12 major ports, notably New Orleans and Mobile. https://en.wikipedia.org/wiki/Union_blockade

2   The Gullah people are known for preserving more of their African linguistic and cultural heritage than any other African-American community in the United States. The distinctive dialect is an English-based Creole language containing many African loanwords and significant influencers from African languages in grammar and sentence structure. Usually referred to as "Sea Island Creole," the Gullah language is related to Jamaican Creole, Barbadian dialect, Bahamian dialect, and very much like the Krio language of Sierra Leone in West Africa.

3   *Target Practice Story*: A folk tale from John's Island that is supposed to be true. Taken from the author's file.

4   John Clifford Pemberton, one of a few northern natives to serve as a general in the Confederate armies was born August 10, 1814, in

Philadelphia, Pennsylvania, to Quaker parents, John Pemberton led forces in South Carolina and fought on James Island. https://www.essentialcivilwarcurriculum.com/john-c-pemberton.html

5    Nathan George "Shanks" Evans was an officer in the United States Army until 1861, when he became a general in the Confederate States Army. He was from South Carolina and first manned troops in Charleston. https://en.wikipeia.org/wiki/Nathan G. Evans.

6    Battle of Secessionville: The Union regiments attacked the Confederate fort (Lamar) at the small summer village of Secessionville, near Charleston, where Col. Thomas G. Lamar commanded 500 men with well-placed heavy equipment. After an intense battle, the Confederate defenders, fought by approximately 1,000 men from nearby units, ultimately prevailed a victory. https://www.battlefields.org/learn/battle/secessionville.

7    Stephen Elliott, Jr. was a Confederate States Army brigadier general during the Civil War. He was a planter, a state legislator in South Carolina, and militia officer before the Civil War. He was again elected as a state legislator after the war, but died before he could fill the office. https://en.wikipedia.org/wiki/Stephen_Elliott_Jr.

8    The Battle of Boydton Plank Road was fought on October 27 through 28, 1864, following the successful Battle of Peebles' Farm in the siege of Petersburg during the Civil War. It was an attempt by the Union Army to seize the Boydton and Petersburg Plank Road in order to cut off the Southside Railroad, a critical supply line into the town of Petersburg, Virginia. https//en.wikipedia.org/wiki/Battle of Boydton Plank Road.

9    The Union was ordered to establish a prison camp at Point Lookout in Maryland, which would hold 10,000 prisoners. Completed in 1863,

Point Lookout was the largest and one of the worst Union prison camp. https;//com/historical/987-point-lookout-prison-camp.com.

10　*The Emancipation Proclamation* was a presidential proclamation and executive order issued by President Abraham Lincoln on January 1, 1863. It changed the legal status of more than 3.5 million enslaved Africans in the designated areas of the South from slave to free. While it did not free a single slave, it was an important turning point of the war, transforming the fight to preserve the nation into a battle for human freedom. https:// en.wikipedia.org/wiki/Emancipation Proclamation.com

11　In 1860, children were often breastfed until they were four or older. Household slaves had duties regarding childcare, and nursing was part of feeding the white children as well as their own. https://www.reddit.com/8pn3e1/daguerreotype_nurse_and_child_1850.

12　Ooman: A Gullah word for Woman: obit, 2.

13　Many healthy men who were eligible to serve in the military during the Civil War never ended up enlisting. The Enrollment Act of 1863 provided that a draftee could pay a "substitute" enrollee as a soldier. Abraham Lincoln was too old for the draft, but wanting to encourage other ineligibles like himself, volunteered to hire a substitute soldier. The national records show that in 1864, Lincoln paid a nineteen-year-old Pennsylvanian, J. Summerfield Stables, to enlist and fight for the Union as his substitute. https://state.com/human-interest/2013/abraham-lincoln.

14　Highway 17 in Charleston County was named King's Highway by King Charles II of England. Most early highways were named by the King in the early settling of the southern Colonies. https:// SC History/ highway.com

15 Chimborazo Hospital was a Confederate hospital built in 1861 in Richmond, Virginia, to service the medical needs for the Confederate Army. During 1862 to 1865, seventy-six thousand injured soldiers were treated there. Over eight thousand of those patients died. https://en wikipedia.org/wiki/ Chimborazo.Hospital.

16 Richmond served as the capital of the Confederate States for almost the whole Civil War. It was a vital source for weapons and supplies for the war effort, and the terminus of five railroads. After a long siege, Grant captured Petersburg and Richmond in early April 1865. As the fall of Petersburg became imminent, on Evacuation Sunday (April 2), President Davis, his cabinet, and the Confederate defenders abandoned Richmond and fled south on the last open railroad line, the Richmond and Danville. https:// en.wikipedia.org/wiki/Richmond in the Civil War

17 The model 1822 of the Springfield Musket was used for almost the whole Civil War by the army. Commonly referred to as the "Springfield," it was the most widely used U.S. weapon by the Northern and Southern armies, favored for its range accuracy and reliability. Archambault, Alan, *Johnny Red, Confederate Rifles.*

18 Confederate prisoners at Belle Plain Landing, Virginia, who were captured with Johnson's division on May 12, 1864, were placed in what was called the "Punch Bowl," the informal name for a series of ravines at Belle Plain, Virginia. It became a temporary holding area for Confederates captured there during the Overland Campaign. Some wounded rebels were also treated there. https://ww w.civilwarfamily. us/2015/09/confederate-prisoners

19 Columbia, South Carolina, was a Southern city of great importance politically, and a supply center for the Confederate Army during

the Civil War. Much of the town was destroyed during occupation by Union forces under Major General William T. Sherman in the Carolinas Campaign during the last months of the war. Sherman was accused in print almost immediately of having destroyed the capital city. His men started many fires, and some drunken Yankee soldiers started other fires. Sherman took as many horses as he was able to find from the capital. https://en.wikipedia.org/wiki/Columbia,_South_Carolina_in_the_Civil War

20 Pluff mud is the mud in the marshes around Charleston and the Sea Islands of the South. It has a rancid smell. A Charleston word.

21 The Battle of New Orleans in 1862 was an important event for the Union. Having fought against Forts Jackson and St. Phillips, the Union was not unopposed to capture the city, and did so with little destruction. At that time, New Orleans was the only city in the South with over one hundred-thousand people. *https//en.org/wiki/Battle of New Orleans Civil War.*

22 Belle Isle Prison is located west of Richmond Virginia. It is a small island located in the James River that was used as a Civil War Prison for captured Union soldiers. The prison only held a few small shacks, called prisoner quarters, and the island afforded no protection from the elements that the Union soldiers had to endure. https://www.civilwaracademy.com/belle-isle-prison

23 Sayler's (Sailor's) Creek Battlefield near Farmville, Virginia, was the site of the Battle of Sayler's Creek during the American Civil War. Robert E. Lee's army was retreating from the Richmond to the Petersburg line. Here, on April 6, 1865, Union General Philip Sheridan cut off and beat back about a quarter of Lee's army. https://en.wikipedia.org/wiki/Sayler's Creek Battlefield

24 Exchange Building, Charleston, South Carolina, The Old Exchange & Provost Dungeon, also known as the Custom House, and The Exchange, is an historic building at East Bay and Broad Streets in Charleston, South Carolina, USA. Built in 1767–1771, it has served a variety of civic institutional functions, including notably as a prisoner of war facility during the American Revolutionary War and Civil War, and later as a US Post Office. https://en.wikipedia.org/wiki/Exchange_and_Provost

25 McLeod Plantation is located at 325 Country Club Drive on James Island, South Carolina, near the intersection of Folly and Maybank Roads. Situated on Wappoo Creek which flows into the Ashley River, historic events have been recorded throughout the period from 1678 when it first appeared on maps under "Morris." Captured by the Union Army early in the war, it was used for a hospital, and offices for the Union. Later it was used as the headquarter for the Freedmen Bureau. https://www.inspirock.com/united-states, Charleston/mcleod

26 A barn-raising, historically called a raising bee or rearing, is an action of a whole community where a barn for one of the members is built or rebuilt collectively by members of the community. Barn raising was particularly common in 18th and 19th-century rural North America. A barn was a necessary structure for any farmer, for example for storage of cereals and hay. https://en.wikipedia.org/wiki/Barn-raising

27 The Battle of Legareville was fought on December 25, 1863, during the American Civil War. Confederate forces tried to surprise Union forces near Legareville on Johns Island but failed to destroy the federal forces or drive them away from Legareville. https://en.wikipedia.org/wiki/Battle_of_Legareville

28  The Battle of Boydton Plank Road was fought on October 27-28, 1864, following the successful Battle of Peebles' Farm in the siege of Petersburg during the Civil War. It was an attempt by the Union Army to seize the Boydton and Petersburg Plank Road in order to cut off the Southside Railroad, a critical supply line into the town of Petersburg, Virginia. https//en.wikipedia.org/wiki/Battle of Boydton Plank Road.

29  Edward Fenwick and his son ran Johns Island Stud Farm, Fenwick's importations of the Godolphin Bloodline via England. The first horse race in South Carolina was in 1734. Anytime there was more than one horse in a place, there would inevitably be a race. It was the Spaniards who brought horses to the new world. www.fenwickhall.com/johnsislandstudhorses.html

30  The Old Exchange & Provost Dungeon in Charleston, South Carolina, also known as the Custom House, and the Exchange, is a historic building at East Bay and Broad Streets. Built in 1767–1771, it has served a variety of civic institutional functions, including notably as a prisoner of war facility during the American Revolutionary War and the Civil War, and later as a US post office. https://en.wikipedia.org/wiki/Exchange_and_Provost